The Village

You might like this.
I truly hope you do.

Rosina *

The
Village

ROSINA GRAY

Matador
9 Priory Business Park,
Wistow Road, Kibworth Beauchamp,
Leicestershire. LE8 0RX
Tel: 0116 279 2299
Email: books@troubador.co.uk
Web: www.troubador.co.uk/matador
Twitter: @matadorbooks

ISBN 978 1789014 297

British Library Cataloguing in Publication Data.
A catalogue record for this book is available from the British Library.

Printed and bound in Great Britain by 4edge Limited
Typeset in 11pt Minion Pro by Troubador Publishing Ltd, Leicester, UK

Matador is an imprint of Troubador Publishing Ltd

For Alex

"I am
because we are."

Prologue

The man was at one with the moment, and with all that surrounded him. His amber eyes reflected the flush of young heather-flowers and ocean of sky that was hung with bright clouds, and as he looked he raised a hand to meet the breeze. Then he lowered his gaze to the sun-warmed earth in search of a beginning.

What he had come for was very nearby. He could sense its great age, and the stillness of its patient waiting. He took a few slow steps on the empty moor, picturing the specimen he had seen before setting out. It had been encased in a glowing bubble of zithilla, and because its time was over he had not been permitted to handle it; but he remembered it clearly, and knew he would recognise it at once.

Here it was already! The man stooped nimbly and plucked a stone from amongst the low vegetation. He laid it gently in his palm, examining its colour and the lines that ran across it. Then he curled his fingers around it and shut his eyes, watching as a multitude of visions blended and separated across space and time – indistinct faces and events that were soon to become dear to him.

His work had begun. The man pocketed the stone and headed out over the moor in the direction of the nearest town.

Part 1

1

September, 2020
BBC Television Centre, London

As the house-lights dimmed, all expectant murmurings died with a hush. Frank Piper stood up to give a short breezy introduction, looking in his element under the hot lights. The man in the other chair remained calm and unmoving.

It was eighteen months into Project *Ubuntu* and until now there had been no official word from "inside." The little settlement craved seclusion, but since it had begun offering weekend breaks and free tent pitches, news, photos and even drone footage had suddenly hit the net and was arousing interest and discussion. It remained a quiet, closeted place, however. Villagers came and went regularly, collecting recycling and old furniture or trading with local businesses. Their faces were open and friendly and their eyes were bright, and yet there was something secret and closeted that clung to them too. Local campsites teemed during holidays, but day-trippers were not permitted beyond the perimeter fence. Many left disappointed, for there was little to see or sensationalise – just an outlying shop where tender was negotiable and staff were not paid – a ramshackle building under a tree, adorned with pigeon-droppings and homemade bunting. There, visitors drank mulled wine under sun umbrellas; picked out cushion covers, greetings cards, preserves and fresh vegetables, and then gave the community something in return.

A lone, shabby outpost bringing a fresh concept to life.

The man in the chair did not invite attention, and the most remarkable thing about him was the steadfastness of his sky-blue eyes. His clothing was understated but there was a self-possession about him – a powerful presence of which he seemed quietly conscious. He had requested to begin the interview already seated as opposed to walking in to applause.

Piper sat down, adjusted his position and crossed his legs. Placing his hands on the arms of his chair, he found himself phrasing his first question with uncharacteristic care: "Paul… You should be aware by now of the growing interest in Project *Ubuntu*. Would you mind first of all telling us a bit about your initial reasons for applying to set it up?"

The man paused for ten long seconds before giving his soft measured response. "Society just isn't working any more. I mean, not for most ordinary people, it isn't. There's too much unhappiness. Too much greed and selfishness. Too much killing. There's got to be a better way. We don't just think it – we feel it…" Emotion fluttered, barely noticeable, at the corners of his eyes. "Are you aware of the actual meaning of the word *Ubuntu* at all?"

"I understand it to be a society living without money," said Piper with a frosty edge. He was unaccustomed to being questioned himself.

Paul continued calmly. "Ideally, yes – but it's more of a *shift* away from that system. We do use money but not exclusively, and we don't aim to accumulate it. We reject the growing drive for monetary wealth and possessions, and the status they hold – or are viewed as holding." He paused, looking up into the dazzling heat of the lights. "But Ubuntu's about way more than that. It's much deeper. It's more about… *interconnectedness* and mutual responsibility. A common translation is 'Humanity Towards Others.'"

"And how does that lead to the down-play of a monetary system exactly?"

Paul smiled slightly at the challenge of the question. "Capitalism rewards selfishness. It's a machine, and it forces us to compete from our earliest years." He stopped, wondering how to proceed. So much to say, and so many ways to say it. "People don't realise how chained they are," he said. "You know – I've got this and I've got that, and I must be this…"

Frank Piper rarely felt uneasy on stage but a strange cavernous sensation was taking hold in his stomach. He had just bought a brand-new Aston Martin and driving it made him feel as if the whole world was at his feet. Paul's words automatically felt like a personal attack.

Paul met the other man's eyes without blinking: "We want to feel free. And we believe a simple non-competitive life can yield true abundance… in all senses of the word. Capitalism is all about the *next thing*, whereas we believe in taking joy in the here and now. People have forgotten what makes them really happy. We've been sold a lie, and what's worse we're passing it onto our children. The time's come for another option – a new way of living. We want to be that change."

To Piper's surprise there were a few murmurs of appreciation here and there from the audience, and a couple of people clapped once or twice. Paul unnerved him, and his own thoughts were fragmented. He found himself having to resist the urge to keep shuffling in his seat. This didn't feel good. The impact of Paul's words – these obvious truths put so plainly – naively almost – was embarrassing: like being corrected by a child. Piper cleared his throat. "Okay. So what exactly do you feel your concepts as a community have to offer what you might term mainstream society?" he asked as silence returned to the room.

The answer came quietly. "Well, everything. Because the things mainstream society is pandering to aren't fulfilling. They obviously don't work. You've only got to look around you. People are insatiable, plus the system as a whole is unsustainable, whereas Ubuntu goals are realistic and easily…"

Piper cut in, changing tack. "But these children you are collectively raising – how do you answer charges that they're destined never to fit into mainstream culture later on?"

Paul knew the audience was listening closely now, and once again took his time to respond. "The village is a home, not a prison. Our children go dancing and singing, and volunteer in town… But no, they probably won't fit in. Just like I never did. Just like none of us ever did."

"So you really feel that badly about conventional society?" said Piper with an affected frown. His smile was a queer upside down one.

"Er… We feel it's largely unhealthy for both mind and body. It's wrecking the planet too."

In response the interviewer quickly crossed his legs and then re-crossed them the other way. "So how do you address things like religion within the village?" asked Piper, leaning back in his chair. He knew it was a lousy question but he needed a stop-gap.

Paul gave a half-hearted laugh. "Look, we've got several religious people in the village, but there's a general understanding that it's not to be preached or pushed onto

8

other people. Certainly there's no requirement to have certain beliefs..."

"But there *is* spirituality, isn't there?" Now perhaps Piper was onto something juicy.

The blue eyes betrayed nothing. "There's some spirituality, which is very much a fluid thing and down to the individual's interpretation."

"But your children have extra subjects in school, and often this involves talking about spiritual issues. Some people would say, of course, that this is indicative of trying to form some sort of cult. How would you respond to that?"

Paul felt a shot of adrenaline and dropped his head for a moment, centring himself. He recalled Ellen's urgent shouts through the hammering rain as he'd got into the truck still eating mouthfuls of breakfast that morning... "Try not to get defensive, Paul!"

"Opinion sharing," he said levelly. "We encourage children to share opinions in the hope that this will continue into adulthood in a positive way. Cults are about brain-washing." He smirked briefly. "*Capitalism's* about brainwashing. How we live is the opposite of that."

Someone in the audience let out a whoop as Piper jumped in quickly. "But Paul – returning to my earlier point: don't you risk creating misfits that are aware of nothing that's taking place in the larger world? You don't have televisions or technology for example. These children's horizons are surely restricted; their aspirations unrealistic. We live in a technological age. Out here the world isn't like your Ubuntu village."

Paul was getting tense again. "No, it isn't. That's the point. Our children are growing up naturally, whereas "out here," as you put it, they're destined to be sexualised at a young age, exposed to graphic violence and hypnotised into money-worship. What kinds of aspirations d'you think *that* kind of childhood puts in place?"

The voice of his ex-wife came again against a background of scattered applause. "And try not to sound too much like an activist… You're our first public face, remember?"

Paul made an effort to return to his more relaxed way of speaking. "Look, I've got nothing against people who want to watch telly. It's not technology itself but *over-use* that's the problem. People need to ask themselves whether they're the masters of it… or are slaves to it – because there's a big difference. We have access to these things if we really need them, but our greatest joy is spending time together by the light of a fire… as opposed to the flickering of a screen. We talk, we eat, we sing. It's what we prefer, that's all."

Electricity was building in the studio as Piper back-peddled to no real avail. "But some would argue that extra subjects are unfair on these children. Don't kids work hard enough already at school?"

"It's not hard work when children are learning naturally," said Paul. "When they're driving the curriculum and expanding their potential. That's not hard work. That's just living."

A few hearty claps split the air as Piper decided to veil his next hit with a short lull. "So you renounce the capitalist way of life. You believe you're offering your children a healthy start…" He paused, faking a cough. "But you did need money to set up the project. You pooled your resources, sold your houses and sold your cars. This is still a completely artificial society then, isn't it – built on little more than collective idealism, and relying ultimately on the very system you're trying to escape?"

"Yeah, but so what?" answered Paul, gesticulating for the first time. "I don't see how the word 'idealism' can even be used in a derogatory way. What's wrong with aiming for an ideal? It's called an ideal because it *is* ideal. We're choosing this life for a reason. Trying to build a new world, you know. You have to start somewhere, and it's based on honourable concepts. Your point is irrelevant. If you can gain that foot-hold, it doesn't matter what clump of grass you have to grab hold of. Or where you put your foot."

With that the audience fell into applause.

2

TWO YEARS EARLIER

Summer, 2018
Norfolk

In time, Foxheath-on-Sea had become Ellen Turner's favourite place – which was a surprise, because as a child she had found it oppressive, with its tall dark Victorian terraces that often transformed the streets into wind tunnels. The town was just large enough to retain a sense of anonymity for those souls who desired it, and its panoramic sea-views and surrounding tree-dotted countryside were amongst the most spectacular and unspoilt in the country.

Every summer the town filled itself to bursting with noise and activity. Children splashed and squealed and picked over slippery rock-pools under blue skies and racing gulls. There was pie and mash or fresh crab salad, followed by a slow drive and the lonely escape of bracken and nightingale. There were pier-shows and shopping, arcades and crazy golf, water-walking and trampolining, and the dazzling lights of the fair. There were sunsets and campervans and kids on scooters, and dogs by the dozen, and fish-and-chip queues right up the streets that had too many teashops to count.

But for Paul and Ellen fullness came with September after the mass exodus, when the town suddenly became more spacious and quiet. With a huge exhalation of relief, Foxheath became introspective again. The exuberance of youth gave way to the peaceful resignation of old age as the campsites dropped their prices. The benches and low walls along the prom were lined with pensioners contentedly eating ice-creams and watching the sea. Dogs wandered freely on open land and the buzz went out of the air and out of the colours. The shops closed earlier and more often in the warm afternoon light, and no one really went outside past six o'clock. And then the beaches became bare and wild, as if man had never set foot on the planet.

On carnival day – the culmination of the summer season – the tall windswept buildings stole the booms and shouts from the long procession of floats and marching bands, flinging them one way and then another, and sometimes swallowing them altogether for a quick moment. Ellen, meanwhile, sat in her small back garden watching the clouds as they moved leisurely over the trees. These days, at forty-five, she was happy to leave the celebrations to youngsters and tourists. Solitude, moreover, had become a sanctuary since her illness, and for her, the peak of the evening was a simple seagull that sailed up and away from her in a sweeping arc. She heard and felt its winged momentum. She sensed a connection as if seeing something of herself in it, and it made her sit up with a jolt.

Ellen knew her doctor would probably think she was becoming unstable again if she told him about feelings of this kind; would peer over his spectacles at her, and then solemnly type the word "delusional" into his computer. But that was just one perspective. Had her doctor been a Hindu for example, he might have been delighted for her, and seen such experiences as a sign of improving mental health. She still retained one or two comforting habits from her breakdown; she still craved the sound of birdsong and lit a candle every day. But during that terrible time the dark had been horrifying, not soothing like it was now, and her bedroom had felt like a cold prison rather than a comfortable refuge. These days – at long last – Ellen was certain she was not only healed, but heading towards better times.

Thoughts of the village had become overwhelming during those weeks of illness, as her brain set about re-wiring itself to cope with the fact that she could no longer stay married to Paul. It had all begun as an innocent distraction from the misery that had gradually consumed them both, and she had spent long hours writing notes, cutting out pictures sourced from the internet, solving imaginary problems and drawing maps. She had rarely felt so driven and interested, and felt sure she could devise a system that combined Ubuntu-philosophy with low-impact living. And then every night, lying exhausted in her bed, she would imagine herself on a sun-lounger outside her simple home, watching the trees and the village grow. She knew she could never set up anything as raw and spontaneous as the African settlements she'd seen online – this was the western world – but she still craved the opportunity.

In time Ellen had come to know every nook, cranny, and makeshift shed in the imaginary village that built itself up inside her head and inside her heart. She knew what it felt like to cycle barefoot past tatty gates and big water butts where the leaves piled up. She knew what it smelt like to pull vegetables from the damp earth as the skylark sang overhead. But when she had finally parted from Paul and moved into the spare room, the village had taken her over and become real. *Too real.* She had believed herself to be an imaginary child within its story, and her friends and family had loomed about her like shadowy strangers. Since then she had shoved the whole concept to the very back of her mind, quietly willing it to fade away as she negotiated the new road she found herself on.

It had been unexpected but comfortable when Ellen had finally realised that she could not continue to move forward without Paul in her life. Without ever discussing the matter they had remained together in the house, and on the back of forgiveness had slowly formed a beautiful friendship. She had even kept his name. Of course they had argued – bitterly at times – but had both come to realise that what they shared was more valuable than what they did not. And it was so much easier *not* being married. For Paul – a beaten child and conscientious, sensitive soul – the gravity of a marriage contract had always been a millstone. What Ellen prized as her own spontaneity, meanwhile, felt reckless to him. Her unpredictability troubled him while his over-protection caged her. But she still owed him much – had to admit that in the early days she had benefited from his steadfastness. Neither of them could deny how much they had evolved side by side, establishing their own world-view and hopes for the future. And so when the emotional chains finally dropped away and lay forgotten, their spirits quickly became eager for growth again, like those of young children.

Ellen often smiled when she remembered how she had surprised him one day with two little dogs. Before, any kind of pet would have been an issue. *Everything* had been an issue. But nowadays their worlds blended and separated like drifting bubbles, and it worked. And the dogs were wonderful – for them both – and had quickly become like the children they had never been able to have. Paul had actually thanked her for divorcing him once. So strange how a simple piece of paper can impact the ebb and flow of life.

As soon as her illness had taken hold, Ellen had ended her long-term art business and refused to consider even a casual return to it. As with the village, what had begun with enthusiasm had died away over time, slowly transforming itself into mind-numbing pressure. Typically for her, this dropping of the ball had been spur-of-the-moment, but the truth was that right from its beginnings she had only ever viewed the business as a stop-gap. Deep down, she had always been certain that it was not where her ultimate future lay.

3

July, 2018
Norwich

Janet dragged her fluffy-slippered feet into the big shiny kitchen where her eldest son sat on his phone wearing a creased school uniform. She ignored him because she knew he was ignoring her. From upstairs came the noise of her two younger boys, shouting amid lost things and bedroom mayhem. She filled the kettle unseeingly and the sun streamed through the window, warming her head. The kettle spluttered and then began to hum.

Outside a robin was singing. His eyes were bright black beads above his tiny soft grey and orange throat. He shook his delicate little body and sang again. His song was loud and wistful, and the wind blew the tree where he sat and the leaves brushed over one another.

It was Wednesday and Janet was busy inside her head. She always felt that happiness was within her grasp on Wednesdays because it was her day off. As soon as the boys were gone she could have some wine, put the telly on and look at the catalogues. For starters, there were those boots she'd seen yesterday. Although she wouldn't be able to wear them until the autumn, she couldn't get them out of her head.

Maybe she'd buy one or two things for the house too. New bright cheerful things, all freshly un-boxed and un-bubble-wrapped. Things that would beg her to keep looking at them, and kindle little sparks of pleasure in her weary heart. But suddenly Janet shivered. Soon it would be the summer holidays. The family would be all together, her husband would take two weeks off work, and she would feel stifled, and tired, and inadequate.

Like an empty room. Like an old woman. Like a lost child.

Alan had apologised stiffly for last night, and had kissed her before leaving for work. The kiss had lingered oddly on her cheek with a slight prickle and smell of aftershave. But Alan's apologies were always self-serving and never tender or loving. He had still managed to make her feel small during his short, contrived little speech, although she could not really remember or understand how. The easiest thing for Janet to do was to fit in with Alan's reality, and so she never listened too carefully to what he said anymore. It was quicker and easier to assume that she was wrong. Feeling wrong had become normal to Janet, and whenever she spoke to people lately she sensed a veil of her own wrongness encircling her. She rubbed at the site of the kiss as she stirred sugar into her tea, and then lightly touched the bruise on her lower back.

"You eaten, Ethan?" she asked the boy. He sat open-mouthed without answering. Janet cut herself a large piece of ginger cake and went upstairs to the bedroom. The thought of looking in on the other two boys disturbed her. It was late and they should be leaving soon… but they could cope alright. No point in fussing – they hated it when she fussed and in any case Ethan could manage things. She shut the world out with the door. Then she opened the wardrobe and moved some shoe boxes and folded blankets aside to reveal a bottle of wine and an unwashed glass. She poured a drink and took out her phone, and its sharp light lit up her sorry face.

Outside a robin sang with passion. He shook his delicate little body and sang again, and his song was a living expression, and the wind blew the tree where he sat as the leaves brushed slowly over one another.

4

July, 2018
Yorkshire

The visitor sat calmly in Dixie's cluttered kitchen, looking strangely out of place. On the table in front of him lay a small roughly-heart-shaped pebble, and a pile of photographs. A warm afternoon sun filtered through grubby windows onto washing-up, wilted plants, dog-hair and half-read books. As Dixie fetched the man a glass of water, he found himself trying to move about in complete silence.

The guest had a clean alien simplicity about him, and although he appeared male he lacked any associated body-language. His head-shape was elongated and statuesque, and his soft ageless skin was mid-tone and greyish. The eyes were striking amber and he had mousy hair, fine like a baby's, lying flat and soft against his head. His nose was slightly flattened with delicate triangular nostrils, and the lower face and jaw was long and square with full, pleasantly-shaped lips. He sat with his legs together and his hands resting loosely on his thighs – but rather than looking affected the way he sat expressed complete ease. He was remarkably tall without any real bulk; wore pale monkish clothing that fell in soft folds, and his large feet were clad in grey velvety slippers with no backs.

Dixie fondled his old black Labrador's ears and looked for a long time at the picture he was holding between thumb and forefinger. It was an eight by ten inch print of a blonde girl aged about seven. At length his guest spoke in a voice that seemed to take on the colours and temperature of the air around him. "I have given her the name Navastri, meaning 'Star Child.' She is older now, but this portrait shows best the nature of her heart."

Dixie studied the girl's expression. "Trust, openness, freedom and joy," he thought. At length he handed the picture back to the man opposite, who placed it on the bottom of the pile and rested his hands in his lap, asking:

"Do you approve of that name?"

Dixie smiled at the question. He knew from their previous conversations that naming was very important to the Companions. "I think it's a wonderful name," he answered. "And do you have one for me?"

"For my people a name is as fluid as a soul. Thus I have re-named you several times since you first touched the mind-matrix. Your present name is Zalyam, meaning 'artist;' but also implying vitality, steadfastness, and the scent of wild apple blossom."

Dixie chuckled with pleasure. "I like that. That's very nice. Thank you!"

Although the visitor did not reply, the intensity of his pleasure and appreciation pervaded the room. These people preferred non-verbal communication – they adored words but used them only minimally – were poets and thinkers before all else, but quietly and succinctly so. Yet there was so much that remained perplexing about them, and suddenly Dixie found himself jumping up as his guest clutched at his own chest in apparent agony. *"Do not think about war,"* the big man gasped with pleading eyes.

Dixie's voice was strained. "Sorry, Omasah… I didn't know I was. I thought I was feeling really good." He sat down again heavily.

The guest re-settled himself solemnly, straightened his clothes. He began inhaling and exhaling smoothly. "It cannot be helped," he said kindly. "I am simply unaccustomed. I will be stronger once the assignment begins."

Dixie re-examined his recent thoughts and remembered that a picture *had* indeed popped into his head, just for a second or two. It was something that had been bothering him all day: a snapshot from the morning news… a screaming father holding a blood-soaked child… the smear of red horror; the gaping torn windows and black billow of smoke. Omasah had mentally received the fleeting image as vividly as though living through it, and it was as shocking and foreign to him as it might have been to an innocent child.

Dixie stifled a sigh as he struggled to control his wandering thoughts. "Who else have you got?" he asked, picking up the next photograph in the pile. "Hey! I know these people!"

He had lost touch with Paul and Ellen Turner several years ago, but now he knew he must find them again.

5

July, 2018
Norfolk

Mr Rix sat in the half-light looking at his wife's favourite chair and studying its worthlessness. He pictured her swollen feet inside her tight blue slippers, and the way she would place them neatly together on the rug. He imagined her white hair swept up from the temples, and the elegance and gentleness that had kept her beautiful to him. He saw her aged hands wrestling with the newspaper; heard her voice and felt the gaze of her eyes that had always worn the same expression: a mix of reliance, compliance and trust. She had been a simple woman, a good wife and companion, and now everything was empty and horribly quiet.

Outside the farmyard was quiet, the fields were fallow and the campsite was closed. The hay-bales in the barns were greying and sagging and had become the dark homes to rats. Lines of dark pines whined against the distant whisper of the sea, just visible as a silvery slice of light between the green slopes of the coastland. As the old man listened, a skylark bounced upward, higher and higher, and began its rapid outpouring. Mr Rix automatically registered it as his wife's favourite bird.

Purposeless bird.

Sage the greyhound sidled up and laid her long pale spotted nose on his trouser-leg. The man caressed the dog's head ever so gently with one big thumb, feeling the delicate bones beneath the velvety fur. "Beautiful girl," he said to the dog. Then he got to his feet stiffly and went to the window. Things were changing, he knew that. A great change was coming. His land spread out before him, growing wild in the afternoon sun. He sat down again and switched on the television, but it was all blaring and flashing colours. It had no place in the quiet room and so Mr Rix turned it off. Shame – Olive had loved her telly.

Purposeless mute grey screen.

The old man and the dog wandered out into the yard and took the rough track-way to the unused campsite. One small caravan sat tucked away in a corner with the tall cobbled farmhouse wall behind and the pines to one side. It was not a new caravan or very big, but it was very obviously a home. There was a whirligig heavy with men's clothing fastened with mildewed pegs, and some scrawny red geraniums in pots. A low stool stood by an old wheel-hub which was blackened from regular fires. Mr Rix smelt toast. The dog trotted up to the closed door of the caravan and stood looking up placidly. "Josh!" called Mr Rix hoarsely, realising that he had become unaccustomed to speaking.

The door swung open, banging noisily against the outside of the van, and a tall, slim figure emerged, fussing over the dog. There was something of the cowboy about Josh, with his checked shirts, jeans, and relaxed bandy gait. His face was narrow and horse-like; the hair greying and unkempt. When he turned to the side Josh looked exaggeratedly long and thin, like a cartoon sketched with quick fluid strokes.

Josh had been living on Mr Rix's land for over a year now. When the old lady had died and the campsite had shut down he had stayed on, tucked into the corner with the grass growing all around. Mr Rix wasn't worried about the law any more: things like that didn't bother him like they had before. He liked Josh and his friends, and they liked him. There was a little rent and the use of his postal address, but none of that was very important. And these were vibrant, interesting people – not run of the mill. In fact, Josh was reputedly a very wealthy man, but he cherished the simple life and was content doing little more than the odd electrical job in town.

When Olive had died, Josh and his friends had immediately become Mr Rix's lifeline. His only son lived in London and was tightly wrapped in his own existence. The old man had been brought flowers and endless cups of tea, invited to barbecues, and serenaded with music until the life had begun to creep back into his veins. It was nice to have people around. They were good, kind, genuine folks, who had nothing to gain from him except for the use of his land.

Mr Rix had often fallen asleep listening to their endless talk of Ubuntu – a society aiming to step back from competition and wealth. At first it hadn't interested him because Olive was still too much inside his head. And Olive had liked a bit of money too; had loved to shop for new clothes and cars and the annual holiday. But little by little he had begun to listen, and eventually to put forward ideas of his own. The woman Ellen had written reams of notes and wanted to publish a book about her ideas. She had showed him her notebook one day, stuffed full to bursting with glued-in photographs. But then suddenly she had got ill and stopped writing altogether... Such a shame. It was as though there was a lull over everything these days, and the weeks rolled into months where nothing happened and nobody came.

Mr Rix sat on Josh's stool, accepting his offer of coffee, and the dog lay on her back in the grass asking silently to be stroked. "What's up?" said Josh, handing the old man a big red mug.

Mr Rix's failing eyes took in the landscape that fell away gently towards the glitter of sea; the height of the black pines and the breadth of the grassy space bordered with tall poplar trees. He looked towards the enormous new shower block that had been such an "investment," with its gleaming array of solar panels. He saw the water butts placed here and there in case of fire, and the power-points for the caravans that stuck up uselessly, choked with nettles. Then he turned and spoke wearily to Josh: "Would you like to buy my land?"

6

September, 2018

Summer was ending, the light had changed and the days were shortening little by little. It was still dry and hot, and the afternoon sun felt like the promise of a long massage. The bright blue sky and bleached grasses dazzled, but there was also a slow light breeze, cooling arm, neck and face, and stirring over the scalp. Neighbours lingered in gardens and on doorsteps with their children, and chatted amiably in the shade. People smiled at strangers, feeling their hearts soar at the simple pleasures of a perfect autumn day. There was laughter in the air, the swish of wheels on tarmac and the lazy barking of dogs, but at the same time a blanket of silence drowsed over everything, and the breeze was not enough to disturb it.

On returning to Norfolk, Dixie had lived and worked cautiously, parking his big campervan up dark farm tracks or on the verges of the most deserted roads every night. The Companions had guided him during regular channelling sessions, assuring him that he was in the right place at the right time. First of all he had bumped into Josh – who he had immediately recognised from one of Omasah's photographs – and had been offered a pitch on his land to tide him over. During their first evening together he had found that Josh already knew Paul and Ellen, but he hadn't yet contacted them, preferring to let things unfold naturally. Josh had mentioned the divorce and that Ellen had been writing a book. "It was about an Ubuntu community," Josh had said, and Dixie had felt a buzz of excitement. Then three days ago Mr Rix had received an important flyer from the local council. Everything was slotting into place.

Dixie had quickly found a good place to sell his wood carvings – in a lay-by on a main road that cut through thick woods – and so-far no one had asked any awkward questions. There was a snack-van there belonging to a local couple who had dropped their suspicions on seeing how his animal carvings drew customers in, and had become quite friendly. He often ate there too, to keep them sweet.

When Paul and Ellen finally drove into the lay-by one glorious afternoon Dixie was both relieved and excited. He had been looking forward to surprising them. He got to his feet and waved as their old blue Rover bounced to a halt. Albert, the ancient black Lab, got slowly to his feet and shook himself expectantly. Five minutes of hugs, slaps on backs, shouted questions and explanations followed, and then Paul went to buy teas.

There was so much to say. Ellen perched on the log where Dixie normally sat to work, rocking forwards and back a little. "We're divorced now you know," she told him. "But it's okay. We're still living together. It's just that he… We're very different you know, in lots of ways. But now the dynamic's totally different. Funny – I feel free now and so does he. It's like we've become something better than we were before… I guess we just stopped trying to change each other."

She studied the ground, remembering things. Dixie rolled a thin cigarette, listening in his calm unhurried way.

There were wood-chips in his thick brown hair, and caught in the pockets of his baggy trade-mark shorts that he wore on all but the very coldest of days.

Just as Paul was paying for the drinks a lurid red Lexus drove into the lay-by, showering the tarmac with loose earth from where it had taken the turn-in too fast. As Ellen turned towards the noise her face changed and Dixie stood up, cigarette in mouth. The Lexus waited, but the driver – a bulky man with a large bullet-shaped head – didn't move. Paul walked in front of the car without looking at it before laying a protective hand on Ellen's shoulder; then he proceeded to stare at the car with a steady cold expression which Dixie had never seen him use before. The driver returned Paul's stare briefly before driving away as aggressively as he had come. "What the hell was that all about?" exclaimed Dixie as Ellen hung her head and breathed out heavily with relief.

"It's okay. Just someone I used to see." Within a minute she had fully recovered, although Paul still looked troubled. Ellen carried on speaking to Dixie as before. "I got really ill about a year ago. Sorry we lost touch. Where are you living? Are you staying down here?"

Dixie smiled and his thick mop of hair bobbed a little. "I'll show you. I'll pack up my stuff and you can follow me."

The friends chatted as they drank their teas steamy-hot, and after the van was loaded they drove through woods and open farmland with the wide ocean to their left. Then they wound slowly through the quiet town, where the cobbled church tower shone rosy-gold in the autumnal light. All around the sky was pierced with the needling cry of starlings and zigzagged with the effortless flight of swifts: darting, falling and climbing between the high Victorian facades.

A long sloping crawl past empty schools and sports fields followed, before Dixie finally turned onto a quiet narrow road with grass growing in its middle. "Surely not?" said Paul glancing at Ellen. They rounded a corner and Dixie's van bounced through the open gateway to Mr Rix's old farm as Ellen fell into raptures.

"I don't believe it!" she cried.

The large camper and the blue Rover pulled up sharply alongside Josh's caravan. Dixie lent on his horn as Ellen and the dogs leapt out of the car. "Josh!" she called, cupping her hands round her mouth.

Josh's door swung open and he jumped down his little steps. "Fancy meeting you here you couple of layabouts! I feel a barbeque coming on!"

He made coffee, the dogs roamed here and there, sniffing contentedly, and the sun sank low over the western line of pines. Dixie unpacked his wood, tools and carvings, methodically wrapping them in plastic and arranging them in a tent. Paul helped him, amazed at the talent that had gone into the eagle with outstretched wings, the sleepy owl and the lithe fox with its enormous tail. Ellen was chattering. "What a shame the blackbirds don't sing at this time of year. I just love them. I'm so looking forward to the spring, but then I suppose everybody does. Sorry we haven't been down, Josh. How's Mr Rix? Is he feeling more himself lately?"

"Ah, now there's a thing," said Josh. He crossed his long legs and blew on his coffee. "I've bought the farm off him. Not the house mind – just this camping bit and that field as far as the poplars." He pointed to the line of tall spindly trees.

"*What!*" said Paul walking up. "You rich sod!"

Josh laughed. "Well, a bit less rich now. But it's given the old fellow a bit more income. He might plant next year… over there." He waved a hand. "But he really doesn't want all the hassle any more, and it was all going to waste."

Ellen looked round at the deserted campsite in the dwindling light; at the smart new shower-block and the big field where grass grew between last year's decaying stubble. "Still *is* going to waste," she remarked quietly.

Dixie unfolded a canvas chair and sat down, yawning. "Not necessarily, Ellen. The council's sent out what they call a 'call for sites.' Tell 'em, Josh."

Josh drained his mug and leaned his bony elbows on his long thighs, grinning. "I was going to phone you, honest. But seriously – it only just sank in yesterday what it really meant. We were up half the night talking about it, weren't we Dix?" He cleared his throat, and there was a gleam in his eyes. "The council wants unused land for building, right? But not just any old building… You can also apply to set up green projects and *social experiments* – stuff like that." He was eyeing Ellen's face keenly.

Paul stared as Josh's words began to take root in his mind. He was normally much faster on the uptake, whereas Ellen was well-known for being slow. Dixie poked her in the leg fondly. "That village you were writing about last year, Ellen… You were only telling me half an hour ago."

Realisation finally lit up her face like the sun from between clouds. "Ubuntu?" Then she gave him a friendly punch. "You bugger – sitting there all that time and not saying a word!"

7

October, 2018

Janet hadn't been able to face work. She had rung in sick with a feeble voice – odd in her own ears – and now sat propped up in bed with her phone, a glass of wine and a sandwich, dying for sleep. It seemed as though her life had gradually morphed into some sort of survival mission where she clung grit-eyed and sag-jawed to the better moments, doing her best to dodge the stray bullets that risked stinging her into clarity. Questioning had become too uncomfortable to bear, and the nights were long and lonely for her as she fought off her screaming doubts.

For the first time in a long while her face lit up: an email from Ellen Turner. Janet liked getting emails from Ellen. These days she didn't hear from her much, even though they lived within twenty miles of each other. But that was alright really, because her own life embarrassed her. Email suited Janet. Phone-calls were strenuous, but conversations with real people were even worse, and fraught with indiscernible facial expressions. She found it wearing, and afterwards would brood over furtive looks and sly smiles, knowing that they had been a reaction to her own inadequacies.

Ellen wrote warmly and with a sense of fun, and it sounded as though everything was going very well for her.

Janet wasn't envious. She knew that Ellen had had a rough life and still struggled sometimes, and felt her friend deserved a break. Since her big breakdown she had changed though, and become more interested in what she called "spirituality." What was more, Ellen and her new friends seemed to live in a completely different world from most people. They didn't use Facebook or watch TV, and had ambitions to start some kind of eco-friendly community. But it was still Ellen – the same Ellen she had nursed through hangovers every weekend with tea and Marmite on toast. The same Ellen whose smile and energy had lit up the floor at a thousand night clubs. The same Ellen whose ankles had been so thin they'd looked as though they might snap.

"*You must try and come up*" she wrote with enthusiasm. "*Ethan's got friends in Foxheath – I saw him in town the other day. I don't know – maybe your family might enjoy it?*" Janet swallowed and blinked heavily... "*The big news is that we're finally going to get to build Ubuntu Village – well hopefully. We've applied to the council and a friend of ours has a perfect bit of land. It used to be a campsite so there's water & electricity already laid on, and if they say yes we're going to start off in caravans just to get going and then build small eco-homes and try to get off-grid. We want to live in a new way & bring up our kids to be healthy in mind and body.*"

"Unlike yours," a cold voice smarted inside Janet's head. Tears stung her tired eyes. Ellen was always careful not to mention Janet's family too much, but Janet knew that somehow her old friend knew *everything*, and wouldn't bat an eyelid if she knew that Alan hit her... Or that she drank.

"*It will be such a beautiful place,*" Ellen went on. "*So peaceful & loving like a real community should be. So maybe you could come and have a holiday round here when we've built it? I do miss you Janet, & hope very much that you're well & happy. Sending much love xxx"*

Janet drained her wine-glass and threw her sandwich in the bin – eating might dull the effect of the alcohol. She drew the thick curtains, and the darkness soothed her against the vision of her husband's contempt at the suggestion of a local holiday. There was stuff to do in Foxheath, but even so. One of the reasons he worked so damned hard was so that they could go abroad and have a really good time once a year... New clothes to travel in and shoulder-wrenching bags of duty-free; the cramped plane journey and the too-hot sun; endless eating and crowds and noise and the frantic upload of photos of everyone having fun; the endless search for something new to do that would banish the scornful frowns of her children. Of course she would never dare tell Alan how much she dreaded it – how it exhausted her, and how she couldn't wait to get home and draw the curtains.

She used the toilet, washed her hands, rubbed a little moisturiser into her cheeks and over her eyelids, sighed as she took off her slippers, and then sighed again as she curled up in bed. And in her mind she tried to picture Ellen's little village.

There was a rustle of trees and a sensation like warm honey, and instantly she fell fast asleep.

8

October, 2018
Norfolk

The fair-headed man sitting slumped in the dining chair looked dishevelled and extremely tired, and his fingers strayed restlessly amongst his hair and over his face and clothes. A gleaming mahogany table reflected weighty velvet curtains, a window onto gardens and fields, and an ancient grandfather clock that clunked methodically against the wall of silence. The table was empty except for a small tumbler half-full of whisky, while the sea of thick burgundy carpet somehow failed to bring any ease to the unlit room.

The man looked up from the amber pool of liquid, eyeing the clock as though wondering vaguely about its significance. Then he looked back at the glass. It had been nineteen years since he'd had a drink. It had been ten days since his wife had walked out on him, and two days since he'd handed in his request for early retirement. The only part of it he really regretted was the whisky. He had not drunk any yet – only smelled it – and wasn't sure if he had loved or hated it.

Doctor Wallace extracted his mobile from his pocket and punched the screen unnecessarily hard. The dialling tone sounded like a death rattle in his ears… "Hello Steve," said a youthful voice; a cheerful voice – the voice of a very old friend.

"Hi Jerry. I just smelled a glass of whisky."

"Ha ha! Done it myself a thousand times! Smelled a bottle of wine I bought for cooking last week and had to give the rest to the next-door neighbour. He was over the moon, silly old sod. Hasn't stopped him moaning about the hedge, though." The voice was eager and confiding, and mirth laced in and out of it. Speaking to Jerry made you feel as though you were walking home after school, giggling with your best friend. "Look, come over for God's sake, mate," he went on. "I promise not to talk about psychology. Ha ha!" The laugh bubbled from the heart.

"I… I don't like being away from home. I like the quiet here."

"Silence is bloody golden. But not so great when your whole life's just fallen down around your ears."

"I wanted her to go, Jerry… in the end."

"I know, mate. But your life's still been turned on its head, hasn't it? That's traumatic, you know. That's why you're sitting there looking at a glass of whisky. You know it wouldn't work but you're in a place where that doesn't matter. Just a break would be nice, and the easiest way is booze. Best pain-killer out there, and it's dead easy. Much too easy if you ask me… Shouldn't be that easy when there's folks like us wandering in the fray."

Jerry's wife Mags seated herself beside him on the sofa, her hawk-like wrinkled face framed in its typical headscarf. Her eyes showed concern as she wiped pastry from her skinny hands very fast, finger by finger. Jerry glanced at her. "Mags's done it too."

"And relapsed like ten times," she whispered very low. "But don't tell 'im that."

There was a hollow pause at the other end of the line. "Steve?" said Jerry. "Mate! Come on over! Mags'll pick you up." He knew that would do it, and suppressed a giggle. One great advantage of Ubuntu Village was no more of his wife's driving – she had vowed to give it up for the sake of the planet.

Steven looked out of the window where pink roses bobbed and felt a fleeting spark of life as a skylark piped up with thrills and spills. "Okay," he said. "I'll come over, you bastard. I bet she's right there… I'll see you in twenty. And yes – I'll dump the whisky." He put his free hand around the glass. It felt familiar. He held it in the air as though toasting the room. It felt *un*familiar.

"Oh, and Jerry! I want to hear more about this Ubuntu thing."

9

October, 2018

Night had fallen by the time Ellen and Paul left the old campsite. They had eaten with Josh and Dixie and been reunited with Mr Rix, who they hadn't seen since the spring. It had been a joyful but exhausting reunion, and now Dixie and Josh sat outside together by the light of a fire as they had come to do most nights. It was a peaceful, comfortable way to pass the time.

Dixie looked into the flames and said: "Fire connects us with our ancestors, you know… and our distant future." He glanced at Josh. "I'm afraid I haven't been entirely straight with you. I've heard about Ubuntu before. It's the reason I came back to Foxheath."

Josh didn't answer. The two men had already formed a strong bond and shared a great trust. He simply watched as Dixie rolled one of his thin brown cigarettes. "Not from Ellen either," his friend continued. "She hadn't even heard of it back when I knew her."

Josh still waited while the other man collected his thoughts. "Ubuntu's got to happen," said Dixie at last. "This one and others around the world – I don't know how many. I've got a friend you'll need to meet. He's… not your average friend. He's come to help, and to make sure things happen in the right way. He's a very… advanced being. Think of him like a seer, maybe. Or a guru. A very powerful person. He's been helping already – kind of behind the scenes."

Josh turned his angular body towards Dixie in the firelight. "Are we talking coincidences? Because there just seem to be too many… as though everything's been lined up for us."

Dixie nodded. "Exactly. It's all got to come together. *We've* all got to come together."

Josh's eyes shone. "You met me and I knew Paul and Ellen and… and Ellen bumped into Carlos after fifteen years, just as he needed a new direction…"

"And you met the viscount through cleaning his windows with Jerry and Mags, and then you all got left all that money…"

Josh interrupted: "To buy this land, which is ideal! And Jerry and Mags are skilled builders too. They used to be property-developers, you know, before drink ruined them." His mind raced over and over. "But if drink hadn't ruined them, then they probably wouldn't be here now," he added.

"Exactly. It all fits together. Ellen always says there are patterns in life, but sometimes you see them more clearly."

Josh collected himself. "So who is he?"

Dixie considered, smoking calmly. "Well, they don't like to think of themselves as 'different' from us, but as far as *time* goes they may as well be from another world. He… *they*… the 'Companions' as they call themselves, are from – well, way ahead, Josh. Tens of thousands of years. Get your head round that if you can."

There was a stunned silence. "Time travellers?" said Josh in a strange voice. "You're… having a laugh aren't you, Dix?"

His friend didn't seem to hear, and went on speaking quietly. "They aren't keen on questions so I don't have an exact figure, but I do know they view time very differently from us. They're from a Golden Age, you see. But he's a hundred percent human, my friend, although sometimes he doesn't altogether seem it." Dixie rubbed his upper arms against the cold. "Look, I'll make up the fire; you get coffee and blankets and I'll tell you everything."

Josh stood up feeling a mixture of emotions. The dark field felt dreamlike, and as he breathed in the night air he felt that nothing would ever be the same again. The sky above had altered, and the wind in the pines sang gently of change. He threw the dregs of his coffee on the ground and said: "You know the viscount wasn't even born into the aristocracy? He just got lucky. Got adopted when he was five, and then ended up wanting to pass some money on to people he really liked and got on with." He laughed softly. "A bunch of crazy window-cleaners… Ha! We all got the shock of our lives. I won't forget that day in a hurry."

They spoke long into the night – long after Mr Rix's light went out and the final glow disappeared from the west. Dixie began by telling Josh how the Companions had first contacted him when he had been in deep meditation. Then about a year ago, he'd begun having channelled conversations with a man calling himself Omasah, and had since met him. It had taken him months to come to terms with what was happening: he had been terrified he was going mad at first, had been unable to work, and had completely isolated himself. He'd even started drinking to excess, although he'd regained control as soon as Omasah had appeared in the flesh.

Josh sat on the step of his caravan sipping coffee. Dixie gathered his blanket around himself, kicking at a log in the fire. "They don't really tell me much," he said. "Just that the time-lines are so bad right now that they've had to... well, tweak things. I think it's like increasing the chances for things to happen rather than causing actual events. The world's in trouble, and if we don't survive they won't either."

"So why you and not Ellen?" asked Josh. "I mean Ubuntu's her baby."

"I was the one they managed to contact, and obviously I'm meant to be a part of this too. They know all about us. I mean everyone, Josh. Omasah gave me photos of you, Paul and Ellen, and Carlos and a load of other people. Said I needed to find them."

Josh raised his eyebrows. "Photos? Not exactly high-tech. Why not just give you a list of names?"

Dixie shrugged. "Most of the folks don't have online presence. I suppose he knew that. And as for the pictures, I haven't the foggiest how he got them. Some advanced technology maybe?" He got to his feet, lost in thought. "You see... according to ancient texts we're just coming out of a Dark Age. That's why we've got so much trouble right now. But in so-called Golden Ages we might be capable of all kinds of stuff... plus living in peace will be a natural state. It's all supposed to go in a huge cycle. Ask Carlos about it – it's very interesting."

Dixie lumbered to his camper over the dark grass. The light clicked on and he could be seen rummaging in a drawer. He quickly returned with a wad of photographs and sat down again. "Look – do you know any of these by any chance?"

41

He lined up the pictures on the grass in the firelight. They included a girl of about seven with a radiant smile; a serene-looking black man in his twenties; a grizzled woman with large hoop-earrings; a blonde middle-aged man in a shirt and tie, and a teenaged boy – handsome and frowning. Josh laughed in disbelief, picking up the one of the fair-headed man.

"Surely not! This is my GP…" He examined it, squinting doubtfully in the firelight. Then he took up the picture of the girl. "I know this one too. Her family have always been keen on Ellen's ideas… these two are her parents, and this is her brother." He quickly surveyed the rest, and cleared his throat. "Most of them used to come up here regularly, before Ellen got ill." His gave a nervous laugh. "So they're kind of all-knowing, then, these friends?"

"Pretty much," said Dixie. "You see, in their eyes, it's how a civilisation acts that's all-important. Advancement's about levels of consciousness, not the tools we use or the toys we play with…" He hesitated, turning concepts in his mind. "We tend to forget that 'technology' means applying knowledge for practical purposes – it doesn't have to be an iPhone or a laptop."

He handed Josh the green pebble that had lain on the table in Yorkshire during his first meeting with Omasah. "That's technology," he said. "Or at least it is to them."

Josh turned the stone over in his palm, and a fleck of crystal caught the light from the dying fire.

Dixie was still eager to explain, relieved at finally being able to share these things. "It's like they exist in a state with much more… connectivity. Universal Mind, Omasah calls it. And stone's a good conductor because it's old and very dense, right? It's like a window into time, but it's kind of ritualistic too. The person who carries the stone has the issue it represents most in hand. That's the stone for this village. And the council *will* say yes, by the way... The Companions aren't about to be thwarted by some dumb-ass councillor."

Josh still gazed at the stone. "Ritualistic? That's surprising. You'd think they'd lost that kind of thing." He went to hand the stone back but Dixie shook his head.

"It's yours now because you own the land. Just don't lose it, whatever you do." He smiled to himself. "Omasah's an amazing person, you know. If he's our future then we really should be celebrating."

Josh pocketed the stone safely and patted the place. "Long way to go, though. But yeah – I guess it's reassuring. So we're going to build Ubuntu and change the world?"

Dixie was searching his pockets for his cigarette papers. "More like giving things a gentle nudge in the right direction," he said. "But not a word to anyone – not yet." He grew serious over his tobacco tin. "This kind of passion... this kind of vision we've created... it's too powerful not to take root. It needs to take root *now*. Like Carlos always says, the world is waking up. No one's immune from the ripples of truth that are seeping through everything, and they're getting stronger. The village *must* succeed, as part of this shift towards a higher state. War, hunger, corruption, greed – its time is over. Other civilizations out there... well, they see us as dangerous. Like kids with a box of matches." He glanced briefly at the night-sky. "That's what the Companions say. But if enough people get in touch with what really matters then everything can start changing. It's like tiny cogs beginning to turn the much bigger ones. Yes, we're just a bunch of drop-outs in a field, but we represent important truths that will grow and grow until they bind the human race together. The time for love and truth *must* come."

10

October, 2018

This wasn't a good mirror. Or maybe it was the lighting. Perhaps Maxwell should ask his father about getting new lighting for the room. He was sure to know the best sort of lighting for a room of this sort. For some reason this mirror didn't do him justice, whereas the one in the bathroom showed off his powerful jaw and paled out the shadows beneath his eyes.

The man ran a big hand through his scant hair and turned away from his reflection. He pocketed his hands and strolled slowly to the window. Such a great house. So lucky to own a house like this, with its bay-window and good position in the town. Ample parking for the Lexus too. The man gazed with pleasure at the gleaming red car. What a find that was. He had his dad to thank for that.

Maxwell moved restlessly about the room for a while before mounting the stairs. He passed his bedroom, where the curtains were still shut, and entered the box-room he called his "office." There were a number of papers strewn about the table and a computer hummed quietly. Maxwell sat down and took hold of the mouse, but he couldn't think of anything that needed doing and stood up again, chewing edgily at his fingernails. Then he went out into the hall, noticing the superior quality of the carpet under his feet, and into the darkened bedroom. He lay down on the bed and laced his big fingers behind his oversized head. The room smelt faintly of stale sweat and urine.

Maxwell closed his eyes and tried to relax but it was no good. He got up with sudden urgency, went to a large grimy antique chest, and opened the top drawer with a jolt. From amongst men's underwear he retrieved a half-bottle of whisky, and took several pulls at the fiery liquid. He began to screw the lid tight but then he stopped, undid it again, and took another generous slug. Then he lay back down on the bed, welcoming the warm comfort as it spread through.

Maxwell slept fitfully for about an hour, snoring loudly on his back. As always when he drank, he woke up angry. He turned onto his side to face the wall, where the rough imprint of a fist showed in the plaster-board. His thoughts raced and he began muttering to himself through clenched teeth. Bloody peasants who lived in this town had no respect. Bloody village idiots, spreading lies That Ellen Turner – she was the worst. He would never forget the insults she had dealt him after their holiday in the Bahamas. To think of the money his father had been forced to fork out for an extra room, when all he'd been trying to do was protect her. She was so naïve it made your head spin. All he'd tried to do was get her back to the safety of the hotel, but she couldn't see danger even when it was staring her right in her stupid face. He'd had to restrain her; he'd had to get tough with her because she simply wouldn't listen. Danger had been all around. He'd seen it in the eyes that had filled the street and he'd sensed it under his skin. It was what he'd been trained for – well, at least for a little while, until there was that misunderstanding. But he'd never forgotten his training. He knew danger, and danger had been all around that night, whispering

People like her hadn't lived. They hadn't moved in the circles he and his father had. She hadn't been to public school and she didn't know how to behave properly. How much she could've learned from him! How much of the world and of life he could have shown her! But she was small-town: didn't recognise quality when she saw it – not quality people, or quality cars, or even quality food. People like her hadn't lived.

Of course he'd never forget the moment he'd discovered that she'd killed his child – the dizzy sickness that had turned his blood to ice in a second. Then he knew that it had all been just a ride for her. A sample of the good-life. Up until then they'd pretty much managed to mend their differences. She'd always seen reason in the end – had been quite good like that. But that day, the light had dawned for him against the horror of what she had done. She didn't appreciate what he had to offer; what his family had to offer. Okay, so maybe he'd mucked up on holiday, but he'd tried his best to make it up to her. He'd bought her a ring and a mohair sweater. He'd taken her out for an expensive meal… Champagne on ice… twelve red roses delivered to her door. But she hadn't appreciated any of it. She'd stopped laughing at his jokes and had refused to eat or sleep with him… and she hadn't stroked his head when he'd cried. All he'd wanted her to do was to stroke his head…

He knew it had been a boy – the little boy he'd always yearned for. But she'd killed it before it even had a chance. Tiny helpless soul. How he'd always dreamt of tenderly stroking a mother's rounded abdomen. His son. Something to be really proud of! Someone to adore him, and to whom he could teach everything he knew. Someone to look up to him, just like he'd always looked up to his own father. He would have been in his twenties now, his boy. A fine figure of a man, no doubt. But she'd killed him – had slipped away one day and returned with an empty sterilised womb.

People in town had no respect for him any more, and it was all Ellen's fault – spreading distorted tales she'd gleaned from other ex-girlfriends. Exaggerated accounts of violence where there'd been only care and protection. Fabrications of an unstable mind that always ignored the reasons behind his actions, or warped them into things unrecognisable. It was unfair that he'd never had a chance to explain how he'd been disrespected, and bullied, and had his nerves shredded. Bloody rural grape-vine: there was nothing like it for twisting the truth. And so nowadays Maxwell had to seek out young fresh things to impress. Groups of youths in pubs and then even younger girls, with their thin tender necks and swelling breast-buds. He'd buy them drinks outside pubs, impressing them with his scorn for the law; would lap up their giggles and smiles, loving the way they found him charismatic despite his age. And sometimes he would haunt the schoolyards just to catch a glimpse and a cheerful wave, his genitals hanging out loose beneath his black frock-coat.

But despite that occasional indulgence he was still stuck here amongst this lousy peasantry since dad had got ill... Couldn't move away now... Wished he could move away and start again with a fresh slate. He loved meeting new people and watching their enrapt faces as he related the elaborate story of his life; the way they would stare wide-eyed at his tales of public school and army life... But he had to look after dad. He owed him everything. Dad had taught him all he knew, and together they had suffered the horrors of his mother's disturbed mind…

Maxwell sat up straight-backed, hearing the pressurized blood whistling in his ears. Without a thought, he kicked his left heel ferociously into the impression in the wall. The plaster-board split raggedly and the carpet collected white fragments and dust. His deep voice trembled round the dark room: "I'll destroy you! You don't know what you're dealing with!" He sat breathing through the searing pain in his foot. He'd get his own back eventually. She was hanging round with a bunch of hippies now, camping illegally in fields and suchlike. He'd get them run in for drugs, for sure. He'd certainly get them for something.

Maxwell used the toilet, spitting profanities into the dirty bowl and leaving it un-flushed. Must get out and have a look around. Must find someone to talk to… Even a bit of small-talk would do. He was good at small-talk… and there was always something to glean about something or somebody so long as you kept your head screwed on.

Slipping on a jacket he slammed the front door hard and locked it with shaking fingers. Then he got in his car and roared off in the direction of the town centre.

11

October, 2018

Home School was literally that – a school in a home. A south-facing lounge with finger-smudged French windows that stayed wide-open whenever the weather permitted. A view onto a tatty garden over threadbare rugs, and the tinkle of wind-chimes amid the faint hum of a road.

Jill clapped her hands decisively. "Art time!" She smacked down some sheets of paper on the table. "Anya – it's your turn for subject."

The girl remained intent on her doodles, immediately answering: "My Ubuntu School." There was a general murmur of appreciation as boxes of felt pens and fat wax crayons were handed round. The children's over-optimistic hopes about the project being approved quickly had soon been dashed. They had been excited about the prospect of lessons in a shed or caravan, but Ellen had rung the council and learnt that the application hadn't even been read yet. A "No" would be devastating, and no one wanted to think about that scenario after the luck of Josh offering up the land.

"Addy's sorted all the pens out," said Jill. "So no duds." The children began drawing at once, and Jill bent her curly head over her book.

"In Burundi," announced Melyne, busily pencilling a tiny building in the middle of her page; "...they fix us good playground with old car and boat. We could make like this!"

"And paint them all really bright colours with spots," said Nadia, whose ideas always ran away with themselves. "And we could have a cave and a pond and a tree-house."

Addy scrunched his face up as he examined his drawing critically. "How do you make a fence go round the corner?"

"Anya, help him, please," said Jill. "Yes, a good playground is a definite must! And does anyone know what birds we'll hear in Ubuntu Village?"

"The black one with a yellow nose," said Melyne.

Nadia giggled and then asked hurriedly: "Are we having a garden? Can it have a trampoline? And can there be a rope-swing?"

Addy's eyes were following Anya's confident strokes on the paper: "Skylarks because of the fields and crows because of the woods and seagulls because of the sea."

"That's right, Addy," said Jill. "And there'll be owls at night too."

Anya settled down again at her own picture. She had divided her page into two halves, and was working on a ground-floor plan of a building alongside an outside view with grass and trees. "Draw a robin on your fence, Addy," she suggested. "They sing all year round."

"How do you draw a skylark?" whined Addy. "Skylarks are my favourite."

Jill was quick of hand with a bird book: "Look it up! So, who can tell me what they're looking forward to most about Ubuntu?"

"Not seeing people walking about staring at phones all day," said Addy. "It's stupid."

Anya spoke without raising her eyes. "Not seeing other kids my age."

"Why?" asked Nadia.

"Because they hate me."

Jill cut in: "That's not true, Anya."

The girl went on speaking softly. "No – it's okay. I understand they think I'm different, but it'll be nice not to have to feel… watched whenever I walk past. That's all."

"When do you see other kids anyway?" teased Nadia, who was younger than Anya but much more savvy and outgoing.

"Well, in the chip-shop…"

Nadia giggled. "They just fancy you."

Anya blushed uneasily. "They aren't all boys," she said sulkily. "Anyway – all they ever talk about is clothes and …" Her voice faded, and gained a tremor: "But they always know as soon as I walk in that I'm nothing like them. I don't think I was made for this world."

Addy's volume was much too high, and Jill gave him a sign with her hand. "We can't have everyone the same, that's what Mummy says." With his eyes on Jill, the boy turned his imaginary volume button to the left before continuing in a harsh whisper: "Otherwise everyone might be like me, which would be awful."

Nadia laughed and Anya smiled down at her drawing.

Jill quashed a sigh as she listened to the chit-chat. It felt like she, Paul, Ellen and the others were running away… was that a bad thing? Was it wrong to want to escape a society that had served them all so well in the greater scheme of things? But that was what was so good about Ubuntu. Like Ellen always said, it was designed to give back, not just to consume: to give to the world and the planet, even if only on a small scale.

Surely it must be time for that, especially with the weather changes and growing strain on resources?

Jill's book lay in her lap as she watched the children lovingly. Yes, they all felt so driven to do it now that there was no turning back. Then she shivered as she heard Paul's angry voice in her head. He rarely lost his cool, so it was always memorable when he did: "If I had kids I wouldn't want them growing up part of this *machine*. Have you seen those little girls in mini-skirts and boots and lipstick, with their little designer handbags? Fucking consumers… already! It's like they haven't even had a choice!" Jill shook herself, visualising the un-blinking power of Paul's eyes.

Addy's skylark was growing in size and intricacy, and black ink had collected here and there in big spots. "Don't press so hard, Addy," Jill told him, feeling hungry and checking her watch. The boy ignored her and continued frowning with effort.

"I don't know any other children too, but that's because I've got Asperger's," he said.

Nadia rolled her eyes at her little brother. "Everything's because you've got Asperger's."

"Well, it is!" argued the boy, as Jill clapped her hands again and the children fell quiet.

Anya sat watching the golden motes swimming in the light that streamed into the old familiar room. The others were still drawing and Jill was eating a sandwich, absorbed in her book. Anya's picture was already finished. She had made her school building circular with large windows, just as she had always imagined it. It had big floor-cushions in each room and a little kitchen in the middle. Anya began sketching a boy's face secretly on the back of her English book, remembering how she had once asked her father: "Am I pretty, Dad?" and how he'd been noncommittal:

"You'll always be beautiful to me, darling."

And so she had studied her face in different mirrors and in different lights. But it had just looked calmly back at her, reflecting how she felt inside. Was it pretty or not? She wasn't sure at all – could not seem to make it appear either one thing or the other. She tried a little face cream one night from her mother's heavy glass jar: it felt cool and smelt of roses.

"Mum, am I pretty?"

Her mother had sighed a little at the question, but then Mary often sighed. "You know Anya, beauty is only luck… a gift… and it's very short-lived. Be thankful, and always remember – it's not clever." Mary's eyes had gone back in time picturing her own mother, who had been both beautiful and cruel. "It really is what's in the heart that counts, Anya. You know that."

And so with this subtle affirmation the subject had been dropped, and Anya was left to wrestle with herself. Night after night she would juggle gratitude and vanity; pleasure and shame, as she eyed her own reflection… until she had remembered that a gift wasn't supposed to be kept hidden away, but shared. Pleased at this loophole, and somewhat released, the girl began to toy a little. Before long, Anya was spending all week looking forward to the chip-shop on Fridays, and the brooding boy who hung darkly on her every move. She came to enjoy the feelings it roused in her young body, and the way thinking about him would suddenly make her giggle. Her pencil shaped the strong jaw and jaunty mop of hair tenderly behind her folded arm.

Later, and the sun was low and the children were in the garden. Anya's fair-haired mother Mary sat talking in the school-room, her pretty hands wrapped round an ivy-clad cup. "You know, Jill. I remember the moment I knew we had to go tech-free. I was at this woman's house… It was ages ago now, when Anya still went to middle school. The two girls had made friends – sort of." Mary sighed deeply and sipped her tea, while outside the children chatted noisily under the old apple tree. "Well, I'd gone to pick her up, and the kids… the other kids I mean… were having this almighty row because an iPad had gone wrong or something. The telly was on and you couldn't hear yourself think – some music video with buttocks and boobs hanging out everywhere!" Mary covered her mouth with one hand as she recalled the scene. "And then the mother yelled, 'Just go on something else!' And, Jill – it just hit me right between the eyes. It was like there was no other option in the entire world. They weren't interested in going outside or imaginary play or anything." Mary repeated the sentence with an added injection of scorn: "'*Just go on something else!*' And it was just screamed at them… and the older sister was sitting there taking photos of herself, pouting like a… Oh, dear! Don't these people realise who and what's parenting their children?"

Jill's folded her hands across her abdomen despondently. "Yes, I know. And then they scold them for looking at the trees and flowers… Drag them along by the arm and tell them to hurry up."

"But it's isolating, Jill. It's like most people don't even see there's a problem. Perhaps there isn't. Perhaps it's just us?"

Jill smiled calmly. These were not new issues. "Well, nothing's ever black or white, is it?" she said. "Technology's revolutionised the world and is a great avenue for truth. Trouble is people see it as a cure-all, and it simply isn't. But it's certainly not for us to dictate to the rest. Stop worrying, Mary. Anya wants to draw and write, and we're giving her a lovely environment to do it in. She'd choose this for herself in any case."

"That's what Anya says," Mary replied. "But I mean Harry's never had any doubts. He never had a telly even way back. He lived in a boat when I first met him, you know – teaching at a posh Grammar school he was, and living in this old boat with a plastic bag of clothes and his guitar!" She laughed lightly.

Jill turned towards the garden where an evening glow played through Anya's halo of flyaway hair. "Nothing must stem the flow of *her* creation," murmured Jill, more to herself than to Mary. Addy was shouting and trying to take control of everything, and Nadia looked over and rolled her eyes again. "Anyway," said Jill quietly; "even if we are freaks, at least soon we can all be freaks together."

12

October, 2018

Mags wiped her hands vigorously on a grubby tea-towel. "There's plenty for 'im," she said, lifting lids and sniffing the air. They had just heard a car crunch to a halt on the gravel outside, and Steven walked in without knocking. After a reality-check in his bathroom mirror he had quickly showered, shaved and put on a smart checked shirt, moss-green cords and brown suede shoes. Jerry burst into his happy giggle. "Hello Steve – you're looking thoroughly middle class!"

Steven fostered a thin smile as he took off his jacket and sat down at the large weathered kitchen table. He felt hungry. He felt grateful too, and said so. But suddenly he was close to tears. "God, I wish I could have a *drink*. What's the matter with me?"

Mags wound her skinny arms around his neck, and she smelt of parsley and onions. "Have some food, Steve. It'll soon pass, trust me." She slid a mug of tea in front of him and began clattering plates and cutlery. Jerry whistled tunefully as he placed mats and glasses, and the doctor stared at a flour-covered raisin on the table. Jerry sat down, watching him through the tops of his thick-framed bifocals.

"You really thinking about Ubuntu mate? You reckon you could... just stand alone in a field, with no labels? No *career*?

Because it defines you, you know – being a doctor. It always has."

Mags shot him a glance that said "What the hell do you think you're doing?"

Jerry continued more gently. "Who do you see looking back at you from the mirror, Steve?" He put his elbows on the table and studied his own clasped hands. "I know I've seen all sorts of people over the years. Admittedly most of them were pissed…"

Steven stared at the raisin intently as though it was a crystal-ball, forgetting to point out that Jerry had promised not to talk about this kind of thing. It was a habit of Jerry's, he knew that; and in any case Steven didn't feel quite so threatened by his own psychology of late.

"I looked in the mirror today and saw… an old man," he answered finally. "And he looked a bloody mess." He waited while Mags served up hot steaming stew, dumplings and rice. "I'm not a doctor any more. It's gone from my heart. But it's an honourable occupation, and I don't regret a minute of it." Steven wasn't sure if he was being truthful; he was more concerned with saying the right thing.

"But it'd swallowed you up whole," said Jerry.

Steven smiled half-heartedly. "How can it not?"

Mags cut in, changing tack: "Ubuntu's completely flexible, you know Steve. We know some people can't give everything up – like you – and other people 'aven't got anything to give – like Carlos and Tali, whose café's just gone bust… and us of course, because we blew everything like the idiots that we are. It is a social experiment after all, although it's a lot more than that to Ellen."

Steve's mind was ticking over, and underneath nagged the suspicion that he was the only person keeping money back.

It made him uneasy and he felt it set him apart. A thought struck him. "What happens about tax?"

"Exempt for the first year. We 'ave to be treated as a business because that's the only pigeon-hole they can fit us in."

Jerry gave a half-laugh. "Ubuntu doesn't stoke the machine, so they're going to want to keep it in check... Horrible world, isn't it?"

Mags scowled at her husband. "Don't say that, Jerry. At least we get to build our paradise. It'll be fun, and like a feeling of going forward. And you never know – with all the housing problems and things, it might get to be a viable option one day... for the government, I mean."

Steven moved the hot food around on his plate thoughtfully. "I definitely feel ready to sell the house," he said. "It was my dream when I was up in Newcastle, but it's ridiculously big – even more so now, with just me there." He was seeing memories, like ghosts. "I wanted peace and quiet and to hear the birds more than anything. Susan was never interested in those things."

Mags nodded. "Yes, she's always been a city girl at heart. Eat something Steve."

He filled his fork. "So how much does it cost to put up one of these... sheds?"

"It's not a bloody shed," said Jerry. "It's a micro-home. Ten to fifteen grand depending on what you want. Peanuts to you. They meet all the building regs – amazing little places. I'll show you some pictures when we've eaten."

"After the homes are built," said Mags, her eyes wide, "we'll keep most of the vans for storage and materials. Just think of all the stuff that goes into a caravan – metal, wiring, wood... wheels."

"Not forgetting the appliances inside," added Jerry with his mouth full.

Mags chattered on. "And there's a big shower block that's going to be demolished. We can use all that for the school and things. That's where our building skills come in!"

The food was good. The sweetness of root vegetables blended with a good dose of cinnamon, and the dumplings were moist and fluffy. As Steven ate he tried to picture himself in a tiny house, with a little plot of land planted with rows of crops. He tried to imagine having no access to a bank account. Ellen was more than happy with the generous donation he'd decided on, but the whole concept was grey and murky in his mind. "You don't *have* to wear sack-cloth," laughed Jerry, as if reading his thoughts.

"There's *oodles* of birdsong up there," said Mags. "You were made for it, Steve. You've just forgotten who you really are."

Steven's private movie rolled on in gloomy monochrome. He saw himself getting up in the morning and making a cup of tea in a cramped kitchen. He saw himself drinking it on a tiny porch wearing a drab dressing-gown. Finally he remembered that he would never have to sit through another of his wife's dinner parties and grimaced, remembering odious people with odious faces. There were definitely things that appealed about Ubuntu – like good genuine people to spend time with. He looked up from his plate. "But what will I *do*?"

Mags immediately became animated. "Ubuntu's about self-discovery, Steve. You can *do* whatever you're good at!" The skinny hands began waving. "Become the person you were born to be! Gardening; teaching; woodwork – anything! Everyone brings his or her *self*, not a bank balance or career. You'll find your niche: trust me."

Jerry was wiping his empty plate with a thick slice of bread. "What did you want to be when you were a kid, Steve?"

Steven froze. He almost answered "a doctor," but as Jerry had pointed out many times, that had been his parents' idea – his parents' world fuelled by his parents' passion. His eyes became watery and he suddenly craved the cool bow of the glass in his hand all over again.

"An artist," he said at last. "Please don't laugh."

13

November, 2018

When Ellen wrote, she sometimes reached a point where she could no longer follow what she was doing with her hands. She felt the pressure of the keys on the ends of her fingers, but was only really aware of the flow of her creation. It was pure and joyful, like a bird's song.

Birdsong and a candle – then and only then had she felt safe.

Birdsong was the sound of Ubuntu. It had been in her imagination from the very first moment. They made music together, Ellen and the birds; and she heard her words in their calls as she typed. It felt as if everything belonged to everything else, and nothing was owned or owed. That was the spirit of Ubuntu, and it burned again in her chest now, making her face glow with pleasure; and her floor was often strewn with notes as she worked on her book late into the night. Sometimes Paul would find her scribbling notes on the floor, like a child absorbed in a drawing.

Ellen's mood was infectious. There was a general belief growing that the council would say yes, and that they would begin moving onto the land within few months. Those who were most optimistic had already put their houses up for sale, while others collected cardboard boxes and waded through adverts for second-hand caravans. The best way to dispel negativity or doubt was a get-together, and so once again the old farm became the venue for barbeques and parties.

Despite his talk with Josh, Dixie still hadn't broached the subject of the Companions with Paul and Ellen. Perhaps he was uncertain of their response... perhaps it just seemed too unreal... but the important thing was that Omasah would be there to help when the time came to build the village. One starlit evening over the fire Dixie decided to sound his friends out a little. "What do you guys think about time travel?" he asked casually.

Paul stopped strumming on his guitar and Ellen looked up at the sky. "I believe it," she said. "There must be species out there so advanced they aren't bound by space or time. And one day we won't be either."

Paul gave her a glance that said "How can you be so sure?" but she didn't notice. Then he watched the fire as he spoke. "There are so many things completely outside our sphere; outside the goldfish bowl so-to-speak. Other dimensions and things. How can a goldfish ever understand a London bus? Well, we're that fish. Our field of understanding is just so limited."

Ellen sat stroking the grass thoughtfully. "Yeah, but scientists still always talk like they know everything. The system doesn't want us to question ways of being."

"I could think about this sort of stuff all day," said Josh. "Just because you can't see it doesn't mean it isn't there. You can't see electricity. Or sound waves."

"Wifi!" put in Paul. "Think of what that's carrying every minute of the day."

Ellen's face was ageless in the glow of the flames. "I love looking at the stars and wondering," she said. Then she looked suddenly pained. "… Although I remember lots of times when I didn't."

Josh leaned forwards to turn over the foil-clad potatoes cooking in the embers, and the group fell silent for several minutes. All around the chatter of other people continued, and the air was full of sparks and the smell of smoke and food. Behind the pines the sky was electric blue. Ellen suddenly resurfaced from where old memories and their emotions had swept her under like a tide. The music coming from Josh's caravan ended abruptly, and gave way to a heart-stopping sense of connection – with the wind in the trees, and the endless galaxies beyond, and with one another.

Everyone had forgotten the start of the conversation – something Paul never did. "I'd love to do it," he said. "Go back to Victorian London, or watch the Romans marching up the beach." He frowned, swigging from a chilled bottle of lager, and the bottle glistened in the red light. "… Or forwards… if we have a bloody future, that is."

Dixie sat sipping coffee with a blanket round his shoulders. His eyes were steady like Paul's, Ellen noticed – but without the slight sadness that only she ever noticed. There was always a hint of a smile on Dixie's tanned face, as though he was forever expecting something pleasant to arrive from very far off, and he seemed to bask in the anticipation of it. "Eyes like Paul's but with more light in them," thought Ellen, as Dixie said smoothly:

"We have a golden future."

Paul blew out disdainfully through his nostrils as Dixie turned to him, adding: "It's just a way away, Paul. But it *is* coming, you can be sure of that."

Ellen shut her eyes, relishing this optimistic thought as

she caught snippets of conversation. People were having fun, everything was rekindled, and things felt like they had last summer. She sighed with pleasure.

The silence waxed comfortable as a long-haired man in his forties approached and handed a joint to Ellen. She looked up. "Thanks, Carlos… I'll bring it back in a minute." The man strolled back towards another fire and sat down, putting his arm round the shoulders of a small dark young woman.

"Well, I'm gonna grab one of these spuds," said Paul draining his bottle.

It was past midnight, and everyone had gone home except for Carlos and his girlfriend, who sat quietly together by the glow of the second fire. Albert slept soundly in the camper's open door, and other dogs dozed here and there on the grass. Paul was fast asleep under his coat.

Dixie had stuffed his thick hair into a woolly hat, and was smoking in his thoughtful way. "The world's gone nuts, Ellen," he said. "We've got crazies running the planet. And then there's the weather, debt-slavery, the health crisis, the lies and the cover-ups… And we've never had such abundance, and yet people have never been more dissatisfied."

Ellen sat hugging her knees to her body, listening closely. "Because society teaches us to be dissatisfied, that's why."

Dixie went on quickly. "The human race is being forced to look in a cosmic mirror – that's what Carlos says. It has to happen like this to trigger change, even in our personal lives. Look, when you got beaten up and had the early menopause and everything, you took it bad, yeah?"

Ellen nodded. "I had addictions too, until I was… Oh, I don't know, Dixie." She glanced at him, trusting him. "I was a mess, anyway. And I had anorexia for eight years. That why my hormones packed up so early and I couldn't have children." She swallowed, and her voice became suddenly strangled. "I got rid of one you know, a long time ago." Her face fell into her hands. "It was a rape, Dixie. It was that man. I had to… I couldn't have…"

Dixie cradled her shoulders and she was as still as stone. "Jesus," he said under his breath. After a stunned silence he went on very gently. "But how have you changed towards life? How have you managed to move on?"

Ellen realised she was being quizzed but felt no need to question his motives. She sniffed and blinked into the dying fire. "I've got my dogs and my writing. Me and Paul are still friends, and now Ubuntu's actually happening. It's amazing."

"Yes, but there's more than that, isn't there? Come on Ellen – say it. I want to hear it. I want the Universe to hear that you understand."

She looked into his face. "Acceptance? Gratitude? Forgiveness?" she offered, not knowing if these were the answers he wanted… "Love?"

Dixie nodded. "Exactly – all of those. And that's how Ubuntu Village can help heal the world – just like you healed your life."

14

2018

It was approximately one year since Carlos and Tali had closed the door on their dream for the last time. The Israeli-themed café and takeaway whose vision had brought them to settle in Ipswich had finally folded. The largely white Caucasian population generally opted for burgers and sandwiches over falafel and spiced aubergine. It had been in the wrong part of town too, tucked away in a side street and reliant on building a regular clientele that simply didn't materialise. But it had been an experience, they had had some fun, had made some friends, and now it was time to move on.

During the period when the café was waning badly, Paul and Ellen had ended up in town on a mission to collect a second-hand fridge, and had entered the café in search of lunch. At first Ellen didn't recognise the long-haired figure loping about behind the hot-counter, although he had clocked her at once. They had met as volunteers some twenty years ago, on one of the last straggling kibbutzim to survive man's inevitable bent for competition: a sunny refuge full of trees and happy children, where vegetables, toilet rolls, cigarettes and bread were free for the taking.

The settlement had nestled between dry hills and green orchards atop the steep Galilee hills, just a stone's throw from the Lebanese border – a place where the sound of gunfire would sometimes carry on hot breezes from the west. Carlos and Ellen had picked mangoes in the stifling heat of the valley, bussing it with others down the precarious winding road at dawn, and then afterwards spending the afternoons getting drunk on cheap Arak in the shade. Evenings were passed in the volunteers' "pub," deep-down in a bomb-shelter that had purple walls and a ceiling painted with stars, or sipping from bottles on the high wall overlooking the vast space between them and the Golan Heights. The deep black valley and hulking peaks twinkled with lights from towns and villages, the air sang with cicadas and mocking hyenas, and sometimes fireflies would flicker in the scattered trees. On returning to England Ellen had written to Carlos several times but received only one response: he was moving to another kibbutz and had met a girl…

On hearing of the couple's troubles, Ellen had introduced her Ubuntu ideas as a matter of course. "It's similar to the original kibbutz idea, really," she had said. "That's one of the things that inspired me. Wouldn't it be *great* to be part of a self-sufficient community, away from this confounded rat-race? Wouldn't it be great to build on values that benefit everybody?"

Following the café's closure Carlos had become self-employed as an astrologer and Tali as a masseuse, helped by a trickle of money from her parents. The friends had stayed in touch sporadically and had met up in the new year. Tali, in particular, had loved Foxheath; and when Paul had happened upon a small quirky house for rent with an attic bedroom and a round window, Tali had begged Carlos to take it. The couple had moved in during the spring of 2018, sleeping on a sofa-bed downstairs with the upstairs given over to their businesses. And roundabout that time Tali had discovered she was pregnant.

As well as being a fully-fledged astrologer Carlos was an inspirational thinker and speaker. He and Paul often enjoyed long late-night debates about everything from ethics to the nature of reality itself. Ellen sat listening one night with Tali's sleeping head resting on her shoulder. As usual Carlos had his beloved charts spread out on the coffee table, covered with criss-crossing coloured lines. "The excitement continues right through this month," he was saying. "We've got that Mars-Pluto thing coming up on Wednesday, and a ton of other stuff. It's potentially strenuous but we're definitely learning and growing from these times."

"But when's it all going to end?" said Ellen. "When's everything going to settle down and stop being strenuous?"

Carlos laughed, showing his array of crooked teeth. "You're asking the wrong question, because in astrology it's never about when it's going to end. It's about... how do I access the fullest potential of what life is giving me right now? It's got to be like, 'Oh, okay – this is intense... and it's restless – so let's use this to transform myself. Let's build some stuff. Let's get some work done.'" Carlos ran his fingers through his straggling hair and there was passion in his eyes. "And what's more, it *can't* ever end until the world actually changes. It can't ever end until we don't see a MacDonald's on every street corner, and until corruption isn't all-pervasive in governments. It can't end until everyone isn't getting manipulated; turned in on one other, and convinced that there are enemies out there... so it's nation versus nation, and Labour versus Conservative, and this religion versus that religion. It'll never end until we start to see these structures, these hierarchies, these powers-that-be *obliterated…*" Carlos paused, examining the paperclip that had held his charts together. "…And die, and be re-born into something that's more organic, and more of the softer, compassionate, humble qualities."

"Like Ubuntu?" said Ellen.

"Yeah, exactly – *that's* something to build. That's some work worth getting done."

Ellen experienced a sudden sinking feeling. This was during the period when she had lost direction and could no longer write.

"Organic's a good word," said Paul slowly. "That's Ubuntu alright. No rule book. Because you can't expect people to cooperate and evolve when they're treated like a mechanism rather than an organism." He sat stroking his short beard. "But have you ever wondered if any of this even matters at all? Maybe this all seems so huge and spectacular to us, but actually it's just a tiny speck in something infinitely vast, like a bubble in the ocean."

"I hate it when you say that," grumbled Ellen.

Tali stirred sleepily, caressing her swelling abdomen. "It means whatever you want it to mean," she murmured in her thick Americanised accent.

Carlos gathered his papers together roughly on the table and yawned. "In a way Paul's got a point. But don't be discouraged, Ellen. Think of it like a dance. No one step means anything on its own, but you put it all together and… Wow! And I say a dance because that can be abstract. It doesn't have to mean anything in itself. It's just *creation*. Expression of one great thing. Expression of the infinite."

Everyone was tired and Ellen got up slowly to go. "But bits of the dance can be meaningful, can't they?"

Carlos grinned at her. "Well, one step lost and the dancer falls. So every step's essential, and sometimes… yes. Sometimes there's a special bit and everyone claps. How's that?" He got to his feet and hugged Ellen warmly. "Don't give up on Ubuntu," he told her. "It might be only one little step that goes unnoticed, or it might change the whole dance. But whatever it ends up as, don't give up on it, yeah?"

15

November, 2018

Mr Rix surveyed the buzz of excitement in the field with great satisfaction. He'd found a tall caravan-flag in one of his barns that had been left on the old campsite – had spent a good half-hour searching for it. He handed it to Josh. "For your new shed," he said.

Josh chuckled. "Why?"

"Why not?" said Dixie walking up. "That's the village's first building!"

Anya appeared in the doorway of the shed and Dixie immediately recognised her from Omasah's photograph. She hung childlike on the doorframe, swinging her long blonde ponytail. Then she addressed him casually. "I'm writing my diary in here. Josh offered me. I'm going to write it for ten years like Samuel Pepys." She disappeared back inside.

It was mild for the time of year and people were congregating in the middle of the flat grassy space, lighting barbecues and unfolding camping chairs. Paul sat strumming his guitar wearing an old floppy hat, and Jerry sat listening eagerly to every note. Carlos was putting up a pup-tent against the breeze, his three-week-old baby strapped sleeping to his front, while Jill was busy with plates and bread rolls on a trestle table. Mags stirred a big pan over a primus stove, dogs sniffed and rolled, and the sweet smell of wood-smoke filled the air.

At last the first proper Ubuntu meeting was underway. They had all straggled round the old campsite counting taps and electrical points, and had paced out hypothetical plots for this and that on the empty grass. Now they sat in a circle with a talking-stick Dixie that had made, and which was mostly failing to be used. "Who owns that shower-block?" asked Graham, a quiet dark bearded man who mainly listened. His son Addy leaned against him, sucking his thumb. The talking-stick moved its way around the circle to Josh.

"Me. We need to rip it down."

Mr Rix winced: the new block had been Olive's pride and joy, but he knew it made sense, and sighed against the pain. Josh still grasped the stick although other hands were reaching for it. "We can use the solar-panels on the houses *and* recycle the bricks, roofing... everything." The circle relaxed – this was more or less what everyone wanted to say in any case, and the talking-stick ensured it was said only once. They were quick to move on.

The doctor ran his fingers through his fair hair and spoke for the first time. He looked relaxed and handsome, and as though a weight had been lifted. "A bloke I know has got a mobile-home he doesn't want. Could we use that? He doesn't want anything for it." He laughed. "A medical-centre perhaps?" He grinned over at Jerry. "Only joking."

Jill took the talking-stick and nestled it between her hands. "Well personally I'd like to think about the shop – I mean the outer shop – because there's so much preparation... Doctor: is it *clean* do you know, this mobile? *Hey* – you aren't supposed to do that!" Ellen, who sat next to her, had snatched the stick and was holding it high in the air.

"The *inner* store first. Paul – tell her. Have you even read my notes, Jill?" Everyone began talking at once and Paul raised his voice:

"Let's break for food, children!"

The air was full of smells and conversation as Mr Rix sat in a sagging canvas chair with a cup of tea. His thoughts wandered and, as usual, settled upon Olive. How happily she would have fitted in with these people, he mused. His wife had never been one to judge – she saw past things like long hair and tattoos, right into the heart of someone. "It's in their eyes, Stan," she would always say to him. Mr Rix felt a lump in this throat. "No," he thought – "Olive wouldn't mind her shower-block being used in this way. Not now."

He watched the children running through the long grass and swinging in the trees at the edge of the woods. And the groups of people were timeless, doing the things that people have always done: eating, sharing stories, crooning over the baby. Ellen sat beside Paul on a blanket, scribbling notes. "We'll need string to mark out plots. Orange string, so it shows up, and a load of tent pegs. And we need to work out everything we can grow and make. I've researched most of that already…"

Paul was lying with his head on his coat watching the clouds, his guitar lying across his legs and his hat hanging on its end. "What're we going to do about food?" he said.

"What do you mean?"

Paul raised himself onto one elbow. "Well, I don't think we should allow meat. I mean as far as I'm concerned, 'Humanity Towards Others' includes animals. Jerry reckons that doctor bloke wants to keep chickens. So do Faye and Graham. Can't say I'm happy about that either."

Ellen felt something gnaw at her stomach. "Oh, Paul – you can't just dictate to the rest. We aren't here to promote our own views; we're here to meet on common ground. I know it's hard, but the whole idea is to get away from that kind of… judgement. It's got to be give and take. We all have to make sacrifices."

Paul hesitated. "I guess," he said, lying back down and muttering under his breath: "Especially the animals."

Ellen pretended not to hear, and hoped that would be the last she heard of it; but she knew that Paul's logical mind struggled with these kinds of grey areas. She sighed quietly. Problems – always problems. Why was it always so darned impossible for people to agree on anything? "Well, I guess we'd better get on with the meeting," she said in a subdued tone. "It'll be getting dark soon."

As the circle began to reform Dixie was surprised to see the incongruous figure of Omasah approaching from the farmhouse, dressed in his characteristic drapery and moving with the poise and grace of a dancer over the grass. He went to meet him, taking his hand for a second in greeting. "What are you doing here?" asked Dixie, glancing over his shoulder.

"A brief visit. I sense a powerful negative presence," Omasah answered softly. "Do not be alarmed."

Dixie felt edgy – especially as he hadn't got round to telling anyone but Josh about the Companions yet. He noticed his friend watching from the circle, and guessed that he had gleaned who the newcomer was. This was silly – he needed to get a grip. It was simply a question of how to introduce the subject. "Come sit with us," he said.

Omasah settled himself cross-legged beside Dixie, carefully arranging his linen clothing. Unreal-looking in the now twilit field he looked alien and alone. People chatted together, looking over from time to time in curiosity. It wasn't that the newcomer was unwelcome – it was simply that he didn't look like anyone they had ever seen before. At last everyone fell silent and the air was heavy with expectation. The children stared at the strange man, and he smiled kindly back at them. Paul looked at Dixie and his eyes asked for an explanation. Dixie coughed a couple of times, and then spoke self-consciously. "This is my friend Omasah. He's going to join us permanently as soon as we start to build, and I'm sure he'll bring great wisdom to the village…"

As soon as Dixie paused Omasah silenced him with a subtle gesture. He proceeded to take in each of the circle one by one – reading them; loving them. They waited, sensing he was about to speak; and when his sweet ethereal voice caressed the air it felt like a blessing.

"I come in love, as an element of the heart of this movement, just as every one of you is. I offer my services as healer and sage, and I bring knowledge and strength that will help the village and its principles grow and continue long into the future."

He fell silent, bowing his head. No one spoke, and the talking-stick lay forgotten in the grass. Wondering how to proceed, Paul cleared his throat. He was struggling with the need to know about this man's identity and origins. "Er… Thank you, um… friend. And yes, words of inspiration." He gathered his thoughts. It seemed as if no one else was going to speak and so Paul continued blindly. "We must never forget the universal truths we stand for. We stand together as a force against hypnotic materialism, and we will never descend into mindless competition." The visitor acknowledged Paul's words with a respectful nod as Ellen's harsh whisper sounded in his ear:

"Do you have to sound so militant?"

Gradually the discussion got underway again, becoming louder and more confident as enthusiasm built. There was talk of crops in the large field, vegetables and fruit trees, and a kind of centre to the village with rooms for meetings. They could build greenhouses out of plastic bottles, and reinforce walls with them too. There were so many things they needed: water-butts, sheds, bicycles, storage units… Addy introduced the subject of the school playground which kindled excitement amongst the children, and Carlos suggested liaising with local businesses in order to "break the ice." As darkness began to fall with a crisp chill, Josh broke from the circle with Anya to collect wood from Mr Rix's big barn. Omasah got up and followed them, reining them in with his quiet presence. He touched Josh's arm. "Please do not be alarmed. Return to the circle. You can collect your wood shortly."

Josh looked towards the farmyard, seeing a hefty figure dart out of sight. Anya saw it too, and gave a little scream. She hid her face in the folds of Omasah's garments and he held her for a moment. "Please," he said, and propelled her gently in the direction of the circle.

In the dark farmyard Maxwell held his breath, straining his ears. He couldn't hear much. Then he heard Ellen's unmistakable laugh. Emotions boiled, and he peered surreptitiously round the corner of the building. The two people who had spotted him were gone, and in their place stood the tall unearthly silhouette of Omasah.

Maxwell edged quickly back out of sight, panting heavily. Who the heck was that? He looked like a blasted druid or something. God, that woman associated with some weirdos. "Well, bring it on," he thought, angrily. "All the more chance the town will turn against them…" He fumbled in his pockets for his hip-flask, undid it with trembling fingers and gulped back a mouthful of burning brandy.

Suddenly a sharp pain sliced through his head like a hot knife and he dropped his flask, hearing it bounce on the concrete. He began fishing blindly for it, but the pain took him again and he staggered and almost collapsed. God, he must be having a stroke. He turned and tried to run in the direction of his car, but a third jolt of pain brought him abruptly to his knees. He held his head in his hands, begging for relief with low whimpers. Out of the corner of his eye he could see that the stranger was closer now, standing watching him like an uncanny statue. A voice resonated deep inside his skull – a voice with no speaker. "Leave this place," it said.

Maxwell struggled to his feet and ran for his car. Falling into the driver's seat he started the engine, floored the accelerator and turned precariously onto the road, forgetting to turn on his lights. Only when he reached the main road did he reduce speed and start to feel safe. Someone honked urgently at him, and he switched on his lights with cold damp fingers. Rationalisation began to take hold. He had better ring his GP. Perhaps he needed a blood-thinner. He must have imagined that voice. Better keep an eye on his health. Should really try and watch the booze. Bloody weirdos. He would have to speak to someone about them pretty sharpish that was for sure. The locals would have a field-day.

Maxwell drove on, beginning to relax at last behind the wheel.

16

November, 2018
Bedfordshire

"Can we have the telly off now?" asked Dick. "I really want to read you Anya's letter. It's so sweet."

Lizzy reached for the remote from amongst the clutter that filled the pine coffee table. She turned the set off and settled back into the sofa, cuddling up to a scruffy ginger and white mongrel dog. "Go on then," she said.

Dick only ever got hand-written letters from his little half-sister because her family lived technology-free. Raised in a house full of music, she was an intelligent, creative, unusual child – forever excited about something and always smiling. Sometimes he worried for her – her life-style was so unusual – and yet whenever he saw her he couldn't help admiring her endless enthusiasm for life. She was thoroughly content, and found beauty and joy everywhere.

"I'll read you the main bits," said Dick in his slow relaxed voice. He cleared his throat, arranging the pages as Lizzy rested her spiky purple-haired head on his shoulder. "We're going to join an Ubuntu village which is going to be on an old campsite. This is a village where you don't need to use money, and you look after the planet by having solar panels and being self-sufficient…"

"Very literate, isn't she?" remarked Lizzy, looking at the pristine handwriting.

"A total book-worm. And of course Harry used to be an English teacher before he took early retirement. She could read when she was three." Dick skipped a couple of sentences before going on. "We'll have caravans first and then micro-homes which are really tiny houses with cupboards in all interesting places, because it's greener that way and it's stupid to have a huge house full of stuff you don't really need. Our school's going to have an old car and playground outside, and sometimes we're going to have discussions about all interesting stuff like aliens and yetis and mysteries like that. We're going to have a room for making tons of things in like mobiles and patchwork quilts, and a library in a shed and everyone can bring all their books to mix up together..." Dick paused as an electronic alarm sounded somewhere in the room. "I'll take them when I've finished."

Lizzy immediately became forcefully maternal. "No, you'll take them now, my sweet, before we both forget. Go on!" She waited while he went to the bathroom, hearing the rattle of pill bottles. Dick returned to the room with a glass of water and they re-settled themselves.

He continued reading quietly: "I haven't told mum but I think you should come and live here with Lizzy because it's much nicer than where you are because of all the fresh air. Please don't think that's silly because of your illness. We going to have a doctor anyway who's given it up – he's really nice. You're so good at building and we will need a lot of builders, and Lizzy could do cooking and things." Dick's face lit up with a wide grin. "Love her," he said softly.

Lizzy's spiky head didn't move as she stared at the page. "Why not?" she said.

"Why not what?"

She sat up straight. "Well, why not, Dick? What have we got here any more? Most of our friends have moved away or are too miserable to even care."

"Yes, but Lizzy. They're going self-sufficient. Mum's already told me about it. It'd be madness. We'd lose all our benefits."

Dick hadn't seen Lizzy's face so bright in a long time. He could sense a battle coming on. "But Dick – what does that money bring us, really? Living near the sea – can you imagine? It would keep us well for longer – that and being with like-minded people. We could feel useful again and it'd be exciting. Don't you want to do something exciting?"

"They aren't even having TV, Lizzy," he shot back, but could already see that the idea had well and truly grabbed her.

"*Exactly!* We're wasting the life we've got left sitting on this blinking sofa!" She smacked it with the flat of her hand, raising dust and making the dog jump down in surprise.

"Well, you're the one who's always turning the telly on. We never have music on any more. I'm always saying we should put some music on."

Lizzy wriggled huffily to her feet, went over to the stereo, and pushed a button firmly. The soft strains of Joni Mitchell's acoustic guitar filled the room. "There!" She sat down again heavily and the dog jumped back on her lap.

"Well, you might not have a stereo either," said Dick, turning the pages of the letter solemnly. "They might get cut off for not paying the bill."

Lizzy rolled her eyes. "Oh, shut up. I don't believe that for a minute. And anyway, Harry plays guitar. What could be better than live music? People pay a fortune to hear musicians like him."

Dick sighed deeply. "I guess," he said at length. He sat up and stretched luxuriously.

"We need to stay positive and happy," Lizzy insisted. "It's the best medicine we could ever have. I think we could be happy up there. I'm fed up with rough pubs with needles all over the toilet floors and people arguing in the street, and nowhere to take Dylan for a nice walk."

The couple fell silent while Dick read the remainder of Anya's letter to himself, trying to find something else that might put his wife off. But the more he read the more appealing it sounded. "The whole thing about Ubuntu is being loving and caring to one another, and being equal, and being on a journey together," wrote his sister. "I think it will be the most fun and happy village in the world, and I really wish you'd come because I miss you and so does mum, and you could always leave if you don't like it, although I'm really sure you would."

Dick laid the letter to one side and rested his head. Lizzy snuggled up again and he wrapped an arm round her, smelling her hair. They listened to the music together. "At least give it some thought, my sweet," she said soothingly.

And so Dick agreed to give it some thought, and found that within a few days he could think about little else.

17

November, 2018

The school corridors were quiet and smelt of floor polish. Ethan sat outside the medical room hunched over his phone. He started as the nearby door opened, slipping his mobile into his trouser pocket. A petite middle-aged woman appeared holding a red folder. "Would you like to come in, Ethan?"

The boy entered the small room which had curtains, a blue carpet, two armchairs and a small vase of carnations in an attempt to render it homely. He chose one of the armchairs and the woman sat down in the other. He hung his head. He had to attend this appointment or risk suspension, but he had already promised himself that he wasn't going to say a word – not a damned word about anything. Staying at school was marginally preferable to suspension because he could see his mates. Suspension meant spending hours in the house either alone, or trying to avoid the sight of his drunken mother.

Ethan sat frowning. Without realising he was picturing his home in his mind. Did Mum really think he didn't realise? That he hadn't spotted the endless wine bottles buried in amongst the recycling and hidden in cupboards? Did she really think he was that dumb? That he didn't see her puffy face and blood-shot eyes? If she was really that unhappy with dad then why didn't she leave? If she was really that dissatisfied with her life then she should take him and his brothers away somewhere. Why did she let dad bully her until there wasn't a shred of self-respect left? She was gutless, and no one wants a gutless mother. He would never marry anyone like her, and he would never be anything like his dad either. Like all bullies, his father was a coward deep down. He controlled everyone with fear and money, and he too thought his kids were too stupid to notice.

The woman was watching the face and body-language of the boy. She crossed her legs and was quiet for a minute or so – which to Ethan felt like an eternity. He kept his eyes firmly downwards. Not only had he vowed not to speak; he had vowed not to look at her either. No worries: he could easily last out an hour.

At last the woman spoke. Ethan didn't trust her – didn't trust any adult – and so to him, her voice sounded affectedly kind. "I'd like to hear in your own words, Ethan, why you think you've been sent to speak with me today."

The boy didn't move, and silence hung oppressively in the stuffy room. He felt hot but didn't want to move to take off his blazer. If he just stayed put, and refused to speak or look at her, what could she do about it? But the woman was unperturbed. "You know, Ethan," she remarked calmly; "the idea of this meeting is that you talk to me about the problems you've been having. If you refuse to speak, then that's effectively the same as not attending."

Ethan's mind began to race. He felt cornered. Maybe an hour was a long time after all. How the hell had he ended up in this lousy situation? Feeling suddenly angry, he began breathing faster. The woman waited, watching him. Finally she cleared her throat and spoke again: "It won't just go away, you know."

Before he could help himself Ethan had looked up scowling, but quickly returned his gaze to the floor. He began picking at one of his fingernails. At last he mumbled sulkily: "What won't?"

"Any of it. The way you feel. Pushing it away won't work – I can promise you that."

"I'm not pushing anything away. I'm just…" At last he moved to take off his blazer, struggling out of the sleeves and throwing it aggressively in a heap on the floor. The woman didn't react and continued looking at her papers. "I'm just pissed off," he said, helplessly.

Once again they fell into silence. Yes – "pissed off" summed it up alright. Let her work it out if she was such an expert. Ethan felt a violent distaste for this woman. How could she ever know how he felt? How could she ever do anything to help? How could she ever know what it was like living in that house, or being inside his head? He knew deep down that how he felt wasn't "right" but he kept hoping blindly that it would go away in the end. Just lately, he had been waking up with a feeling of impossible black despair. Despair at the thought of school; despair at the thought of even going downstairs. It had got so bad that he was spending as much time as possible in bed, distracting himself with action movies that carried him away to a non-participatory world. But, much as he was scared to admit it, she was right: it *wasn't* working. He was increasingly beginning to feel as if there was no escape. He was increasingly craving the warm oblivion of sleep.

The woman crossed her legs and breathed slowly. This was going to be a tough one. She changed tack. "Can you think of anything that might change to make you feel happier, Ethan?"

Much as the boy wanted to remain emotionless; wanted to get the hour over with, he felt something stir inside. Much as he wanted to blot everything and everyone out, there was a kind of sick dizzy feeling churning in his stomach that was getting a hold.

The woman prompted him gently, and this time her voice sounded genuinely kind – he didn't know why. "Can you think of anything, Ethan?"

The boy squeezed his eyes shut. It felt as though he was standing on the edge of an abyss and seeing himself at the bottom – small, distant and broken. When he finally looked up his face was desolate. "I suppose I'd kind of like a girlfriend," he muttered. His head swam with some kind of memory, and suddenly he was sobbing so hard that the convulsions twisted him in his seat.

18

November, 2018

After hearing the car roar away from the old farm, Ellen sat empty-faced on the grass. "It was Maxwell," she said to Josh and Anya. "Definitely – he's the only person who drives like that." Omasah approached noiselessly and seated himself at her side.

"You have nothing to fear, Kaphalya," he told her with sympathy that seemed to pervade the space around him. Ellen turned to meet the strange amber eyes, sensing peace there. Peace and something more – something that felt like a very great distance.

"Why do you call me that?"

"It is my chosen name for you. It speaks of flowering and great depth." He settled himself, arranging his clothes neatly again. Anya put out her little hand shyly and Omasah took it.

"I don't know who you are," she said; "but we're very pleased you're here."

"Thank you, Navastri – our Star Child," he answered, and Anya gave him her widest and most beautiful smile in reply.

Ellen's arms were folded protectively across her chest. It was colder now, and nearby Carlos and Mags were busily building a fire. She winced as a log crashed onto the pile. Tali sat in the pup-tent nursing the baby under a blanket, and others stood about in hats and coats waiting to get warm. In the darkening trees a lone crow was cawing, and somewhere far-off a fox barked sporadically. Dixie and Paul approached and squatted down in the darkness. "What's going on?" asked Paul with a frown.

"Maxwell," said Ellen. She took her head in her hands. "Why the hell's he hanging around all of a sudden? God, it's been about eighteen years…"

Since settling in, Dixie had heard all about Ellen's traumatic relationship with Maxwell from Jerry – a dedicated armchair psychologist who couldn't help finding the case interesting. In his opinion the man was seriously deluded and narcissistic – a "chameleon," who became exactly what his victims needed and wanted before beginning to exert control. But Jerry had also mentioned that narcissists tended to be strictly "on or off." They were inclined to be stalkers, but not after moving on to a new phase. "Why d'you reckon it is, Ellen?" Dixie asked her.

Ellen's face clearly showed the effort and unpleasantness involved in thinking about Maxwell. She sighed hugely. "Oh, I don't know… I heard his father's ill and he has to care for him now. His father's exactly the same – scared the shit out of me. That's why Maxwell's like he is I guess. Plus his mother ran off when he was about twenty. Maybe the prospect of his dad dying has brought things to the surface. He thinks of him like a god. Worships him. He must be feeling vulnerable."

"Have a chat with Jerry about it," suggested Dixie.

"Oh, I already have," said Ellen. "There was a time when I couldn't talk about anything else. I know exactly how his mind works. But it's really not something I want to think about right now. This was supposed to be a special day."

Josh touched her shoulder. "It still is."

The fire began to leap up and Ellen immediately felt a little better. Darkness fled, and a cheering crackle accompanied the drift of smoke. Anya gazed into Omasah's eyes. "Please say something nice," she said.

The man considered before addressing Ellen with great tenderness. "Kaphalya: are you aware that this is a vibrational reality, and, as your great scientist Planck so accurately expressed, were it not for consistent vibrational interplay on a vast scale this universe would cease to be?"

She smiled in some surprise as she tried to adapt to his flow of thought. "Well, I've seen videos about that sort of thing. I know roughly what you mean."

Omasah took her hand and paused as he considered how to proceed. He thought so differently from these people – inhabited an altogether dissimilar world. He wasn't yet accustomed to meeting their needs; to putting his knowledge into words they might make use of.

He continued slowly: "Your human emotions are an extension of this system, Kaphalya. As such, they all derive from two opposite base vibrations – those of fear and those of love. The man of whom you speak is rooted in the fear vibration."

He waited, watching Ellen's face and assessing her understanding. "I thought hate was the opposite of love," she said.

Dixie waggled a finger. "I've heard this before. Hate has its roots in fear, although of course the haters themselves will swear otherwise."

Omasah gave him a nod before speaking softly again. "The original thought that began all things was creative, and hence loving. Love, therefore, is the more powerful vibration. Do you see? This man is weak; you are strong. Speak the truth and he cannot harm you. Foster love and he cannot harm you."

Ellen looked doubtful – almost offended. "What, so I must love him?"

As Omasah's brain activity approached light-speed she thought she saw him flicker for a moment, like an image on an old TV set. She rubbed her eyes, convincing herself it must be down to the heat-haze from the fire. The man's voice came tenderly on the night air: "Forgive his errors and foster love as your bodily vibration. Feel it empower you and bring you joy. He owns his destiny and I am here to protect you. Do not allow fear to pollute your heart."

Ellen was touched then, and undertook to put the matter from her mind and focus on planning the village. She didn't know what Omasah had said to Maxwell, and felt uneasy about asking. In a way she didn't want to know – didn't want any kind of scenario playing through her head. It was as if by picturing the scene in the farmyard she might experience some of it herself… might see Maxwell's face. But whatever had happened he had gone – and in a big hurry. Questions crowded her mind. Something was extremely strange about this new friend of Dixie's, but it was a positive, serene, magical kind of strangeness that left her feeling positive and serene herself.

"Thank you," she said to him brightly, and meant it from the bottom of her heart.

19

November, 2018

"I still can't believe I'm doing this," grumbled Steven. He and Jerry stood side by side looking into the cluttered garage, hands in pockets.

Jerry was cheerful as ever. "The whole lot's got to go with you and into storage on-site. You're not getting rid of anything exactly, so cheer up. I just need to see what's here so I can tell Ellen."

Steven walked over to a pile of plastic crates, on top of which sat a ragged shoe-box. He picked it up. "Photos of Ben when he was a kid," he said despondently, lifting the lid. "He was such a happy affectionate kid… Now he's turned into rather a cold-hearted bastard, I'm sorry to say."

Jerry was examining the tool-boxes, tins of car-wax and tubs of paint that crowded the sagging shelves. "That's the kind of thing you keep. But all this kind of stuff will be pooled with everyone else's. From what I've seen so-far we'll need a pretty big tool-shed." He took his notepad out of his jacket pocket and began writing.

"But won't most of it be superfluous?" asked Steven, still sifting through photos. He held up a big one. "Look: me when I got my doctorate. Speaks volumes that I never hung it in the house really."

"Ha! What a handsome bugger!" Jerry took down a pot of paint-brushes and began testing their bristles. "Everything will get end up getting used somehow, some way. For bartering or selling or materials. Or… fire-wood." He responded to Steve's pained expression by holding up a solidified brush. "Apart from this sort of thing. This is the sort of stuff you need to dump, and you'll find surprisingly little of it to be honest."

"So all my furniture?"

"Yes, all your furniture."

Steven sat down on a box and breathed deeply. Jerry looked at him with fondness. "You're getting yellow again, aren't you? If it means that much to you, I can honestly say that Ellen has more sense than to burn your mahogany."

His friend rolled his eyes. "Yeah, I know. Cowardly, aren't I? Clinging to a bunch of antiques like my life depended on it. And nearly all of it's stuff that Susan wanted anyway. She'll probably want most of it back too, knowing her."

"What's happening with the settlement?"

"We'll be divorced in two months. It's that quick these days. The house should sell easily and then she can take whatever she wants. I'm not going to tell her about Ubuntu yet – she'd probably die laughing." He looked up at the garage roof and then at Jerry. "I can't go back now. It's just that I've been this way for so long now."

"Been what way?"

"Well, you know – believing that *things* make your life better and are a mark of success. I mean, surely the best measures of achievement are… well, the strength of you marriage for a start; how content you are, and what your children turn out like? If I use those criteria then I'm a dismal failure."

Jerry sat down next to him and crossed his legs. "Ben's just Ben," he said. "He's a decent enough chap; he's just in a different place from you, with a different view of the landscape. So stop beating yourself up for heaven's sake. Life doesn't have to be such a chore as we're led to believe, you know. It's really all about the *experience* of being alive: the living moment! And its expression! Focus on that and you'll begin to feel free."

Steven stood up and stretched himself. Lately he often found it difficult to follow his friend's train of thought. He sighed, feeling a distance between them. "Okay – I'll try." He replaced the old box on top of the pile. "Come on – let's have a cuppa." Then he stopped, suddenly thoughtful. "Free." He repeated the word, savouring the sentiment of it. "I do feel as if I've spent my whole life in chains, you know. Chained to my job especially; but chained to Susan and her world too. I guess that's why I've got this urge to do something so completely different." He closed the garage door with a clang and they went into the house.

Jerry sat at the dining table writing in his notepad again. "So how's Ellen's book coming along?" Steven enquired. "I'd be interested to know exactly what this system is that she's supposed to have come up with."

Jerry pointed at him with his biro. "Forever the doubting Thomas, aren't you?" He laid his pen down with a chuckle and picked up his mug. "She's still typing like mad, Paul says. It's in two parts, the book: first, the philosophy of Ubuntu – which is actually the most important bit – and then the trading system: what we can make, grow, recycle and sell etcetera."

Steven sat gazing out of the window. In Susan's absence he had taken off his shoes and crossed his feet on the edge of the table. In Susan's absence the table was dusty too. "I just don't see how the village can possibly get enough back to survive. We'll have over twenty people to feed," he said.

"Well for a start, *Thomas* – have you seen Dixie's work? Most artists as good as him yearn for a bunch of toffs sipping Champagne in a Mayfair gallery. Luckily for us, that's not Dixie."

Steven raised his eyebrows and watched as a few flakes of light snow flurried slowly around the shrivelling roses outside. "So what happens to all our furniture and spare pots and pans and other junk? There'll be enough to fill ten storage units I should think."

Jerry put down his pen and took of his glasses, rubbing his eyes. "Yes, total pooling of resources. We acquired it all, and now we can make use of it – instead of casually shipping everything off to landfill it'll see us through the next ten years. And when the handle drops off your frying-pan there'll always be another one handy."

Steven began sparring with him. It was a way of voicing the doubts that kept coming and going in his mind, and disturbing his sleep. "So half-way through frying my breakfast I have to go out in the mud and search through a freezing storage unit? I can't help feeling it's all a bit… war generation."

Jerry was suddenly tired of the way Steven kept continually expressing his reservations and, uncharacteristically for him, became very annoyed. "God, you're so… fickle. So don't come, Steve! Stay here! Get in your expensive car, drive to a crowded supermarket and search frantically for a parking space to lose yourself in a queue of miserable faces checking themselves out on machines that keep repeating themselves over and over if that's what you really want."

"I do my shopping online," remarked Steven blandly and without thinking.

"So go and sip Champagne in some sodding art gallery and talk about nothing! You just haven't got it at all, have you? You've been too long in *this*…" (he waved a despairing hand around the lush room) "…to realise the joys of living a simple life. I pity you. I mean it's not like it's even made you happy!"

Steven was stunned, and kept his eyes on the table. He had never seen his friend like this before, but of course Jerry had not long given up drinking. He remained the same in many ways – always buoyant and fun – but with this underlying serious edge that was completely new: this mysterious passion for what Steven felt were elusive, poorly-defined things. For the second time that afternoon, he experienced the same painful gulf between them.

Jerry was getting ready to leave, but as he wrestled with his jacket he was still eager to put his case. "There'll be a store in the village," he was saying. "It'll be stocked with everything you'll ever need. Just walk in and take it… if you can manage to lower yourself to the task, that is."

Steven stayed sitting, feeling frazzled; and before he could think of what to say the door had slammed and Jerry was gone into the gathering snow.

20

December, 2018

Janet was her oldest friend, but Ellen couldn't help feeling her heart sink when she saw her name in her inbox. It wasn't that things were going badly, but they had more or less stopped moving and it made Ellen despondent. She was still writing – editing and typing her notes onto her laptop – but her output had begun to drop. And they were still waiting, waiting, waiting for the council's decision.

Dixie had insisted again and again that the answer would be yes – couldn't possibly be otherwise because of the influence of his strange friend. He had filled her and Paul in somewhat as to who Omasah was and why he was here, but they both had to admit they were struggling with it. Paul certainly had his suspicions. "What if he's just some lunatic?" he had said to her with his typical frown.

Ellen wanted to believe Dixie's story, especially as it was so fantastical, and felt that the photographs were adequate proof. Many of them, like the one of her and Paul posing in front of the Acropolis, were old – had never even existed in digital format, and any negatives were long-lost... so how could the man have possibly laid hands on copies? Surely it had to be via some supernatural force, or incredibly advanced technology?

Ellen knew that Janet had been unhappy for many years – that her marriage was failing and that her children were developing problems. What she had gleaned here and there came in a flood of unhappy admissions now in this new email. Ellen's face fell as she read, and the weight of it sapped at her already declining strength.

"*Hiya Ellen,*" wrote Janet. "*I hope you're well and everything is coming along O.K. with the plans for your village. I was glad to hear you are writing again & I'm sure you'll come up with a great book about your ideas and that people will want to buy it. You've always been so clever & I'm so glad you're doing things you enjoy. As for me I've not been in such a good way to be honest. I know you never liked Alan even though you were nice enough not to say. But anyway we really aren't happy and he is very controlling and aggressive. I am sorry to tell you this my lovely but I feel the time has come for me to tell somebody. I don't want anything from you or to spoil your day, just to read it will be enough and for me to know you are there.*

The even worse thing is that Ethan's not in a good way either. He keeps getting in trouble at school and stays up half the night watching violence & sometimes he goes out and won't take any notice of me saying when he has to get in. I don't know who he's hanging round with and I feel sure he's drinking and definitely sleeping around because I found a girl's thong in his pocket. He's only 14, and I know a lot of them do at that age but that doesn't make me feel any better, & I found porn under his mattress, really nasty hardcore stuff, and god knows what else he watches online. I know I'm a disappointment to him because I often have to hit the wine to cope. Josh is not good either, he just plays computer games and lives on coke and crisps – it breaks my heart, but they barely speak to me let alone trying to eat together. I have lost control and

Alan just doesn't want to know because I think he likes seeing me not coping. I half wish he'd leave me to tell you the truth, but I think he likes making me unhappy I really do. I saw my doctor and he gave me tablets but they made me feel so nervous that I stopped them. When I told him he got quite angry & said I should have kept on with them and so I daren't go back now.

Ethan is seeing an educational psychologist but he won't tell me anything and it doesn't seem to be doing any good. I am so sorry to have to tell you all this and I would never want to burden you, but I know you care and it makes me feel less alone to know that you are aware of what's happening, but I don't want anything from you honest Ellen. In any case it's my mess and it's up to me to deal with it somehow. Please try not to worry about me and thanks for reading this. Love you lots and stay happy, you're a lovely friend to me – Janet xxx"

It took Ellen almost an hour to word her reply – cutting and pasting this or that word until she could finalise something that was balanced between empathic and constructive. It was the best she could possibly offer Janet without insisting her that she leave her husband. She knew *that* would fall on deaf ears, at least for the time being. Ellen was well aware of the degree of power this species of man could wield, and as she clicked "send" she sighed heavily, sensing the weight of her friend's situation.

Not feeling up to writing she knocked on Paul's door to find him battling with online bank-accounts and cursing. "Fucking robbery!" he exclaimed, and she saw that his hands were trembling. "Failed to send so I re-sent it, and now both payments have gone but nothing's arrived the other end. And you always get to speak to some heartless bastard who makes you feel it's your fault… And do you know what else?" Ellen didn't answer, and got ready to shut the door at the first opportunity. "They want me to *appeal* with a bunch of forms that won't even be sent out for five days! Call this the communication age? They want me to ask for my *own* money back by *snail mail* for Christ's sake!"

"Sorry – I can't do this right now," said Ellen, and closed the door as softly as she could. A moment later Paul's rather red face appeared round his door.

"Sorry," he told her. "It's just so scary. It's five thousand quid I'm trying to move and… Oh – never mind. You alright?"

"Not really. I feel totally flat. And I got a really tragic email off Janet. Why don't you take a break? Maybe it won't look so bad when you come back to it."

He immediately joined her in the hallway, obviously wanting her company. "Let's make some tea."

They went down to the kitchen and sat at the breakfast bar, sipping gratefully at their mugs. Paul was coming back into himself again. "Ridiculous, isn't it, how we sit and sweat over a few digits? Truth is that that money doesn't even exist. Especially not these days. Pixels on a screen! A mere concept! And most people haven't a clue how tenuous it all is either. One big solar flare could bring the whole system down."

"Well, soon Carlos will be overseeing the finances," Ellen reminded him. "You won't have this kind of stuff to worry about."

"I know."

"So why are you so up-tight? You'll get it back okay."

Paul gulped thirstily. "Principle of it," he said, gruffly. "And the fact that whatever you try and do these days they seem to bugger it up. Give me a physical bank any day – a friendly old codger with a pencil behind his ear." He smiled introspectively. "That money's for the village you see... it could be a while before this house sells. But then again I wish we could ditch the money side of things altogether – I'm sure it's possible."

Ellen looked at him fondly. "So am I. But it's got to happen gradually. We have to be a system within a system – at least for now." She held the warm familiarity of his hand in hers for a moment. "Thanks!" she said suddenly.

"What for?"

"Oh, I don't know. Everything. Staying with me on this idea I guess. It's a hell of a thing we're about to do."

"Can't wait," said Paul. "Biggest risk I've ever taken, I know, but... got to unplug you see – it's the only way to stay sane. No more virtual bank accounts. No more speaking to machines and heartless bastards." From somewhere nearby a car alarm started screeching, and the noise echoed round the town. Paul looked up and sighed. "Just the wind in the trees and the smell of the earth."

Outside mighty Orion crept upward, clear and spectacular beyond the rooftops of the town.

"Yeah – I can't wait either."

21

December, 2018

Mr Rix's kitchen table was scattered with home-made Christmas cards: snowmen with carrot noses, Santas with big sacks, and kings riding camels under golden stars. Faye sat drinking a glass of water: a slight, pale, plain woman, so quiet as to seem on a first meeting insubstantial – although in truth she fostered an inner-strength as unshakeable as it was understated. "The children made all those in two days," said Faye. "Jill wanted you to see. They're for the village shop… for next year of course. They're starting decorations tomorrow. The children want so much to be getting on with things."

"Don't we all?" groaned Ellen. "I've had enough of sitting about talking. I want to run but I feel like my feet are glued to the starting block."

Mr Rix entered, carrying a pea-green teapot and some cups on a tray. "Well I saw a little chap in a suit looking round the site on Thursday. Must've been from the council don't you think?" He admired the Christmas cards smilingly. "It's wonderful that they're so enthusiastic, isn't it? My Olive would have wanted the whole lot. There's nothing so lovely as a child's drawing."

"Yes, sweet, aren't they? Anya's are very accomplished," said Ellen, picking up a sophisticated silhouette of the stable scene against a night sky. "She's quite brilliant, isn't she?"

Faye was never one to judge. "Well, I'm certainly pleased there's such a variety," she remarked.

There was a heavy slopping noise as Jerry's large soapy cloth hit the window from outside. He proceeded to wipe energetically and then to squeegee with a quick and practised hand. Mr Rix stood and watched as the grey water ran down. "I wish he'd let me pay him," he mused. "I'm used to paying my way you know. Doesn't feel right."

Faye looked at him in her quiet way. "You accepting his services as a gift makes him happy. We're your friends Mr Rix." As she spoke Jerry's head turned towards the sound of running feet and his eyes looked in at them over the windowsill, somewhat alarmed. Faye's eldest burst into the room and her words tumbled over one another breathlessly.

"Mum – Melyne's crying her eyes out in Dixie's van 'cause he's got a picture of her brother but she doesn't even know where her brother is and she thought he was dead and she won't stop crying…"

Faye got to her feet and held the child close for a moment. "Alright Nadia – I'm coming."

"She won't stop crying," repeated the girl, and headed out into the farmyard again as quickly as she had come. Faye and Ellen followed watched by Jerry, dripping cloth in hand, and Ellen's two Jack Russells scampered in circles, sensing the tension and barking. Inside the farmhouse Mr Rix sat down in his favourite chair with a biscuit, tutting softly to himself. Addy had made his way to the house and entered the room, saying glumly:

"Can I sit with you, Mr Rix? I don't like screaming."

Outside on the campsite Dixie was standing on his steps looking worried while the sound of wailing came from inside his campervan. "She's in absolute bits," he told Faye. "I'm so sorry. She just picked up the photo and that was it."

"She suppresses a lot… she has to," Faye said as she shut the door, hemming the three of them and the two dogs into the tiny kitchen. Nadia was sitting with her arms around the curled-up figure of her adopted sister, while Dixie's Albert sat flat-eared and forlorn on the floor. The wailing continued, and it was like nothing anyone had ever heard before. Faye looked into Dixie's eyes. "Where did you get it?"

Dixie put a hand over his face as Faye sat down quickly with the child, burying her mouth and nose in the woolly hair. The girl clung to her mother's pullover, and the wailing subsided into sobbing interspersed with violent intakes of breath. "Where did you get it?" repeated Faye. Dixie took a seat opposite, retrieving the photo from the floor. Nadia sat open-mouthed, pale and unlike herself.

"A friend gave it me," Dixie began, weakly. "He gave me several pictures of people who… who might be good choices to help build the village." They looked round as Josh pushed his way in the door, heavy-eyed and trying to make sense of everything.

"Anything I can do?" he said, scratching his head and squashing himself into a corner. "I was fast asleep."

Ellen laid a hand on his arm. "It's okay, Josh."

Melyne was repeating the same words over and over, hoarsely between sobs. "C'est impossible. C'est impossible."

Her mother rocked her slowly. "Doucement," she murmured into the soft hair; "Doucement." She addressed Dixie again. "Your friend from the meeting?"

"Yes. He's a good man."

"I could see that."

"We can trust him absolutely," said Dixie, fighting his own awkwardness. "I'm just so sorry that this has happened like this. I should have said something earlier, but it's just so... difficult."

"Is it definitely him?" asked Ellen examining the picture. It showed a young man whose expression blended strength and wisdom with smiling benevolence. Melyne spoke fiercely into her mother's pullover:

"*C'est lui!*"

Faye looked firmly at Dixie. "I need more."

Dixie shut his eyes for a second or two. The girl raised her tear-stained face to him for the first time, and he addressed her in his kindest tone. "My friend who's going to come and live in the village with us – he's a very good, wise man who comes from a long way away. He gave me that photo, Melyne. So please believe me: this means that your brother will come."

Faye wiped Melyne's face tenderly with a handkerchief. "C'est impossible," said the girl again, although with less conviction than before.

Ellen's more excitable dog, Jack, was licking Melyne's hands all over as though desperate to ease the situation. Faye looked at the others, and explained in a flat monotone. "Jean was working as a missionary in Somalia when their village was attacked. If he ever returned there he'd have found nothing."

"Could he ever trace her to England?" asked Josh.

Faye shrugged. "It'd be difficult and slow, but not impossible. We've tried to find him several times..." A gentle knock at the campervan door interrupted her, and an elongated head appeared. Omasah entered silently and

Faye and the two girls moved to make space for him without speaking.

"Thanks for coming," said Dixie in relief.

Ellen stared in amazement. "So it must be true," she thought. This was definitely beyond coincidence.

Omasah swept his clothing aside and sat down, taking Melyne's hands warmly and looking into her swollen eyes. She held his gaze and was pacified by it. "Loveliest child," he said; "I beg you to trust that your brother is alive and looking for you. The road will find him, and you will soon be reunited. I am deeply sorry for your tears. Please be light of heart."

Melyne hesitated and then laid her head softly against the man's heart, closing her eyes. Faye looked on in mild surprise and Nadia smiled tearfully. Omasah placed a large hand on the back of the girl's head; his eyes focused inwardly and twitched a little. Then, in little more than a whisper, he repeated his recent words in fluent Kirundi before returning Melyne gently to the arms of her mother. And suddenly he was gone with surprising quickness before anyone had fully adjusted to his presence, and the friends sat bemusedly on the cramped seats, listening to the beginnings of a soothing rain.

It was dusk and Melyne was herself again, happily playing ball with her brother and sister on the darkening field. Mr Rix had led everyone between ramshackle buildings to where three caravans had been stored and then abandoned. "People don't want the hassle of selling them, and so they just stop paying and never come back," sighed Mr Rix. "Unbelievable really, isn't it? Anyway, I know they've gone a bit green but do you think you can use them at all?" The two girls ran up, all gangly legs and flapping feet.

"Me and Melyne could have this one to use as our little house at the bottom of the garden and we could sleep in there sometimes, couldn't we, Mum – *please?*" said Nadia, her words tumbling over one another.

"Well, possibly," came the measured response. "We'll have to see."

"You always say that," complained the girl in disappointment as Mr Rix unlocked the door and Melyne clambered inside. She began opening cupboards and shutting them again with an enchanted expression. She peered into the little fridge.

"So beautiful," she said, stroking the pink velveteen curtains with a smile that lit up the tiny room. Faye and Ellen exchanged glances.

"Well, so long as no one else desperately needs it, then," agreed Faye. The two girls cheered and clapped and hugged and then sat chattering together, making plans.

Ellen went over to look at the largest of the vans. "Hey, Faye! What about a tea-van?" she called. "Look – we could remove the seats here and take the front out and make a fold-down counter – like they've got in your lay-by, Dixie. That must've been an ordinary caravan once."

"I guess so," he said. "Although don't ask me how it's done."

"We could do food for people visiting the shop," Ellen beamed. "Good food. Fantastic food! Mags can do the cooking. She'll love it! What a shame Jerry's gone home. I'll have to ring him up and tell him. Maybe he could do the alterations? We could have tables to sit at and everything."

Dixie stood with his hands in the pockets of his shorts, legs apart. "Sounds a good idea," he said. "The more things we can offer visitors the better. Mags is certainly a very good cook." And Mr Rix listened and looked on, rubbing his hands together in delight.

Dark fell, and the night was black, wet and moonless. Mr Rix dropped Ellen near the seafront where the lights from boats and wind-farms hung in strings on the invisible sea. Walking the dogs home through misty lamplight and rain-washed streets, Ellen stooped to remove a snail from the centre of the footpath. She turned it round to face the hedge. "Go that way, little chap."

She found herself gazing through a window at a ceremony playing out on a screen. The many many flowers of Remembrance Day. As the elaborately dressed archbishop began speaking, brandishing his golden crook, Melyne's heartbreak flooded back. The rain increased. The pomp and flag-waving became ridiculous. The celebration of Empire and its soothing words of God were drowned by the rain. "Remembering them isn't enough," Ellen thought, as she moved quickly on.

Passing through the quiet house in reflective mood, she stopped on the stairs by a photo of herself as a little girl that hung there. She could vividly recall her father taking the picture – she had been eating a plum. Her mind substituted the happy little face with that of Melyne – Melyne looking into the eyes of her own father as he took her picture. It might have been taken the day before he was slaughtered in front of her in a shower of blood. Everyone had died in that house except for her. No: war was not an inevitable fact of life; no empire was truly glorious, and no parent should ever have to find a way to tell a child that it's a killing world.

Ellen spoke despairingly to her empty bedroom. "Oh,

when will we ever stop *fighting?*" She bent down to take off her boots and then jumped in surprise as Omasah's unmistakable lullaby-voice answered in the very centre of her head:

"When you remember that you are One."

She turned quickly, almost losing her balance, but of course she was alone. A liquid serenity began to melt all tension, like lying back in a hot bath. She breathed in smoothly and the room became beautiful, and it was as though she was seeing the whole of life and its wonder for the very first time.

Omasah had heard her... had answered across the vast gulf of time.

She was still up and yawning long after midnight, having busied herself for several hours with plans and menus for the little café. It was ridiculously premature but she couldn't help herself, and knew she had no chance of sleep with so many ideas whirling round her head.

Just as she was getting into bed, she remembered the green stone that Josh had given her that day. She fetched it from her jacket, and laid it in her hand. "It looks like a heart," she said, watching the chips of crystal glinting like distant stars. Ellen slipped the stone beneath her pillow, blew out the candle, and cuddled up drowsily with her dogs. And as she drifted into a peaceful sleep she heard once more the comings and goings of a soothing rain, and felt that there was nothing in the world so wonderful as the love she shared with her dogs, and the sound of the rain.

22

December, 2018

Dick watched as a tiny wren perched on his balcony like a little puffed-up ball of brown feathers. The dialling tone rang on and on in his ear, but just as he was about to hang up, Anya's breathless voice answered. "Dick?"

"Hi, Baby."

"Sorry, I was in the garden

"What're you doing out there, then?"

"Filling up bird nuts. How are you? How's Lizzy?"

"Oh, we're alright."

"Did you get my letter?" she asked, eagerly.

"Of course."

"So what do you think?"

"Well, Lizzy's keen," said Dick. "I guess we both are."

"Really?" She sounded thrilled.

"I'd like to know a little bit more, though. Like who pays the bills?"

"Well, everyone does. Everything's pooled. Carlos is doing the books because he's used to it, and when we go off-grid there won't be any bills anyway apart from water, but we're going to use rainwater whenever we can because Paul's got loads of ideas and one day he wants to build a well. And anyway, the houses are all tiny and really cheap to run."

"But Lizzy and I haven't really got any money to bring,

109

Anya."

"It doesn't matter."

"How can it not matter?"

"It just doesn't," she said. "It doesn't mean anything in Ubuntu. What matters is that you bring yourself. It's all about being in nature and being creative and all that sort of thing, and caring for one other and the planet, like life should be."

Dick hesitated, feeling affection for his little sister flood through him. "But how can we be sure we'll be able to survive?"

"We just will."

"That's not really an answer is it, Anya?"

"Well, we'll be growing everything and making loads of things to sell and recycling things which helps the town get rid of their rubbish; and we can sell vegetables and herbs and flowers and all that kind of stuff too… plus bags and cushions and cards and Ellen's book… and Dixie's carvings are worth loads."

"Yeah, Mum told me about him. So who's this Carlos guy?"

"Ellen met him in Israel. He's got really long hair and he's an astrologer. We've got lots of skilled people. Maybe Lizzy could do massage later on because Carlos's girlfriend does it too."

"For visitors?"

"Yeah, maybe. Please come. It'll be so nice with everyone together. We can have barbecues and camp fires, and music every night."

"Well, like I said: Lizzy's keen."

"And what about you?"

"I'm keen too, Anya. It's just a really big step. Can we bring the stereo?"

"Of course!" laughed his sister. "Music's one of the most

important things to have. It's like an experiment, you see. But if we really need a computer or telly we've still got Mr Rix, who owned the land before."

"But isn't that cheating?"

Dick could picture her little frown. "No – because there aren't any rules. Paul says we've thrown the book out."

"So it's like making a statement?"

Anya considered. "Not really. It's more because we want to. Carlos says it's like taking a step back to take a step forward. We want to reconnect."

Dick paused. "Lizzy's phone separates us, I know that much."

"That's awful. You're real – that's just pixels… Is she on it a lot?"

"Constantly. It does my head in. I mean, I've nothing against people keeping in touch, but she's… well – addicted, I guess."

"But she doesn't mind giving it up, though?"

"I guess she feels it's time," said Dick. "It was her who first said about Ubuntu, not me. And she wants to do the cooking."

"Oh great, because we're going to have a café too!"

"She's even been looking at recipes."

"Oh, brilliant! Please think about it Dick, because if it goes wrong you'd be re-housed anyway with your… you know."

"True."

"And life's all about the experience because Jerry said. When it's all quiet and peaceful like in Ubuntu you can have a lovely experience, but when it's all noisy and rushed all the time you lose yourself, and then the day's gone and you can't remember any of it. It's like when you see stuff on telly and it's just shown to you, but real life's a two-way thing and you add part of yourself to it, which is like a connection with all creation."

"I see," he said, entertaining her. "And how d'you know all this, then?"

"Oh, I don't know. I'm reading Treasure Island. Have you read it?"

"I've seen the film," answered Dick, before he could stop himself.

"That's not the same. See, that's what I *mean.* I've got my own characters inside my head and my own island. How can you ever expand as a person if your brain never does anything for itself?" Her voice dropped. "It really upsets me. Seems to me like everyone's told what to be and how to look, and they can't fight it because they've forgotten how to think for themselves. Or maybe they're scared of being different. Or maybe they're just happy that way, I don't know. Anyway, never mind. I suppose I'd better go and see my dad."

"How is he?"

"Same as always. Playing guitar in his dressing gown." She giggled. "So you will probably come, won't you?"

"Yes, my lovely. We'll probably come…"

23

December, 2018

Harry lay with his head nestling in a pillow that had been fluffed up and propped with great care against the headboard of his single bed. The darkened room was cluttered but tidy. More than tidy, in fact: only Harry saw or appreciated how every part of it was carefully balanced, from the positions of the pictures on the walls, right down to the order and heights of the jam pots and sauce bottles on the shelf. The man in the bed breathed sleepily and listened for winter birds with his eyes shut, waiting for exactly the right moment to get up and make his tea. The house was silent: Mary was at work and Anya was at school.

When exactly the right moment arrived he sat up, yawning loudly. He wrapped his dressing gown around himself and fetched the only two mugs he possessed: one that Anya had bought him, with a Japanese painting on the side, and a second one, hand-painted with a play of multi-coloured stripes. He turned the light on, filled the kettle, and went out to use the lavatory. After a rinse of his fingers he returned to his room, taking with him the fresh newspaper that lay faithfully on the polished hall table. He stood enjoying the drone of the kettle and the occasional little tweets of birds from the hedges and trees outside. Then he sat down in his overly-large black swivel chair with his double helping of tea and the newspaper. He proceeded to complete the cryptic crossword in around twenty minutes, swearing under his breath every now at then at the composer's ignorance, and occasionally cackling with delight at his own. When he had finished, he folded the newspaper in half and dropped it on the floor without so much as a glance at the front page.

Harry left the blinds shut. Mary had recently become fearful about his lack of sunlight and had given him a bottle of vitamin D tablets which he took religiously every day with his breakfast. But it wasn't time for breakfast yet – breakfast happened at around six o'clock in the evening, and before breakfast he had to get in at least four hours' solid guitar practice. He straightened his bedclothes a little, and tightened the cord of his old grey dressing-gown. Last Christmas, Mary and Anya had bought him a new sky-blue dressing-gown in the hope that he would wear it and appear less "depressing." Although their sentiments were beyond him, he occasionally humoured them... but he liked his grey one much better because it felt like part of him. Harry sat down on a padded dining-chair and picked up his priceless antique acoustic. It felt like an extension of his own body.

The man became like a bird then amid a torrent of art that needed no audience to either drive it or render it worthy. Every now and then he would stop to scribble in a little flowered notebook: obscure symbols of his own invention whose meaning would die with him. The man was a genius, but no one knew it less than he did. And in any case, being an well-known talent would be a most unpleasant way to spend his life – having to get up early; meeting people who talked too much, and travelling about all over the place to play music that didn't altogether thrill him. No – this bird beat its wings to its own rhythm lest it become mute…

The only other time Harry laid down his guitar was when Anya came home from school. She was his impossible love, and his wonder at her never ceased. They shared an esoteric world of impromptu stories and oddball drawings embellished with their own made-up words. Anya always spent twenty minutes or so with him when she arrived home, talking and laughing happily… until she sensed the inevitable ache to continue with what he termed his "work." His attention would begin to waver ever so slightly, and a subtle anxiety would creep into his eyes and cloud them. She would leave him then, to settle herself downstairs with her own artwork, book or diary.

Harry had a mini-fridge, camping-hob and small worktop in his bedroom, plus one plate, one bowl and a set of cutlery. When it was time to eat (just two meals per day, and very meagre) the main pleasure lay in the preparation. Because having to eat annoyed him, he turned it into a creative process that he could enjoy. Willow-pattern plate, knife, fork and silver-ringed napkin would be lined up carefully. Then salad would be neatly chopped; half a slice of bread buttered with purposeful blobs; cheese cut into perfect cubes, and two sardines lifted slowly from their oil so as not to blemish their silvery perfection. Lastly, the whole colourful arrangement would be profusely peppered with a satisfyingly loud grinder. Harry didn't eat breakfast food for breakfast – he ate whatever he really fancied, and it was often exactly the same thing that he had eaten for days.

At some point during the evening he would always pay his beloved Mary a short visit, first sniffing her hair and kissing her forehead, and then taking an armchair and wondering what to say. She would sit quietly knitting or doing a crossword, occasionally asking him about a clue or bringing up an old memory they shared. Later, Anya would come upstairs for an hour or so before she went to bed – by now he was musically satiated, and they often became noisy as they laughed about life and each other. "Are you looking forward to Ubuntu, Dad?" she asked him one night from his big chair.

"Well, of course I am, darling. Although of course it won't make much difference to me."

She giggled. "Do you think you'll get dressed sometimes there, because people might think it's strange if you never do?"

Harry tackled the concept with some difficulty. "I can't see why. It doesn't do anyone any harm if I don't get dressed," he said, hoping he wasn't being criticised. He didn't like being criticised and couldn't understand why people did it.

"I think it'll be lovely and you'll really like it. You won't be able to hear any traffic – just nature."

"Lovely."

"D'you think you'll sit near the fire with us some nights, because it's really atmospheric?"

Harry ran the scenario through his mind and approved somewhat. He had been a keen hiker in his younger days, and had loved to light a fire outside his one-man tent. "Yes, I might like that," he conceded. "It's a very ancient thing, you know – to sit by a fire."

Anya swivelled the chair, propelling herself from side to side with her bare toes. "And that's why everyone likes the smell of the smoke because it reminds us of when we were cavemen."

His face lit up. "That's right. And the light on the cave walls made shadow-pictures, and then the men began to make them look real using bits of charcoal. And that was the beginning of art."

"I know. Would you have liked to be a caveman, Dad?" Then she laughed. "Mum says you are anyway, and this is your cave!"

His reply was free of annoyance. "I can't see anything wrong in that."

Anya jumped up and kissed him goodnight. "It isn't wrong – it's just different. You're much better than other dads and I love you. I hope you'll sit by the fire with us sometimes. It'll be nice. See you tomorrow." And she left the room with his little shopping list to give to her mother.

Harry's evenings began at precisely midnight when he poured himself a large malt whisky and picked up James Joyce. He loved the night – always had done. It eased something within him with its timeless silence. Only when he heard the early-morning stirrings outside did he think of sleep, and then he would snore loudly for exactly eight hours without moving a muscle.

The only other notable aspect to Harry's life was his weekly bath – a process so convoluted that it seemed to take over the whole house. For Mary and Anya, it meant slight amusement mixed with frustration at being denied access to a toilet for an hour. The water would be luke-warm and very deep. Sounds of splashing and sloshing would be followed by the profuse pourings from a jug as he washed his hair, and a cacophony of spitting and coughing. Then came the wet-shave, bringing with it outbursts of swearing as blood streaked the white foam. Eventually the door would unlock with a loud purposeful CLICK and he would emerge with bits of tissue stuck to his chin, reeking of aftershave.

And this was Harry's life in its entirety. He enjoyed every second of it, save perhaps the shaving: relished every breath that he took and every note that he plucked. Mary knew that the only thing Harry could ever really bring to Ubuntu was his music, but would he agree to share it? She couldn't help hoping so, because his increasing seclusion concerned her. In their early years he had been the life and soul at parties – had been fired up by people's enthusiasm for his talent. But no one could change Harry – not then, not now and not ever; and so the matter was necessarily laid to rest.

24

January, 2019

The council's planning commission office was a small square one, and the chief planning commissioner was a small square man. The council buildings had recently exchanged a spectacular panorama up on Foxheath cliffs for a lifeless view over flat featureless fields and the drone of relentless traffic. So much for good planning.

Seated in his office, early as always, Mr Rankling held a drawing in his stubby fingers. He peered through his glasses at the neat text in the bottom right-hand corner: *"Artist's Impression – Project Ubuntu."* No doubt it was a very good drawing. He held it up to the light, examining the little coloured strokes that made up grass, trees, clouds and little houses. "Very nice," said Mr Rankling out loud.

At that moment Mr Rankling's gaunt colleagues drooped into the room and arranged themselves half-heartedly around the table. Mr Rankling got up, scraping his chair loudly, and stood squarely before them. He picked up Ellen's sketch of Ubuntu again and waved it in the air. "Okay. Call for sites, case C12." He pressed a button with one stiff finger and requested tea and biscuits. "Right!" he continued, speaking quickly. "A green-build-stroke-social-experiment type thing. Living off-grid without technology. Aiming for self-sufficiency and encouraging recycling and bartering. Ha! Would you believe it? The ideas some people come up with!" The youngest and gauntest member of the group said "Cool," without really knowing why.

"Won't there be rubbish and horses and a huge big disgusting mess?" asked a prim, tidy young woman with her hair scraped into an enormous blonde bun. Mr Rankling put a folder on the table in front of her.

"Take a look," he told her, and began strolling about the room craving his biscuits. "I've seen the land. It's not overlooked or visible from the road. Thing is, government's demanding these green builds now – that's the first thing. And it might even get touristy because they want to open a craft-place shop-thing… all dingly-danglies and what-not no doubt."

"But the tourists won't spend anything if they're bartering," said Youngest and Gauntest around a yawn.

Mr Rankling tutted loudly. "So you haven't read the application either I see, Guy. You don't have to barter, but you can if you want – it'll be a novelty. Any attraction's a good thing – gets people circulating. And they'll be trading with local businesses too. Going to plant a load of crops apparently."

"But what about the mess?" repeated the blonde woman. "What if people complain?"

Mr Rankling's blood-sugar was very low. "Don't keep banging on about mess, Caroline. They're fanatical environmentalists for God's sake." He checked his watch just as the door opened on tea and biscuits. A big flowery woman slammed a tray on the table and left without speaking. Mr Rankling frowned after her for a second and then grabbed three ginger nuts. "*And* we get extra funding for a social experiment." He munched contentedly, strolling about on his stiff little legs. Outside a skylark sang distantly and unheard. "Nice picture, I thought. Take a look."

Mr Rankling didn't realise how much Ellen's sketch was swaying him in favour of Ubuntu. He didn't altogether register the way the light filtering between trees and over rooftops had stirred him. It was a beautiful drawing of a beautiful place, and in a small unaccountable way it reminded Mr Rankling of something to do with his childhood days. *And* they got extra funding for a social experiment. A few extra perks here and there to wangle for him and the wife...

Guy was looking at his phone under the table. "How the hell can you live without technology?"

Mr Rankling laughed gooily around a mouthful of biscuit. "That's their problem." He checked his watch again, took out his handkerchief and blew his nose loudly.

"Well, they must have some kind of plan," said a dark-suited bespectacled girl with the air of one who finds everyone and everything ridiculous. Mr Rankling didn't answer. He had already made his decision with uncharacteristic speed. Often applications were discussed several times before reaching a final decision, but for some reason he was compelled to get this one out of the way. It was almost as though someone was hanging over his shoulder, whispering persuasive words in his ear.

"Yes, of course they have a plan, Sally. It's all in the notes which *you all should've read*." He clapped his hands together and then rubbed the crumbs off them. "Vote on Project Ubuntu..."

"But we don't know the plan," said Guy.

Mr Rankling felt hot after his biscuits and tugged at his tight collar. "Well, read it then!" he croaked. The lad was a waste of space. "You can read, I presume?"

The young blonde woman finished her cursory glance at the folder. She closed it and slid it in front of Guy. "I vote yes. It sounds sort of interesting." She selected a biscuit very daintily and pulled out her phone.

Fifteen minutes later the forms Ellen had struggled so long over, along with her picture of the light through trees falling on the rooftops of Ubuntu, were sitting in the APPROVED tray in Mr Rankling's office. Guy still held a page of Ellen's typing in one hand. "Sounds a load of crap to me," he thought vaguely.

As he glanced out between the slats of the window-blind he thought he caught sight of something pale moving against the barren fields outside. Instinctively the boy stood, pulling the slats apart for a better view, and then watched in bewilderment as the wraithlike figure of Omasah began to drift away between the low bushes before abruptly vanishing in a bright flash of light. Guy blinked rapidly, rubbed his eyes and flopped back into his seat. He proceeded to stare open-mouthed at the wall until lunchtime.

25

Sundara
The Distant Future

The tall slender man sat overlooking endless forest, one hand resting on a large mongrel dog who curled close against him. Below him, tangled trees of many heights and shapes harboured unseen birds and creatures of all kinds, their chests pulsating with the undulations of screech, call, whistle and song. Towards the west, the vast dark sweep of vegetation was broken by a snow-white pyramid that blushed pink now in the twilight, its golden cap flaring like a second sun. On the ridge of ground where the man sat, the long pale grass was undisturbed except by his recent steps, and the scents of dog rose and sweet honeysuckle blended with nutty gorse from further up the dry hill. All around the warm air hummed with the sleepy drone of insects as they drifted this way and that, trailing scribbles of golden light.

When the man eventually stood there was a feminine grace in his movements and his stance. As a ruddy half-moon crept above the horizon he began to collect rocks and firewood, and to clear a space. Cool winds stirred the encircling trees like a mother's hush to sleep as the dusk began to subdue the passion of the forest creatures. Omasah crouched for a moment beside the neatly piled wood, and stared intently at its centre. As the wood caught fire he stood, and savoured the smells that hung in the cooling air – looked again with emotion at the darkening sea of foliage. He was going to miss this place and this time.

As darkness fell he lay down in the grass to sleep with the dog, one arm bent under his head. The sky above was awash with stars, while to the south-west the crystalline band of the Milky Way rose in unearthly pinks and browns; and the small fire became a tiny speck of orange in the vast black land, and the black land lay still save for the wind that moved in the leaves.

Omasah awoke next day to the songs of a thousand birds. He left the space clean and undisturbed, softly kicking the powdery ashes into the grass and replacing the rocks beneath the trees. Taking a handful of berries, he set out for his settlement: several hours' journey broken only by brief meditations, during which the woodland creatures came close, sniffing at his clothes with wet twitching noses, and sometimes resting their heads upon him in gentle curiosity.

The village consisted of a cluster of roughly twenty circular dwellings of stone or daub and thatch. It stood on a grassy plain at the edge of the forest, where wild slopes, busy with bees and butterflies, gave way to a rocky valley and meandering river. On the far side of the river, more forest receded towards mountains whose peaks were shrouded in heavy cloud, dark and unmoving. Here and there, alongside the snaking river or from within the sweep of trees, spirals of smoke indicated other settlements; while to the north-east a remote step pyramid dominated the hazy distance.

As Omasah approached he could hear chimes of wood and metal playing in the light breeze, and from close-by came the soft beat of a drum and the caress of a lullaby. A number of diversely-dressed people emerged, some hand in hand with children. Several wore long plain robes like his own; others favoured knitting or patchwork. A few had worked colour and pattern into hair or skin, and there was the occasional glint of polished metal from bead or bracelet; buckle or button. All shared his remarkable bone structure and tranquil grace, and their wordless greetings took the form of a brightening of their eyes and a softening of their faces. Much lay between them, all deep unspoken

One man drew close then: a keen-eyed elder dressed in a short brown tunic that exposed strong wiry legs well-used to walking. He carried a melon-sized globe of zithilla in one blue-tattooed hand, and within its silvery void could be glimpsed a small green pebble. The man's other hand stroked his white beard as he presented the shimmering orb. Omasah watched as the stone slipped and slid very smoothly about the shining curve that held it, before re-settling.

"You are at peace, Rta," said the man. "Come."

The two men turned towards the forest, with Omasah carefully bearing the globe, and behind them the people came quietly together to form a file. A few dogs followed at a trot along the path, which was well-worn and bordered with lush ferns. Ahead of them the golden tip of the pyramid mirrored the summer sky, and ten minutes brought the villagers to its northern face. Omasah looked up at the towering white perfection, and laid his palm against the coolness of its shining wall. A dark aperture whispered open, and the procession entered with bowed heads.

Built for healing and gatherings, the pyramid was empty inside, and large enough for a congregation of several thousand. The centre of the gigantic floor was freshly-laid with a carpet of sweet-smelling straw and dimly-lit from an unseen source, and it was towards this spot that Omasah headed. In the middle of the straw sat an engraved metal bowl of fragrant oil, with which he anointed himself before sitting down. The rest of the group did likewise, forming a circle. The entrance had closed, and it was as though the vast surrounding floor-space and soaring walls were lost in boundless starless night.

The company began a slow harmonized mantra then. Omasah alone remained silent, with the glistening sphere resting in his lap. As the pyramid began to receive the sacred tones, they blended and swelled into resounding, peaceful, healing vibrations that swept through body and soul. As echo overlaid echo, the chant became louder and more complex, until everything and everyone surrendered sweetly to its inexorable power. This was Omasah's final preparation for his journey across time.

Following the healing ceremony they returned to the settlement at a leisurely pace, and the bearded man led Omasah beyond the huts to a heavy wooden door set alone as though leading into a bunker. All around it and upon the slope to its rear the grass grew thickly and undisturbed. The dark wood of the door was carved with intricate depictions of flowers, leaves and birds that wove a living frenzy, and yet here and there sat an empty space or simplistic form that balanced what might have otherwise been a jumble. In the centre hung a heavy metal hoop bearing a monkey's head, which the older man turned with a loud clunk.

Still carrying the globe, Omasah followed the way down ten steps hewn from the bedrock and into a domed chamber that gave onto a spreading network of natural caverns tunnels. Everything was bathed in warm subtle light, ‹ again from an unseen source, and a few people came and went quietly along adjoining passages. Here, he was immediately greeted by a woman dressed in blue-grey robes embroidered with large white swirls. Her salt-and-pepper hair was neatly braided and piled high upon her head, and a blue star shone at her brow. Stepping forward to take Omasah's hands she shut her eyes in order to connect fully with him. Then she smiled and placed a small flat package into his hand before indicating one of the exits.

The three of them passed by several grotto-like chambers where groups could be seen sitting around zithilla globes – some in silence; others in deep discussion. Then they skirted a larger loftier space stacked with crates before arriving at their destination: a small room that was empty but for a short icy-white pillar. As they entered, the doorway hissed seamlessly shut, and the ancient stony walls enclosed them.

Omasah placed the glowing orb on the pedestal and turned to his companions, heavily aware that he had a difficult transition ahead. For them, barely ten minutes would pass before his scheduled hour of return. They would wait there with medical personnel, ready to nurse him through the recovery, and comfortable in the knowledge that their Golden Age – along with others past and future – would continue to flourish.

Omasah had informed Dixie of the date and time of his arrival, and had explained the difference between his previous brief visits – where he had bi-located across the continuum using his light-body – and this more permanent one. The first few days existing in what he understood as a lower density would be difficult, but he was accepting, and honoured at being chosen for the assignment.

He held his friends' hands about the pillar and exchanged glances with them. The loop of time he was about to exist in would become rapidly more isolated as its frequency was temporarily stepped up, and he had undergone intense training in order to deal with this vital but burdensome work. He would be alone now – fully immersed in the past and its time-frame – and the only information he would be able to access with any ease would come by way of the stone. However, even that would lack coherence and clarity, and Omasah was destined to experience a sense of blindness and separation that would, at first, be crippling. The mind-matrix would be weakened and likely to glitch, but he had a healthy confidence in himself and in his allies at both ends. He was ready.

As Omasah shut his eyes, the inside of the globe began to flicker and change. First, random speckles of light darted and danced. Then they coordinated into multi-coloured threads that formed a three-dimensional geometric shape. The apparition turned silently upon its base with increasing speed before rising slowly into the air. As the colours blended into white light, the shining whirling sphere appeared to hang motionless, and Omasah's body started to vibrate. Then his eyes rolled up and backwards, and he faded in and out of sight several times. Suddenly his whole body lit up dazzlingly bright, and with an enormous pulse of energy that faintly disturbed the hair and clothes of the onlookers, Omasah was gone.

26

January, 2019

Ellen opened the oven, pulled out a baking-tray using a tea towel, and turned over slices of aubergine and red pepper sizzling in oil. Then she slammed the oven door without meaning to and went to start the washing up.

Paul came in with his hands in the pockets of his baggy trousers. "It's blowing old boots out there. The dogs will hate it. That was the council on the phone…"

She turned round – transfixed.

Paul's face lit up.

Ellen cupped her mouth with her wet soapy hands. "Oh, my God! Oh, my God!" Then she bit her lip, looking at Paul in disbelief. From outside there came the sound of the wind rushing through empty branches and the warning "chak chak chak!" of a blackbird amongst fallen leaves. Instantly she recalled how the trees had whispered and the birds had sung her to sleep when she was ill. Sounds of life: sounds of Ubuntu.

"Well!" said Paul, filling the kettle. "It's actually happening!" He spooned coffee into a mug. "They're eating at the farmhouse tonight. Shall we go and break the news in person? I don't feel tired any more."

"Oh, definitely!" cried Ellen. "With the guitar… I'll make some of my burgers!" She began taking things out of cupboards and slicing up an onion. "What did they say? Anything?"

"Not a lot. Just that it was 'yes,'" said Paul, watching her thoughtfully. "What a string of luck, eh? What a bloody string of luck. I mean the land especially… And then the call for sites. Honestly – sometimes you really have to wonder."

"What?"

"Whether this is all some kind of game. Whether any of it's even real."

"It is and it isn't," said Ellen quickly.

The way she rarely thought before she spoke had annoyed Paul when they were married, but now it simply amused him. She continued excitedly: "It's an illusion of sorts, this reality… But its importance – its purpose – is very real."

She stopped chopping, suddenly absorbed in the racing of the grey sky outside. "Every one of us is a key player. We all help create it."

Paul blew on his hot coffee. "But sometimes it feels as though someone… or something else steps in."

Ellen was thinking now – thinking about Omasah. She began scooping handfuls of onion into a glass bowl. "Maybe sometimes someone or something else has to," she said.

Part 2

1

7th March, 2019
Anya's Diary

I really like it here. The skylark sings all the time. It's been singing ever since I arrived and it never even gets out of breath. Paul says that they get so happy up there that they go into another dimension and that's why you can't ever find them in the sky. I'm sitting in Josh's new shed again which smells really nice. There's nothing in here yet except for me, a box of tools, and two huge orange cooking pots belonging to Mags. Soon I'm going to have my own brand-new shed here to use as my own place for writing with all my books on shelves and a big beanbag! It will not be real wood though, but it will have a balcony and hopefully a round window. We don't know what we're going to do about all Dad's snoring in such a small space, and he never opens his blinds or windows and it's not fair on mum because she likes a lot of light and fresh air. But we'll find a way because that's the spirit of Ubuntu. It's all about finding ways to get on together even if sometimes you have to back down or let one person not do as much as the others – like Dad, who doesn't do much at all really except guitar – but everyone has a gift or can just bring him or herself because everyone's different. These are the sort of ideas that Ellen and Paul hope will gradually leak out into the culture and help to make the world a nicer place.

Today we can begin moving here so it's the first official Ubuntu day although nothing's really happened yet. We had to wait 4 weeks in case anyone objected but they didn't so that's OK. Ellen was really worried but today she's really happy and her and Paul and Jerry and Mags are at the other side of the field with balls of string to mark out plots. They are making an awful lot of noise. I hope I will be that jubilant when I'm that old.

So when the plots have all been marked out we'll begin to put the caravans on which will be this weekend probably. We've had a few people look at our house but no offers yet and Mum says it doesn't help that Dad won't get out of bed. Dad saves most of his money so he's bought my shed and our caravan which is a four-berth second-hand one. I think I'll sleep in my shed anyway because it is plenty big enough for my bed and lots of other things. Josh says I can have electricity when they get time because he was an electrician before, so it will be like my own mini house but until then I can use candles on plates.

There are a lot of things we need to plant quickly during March or it will be too late, and Jerry and Mags and Mr Rix know a lot about all that kind of thing. Mr Rix is always around even though he's not even doing Ubuntu, and Ellen says he is like our outpost because we use his phone and things. I love his greyhound Sage and she really likes me too. She is a beautiful gentle soul because you can see it in her eyes which are very beady, and her nose is ever so long and her head is very soft. I want Mum to get me a greyhound from the rescue place in town and she says she might.

So anyway, we are in a big rush because of all the things to plant. Everyone's been saving plastic bottles since the summer, and all their friends have been saving theirs so we've got hundreds, and Paul's going to make a greenhouse out of them as soon as *possible for seeds. You cut the bottoms off and then you thread the bottles on canes so one bottle slots into the next and then you make a frame. Ellen says she's never seen Paul so happy as since he's been inventing things for the village.*

Last night was really good because all the people doing the village came to Mr Rix's house except for Dick and Lizzy who aren't here yet, and even Dad came. So that was about twenty people and 4 dogs and it was a huge squash. Ellen drew a plan of the village and everyone decided where they wanted to live which took ages and a lot of talking and I was totally worn out by the end of it. Dad quite enjoyed himself and played blues on Paul's guitar and sang his Squeeze my Lemon song which embarrasses mum like anything because it's rude.

The houses are going to be in 3 rows on the right side facing the woods so they get sun all day. Our plot is going to have Dick and Lizzy behind (because they are in our family) and Jerry and Mags on the right, because we've known them all our lives, and then on our left will be Nadia's family because Nadia and Melyne are my friends. The people with chickens will be in the corner because it annoys Paul and my shed will be on the plot next to Jill which will be nice because she has a great affinity with me, and I am going to have my own allotment with lavender because of the smell. We are going to be organic and use marigolds to get slugs away from our lettuces and things, and in November we are going to plant a load of daffodils.

Our school's going in the corner of the playing field on the left as you walk in and Paul says it can be round if we want. In the middle of the village will be a centre with fruit trees on one side and willow on the other so we can get fire-wood and fences one day. There's going to be a gravel path right up the middle to the centre, and decking outside to sit on with steps going up, and we're going to put eucalyptus trees on either side of the drive because they grow fast and sound nice in the wind. We're going to have a living fence all round the village because of the foxes which starts off as just woven sticks but then gets shoots, and it grows really fast too so it's a constant supply. At night here you get a lot foxes which sound scary, and owls which are awesome and look right at you as they fly past. Inside the fence will be a cycle path and we're going to have a bike shed near the gate and another one near the centre, and anyone can use the bikes whenever they need. I'm donating my red and gold bike which I've never ridden much because I'm not really a bike kind of person.

Opposite our school will be the craft-room and village store where you can walk in and take what you need. Behind the orchards will be the horrible buildings like the storage units, the wood store and stuff like that, and then the bit between the orchards and playing field is for extra allotments and Mr Rix is going to plough it maybe even tomorrow, and it will have a big tool shed for sharing. And that's the plan for Ubuntu village, all except for the outside which will have our electric truck and tractor and bins. Hopefully most of our rubbish will get reused and we're going to have loads of compost heaps which Nadia says will get full of snails for racing. Under the big tree outside will be the visitors' shop and café and Ellen says I can work in the shop if I like, and that's the plan for Ubuntu Village.

2

March, 2019

Maxwell pulled the clinging brambles from his trousers in annoyance. He couldn't believe he'd had to lower himself to skulking in the woods, but every time he had tried to come via the road his car had stalled without explanation and would only go in reverse. It definitely seemed as if some witchcraft was at work, although he didn't really believe in that kind of rubbish. The whole thing was making him paranoid and scrambling his reasoning, but at the same time it was driving him on.

In front of him the big field stretched away towards the old farmhouse. Ellen and her friends were quite close, but much too preoccupied to notice him, and looked as though they were marking out the ground into sections. Whatever was going on he needed to speak to the council about it because it was bound to be illegal. Maxwell and his father had always considered themselves to be great bastions of the law.

He turned to go, catching his clothes again. Bloody woman – trust her to bring him into this lousy situation. He heard her laugh, and as always it sickened him. How could she laugh after what she'd done? How could she even live with herself?

At last Maxwell reached the grassy track that led to where he had parked his car. He trudged along deep in thought and hands in pockets, scowling to himself. Then he heard a pheasant's sudden grating alarm call, and automatically glanced between the pines. There he stood again: that huge spectre of a man – the druid – but this time he seemed to flicker faintly as if only half there. Maxwell immediately looked down, quickening his steps and feeling a surge of nausea… he must have a migraine threatening. He resisted the urge to glance back over his shoulder, willing the strange apparition away. For the umpteenth time he considered going to the police, but no – they were bound to think him insane. What was more, the police had recently visited him after two local school-girls had been flashed at. What bigger insult could be dealt a bastion of the law? But he had easily convinced them of his innocence – had used his well-mannered charm and easy humour to dispel their doubts.

Panting furiously he reached his car and drove away, quashing the powerful urge to spin his wheels. He passed through the town and out the other side, pulling up sharply in front of the smart new council buildings. He took a nervous swig from his hip-flask and then popped a Polo into his mouth. With a deep breath he got out of the car, brushing any remaining bits and pieces of vegetation from his clothes. Then he headed self-importantly for the big glass doors.

Three minutes later Maxwell was eying the spotty chinless youth opposite with all the scorn he could muster. Was this really the best they could do for him? He took a chair reluctantly, clearing his throat. Guy looked blankly back at him over the desk. "How can I help?" he said.

"How might I help you today, *Sir?*" blustered Maxwell with such suddenness that Guy was visibly shaken. The big man leaned forwards, jutting out his chin and speaking between his teeth. "Social skills are a complete mystery to you kids these days, aren't they?"

"Er... sorry," said Guy, feeling a whole swarm of butterflies take hold of his stomach. "...Sir."

"You aren't the head of this department, are you? God only help us if *that's* the case."

Guy felt a mixture of shame, fear and anger. His voice sounded squeaky in the stuffy room. "Mr Rankling's out on site. What can I help you with?"

Maxwell shot him a murderous look.

"*Sir!*" Guy added with urgency.

"Right. Now, there's this farm on the periphery of town that's gone largely to seed. I've been doing a bit of reconnoitring recently and have gleaned possible breaches in regulations. There's a group of layabouts camping illegally down there and lighting fires. What've you got to say about *that?*"

Guy relaxed a little in his chair and folded his hands in his lap. "Oh, that's just Project Ubuntu," he said with mild satisfaction.

"The... *what?*"

"The Project Ubuntu, *Sir*. It's going to be a whole village eventually you know. An experiment thing about living without bank accounts and phones and with all windmills and stuff. It's been in all the local papers."

Maxwell was hot and speechless. He didn't know which part to get angry about first. As if he'd ever laid so much as a finger on a local paper... as if a bunch of layabouts like them could build *anything*… "But… but why wasn't I told? I mean, why wasn't the town informed? I mean *you* obviously know all about it!"

Guy went on, beginning to gain a little confidence. "Oh, it went through all the proper channels, Sir. You had eight weeks to raise an objection, Sir."

Maxwell stood up, seeming to fill the room. "How can I raise an objection when you don't tell anyone what's going on?" He hit the desk with a big red fist and began marching to and fro, muttering under his breath. "This could affect the entire status of the town for Christ's sake."

Guy was beginning to lose a little confidence. "Well, Sir – the sign's been outside the location since January, Sir."

"*Sign?* So I'm supposed to notice some bloody invisible *sign* that's five inches square am I?"

"Exactly, Sir – except it was A4 and bright yellow. And then you're supposed to stop and read it, Sir – to see if you object." Guy dearly wished it was lunchtime. "You could have looked at the plans then you see, Sir."

"Well, can I object in retrospect?"

"You what, Sir?"

"Can I… Oh, never mind. Can I make an appointment to see your superior?"

"Well, I s'pose so, Sir. But Mr Rankling's quite enthusiastic about the project. You see it can't do any harm out there and it's good publicity an' all. And the Prime Minister likes this sort of thing, Sir."

Maxwell's head reeled suddenly with the realisation that he had tried to drive past the place at least five times during recent weeks. His car stalling wasn't random after all, and he wasn't imagining things. He was bewitched. That woman and her druid friends had bewitched him… A tightness grabbed his chest and arms as anger poured through him. He must leave immediately or risk becoming violent. "Forget it," he growled, leaning over the desk. "But don't think you've seen the last of me. I've got a very high profile in this town." He strode towards the door.

"Thank you, Sir," said Guy confusedly.

Maxwell turned to him with an ugly expression and then slammed the door so hard that the whole office vibrated. He marched out to his car. Sitting in the driver's seat he tried to collect himself. He would have to come back when he'd calmed down – see if he could appeal against the decision. He wasn't having it – simply wasn't having it. Bloody woman, giggling in the field with her *friends*. He thought of her broad smile and the way she had been gentle with him in the beginning. Then he thought of her face when she'd told him what she had done, and felt the memory of the ensuing violence sweep through his veins like a torrent. He flexed his large fingers, swallowed another slug of brandy and drove away with a satisfying spin of his wheels.

Maxwell cursed furiously amid the queuing traffic in the town centre: he was late for his father by almost half an hour. When at last he turned into the gravel drive of the large squat bungalow and turned off the engine he resisted the urge for more alcohol, and extracted another mint from the packet with difficulty. No good if he got arrested for drink-driving – if that happened again he'd lose his licence for good and then where would dad be? He heaved himself out of the car and went to unlock his father's door. Old familiar smells greeted him – something like boiled milk mixed with fried eggs and biscuits. "Dad!" he called, suddenly feeling more cheerful.

"Dad, sorry I'm a bit late." Maxwell felt young again now, and homely, and full of purpose.

He went into the sitting room where the old man sat asleep in a high-backed armchair with a blanket draped over his knees. Maxwell stooped to pick a couple of crumbs from the rug and went to straighten the heavy curtains, but then froze as an unexpected horror jolted him into a state of terrible knowing. The stillness that had lain to rest the dust in the sunlit room was not that of a sleeping man, but that of a dead one.

3

March, 2019

She had completely removed the letter from its envelope before realising that it wasn't addressed to her – but to her husband. Fear drained Janet's body, leaving her weak. Whatever would he say? She stood freezing cold in her thin nightie, wondering what to do next. It was his credit card statement. She waited, realising the power of it. What had she got to lose by looking? Now it was open she simply must look.

The figures stood out, punched small and black and unmoving on the page. Her eyes bored into them, as if that might change them. Her hand went to her mouth and hovered there – Alan owed over twenty-five thousand pounds. When she eventually folded the letter and replaced it in the envelope she had no idea how long she had been standing there.

She took a long hot shower and got back into bed, making herself comfortable and trying to relax – to tune into the wind and the birds like Ellen had advised her in her last email. But it was no use: a movie was playing in her head – a movie that carried on regardless of whether she wanted to watch it or not... Alan stroking the lines of the new car like a woman's hips. Alan on holiday, downing cocktails and shovelling food and racing the boys down the beach. Alan at

Christmas, arranging huge glittery boxes under the tree with exaggerated care...

It was all a sham. No wonder he was always so tense lately. He was quite well-paid, but even so... hadn't she sometimes wondered where all the money came from? She had never dared wonder very much, let alone ask. Could he really blame this one on her? Of course she expected him to try...

The front door slammed like a rifle-shot. Janet jumped as though bitten, and then eased herself back into her soft pillows to wait. She could hear the rustling of the letters and then his footsteps over the kitchen tiles... the very expensive kitchen tiles. The noise as he ran up the stairs was like a roll of thunder.

Janet breathed now like Ellen had said. All she needed to do was breathe – to keep on breathing in and out rhythmically with closed eyes. She didn't need to look at him, or listen to anything he had to say. She heard the wind buffeting the window, reminding her it was there. Her breathing blended with the gentle sound and a slight smile played about her lips. She heard a little bird pipe up, and pictured its fragile body and its little black eyes, and her smile became serene like her breathing as a feeling of peace settled in her weary chest.

She had expected some kind of verbal confrontation but she was wrong. Any excuses were swallowed in his ferocity at her transgression and his panic at what she now knew. Janet spent her own money on her little foibles, relying on him for the "big" things. He liked it that way and had cultivated it – it gave him a sense of purpose, and kept his wife in a state of obligation. But now she knew it was all a facade, and his anger at the naked truth of it crashed upon him, unstoppable.

As he beat her she became limp and fearless, and sensing her fearlessness he beat her still harder until he realised the burning pain in his hands and shoulders, and the fire in his throat. Janet's fear subsided. Long weeks of uneasy watchfulness and half-hearted pretence were finally over, and she half slept in welcome surrender. And Ellen's voice came to her tenderly on the rushing of the wind: "I had an experience once Janet. I can't really explain it except to say that it was beautiful beyond words, and that it told me

that I must never

ever

be afraid."

4

March, 2019

Day two and still none of it seemed even half real. Ellen sat drinking tea and looking out at the huge expanse of field. It remained unchanged except for Josh's caravan in front of her own and Dixie's camper to one side. As she sat there she could faintly hear Paul moving about next-door. She smiled to herself: what a funny thing to do – sit about in little boxes in a field. But her contentment and excitement was mixed with impatience – impatience to get the big storage units on site to start with, so that they could begin transferring their possessions. The house had finally sold just two weeks ago. She pictured it standing so big and silent without them there to animate it, but felt no regrets. She had gone through some major changes there, and it felt good to finally close that door and take the first step on the other side.

As she watched, a big red tractor emerged from the farmyard with a silver plough glinting behind it. It began to move over the grass, bouncing and juddering as it went. She heard Paul leave his caravan and saw him begin to walk to meet it. Ellen checked the clock – it was still only seven thirty. Hurriedly she washed in her impossibly small bathroom before pulling down the blinds so that she could have ample room to get dressed. Russell and Jack tumbled joyfully down the small steps as soon as she opened the door and began chasing each other round and round on the grass. Josh's and Dixie's vans were still tightly shut up and silent with sleep.

Mr Rix and Paul stood by the tractor shouting over the rumbling of the engine. Mr Rix looked radiant. "Morning my dear! Going to plough over the big allotment first!" He mounted the cab and roared off over the crisscrossing orange strings. She joined Paul and they trotted after him.

"Sleep?" asked Paul.

"Not much," she said.

"Me neither."

They watched for a while as the huge blades split the heavy ground and began turning it effortlessly; stood breathing in the rich fertile smell. Then they sauntered back to where Josh was sitting on his step with a coffee. "You're early birds," he said. "Woke me up with that bloody thing." He saw Ellen's face drop and got up to hug her affectionately. "Joking!" he said. "I'm so glad you're here." He disappeared inside to fetch the camping chairs and set them out on the grass. "So what's the plan for today? You want my help with a load of plastic bottles so Dixie tells me?"

"That's the tip of the iceberg," answered Paul with seriousness. "The storage units are coming the day after tomorrow, so we need to make sure the ground's level up there. We've got two sheds arriving at four-thirty, so we need to pave ready for them. Mr Rix has got a load of slabs in his yard, so I hope your back muscles are feeling in good shape. We'll need to load the lot into the truck." He looked at Ellen. "What else?"

"Jerry said he'll start digging the main drive as long as he's not needed anywhere else. He and Mags and the doctor are arriving later today, but I'm not sure about Carlos yet because the baby's got a cold… Oh! And the living fence is coming tomorrow."

"I've been thinking," said Paul. "We ought to fence round the truck and tractor outside too, in stead of having them on show."

Ellen thought for a second. "Good idea. Can you ring them now and ask? The number's on my fridge."

Paul got to his feet and pulled out his phone, checking his credit. "Eight quid left," he announced. "Then I'm dumping it!" He strode off purposefully.

Josh looked at Ellen. "How you feeling?"

"Oh, great!"

"Got the stone still?"

"Of course." She held it in her palm to show him. "I have it in my hand all the time – it's comforting."

"How's the doctor these days?" asked Josh. They all knew about his argument with Jerry a couple of months back. Jerry hadn't stayed hostile very long – it wasn't in his nature – but Steven had struggled with himself for several weeks afterwards.

"Fine… he's worked it through. Paul calls him 'Pseudo Ubuntu' because he's kept money back, but I think that's unfair. I keep telling him that by saying that he's just showing *himself* up. Steve wanting to keep chickens doesn't help either. But that's Paul: it's all or nothing with him. I think it must be hard for a career person like Steve. Personally, I've never had much direction until now. Funny how some of us follow such rigid paths while others just… drift."

They looked round as Dixie approached and sat down with a freshly rolled cigarette. "Hi," he said, and lit up with a cough or two. "I've just seen Paul. He wants me to do the rounds with my camper and get all those bottles. Never thought I'd be called on to help build an emergency greenhouse…"

They fell into silence, watching as the tractor continued to shape the land. The gulls gathered behind it on their pale wings as the sun climbed slowly behind thin grey clouds. And all around the morning breeze blew at the little orange strings, shaking them.

By the afternoon anyone with time to spare was there to help. The children sat together threading bottles onto canes while Paul deftly put together neat timber frames. "We must have way too many bottles," said Nadia, looking at the enormous piles.

"Doesn't matter," Paul told her. "Cut in half they can be used for pots, and cloches for cold weather." Ellen smiled to herself, feeling the thrill as life was breathed into her ideas. Mr Rix had rolled the allotment area and moved across to where the first caravans stood. The paved areas were almost ready for the new sheds, and Addy was in a rotten mood because they were going to be used for tools and equipment rather than his beloved library. As fast as problems were solved new ones arose, along with a flush of new ideas. "When we go off-grid," said Paul around a mouthful of nails; "I'm going to build a laundry room. Solar and wind won't run washing machines, so we'll need to make our own."

Ellen was holding the long struts of wood straight for him. "What? How on earth can you do that?"

Like all engineers Paul loved a challenge and welcomed the question with a big grin. "Bike power. Perforated drum inside a square tank. Easy! And in winter if the panels don't chuck out enough heat you can just bung a few hot stones in the water."

Ellen was impressed. "Sounds great."

"Three thirty gallon drum set-ups should be enough. I've looked at a ton of videos – only needs half an hour's pedalling…" He paused, banging in nails. Then he nodded his head towards the farmhouse. "Who's that?"

Ellen turned to see the figure of a tall grey-haired woman marching towards them as though on a military exercise. "I don't know, but she doesn't look very happy."

The woman spoke to Jerry who was working on the trench for the drive. They heard him shouting over the noise of the digger and then saw him point in their direction. The woman began a determined beeline just as Carlos wandered up with baby Noah swaddled at his front as usual. Ellen felt relieved: "Strength in numbers," she thought.

The woman began speaking harshly as soon as she got within ten feet. "Ellen and Paul? My name's Sandrine from the RSPCA shop in town. Look, I really have to make our case to you. My area manager is absolutely distraught. This set-up is totally unacceptable!"

Carlos put out his hand and smiled engagingly. "I'm Carlos. And how are you today?"

She ignored him and wasn't in the slightest disarmed. "Look – you can't just expect to set up business here in direct competition with the town's charities. It's a terrible thing to do!"

Paul walked forward, calm but puzzled. "Sorry, but I don't get what you're saying. We aren't a business, and we're not in competition with anyone. That's exactly what we're trying to get away from…"

Sandrine cut in sharply. "Apparently you intend on taking people's spare items for your own use – clothes, furniture and suchlike. Well what about us? What about the animals we're trying to save?" She stood with her hands on her hips, glaring.

Ellen stepped forward. "Look, Sandrine. The last thing we want to do is to take your trade. I'm sure we can come to some arrangement…"

The reply was spat rather than spoken: "And just how do you intend on doing that?"

"It's simple," said Carlos, and Paul and Ellen eyed him sideways. "We'll give you things to sell: unique craft items made here. We're going to have a very busy craft-room you know. And any extra stuff we acquire we promise we'll let you have that too. How does that sound?" Sandrine attempted to process what she'd just heard while Carlos continued coolly. "And when we get more established we can think about rescuing some animals. The village could do with a couple of cats. We don't want mice in our food stores."

Ellen dipped her head a little to hide her smile, while Sandrine was softened but nowhere near subdued. "Well, it's not just us – there are several shops in town and they're all up in arms about this."

"We'll be opening our temporary craft-room as soon as possible," said Carlos. "I suggest you come back in a couple of weeks. We'll show you round and discuss things further."

"We're going to be making a ton of stuff," put in Ellen. "And one of our men is an excellent sculptor. I'll show you now if you like."

Sandrine shuffled from one foot to the other as if trying to decide which to stand on. She couldn't help liking Ellen's full and generous smile. "Well…" she wavered. "I'll give it two weeks and then come back. Can I bring some of the other managers?"

Carlos put a hand on her shoulder and she flinched slightly. "You can bring whoever you like," he told her.

They stood together in silence as the woman picked her way back over field towards the farmhouse at less than half the speed of her arrival. Ellen sighed. "Oh my God – I can't believe I never foresaw this." She looked up at Carlos, wan-faced. "Thanks!"

Carlos laid an arm across her shoulders. "No worries. She's got a point, though. And I've only placated her temporarily – this needs some serious thought on our part."

"I feel such an idiot," said Ellen, covering her face. "How can we ever meet that kind of demand? Oh dear – I must go and talk to Faye and Jill…"

Paul looked gravely after the disappearing figure of Sandrine. "We'll do it somehow," he said, looking up suddenly as a lark began to sing. "Humanity Towards Others… remember?"

5

April, 2019

All he had requested was a small wooden garden shed containing a single bed, a table and a chair. Jill however had insisted on a rug upon the floor, and Faye had made a pair of curtains and a duvet cover in various blues for the bed. There was also a small cupboard containing a plate, a cup, some cutlery, two napkins, a dustpan and brush, a box of candles and some matches. The simple home stood at the far left end of the front row of caravans near the newly-planted willows. They had prepared the plot with lines of broad beans, cabbages and some herbs, and there was a water-butt behind the shed with a watering can.

The weather was windy and cold. "It's ridiculous. He'll be freezing," said Ellen, hugging herself.

Dixie checked his watch. "Stop worrying, Ellen. He doesn't have the same needs as us. We'd better fetch Steve."

The doctor had been told of Omasah's impending arrival but had been kept in the dark as to the exact nature of it. All he knew was that the man might be unwell and in need of medical attention. He clearly sensed the secrecy surrounding Omasah and it left him slightly dispirited, but he tried to let it go. The man was not his friend, and he shouldn't expect to be told the details of his life unless they became relevant.

"Here comes Steve now," said Ellen, catching sight of the doctor's fair head as he threaded his way between the patchy green allotments. Steven was feeling a little odd carrying his ancient brown leather medical bag once again. It had originally belonged to his great grandfather – a treasured heirloom dad had solemnly handed to him when he'd first become a student. They all went into the little house leaving the door open. "It's quite cosy actually," said Ellen, looking round. She took out the stone and laid it on the table, as per Omasah's instructions.

Dixie studied his watch in the semi-darkness. "Any minute now…" The three of them sat down and Steven placed his bag gently on the floor near his feet. No one spoke. The wind hummed between the pines and the birds were quiet except for the occasional pigeon from deep within the woods. Dixie checked his watch yet again. "What time have you got, Steve?"

"About four minutes past."

Ellen moved to the door, hearing voices. "Quickly, Steve!" At the edge of the new orchard Paul and Graham were struggling to support the figure of Omasah between them. He looked barely conscious; weak and ashen. Together they began half-dragging half-carrying the enormous man towards the hut, ruining a swathe of young plants beside the narrow path. Nadia rode up on a bicycle and skidded to a halt. "What's happening, Daddy?"

Graham spoke urgently. "Go and ask Jill for some blankets. If she's not there, find someone else." Nadia peddled off towards Jill's caravan on the other side of the vacant plot next-door. With a final effort the men hauled Omasah through the door and onto the bed, and Steven immediately felt his pulse.

"Should I get him a drink?" asked Ellen.

Steven didn't answer at first – he was checking the man's eyes with a light. Omasah seemed comatose, and the doctor set about testing his reflexes. "Yes please, Ellen," he said finally, slipping a blood pressure cuff onto the patient's arm. "He might be dehydrated. He's certainly exhausted."

He started to inflate the cuff as Nadia hurried in carrying blankets. She waited while Steven finished. "Let's cover him," he said. "Roll a couple of those up and raise his feet." He began to re-pack his bag. "He'll be fine I'm sure. He needs to warm up though, and get some sleep."

Jill's head appeared round the door of the crowded little room. Ellen brought water and lit a candle but realised she had nowhere to put it. She went outside and found a brick and stuck it on that. The panic had subsided.

Everyone took turns to sit with Omasah until the doctor was happy with his vital signs. Dixie went first, sitting silently on the wooden chair and wondering vaguely about the distant future world his friend had left in order to come and help them. He supposed it must be as difficult to envisage as an iPhone or pair of trainers might be to an ancient Greek… He watched the tall man sleeping peacefully beneath the warmth of the blankets – he did not stir except to drink a full glass of water, and as he propped himself up to do so, the brown packet he had brought with him slipped to the floor. As Omasah drifted back to sleep Dixie picked it up and peeked inside. Quietly and carefully he pulled out a pristine British passport and national insurance card both bearing the name John J. Mellor, along with a couple of other folded papers. With a mystified smile he quickly returned them to their packaging and placed them on the table.

The man slept until dawn, awakening to what sounded to him a very scant chorus of birdsong. He was immediately overwhelmed with the oppressive intensity of what we know as the modern world – a state with a far greater sense of separation than he was used to. It felt acutely lonely; but at the same time an endless jumble of sights, sounds and emotions inundated his mind and seemed to crawl beneath his skin like static. Still too weak to sit up, Omasah entered a profound state of meditation and lay silently until the village begin to stir around him.

6

April, 2019

"Ask yourself this: What is *real*? What's real right now in your life? I'll tell you the answer! I tell you that right now the wind is blowing. The stars are out and it's cold. The food's good and the fire's warm. We eat in gratitude and companionship tonight: this is the truth. Division is an invention of the human mind. Our differences are perceptual: I'm right and you're wrong; my God's different from your God and my God doesn't approve of people like you; this is my land and that's yours – No! Because no one owns any land. No one owns anything. A piece of paper or some pixels on a screen aren't ownership. We can't own what's divine and timeless, and we certainly can't put the nature of God into human terms. The land's a gift; the moment's a gift, as are the beautiful stars and the good warm fire. When we're united in loving appreciation of these simple blessings nothing can divide us." Carlos reached forward and took two bottles of beer from the grass, offering one to Steven.

"No thank you – I don't."

"These are the things this village is really about. That's why I'm here, Steve: I want to cherish these things with people who feel the same way. It's where I'm at – this leading-edge moment… not some yearning for the future or some pang about the past."

Steven smiled contentedly. He liked Carlos and the way he thought. He wasn't so keen on the astrology part but he found him stimulating company, if a little confrontational. "The truth is I still don't really know why *I'm* here," he remarked.

"Think, Steve. You could be anywhere in the world right now but you're right here, talking to me. We each bring our reasons and our own stories."

Steven fell to questioning himself – something he was becoming much more used to. "I'm definitely drawn to it," he said. "It's very liberating."

"Good answers." Carlos swigged his beer and grinned into the fire.

Steven had expected more. "Don't you want to know *why* I'm drawn to it?"

"Only when you've explored that."

Steven looked around at the faces of the people and felt the crackling of the fire stirring him. Why did this feel so much safer and more joyous than his previous life? What was it that shone in the eyes of these people and which he so rarely saw anywhere else? He thought of the big room with the polished table and the ticking clock, but it was the roses at the window that he missed if anything, and the birds over the fields. Looking back, the big house and up-to-date car seemed like awkward, difficult things that had seemed necessary in order to uphold some vital concept. They were things he had felt he must have, and must never lose – and yet now they were gone he was glad. Now life was about simpler everyday things, and how they played out. His face and eyes lit up in a new way as he not only understood Carlos's words, but felt the exhilarating accuracy of them. "This is real," he said to him.

"This is life. And looking back… so much of it was passing me by." He checked his watch – an ongoing habit with him. Then he said: "Time goes slower here. Have you noticed?"

Carlos laughed with pleasure as he adjusted little Noah in the crook of his arm. The baby slept peacefully, and his father watched him for a while. "I want his childhood to be free and easy. I want him to grow up happy, you know. Not some desperate grasping happiness that he chases blindly all his days only to realise it's failed him when he's old and sick. Because joy is right here, all around us, Steve. The art is to know how to tune into it. And it's free – *free* – *in all senses of the word.*" He stroked the tiny cheek with his finger. "That's why all of us are here: to live out these ancient truths."

Steven lay back on the cool grass away from the burning heat of the fire as Paul and Harry began to play guitar. He watched the sparks spiralling upward into the pale smoke that filled the dark sky, and then shut his eyes. He was beginning to feel a sense of belonging that he had never felt before. Even his childhood had been cold compared with the sense of comradeship that was building in him now, day by day. He had been worried about feeling useless and out of place, but it wasn't like that at all; and living in a caravan was warm and cosy, not uncomfortable and inconvenient like he had imagined. His vegetables were planted and he was enjoying the easy satisfaction of caring for them. Dick had been helping him build a chicken coup, and the work and fresh air was invigorating, while Ellen had promised him some watercolour lessons as soon as there was time – had even given him all her old art materials. He was also keen on Dixie's new idea of building an iron-age-type roundhouse on the new playing field. The children, what's more, were a delight. Only yesterday Nadia had surprised him with a rose-bush for his garden, accompanied by a little note, saying "I know you miss your roses so I got you this xxx." He thought coolly of Susan as he lay stroking his bristled chin… she had always forbidden him to grow a beard.

From somewhere outside the circle there was a sudden shout – an unfamiliar voice that came urgently on the breeze. The atmosphere shifted as the cry split the night air a second time. Steven sat up as someone began yelling foreign words, seemingly in panic. Faces turned and questioned one another in confusion before becoming a sea of eyes that searched the darkness enveloping the main gate. Melyne broke free from the group like a wild thing, running onto the newly-laid drive and scattering the gravel. As she disappeared into the blackness Paul turned his torch on her, and the people gathered together with their backs to the fire. The bright white light picked out the fleeing child just as she fell passionately into the outstretched arms of her brother.

Just a few hummed notes and Harry had it completely, and could play endlessly with it in beautiful ways. As Carlos began to sing the Hindu mantra people began to congregate again at the fire. Tali sat with her eyes closed, her face and body softening little by little until she joined him in a relaxed bird-like trill that complimented his rougher voice perfectly. Jean sat listening with his arms around his smiling sister, mystified as to the origins of what he was hearing and yet at one with the eternal sentiment. Here was humanity in its true element: united in heart-felt celebration of all that is.

7

April, 2019

It was the end of the week and Ellen and Josh were making a concerted effort to create some sort of order in what was known as the "store." The mobile home that Steven's friend had donated had been chosen for the purpose, and had been placed opposite the temporary school near the caravans. Unlocked and un-staffed, it was to supply everyone with day to day items from food, clothes and crockery to batteries, bulbs and toilet rolls. Ellen had volunteered to be its supervisor which meant ensuring it remained stocked at all times. There was a long table in the middle which they had filled with shallow boxes ready for food, and they had placed several shelf units around the walls, plus a stand full of empty clothes hangers. The floor was choked with miscellanea which Ellen was sifting through bit by bit, while Josh was busy cleaning out the chest freezer ready for conversion into an energy-efficient fridge.

Ellen stood up and checked her watch as Anya wandered in carrying school books. "Aren't you supposed to be on holiday?" Ellen enquired.

"I'm getting my homework done so I can forget it," said Anya.

Every Friday Mr Rix would ring in a big order for chips at five o'clock – a kind of custom that had grown up over the past month or so. "It's time we two took a break. Would you like to come with me to the chip-shop?" asked Ellen.

The girl seemed to shy away and sat herself quietly on a big box. "I'd rather not. Can't Nadia do it?"

Anya had seen the boy again last week but this time she hadn't liked what she had seen. He hadn't noticed her as he flirted noisily with two girls – girls in very short skirts who giggled and wiggled and played with their hair. With an icy pang to her heart Anya had realised the scale of her own stupidity. She had quickly escaped to the pier toilets feigning nausea, and had vowed never to go near the place again. Ever since, she had turned her attention to writing heart-breaking poems that she would burn ceremoniously after dark in the corner of her allotment.

Anya kissed Ellen's cheek softly. "I'll ask Nadia," she told her, and left the mobile hurriedly. She was eager to be alone with her aching emotions.

"She's not herself lately, bless her," said Ellen, sitting down beside Josh. "I like your pendant."

Josh touched it with his long fingers and smiled. It was a small rounded beach pebble with a hole in it that had been threaded onto black cord. "Jill made it for me," he said. "You don't find many little stones with holes in, you know."

Ellen grinned. "She likes you."

"I know," he replied softly.

"So is it… reciprocated?"

Josh studied his knees thoughtfully. Then he looked at Ellen happily. "She's nice," he said simply. "It's a long time since I've really thought about being with a woman… but yes – she's really nice."

Nadia burst in noisily. "I'm doing chips with you, Ellen. Can we go now 'cause I'm absolutely starving?" She stooped and picked something up from the floor. It was one of Anya's school books. "Can you drop this off to Anya?" said Nadia, handing the book to Josh. "It's her English book." Ellen got up, stretched and then rubbed her lower back, and went out with Nadia into the sunny afternoon.

Josh turned the blue exercise book over in his hands and stared at the head and shoulders sketch of a boy – handsome and frowning. It looked oddly familiar. Where had he seen that face before? Unable to place the memory, he tucked the book under his arm and headed for the caravans.

"How do you know when you're in love, Dad?" Anya asked from her beanbag. It had become a habit nowadays for Harry to visit her in the shed in the afternoons instead of squeezing into the van. As he sat in his big old swivel chair which he'd given her, he suddenly noticed his daughter's small breasts beneath her T shirt, and saw that her face was becoming beautiful and structured rather than girlishly pretty. Without realising he began drumming complex rhythms with his fingers on the arms of the chair. He tried to remember how he had felt some thirty years ago, and frowned as he thought how to answer.

"There are many different kinds of love you know, sweetheart. But they're all wonderful and very thrilling."

"So how do you know?"

Harry experienced a brief wave of sorrow. Things were changing, and change was always uncomfortable to him. He looked at Anya again. She looked a lot taller than she should do. "You feel the thrill," he said. Then he smiled.

"What?"

"I remember my first real love… Molly Leason. Dark and sculptural, she was. I called her my Tibetan Mystery Lady, because that's how she felt to me. We used to meet at this certain bench on a hill, and almost every time I'd go there she was already waiting. But we never fixed a time – we never had to."

"So what happened?"

"Her dad wouldn't let her see me any more. I wasn't posh enough. Ha! I used to lie in a barn and cry for hours. But there was a kind of thrill in that too."

"Do you think it's only thrilling when you look back on it, though?"

"Very possibly," he said.

"So how do you get through the horrible bit?"

Harry drummed some more, thinking. "All things pass, darling. And you know what the Buddhists say? 'Pain is inevitable; suffering is a choice.'"

The girl considered. "Oh, that's good – I like that… I'll have to write that in my book. Anyway, let's play cards." The girl went to her little bookcase and picked up the deck, and within five minutes everything felt the same as it had always done.

8

29th April, 2019

Dear Janet

I'll be writing to you by hand from now on because I've finally finished my book and sold the laptop. The book is called *Ubuntu: a System within a System*, and one of our children, Anya, designed the cover. I really can't wait to see it! I've ordered 100 copies to begin with – it didn't cost that much really, and we still have money pooled which we're spending on various things around the village. It's really beginning to take shape which is just so exciting, and I wish you could see it. Mr Rix from the farmhouse was a great help doing all the ploughing with his tractor. All our planting's done in our plots (I've got carrots) and we also have a field next door where we're experimenting with chick peas. So-far they are doing great, which is good news because they keep dried for a year, and Mr Rix has been researching all the other pulses and beans we can grow. Paul's made a really long greenhouse using plastic bottles with connecting doors through the middle. He's tied it down with ropes and is now planning a root cellar for storing fruit and veg. I've never seen him happier. Ha ha – at last all that problem-solving energy is going into something other than me.

This week the first concrete areas were laid for micro-homes and the ground dug up for pipes. Our resident doctor, Steve, has *already has his built. It's just lovely – so beautifully designed, and I just can't see why anyone would ever want more. All the rest of us are still in caravans or campers which is getting a bit tedious to be honest, but we've had so much to do. Dixie and Josh are staying with their vans but the rest of us are going for the new homes. Three of the children have decided to more-or-less live in what they first planned on using as their "hanging-out" places. Anya's got a shed which is a great little building – fully insulated etc. Nadia and Melyne have an old caravan which they've covered in stickers, and you can always hear them giggling in there as you bike past. I think it'll be good for the children to have their own allotments to care for too.*

The few of us who owned homes have sold up now and all the cars are gone too. Paul and I gave our old Rover to the school because it was only valued at 50 quid and the kids have painted it all over – it looks amazing. Our friend Dixie has always wanted to build an Iron Age roundhouse and so he bought a book about it, and that's taking shape too on the playing field near where the school will be (at the moment the children use a mobile), although we don't know what we're going to use it for yet. Also this week some guys are coming up from London to install an extra composting loo near the allotments and one for the 3 girls so they don't have to keep using their parents'. All the homes will have these loos too, and amazingly they don't pong at all.

We had a bit of trouble at first with the local charity shops, but we've pretty much sorted it out now. They heard that we planned on collecting old clothes etc. and other unwanted stuff and they got really snotty. So we have kind of done a deal by offering to relieve them of all the rubbish stuff they get and can't sell and which goes to landfill in exchange for items that are better quality – we mainly only want the fabrics for our craft centre in any case. We'll also give them any excess stuff we get and some of our craft items to sell in their shops. We really don't want to be on the wrong side of the charities because we are supposed to be an ethical community. As long as we have plenty the rest can go elsewhere.

We had a huge surprise a few weeks back when little Melyne's brother Jean arrived from Africa. Melyne is Faye's adopted daughter – I'm sure I must have mentioned Faye to you. She is our sewing lady and does a bit of teaching too. Anyway, he just walked into the village one night, and Melyne's practically not left his side since. He's a priest and missionary, and managed to get here with the help of online Christian networks. Then he traced his sister to Faye's house only to find it empty. So the next day he went to the parish church and asked if they knew her. Well, Faye takes Melyne every Sunday without fail, because her faith was always such a big part of her life before she came here.

I really am in total awe of Jean – while there was war and famine in his own country he was in Somalia spreading the word, even though Christians are persecuted there. What's more, he can drive a tractor, build practically anything and works every hour that God sends. He can even thatch a roof. Oh, and he's also refused a micro-home – insists on building his own house using materials from the old shower block (which is still mostly in a big heap outside the fence) and there was even a vacant plot sitting there waiting for him! Paul and Jean get on like a house on fire even though Paul's a bit anti-religion. They share so much common ground that the one difference doesn't matter, which is great, and in keeping with the spirit of Ubuntu. Jean is such a beautiful strong calm and wise person, and we're so glad he's joined us.

So that's how far we've got to date. It's exhausting but rewarding, and we are all so close and like a big family. It seems like there's always something going on in a quiet way – a barbecue or some music or a nice discussion – but there's never any pressure, and you can take it or leave it. The evenings round the fire never fail to feel magical, and on clear nights you can see every star in the sky. It's everything I always imagined, and it's changing me in ways I never thought were possible. There's still a lot to do and build and it gets quite nerve-racking at times. I get so tired I never have trouble sleeping like I used to, which is good. When all the building's done we have to look at going off-grid, which will be a whole new ball-game. We have some big tasks ahead but I know this is my path and why I've been put here on this planet. Self-belief has never really been my forte up until now. It's like I've been waiting in the wings all my life, but with this project I've finally walked onto the stage.

I hope this letter finds you feeling a little more comfortable at home Janet, and that you are managing to find some of the peace and happiness you deserve. Come and see us any time. Much love – Ellen x

9

May, 2019

It took time for Omasah to adapt to his new life in the village: a challenge he met methodically and with composure. There were many things that deeply puzzled him about his new companions – they were obsessed with time-keeping, ate too much and too often, and hardly ever stopped talking. But they found him equally mystifying, with his continual need for solitary walks in the woods, and long hours spent in meditation.

Every morning when Omasah got up he would first wash and dress in one of the simple cotton outfits – trousers and tops – that he had asked Faye to sew for him. After a drink of water, he would sit silently and tune into the feelings and dreams of those around him as they stirred or lay sleeping. In this way, he determined where he could best be of service during the coming day. Where there was anxiety, doubt or the beginnings of conflict, Omasah would always appear to smooth things over with his quiet and indisputable wisdom. This was his work.

Because of Omasah's intervention, Paul had grown to accept that two house-holds were keeping chickens. At first he had been up in arms, shouting at Graham while Ellen stood tearfully at his side: "It's exploitation, pure and simple!"

Unperturbed, Graham argued calmly that it wasn't like factory farming where birds suffered and died. Omasah had to keep this conflict in check for two weeks until the two men at last regained their mutual respect. On one occasion he had requested that they sit looking into each other's eyes for as long as they could manage.

"You are like two candles lit from the same flame," he had told them. "Know that the other person is you. Hurt the other and you hurt yourself." Paul was already familiar with concepts of this kind, and had cursed his own inability to live by them – but eventually he had won through, and to Ellen's great relief his anger had melted away for good.

Omasah had been concerned for Anya during her brief episode of heartbreak, and whenever she had failed to visit him he had gone in search of her, sensing her emptiness. Sometimes she would accompany him on his walks, and he enjoyed her bright eyes and smilingly tolerated her energetic chatter. With her great capacity for joy, she was a kindred spirit.

"Have you ever been in love, Omasah?" she had asked him one day as they collected pinecones for the craft-room. He had crouched down to look into her face, reading her meaning – and she had meant something yearning, agonizing and physical. He had puzzled how to answer.

"All is love," he had said to her tenderly. "I cannot fail to feel it. But pain is a different vibration. Where there is pain, love is compromised."

Anya had eyed his face in emotion as he stroked her hair: "Be at peace, Navastri. You are like a forest flower learning to grow towards the light."

Omasah was also heavily aware that Ellen often did far too much, and put herself at risk of nervous exhaustion. He paid her a visit every day to make sure that she sat in meditation for at least twenty minutes, ignoring her excuses and sitting with her if necessary. Such were his healing abilities that Carlos suggested making one of the rooms in the centre a special healing and massage room. Although known as the 'centre,' this building had somehow been shoved to the very back of the queue, and all that marked it to date was a rough circle of faded orange string. Ellen was enthusiastic. "Perhaps we could even offer healing therapies to visitors one day?" she had said, and they had both taken this thought and pondered on it.

One day Ellen had offered the stone to Omasah feeling that it was his place to hold it now, but he had refused. "You are the vibrational heart of this place," he had told her. "I can read it whenever I need." Ellen had puzzled long and hard over the significance of the stone, and would often gaze at it and wonder how it could be so important.

"I don't understand," she had said to Omasah one evening. "How can you get information about the future from this stone when it only exists in the present? Surely you can only get things about the past from it?"

Ellen thought Omasah was actually going to laugh – something no one had seen him do yet. She laughed in his place. "What? Please say!"

As always, the man paused to think. "Time is not linear across all dimensions, Kaphalya." She looked blank, and so he tried to elaborate. "The stone marks the beginning and end of this particular loop of time, and therefore contains the whole within it." Another pause. "Not only the whole, but every possibility within the whole."

"But why this particular stone?" she frowned, turning it in her palm. "Wouldn't any one do?"

Omasah nodded slowly – more a gesture of respect than an affirmative. "There are many stones that would have sufficed, but that *is* the stone for this village."

"Did you choose it, then?"

"Do not juggle scenarios, Kaphalya. In this time-line I simply recognised it and picked it up."

"Recognised it from where?"

Omasah smiled in his gentle way. "From my own time, where it lies protected."

Ellen was mystified. "It makes my head hurt," she said. Then she asked a little tentatively: "Does the future look okay?"

"The future looks golden," he replied, knowing this to be the best answer for helping Ellen achieve her desires. "Here," he said, folding her hands around the stone and cupping them in his own. "Let me show you how things are."

His hands were warm, and they pulsed with a buzzing energy that trickled up her arms. Ellen bowed her head, closed her eyes, and then gasped: "I'm flying!"

Her mind was a high sailing bird. She could feel the power and manoeuvrability of her wings and tail. Wide white wings… Warm clear air… Diving down over houses, trees and walled gardens, recognising things in a strangely undefined way. In the distance glittered what she knew to be the sea and yet she had no words for it, and sensed it merely as an invitation. As she glided with speed, hearing loud indistinguishable noises over the rushing wind, she suddenly accelerated upwards and opened her eyes with a scream. "It was me!" she cried. "I saw me sitting in the garden last carnival day! I remember seeing that seagull… I felt the connection!"

"You recognised yourself. All is One Kaphalya, even across time."

Jean's and Melyne's memories of brutality and loss presented the most difficult aspect of Omasah's ongoing mission. He saw great strength and goodness in Jean, and welcomed his blossoming relationship with his sister. But whenever he encountered the girl it was hard for him to contain the emotions that swept over him. Omasah had spent time observing her memories, in the hope that by playing them out again and again he might begin to adjust. He felt it was unfair to mind-block them when his job here was to encourage sharing on all levels. And he wanted to understand. But although the villagers' pain was his pain, he had still blocked the multitude of sensations he had first picked up from beyond the village gates – had he not done so, he would have found it impossible to function. He was of course aware that there had been many ages of this dark and violent type throughout the long cycles of time: it was a necessary part of a vast and natural ebb and flow, but it was not easy for him.

Dick and Lizzy were always Omasah's last port of call for the day, so that he could spend as much time as needed without being required elsewhere. Lizzy would prepare him a hearty salad using various oils and seeds mixed with avocado and olives as well as the more basic leaves and tomatoes, and he would eat it slowly and daintily at the table. Then he would join them in meditation and offer healing where needed. Lizzy had told Steven enthusiastically about how well they both were feeling since their treatments, and had described how the heat was palpable from Omasah's hands. She also claimed that while her eyes were closed during sessions, she could see a soft light that surrounded her. Of course Steven had remained sceptical, but was nevertheless pleased for them and the all-round positivity of what he privately deemed a placebo effect.

Contentment flowed easily to Omasah. He needed little sleep and could often be seen watching the stars from a canvas chair late into the night, pleased that his work was proceeding well. With his quiet composure and placid ways, he gradually came to fit into the fabric of the village like a delicate hand into a soft glove.

10

June, 2019

"God is with you when you create," observed Tali, her chocolate-brown eyes slightly crossed as she focused on her needle. "God is not with you when you destroy." The new craft-room was a hive of activity, and Tali sat stitching gold sequins onto a freshly-made shoulder-bag.

"And yet people kill for their God," sighed Faye at her sewing machine. She glanced at Melyne, who sat peacefully at the table weaving friendship bracelets with her sister.

Jill asked softly: "Did you see much conflict in Israel, Tali?"

"A little. I been in shelters a lot and evacuated from rockets. But I mean… it's just all the time an… atmosphere, you know. It's difficult to realise unless you been there."

Melyne sat unmoved. Faye was watching her fondly, and for the thousandth time welcomed Jean into their lives.

"I know what we should make," piped up Nadia. "Anti-war dolls. Special Ubuntu ones. Mix up the races."

"You mean like pink golliwogs?" said Jill. They all giggled.

"Kind of…" Nadia mused. "We could mix up the religions too."

Tali said quietly: "Mix Jew and Arab and a war will erupt."

Nadia's imagination immediately blossomed. "It's like having the human shape with all different things in it but to show it's still human. We could have ones with lovely saris and then all things from different countries, like a pair of clogs or a string of onions, and ones with ginger hair and Chinese eyes and a bindi. And some of them could have a disability too, like only one arm… or one eye."

Melyne chuckled happily. "And all must be smiling," she said.

Jill picked up her notepad in mild amusement. "Well we can certainly think about *something* of that sort, Nadia. Make an anti-racist statement. We do need special Ubuntu ideas – things you can't get anywhere else…" Her pen looped across the page.

They fell silent, and Melyne's thin fingers worked methodically at her bracelet and her mind was far away from the images it fled.

"Not a breath of wind out there," announced Paul entering the room. "You lot look busy." He began doing the rounds, picking things up and turning them over. He examined a patchwork bag. "These are fantastic! How long do they take?"

"Not long at all really," Faye answered over the whirring of her machine. "Tali's getting really quick with her sequins." She plucked another coloured fabric square from the pile next to her.

"We need more ideas," Nadia told him. "Can you think of anything we can make apart from bracelets, bags, cushion covers, quilts and dolls? We want to do dream catchers but we need to find out how…"

"Stop just a second," interrupted Paul. "Everyone just stop what you're doing and listen." They obeyed in puzzlement.

"Silence…" he said. "The sound of Ubuntu."

176

"Beautiful," whispered Tali.

"Golden indeed," agreed Jill.

Paul thought for a second. "I was thinking about pottery, but the problem's running a kiln. They use a hell of a lot of power. Don't think it's really ethical."

"There's one in town," said Faye. "Maybe they'd let us use it if we gave them some stuff to sell."

Tali's eyes brightened. "Send Carlos the diplomat! He can persuade all!"

Paul opened the door onto the calm misty afternoon. "Still better, we could build our own kiln... yet another challenge!" The door slammed shut. Somewhere nearby a blackbird began to sing.

Melyne slipped her finished bracelet over her tiny wrist and tightened it. "I like the birds most. Silence is sad."

Nadia suddenly let out an excited squawk. "Oh my God – I know what we should do! A 'Sounds of Ubuntu' CD! We can put all the lovely sounds on it for people to relax with and then put it in the shop. Can we, Jill – *please?*"

"With the birds!" smiled Melyne.

"And the crackle of the fire," added Tali.

Jill began writing again. "Well, I'll speak to Ellen. It'd be in keeping with our values and everything, so long as we can afford it. Wow! Our own CD! It could be brilliant if we get it recorded properly."

"Wind-chimes tinkling and trees rustling," suggested Faye.

"Pigeons cooing and Jill running on!" laughed Nadia, as Anya entered the room with Ellen, both fresh and glowing from walking the dogs at low tide.

"We've got loads of stuff," said Ellen, putting a sand-covered bag on one of the tables. "Look at these stones. And we've got feathers and shells and some great bits of driftwood – look at this!" She held up an elaborately twisted stick, smoothed by the sea.

"Gratitude stones," said Faye, picking up an oval piece of brick-red jasper. "Have you heard of them? You get a nice stone that fits into the palm of the hand, put it in a nice little bag with a note saying what it's for, and that's it!"

"Well what *is* it for?" enquired Jill.

Nadia answered for her mother. "Oh, yes – It's for reminding people to be grateful for everything they've got in their lives. You keep it in your pocket and whenever you feel it in there you're reminded and it gets to be a habit."

"The little bags will be easy-peasy," said Faye. "Good job we've got another sewing machine on the way. And Anya – you can do the writing all prettily."

Jill began scribbling again on her pad. "Wonderful; just wonderful…"

11

June, 2019

Steven had been the first person in the village to have his micro-home built: a three by four metre wooden structure that had arrived flat-packed on a lorry, and taken just a few hours to assemble. He had insisted on ordering it early using his own money, feeling secretly unable to wait like a child at Christmas. It was cleverly designed, with the double bed forming the ceiling of the sitting area, and a raised kitchen with lots of storage underneath. The house had an under-floor heating system and was well-insulated against both heat and cold, although he had to admit he did get warm at night sometimes – but then he would open the window wide and watch the stars creeping over the trees.

There was a narrow bathroom with a gravity-fed shower at one end and a composting toilet at the other; and the sliding doors could be left open so that a tall frosted window let in extra light. He had placed mirrors here and there to add a sense of space, and hung a few of his favourite paintings. Everything was still running from the old campsite electrical point, but Steven had a private ambition to be the first house to get off-grid. Two solar panels from the demolished block wouldn't do much, and so he had set about trying to design a wind turbine ready for colder, duller weather. He would no doubt need advice off Josh and Paul, but he wanted to give it a go on his own first to see what he could come up with.

It was late one Saturday afternoon and he was resting his sore muscles after a shower. He had never done so much hard physical work before, and although he was getting a lot more used to it he'd definitely overdone it this past week, swept up in the mass enthusiasm for completing the roundhouse.

Jerry's cheery shout reached him from outside: "Steve!"

Funny how to this day he still couldn't get used to the way everyone called him Steve... He sat up, stretching. "Steve! Someone to see you."

He dragged himself to his feet and looked out of his front window, and was flabbergasted to see the figure of his son making his way awkwardly up the little path and frowning at the chickens. Seconds later there was a knock at the door – as if he needed to knock. "Hello," said Steven, feeling profoundly nervous. "Come in."

Ben entered the tiny room looking enormous and inappropriately dressed in an expensive-looking brown suede jacket and smart navy chinos. Steven shook his hand, and they glanced briefly into each other's eyes. "Take a seat. What are you doing here?" asked Steven. "Anything up?"

Ben didn't sit but stood with his hands clasped behind his back, pretending to examine a small Turner print beside the window. "Mum told me," he said in a loud voice. "I just had to see it for myself..." He turned and looked down at his father, who was sitting on the sofa. "She's decided she wants the old clock and the dining table. I don't suppose you've got them any more though."

Steven felt suddenly tired. Of course he'd had to inform his ex-wife of his whereabouts, but he hadn't expected this in a million years. Ben never visited, and hardly ever phoned.

"They're here in storage. It'll take me a while to lay hands on them, but she's welcome… Tea?"

"No thanks." Ben looked around the little room with a pinched expression. "What the hell do you think you're up to, Dad? Everyone's laughing, you know."

"Everyone?" Steven's eyes widened. "Who's everyone?"

"Tim. Marjorie and James."

"That's not everyone." Steven mounted the steps to his kitchenette and filled the kettle with trembling hands. Ridiculous how his own son could make him feel this way. Ben sat down at last, stroking the fabric of the seat – assessing it.

As the kettle boiled Steven perched on one of the kitchen steps. "Look Ben – those people never felt like friends to me. They never interested me like these people do. I've got every respect for you and Mum and the lives you choose to live. All I ask is a little in return."

Ben snorted in reply and fell to looking out of the west-facing window that gave onto Dick and Lizzy's caravan next-door. Lizzy could be seen busily pulling weeds from her allotment and tossing them into a bucket. She was wearing her brightest patchwork dungarees over a small pink vest-top that exposed her numerous tattoos. Ben's voice was frosty and exaggeratedly public-school: "Who're your neighbours, then?"

"Dick and Lizzy. They've both got HIV." Steven was angry now. He made his tea noisily, spilling big drips. "Look, Ben – if you're just going to take the piss please go. Come back tomorrow and I'll give you the things."

Ben was feeling just as awkward as his father, and so got up hurriedly with a degree of relief. It had been a mistake to even come inside, he saw that now. But as he stood there a pang of rejection undermined him, turning him sulky. "You haven't even asked me how I'm doing."

"Sorry," said Steven. "How're you doing?"

A pigeon began cooing loudly from the roof. Ben felt stupid now, as well as irritated and contemptuous. "I'm doing well. Very well…"

"That's good. I'm pleased. So am I."

Ben lumbered towards the door, consumed with the urgency of getting out of this place. The door swung open onto a mishmash of greens, greys and browns and a rush of fresh air mixed with chicken dung. For a second it transfixed him. He searched inside himself for something but there was a blockage there. He turned to his father. "See you tomorrow," he said gruffly, and strode down the path.

Steven didn't move. He sat watching Lizzy, suddenly overcome with fondness for her. He finished his cup of tea without tasting it, put his slippers on and went outside, stepping over the little green wire fence that she had insisted on from day one. He went up to her. "Hi," he said.

From inside the van Joni Mitchell warbled bird-like over her piano. Lizzy rubbed earth from her hands. "Who was that bloke?"

"I don't know," said Steven, inexplicably. He didn't want to think about it right now. Lizzy eyed him carefully and then took his hand.

"How about a nice big bowl of your favourite curry?" she smiled, and led him towards the caravan steps.

12

July, 2019

Saturday afternoon, and Ethan lay stock still on his bed listening to the unmistakable sounds of violence coming through the floor from downstairs. He daren't move a muscle – could hardly even breathe. This wasn't how life was supposed to be, and the boy couldn't process it or assess his own role within it. He simply waited for the noise to stop, studying the artex overhead with its pale shadowy rivulets that formed shapes like winter trees.

His parents never knew if he was out or in these days, and it was good. He had told them that he ate tea at a friend's and then did football twice a week, which was a lie; but it was worth it to get more time out of the house. He had to purposely dirty his carefully folded shiny blue kit with varying degrees of earth, mud and grass depending on the weather. It was a way of gaining a bit more control and freedom, and his mum's face looked happy when she thought he'd been playing sports. But often as he mounted the stairs he would have to fight back the tears that her pleasure unexpectedly raised in him. Keeping that kit pristine was one of the few ways his mum still managed to show him love.

The noises had stopped. He couldn't hear his mother crying. Maybe it was a mistake. Maybe they had been moving furniture or something. He sat up slowly and listened. The whine of traffic, bark of a dog and rustle of trees outside sounded cutting and sharp through the crystal-clear air. Then the front door slammed with a crash, and he heard his father walk to the car and drive away at high speed. He sat listening. He really should go down and see if she was okay, but for some reason he didn't want to look at her or to help. He felt sick under the weight of his own wrongness. Why didn't she feel like his mum any more?

She was moving now. He heard the wardrobe doors sliding and immediately lay down again, stiff with tension. She was all right. He was staying put. He didn't want her to think he was there. He was thirsty, and fished on his bedside cabinet for a sports-bottle which had an inch of Coke in the bottom. He swigged a mouthful – it was flat and tasted of plastic. The toilet flushed downstairs. In the silence that followed he was alone in the world. His mum still wasn't crying. She must be okay. He studied the pale shadowy trees that crawled overhead, and nothing felt altogether real. He grabbed his phone.

Scrolling down and down and down and everything was bright chatter, motion and flaunting girls. By now Ethan had an escalating problem with girls, and it seemed that wherever he went at least one pair of doey painted eyes followed him. At first he had been embarrassed and would blush innocently… but that was a long time ago now. Later he had tried to establish some kind of footing – had experimented with friendship, tenderness, love, conquest and sex. But it had all become painful in complicated ways – had laid demands on him that were beyond his understanding.

Nowadays his loins ached and his blood boiled with dark emotion as he posted pictures of himself, sitting online for hours on end until a sudden pang of hunger or thirst roused him. His followers had recently begun an exponential increase, and they were ninety percent female. He disrespected the girls' neediness, but it was so easy – like gorging on endless chocolate ice-cream. The whole thing had become some kind of obscenity which he both craved and repulsed. Endless chocolate ice-cream until nausea set in. And when he took them roughly in unfamiliar bedrooms or against dark alley walls, he did so without looking into their faces.

The boy couldn't focus; couldn't seem to be able to read. He ignored his notifications and let his phone fall to the floor, leaving one arm hanging. Lately, he kept feeling as though something unthinkable was hunting him, and it was gaining ground. Whatever it was, he was certain that he must somehow keep just ahead of it. Some nights it would almost take hold of him, and he would jump awake in sweaty panic. A deep-down part of him yearned for a clear sunlit space that he could run headlong into, but everything felt compressed and oppressive, and the world's chaos crammed his mind.

Where and who and what was he amongst all of this? Was his role to outwit the relentless pursuer, no matter what? That was how it was beginning to feel – that it might lay a chilly finger on his neck at any moment. And so he must keep going, little by little and step by step, amid relentless noise and confusion. It didn't matter how meaningless things might seem, just so long as he could keep ahead and not look over his shoulder.

Don't stand still.

Ethan began sifting through his DVD collection,

scattering discs on the floor and forgetting that he didn't want his mother to know he was home. Then he thought better of it. He reached beneath his mattress for the most recent porn movie his friend had lent him, and his hand shook as he slid it into the player.

13

18th July, 2019
Anya's Diary

When it's quiet in the mornings here and the foxes bark in the woods and the wind makes a shushing sound you can feel some kind of ancient spirit inside you, which is probably nature. Today it is a humming wind which will be lovely to listen to in the night. A humming wind is quite rare and is my favourite sort of wind because gusty winds wake you up with a jump but humming winds make you feel all nice and sleepy. Most of all I like the rain on the roof which you don't get to hear properly in a normal house, and this weekend Mr Rix says it will be very rainy so I will be in here all cosy in my bed. I've been writing some poems in my poetry book and I wrote one called Ubuntu Morning which is about all these kinds of things.

Jill has flu so Faye is teaching us tomorrow. Hopefully Jill will be better next week, and Nadia saw Josh going into her house and thinks they are in love which is quite nice I suppose as long as it doesn't change her. I don't know if she is too old to have babies but it might be nice to have some more babies here because Noah is lovely and I really like helping Tali with him, and on Tuesday she asked me to look after him while Lizzy massaged her back because Lizzy is also a masseuse and so we have two in the village.

Last night before she went to bed all sick Jill gave me a rocking chair that used to be in her house and which is too big for her porch and wouldn't rock properly on it because there was no room. So now I have that as well as Dad's swivel chair in my shed. It just looks so lovely now in here that I am really glad I don't have to live in the main house, although the main house is also very nice and Dad has his own kitchen bit so he can keep his life as it is and eat in the middle of the night. I got a really nice rug from the storage which I put instead of the first one which wasn't very nice, and yesterday I went into town and got a string of little birds with a bell on the bottom and I think we should make that kind of thing in our craft-room. I have my table near the window so when I am writing or drawing I can see what's going on, and in the evenings I can smell the lavender if it's dewy. I am still using candles because I really like it and I have a primus stove to make tea with, and best of all I have some new solar-powered fairy lights that Mum bought me and they are just about the best part, and they give out a nice soft light too so I don't think I need to be connected to the grid.

Tomorrow we are having a meeting which we do most Fridays after chips, and I am going to suggest doing some flyers to print on Mr Rix's computer so that we can let the town know all about us and build up a relationship, because soon we want to open the shop and café. Carlos is very into the idea because I asked him, and it will let the people know how we can take some of their recycling away and old rubbishy clothes because people get so much stuff in their houses and garages and we can use a lot of those things. Mum is going to work in the shop whenever Jill is teaching and I'm going to help in there after school and I think I will really like that.

I think Carlos is just about the most interesting person here apart from Omasah, and yesterday me and Melyne sat with him on the field while some people did cricket which I don't like because I am rubbish. We had a long chat all about how the world is, and he said that if every single person on the planet believed in the well-being of us all and felt that we are all one, then all the problems would stop tomorrow. I said that it's hard to do that if you're starving and then Melyne said that we should get rid of all the weapons and I agreed, but Carlos said that people will always invent new ways to kill one another, which I guess is true, and that what must really stop is the urge to kill. He said it's a gradual thing which he believes is already happening because we're in a new age, although I can't really see it but I really hope he's right.

Omasah lives in front of Dixie in a really small hut and I visit him a lot and he is a very calm and peaceful person, and he always says beautiful things. He is a poet and not from here but I think that if he was from here he would be something like Daddy and me, and I like to give him little presents. Last week I gave him two geraniums for outside his door, and I painted stripes on one pot and spots on the other. Omasah likes birds and things like I do and he only eats raw food, and he says that he comes from a place where there are a lot more birds than here and enormous forests, and that's why he likes the woods and sometimes I go for walks with him. He says it's called Sundara where he comes from, but it's not in my atlas and Nadia thinks he's making it up although I don't think he would ever do that.

Jean is teaching Dixie how to make African masks by drawing for him all the different kinds of designs they use, and this is a really good idea because they are quite easy and very popular these days. Jean is also helping build the school and it's going to be so cool because he is using plastic bottles in one wall to make a pattern like they do in Africa sometimes and it will look great because the bottles are all different colours and the sun can *shine through. Because we are hoping to be self-sufficient we've decided to chop down every fifth poplar tree by the chickpea field and replace with saplings which will grow ten feet a year. They are enormous the poplars and will last ages, and we are going to store them in the school mobile after the proper school is built. Paul says the wood doesn't get very hot but we'll have to make do, and that we might use it for helping heat water because someone gave us a big metal bath and Paul is going to put it in the laundry room when it's finished behind a curtain so we can have a hot bath, which Ellen is very pleased about because it's the only thing she misses. Poplar wood is okay for carving too so we're really lucky to have those trees. Dixie likes to work by himself so he has a little workshop which Dick built from breeze blocks with a tin roof, and it's nice to go and watch him as long as I don't talk too much.*

I feel much happier now that we are all getting set up and everything and I have started eating tea twice a week with my brother because Lizzy cooks amazing curries and says she will teach me. I'm pleased I've more or less forgotten about that boy because now I don't see him any more so it's stopped hurting. He was very gorgeous but he would never like a girl like me in any case and all he ever talks about is stupid stuff so I am glad I'm getting him out of my system, but I don't know how I am ever supposed to get married and things being in this place. Mum says not to worry because soon I can get a volunteering job in town looking after babies or something and then I will meet more people, except I don't see how you can meet boys in that kind of situation. Anyway, Ellen says that there's someone out there for everyone and that it will be sent to me exactly when the time is right.

14

August, 2019

Maxwell stood staring at the SOLD sign through his window in disbelief, still unable to get his head round the enormous blow his father had dealt him. All those years of bravado and yet the old man had died penniless. Worse than that, he had died so vastly in debt that Maxwell had been forced to sell the house in order to sort everything out and pay for an adequate funeral. This wasn't what he had expected in a million years. Apparently his father had not been the man he claimed, and yet Maxwell still couldn't find it in his heart to disrespect him. The brain-washing had been far too thorough for that, and nothing concrete existed beyond it.

Because he had been unable to face the truth, and, finally, even to comprehend it through the fog of dementia, the old man's troubles had grown as exponentially as the piles of letters stuffed into the bedroom drawers. He owed rent on the bungalow and money on Maxwell's car. There were credit card bills for meals out and tailored clothes from years back; nights in hotels and first class flights abroad. As he searched through endless unopened letters and crumpled statements, Maxwell recalled accompanying Dad on many of what they had indulgently referred to as "little days out," remembering clearly the swelling pride as he had walked into luxurious rooms hung with sparkling chandeliers. The atmosphere that pervaded those kinds of rooms was unforgettable.

It was true that the old man had been reasonably well-off following his military career, but he had owed money for years now, occasionally dodging the bullets with consolidation loans that served to stack still more on the mountain of balance due – and he had always thrown up the family home as security. It hadn't helped that when the house had been handed over to Maxwell it had come rent-free and with a regular income. Maxwell's nerves had always interfered with his ability to hold down a job, and his father had considered working beneath his son in any case. With no savings of his own, Maxwell was left with too little to buy even the smallest bungalow, but too much to claim benefits, and the future looked unavoidably bleak. He couldn't believe that he hadn't checked these things after Dad's first stroke – but then Maxwell had never really got used to thinking for himself, and had certainly never dreamed of questioning his father's solvency. That would have felt like an affront.

Part of it was his mother's fault of course. Trouble had always followed her like a bad smell. Maxwell knew that at one stage his father had paid out huge sums for private therapy… what a mistake that had turned out to be. She had proceeded to twist the truth so convincingly that the therapist had begun to ask *them* awkward questions, as though her neuroses might have something to do with *them*. Dad had been furious; had threatened to throw her out – but then they had woken up one day to find her gone. For Maxwell it had been the final insult, and he had mentally disowned her from that moment. He had been just twenty-one at the time.

Maxwell studied the SOLD notice as it wobbled in the gusty wind. His drinking had escalated since his father's death, but that was understandable. He needed something to numb the pain for God's sake. He poured himself a large measure of whisky and sat down at the table, remembering how they had eaten there together years ago like a proper family. His father's far-away voice came into his head: "Keep your back straight, son. Don't bang your cutlery on the plate." He blotted out the figure of his mother who had used to sit opposite him, feigning oppression and vulnerability where none had existed. She had never realised what a fine figure of a man she had married – had never respected his clear-headedness and leadership skills.

As he sat there Maxwell caught wind of footsteps on the gravel outside and saw two male uniformed police officers strolling up his driveway. They hung back to look at his car before proceeding to the front door. Maxwell's heart immediately began to race. Why couldn't they leave him be, especially after what had happened? A loud pounding knock filled the room and Maxwell's head. Hopefully if he stayed quiet they would think he was out, so he crouched down between the dining chairs, clutching his whisky glass tightly. The pounding was repeated. "Mr Hood!" said a baritone voice. "Open the door – we know you're in there."

From where he sat, Maxwell could see one of the officers shading his eyes and peering into the room through the bay window. After ten seconds or so the man gave up and moved off. Then there was a familiar clunk as the latch to the side-gate was opened. Maxwell listened carefully, hearing both pairs of feet making their way round to the rear of the house. He froze and held his breath, suddenly realising the kitchen door was unlocked.

Acting on instinct, Maxwell extracted himself clumsily from his hiding place and grabbed his bottle and wallet from the sideboard. He rushed for the front door, opening it as quietly as he could. Once outside he began to run, heading out into the main road and crossing it without checking for traffic. A car slammed on its breaks and blew its horn in alarm. Maxwell took a sharp left into a long walled lane that led towards the church, and his footsteps resounded heavily in his ears as he careered headlong towards the bright green patch of graveyard.

At last he stopped, his chest heaving and thoughts whirling round his head. Did they have a warrant? Could they enter his house legally if he wasn't there? Would they even care... they could easily make up some tale? His throat burned and he spat into the weeds. Those pictures on his computer... he must go back somehow and delete them. No – that wouldn't work... must remove the hard drive. As if a few pictures could do any harm... but what if they were watching the house? Was he over-reacting? Or was he in real trouble? He couldn't go to jail. He'd never survive it. His hands shook uncontrollably as he sank sobbing onto the damp grass.

15

August, 2019

As summer moved on Jill had seized the helm of the village shop, and was enjoying it thoroughly. She was heady energetic company, full of laughter and ideas and very popular with the children. The stock was steadily growing. She didn't want a half-empty shop, but one bursting at the seams with invention and colour. The stark blank-windowed building that Jerry, Mags and Dick had erected on the site of the old shower block was already transformed in her mind's eye. On the bare concrete floor was thrown one of Lizzy's rag rugs that she had taken to working on in the evenings. To the imaginary smell of fresh fruit and vegetables was added that of flowers and lavender bags, and on the chairs carved by Dixie cushions and dolls jostled for space. Jill stood with her hands on her hips eyeing the floor and wondering how a wood-effect lino would look – it wouldn't be too expensive, and she was fast becoming sure that it would fit just right.

She heard footsteps and Mags appeared in the sunny doorway. "Come and have tea with us?" she offered. "First pot of tea the café's ever made." Jill smiled and followed her out into the hot sun where Jean was working on a little playground for visiting children. He had started by laying woodchips and building a swing using wood from the newly-felled poplars, and today he was busy constructing a kind of climbing frame from brightly-painted tyres.

"The bloke never stops," said Jill. "Hey Jean! Fancy a drink?" The young man got to his feet and joined them under the tree. Jean always drank coffee so Jill went to the caravan to make him one, forcefully resisting his requests to do it himself. Jean sat down cross-legged on the grass where Ellen lay looking at the leafy canopy.

"Jill's worried about pigeon droppings," she murmured lazily. "On the roof."

"She worries too much," said Jean.

Ellen raised herself onto one elbow. Skipping subjects was one of her habits. "How did you meet Steve – you and Jerry?" she asked Mags, guessing it was bound to be some dramatic tale: the couple had always led reckless lives until relatively recently.

Mags gave a snort of laughter as she re-tied her headscarf. "Well," she said; "Jerry went to the surgery one day with some problem or other. I think it was his stomach. This was way back when we were completely wild, and Steve was still new to his practice. They got chatting and kind of got to realise quite quickly that they were both a couple of piss 'eads. Jerry's medical problem got kind of side-lined and they went way over the time for the appointment apparently, laughing and joking like a couple of idiots." She glanced at Jean fearing disapproval, but his face and eyes spoke of acceptance as clearly as any words could have done. Mags took a sip of tea and continued, although a slight restraint had crept into her voice.

"Well… they met up later on 'cause he actually lived quite near to us as it 'appened. Jerry went round there but for some bizarre reason Steve didn't 'ave hardly any booze, and neither did Jerry. So d'you know what they did? They drank cough medicine… out of a couple of wine glasses."

Ellen stared and then gave a sad smile. "I've done things like that," she said. "Sometimes pain is just too hard to take." She looked hurriedly at Jean. "You must think us terribly weak."

Jean took the mug of coffee that Jill handed him and shook his head gently. "There are many sources of pain and I would be a poor priest if I were to judge how people face their sorrow."

Someone was coming along the hot and hazy track from the farmhouse. Ellen got to her feet and shaded her eyes, making out the figure of small stout man wearing a suit and carrying a briefcase. He looked decidedly overheated and flustered. "I'm Mr Rankling from the town council," he announced as he came close, pulling a large handkerchief from his pocket and dabbing at his forehead.

"Heavens – it's nothing bad is it?" said Ellen at once.

"Not at all, my dear. In fact it's quite good news I'd say. Who's the er… head of this place?"

Ellen's mind raced. Paul would do best with this kind of thing – much better than she would. She was inclined to get lost during conversations with strangers, especially if there was any kind of officialdom involved. She turned to Jean. "Would you mind taking this gentleman to see Paul? He's in the root cellar."

Mr Rankling eyed Jean – who was in the process of taking off his shirt – with a degree of suspicion. "Come," said Jean, tying the loose sleeves around his slim waist.

Mr Rankling followed at an awkward trot along the rutted track towards the main gate of the village. They had certainly got a long way with everything he thought to himself, reaching for his handkerchief again and hurrying to keep up. How on earth had they managed to grow such a big hedge in that short time? When he had last been here it had been no more than a huge empty field.

On passing through the large open gateway Mr Rankling felt as if he had entered another world. There was a big green playing field where some children were kicking a ball, while opposite were little houses and allotments – and through the windows of a park-home he caught site of people working busily at heaven knows what. There were lines of crops and a great long greenhouse, and in the corner of the playing field sat a big round thatched building that looked as though it had been transported straight from the year dot. Mr Rankling's head swivelled from side to side as he followed Jean up the long sweeping driveway bordered with young trees. They reached the centre building, as yet still incomplete, and went around it to the rear. Mr Rankling stared at the long lines of fruit trees and willow, discerning sheds, caravans and trailers beyond them. "My, you have been busy," he exclaimed. Jean gave him a gentle smile and then indicated Paul, who was painting the inside of the new cellar.

Paul put down his paint-pot and came squinting into the sun. He offered a hand to Mr Rankling and then quickly withdrew it, realising it was covered in paint. "I'm Paul Turner. How can I help?"

Mr Rankling seemed absorbed in the root cellar. "What exactly are you building here?" he enquired, peering inside and up at the ceiling.

"It's a cold store for fruit and veg and stuff. All that earth over there will go back on top eventually – bit like a bunker." Paul paused. "And you are..?"

Mr Rankling seemed alarmed at his own lack of manners and became suddenly professional: "So sorry. I'm Mr Rankling from the town council," he said, offering his hand and then quickly withdrawing it. "I've come to talk to you about your grant."

Paul rubbed his hands slowly on his overalls. "Grant? What grant?"

Mr Rankling became immediately verbose. "Well, because you're a green low-impact project, which the government is currently insisting we encourage and support, and because you have the potential to benefit the local community, especially with it being a tourist area – well, we have a grant waiting for you whenever you'd like to take it up. It's a very simple application I assure you. I did inform the young lady in my letter and because I haven't heard anything, well – I thought I'd better pop over and have a word in person, with you not having a telephone or anything."

"We're fine," Paul answered levelly. "We don't need the money. Use it to help the town in some other way… not that we're ungrateful or anything."

Mr Rankling was taken aback. "But… Er… What if..? Surely you…"

Jean was finding the little man amusing, and Paul had to try hard not to meet his eyes over Mr Rankling's shoulder. "You see we pooled our resources when we started up and the village is nearly finished. We're aiming for self-sufficiency, not capital gain – it's an important part of what this is about. We don't need any extra money." Then he looked hard into Mr Rankling's eyes. "I'd appreciate hearing about where it's gone though."

"Of course! Um… Of course I can certainly relay that information to you, Mr Turner." He picked up his briefcase and became jovial. "Well, that's fine Sir, if that's how you really feel about it. That... er, all sounds just fine. What a lovely lot of trees you've planted. It's all looking very nice I must say. Well, I suppose I'd better be off then. Good luck with your shelter. Not the best weather for working in though, I must say." He extracted his handkerchief once again. "I'll see myself out."

Jean began chuckling quietly to himself as soon as the man had gone. He looked at Paul. "Why you so serious?"

"Because I know damned well he'll probably take a golfing holiday with that bloody money – that's why."

Jean laid a hand on his shoulder. "No worries. We live our lives – he lives his."

Mr Rankling strode back along the gravelled path with a distinct spring in his step. Well this was a turn-up for the books. He thought they'd just over-looked the offer, or simply not got round to it. It was a mystery to him how anyone could turn down money like that. Oh, well – their loss was his gain... at least in the odd little way – just here and there. He decided to pop into town and buy his wife a nice bunch of flowers. She'd like that. It would make her day. The ones with the big coloured daisies. Funny though: he still couldn't help feeling a slight admiration for the villagers as he got back in his car. It was a fleeting emotion, and not sustained by any real need to understand them. But he did have to admit it: they'd worked hard on that village, and they seemed like quite decent sorts underneath it all.

Omasah moved smoothly up the drive to where several villagers were shouting and waving their arms. Lizzy and Graham were furious with Paul for turning down the offer of the grant, insisting that he should have called a meeting to discuss it. Josh had suggested ringing the council to put it on hold, while Carlos sided completely with Paul. "Making this gesture at this early stage is important," he was saying. "Even if Paul was wrong to decide on his own, I can see where he's coming from. That money should go where it's most needed – that's Humanity Towards Others for God's sake." Ellen stood apart from the rest, glum-faced. This was the kind of scenario she had always dreaded.

"Yes, that is what we're supposed to stand for," she said quietly as Omasah took her gently by the arm. The group immediately turned to him, moving in close. Silently, he encouraged them to join hands and form a circle, and Ellen gave Paul's hand an affectionate squeeze.

As Omasah spoke Ellen wondered if the others felt the depth of the compassion that pervaded his words and his look. "There is rarely a course that pleases every individual," he began. "Thus, we must consider ourselves as one, and as standing upon the foundations of one principle."

Graham immediately interjected: "But to uphold the principle we need to survive."

"We are surviving," Ellen remarked flatly.

"If we go the principle goes," argued Lizzy. "It can't exist without us."

Paul's voice was strained. "Look – no one was worried before he came. You've invented a whole imaginary disaster from nothing, just because there's the scent of a little bit extra. That's the kind of dumb fear that fuels capitalism and quickly turns to greed…"

Omasah raised a giant hand and waited for the group to become still again. "The village is running well, the living is good, and you need nothing extra at this time," he said. "Thus the surrender of this money reinforces the values upon which this place is built. Return your thoughts to all that unites you, and do not allow the seeds of disparity to take root in your hearts." He turned to Paul. "You must undertake to create a decision-making procedure that everyone considers fair."

And with that he was gone with the customary swiftness that always left a heavy silence in its wake.

16

Autumn, 2019

Since discovering her husband's debt Janet had become like a prisoner in her own home. There was no apology on Alan's part – far from it. He saw her opening his mail as unforgivable, and on the back of it the beatings had become more frequent. He revelled in her fear of the inevitable.

Janet had eventually mustered up the courage to visit her doctors' surgery again, and been fortunate enough to see a kindly man who had given her a sick note valid for three months. She had handed in her notice at work, knowing in her heart that she could never go back and that that part of her life was over. One rainy afternoon she had managed to curl up on her bedroom floor in the semi-darkness and fill in an application for benefits. This small income enabled her to carry on buying wine, which she ordered online and had delivered when no one was in the house. Her social networking had become limited to browsing, and she would often spend hours immersed in the photographs, memes and texts that out-going good-looking people exchanged. She kept the house spotless because it gave her something to do, although she mostly avoided Ethan's room for fear of what she might find. It didn't occur to her to ask for help with either the beatings or the drink, and so in this way her life continued devoid of any conception of release or change.

Such was Alan's psychological make-up, that by now he was experiencing continual feelings of anger that his deep unacknowledged fears prevented him from questioning. Had he been blessed with more insight and courage, perhaps he might have examined his family's situation and his own role within it; but all he experienced was frustration and rage. It bubbled and fluttered in his chest, and caused him to cough and splutter, and worry and curse. He barely spoke to Janet and the boys, spending his time either in the garage or fiddling with the computer, which he would experiment with until it obliged him with a problem he could fix. The family holiday had been cancelled without explanation, but Janet did not dare ask whether he was doing anything else to help clear the debt.

Just getting through the day had become a challenge to Janet. She had her routine and was aware that she was no longer living a normal life, but it was paramount that she stayed focused on the few tasks that were essential. She needed to keep the house clean and to supply herself with food and drink. Alan had taken to doing the weekly shop at the supermarket, and Janet felt crushed by the shame of her failures. She kept herself clean, but rarely bothered to get dressed any more. One by one her friends had all dropped away – not because they didn't care but because she had cut them off, feeling she had nothing to offer them. Ellen still wrote, but Janet couldn't imagine ever seeing her again. It was nice that she kept in touch though, and she savoured the letters which she stacked faithfully in a box beneath her bed.

The summer holiday had been long and tedious because her two younger boys had needed her. She had struggled through it a day at a time; had undergone flustered conversations with friends' mothers over the phone, and driven to various houses in her slippers and pyjama bottoms to pick up waiting children. She had fed unfamiliar boys with fish fingers and oven chips and retired to her room while they sat absorbed in war games. She had kept out of the way wherever possible, and it had been a long hard dreary haul. Finally September had arrived and she could go back to hiding away as much as she needed. The relief was overwhelming but so was the guilt, and she would often cry for lonely hours about everything that she was, and everything that she wasn't.

Although Janet failed to see the point of hoping for change, let alone attempting to initiate it, change was heading her way. At the end of August Alan's uncle had died – a man practically unknown to rest of the family – and Alan had attended the funeral alone. Then two weeks after the boys returned to school the change caught them up with an unexpected inheritance that covered a big chunk of the debt. A re-mortgage would clear the rest, Alan had told his wife with characteristic coldness – although she had noticed the spark of relief in his eyes.

During the following weeks, Janet was surprised and disturbed by the difference in Alan: surprised because it was so completely unforeseen, and disturbed because she couldn't find it in her heart to trust it. The change was there however, and he walked about like a man in an ill-fitting new skin. Suddenly he interacted more with Janet and the boys, and they found themselves accommodating him rigidly out of fear. Suddenly he was around more often, sitting in the lounge and wondering where his wife was. He had begun to touch her again, and her skin crawled at the possibility of a renewed physical relationship. The beatings stopped abruptly... which made the dread of them pile up all the more, like a mass of water against a dam.

There were a few hundred pounds remaining following the re-mortgage, and Janet dearly hoped that Alan wouldn't suggest a winter holiday somewhere hot. He didn't, and she gradually began to relax ever so slightly into her new role. It wasn't any better; just different. Her routine had changed a little, and her cage had enjoyed a cursory coat of cheap gold paint – it was really no more than that. And so Janet continued blindly, as though dragged along by a thick chafing rope.

17

September, 2019

Crows and light rain and the wistful song of the robin: these were the sounds of Ubuntu in autumn. At last work on the outer shop was complete, although the deadline had been missed by a fortnight and the children were already back at school. However, Ellen had assured Jill that come the October half-term everything would pick up with an influx of late holiday-makers. The shop was fully-stocked with a selection of seasonal vegetables along with everything they had made during the past six months. With the arrival of this landmark struggles and mistakes were forgotten and filed away for future reference, and there were mixed feelings of completion and beginning; of relaxation and expectation.

"I wish you'd stop walking around all the time. It does my head in," said Nadia.

Jill stopped, hands on hips. The shop was due to open in under an hour. Anya sat at the small counter next to an enormous old-fashioned till that Faye had discovered in an antique shop. Beside the till were baskets of lavender bags and gratitude stones.

"It looks great, Jill," she smiled.

Jill slapped a piece of paper on the desk in front of the girl. "Another sign!" she said, looking into the air as though seeing it. "Halloween Pumpkins Coming Soon… And draw some bats and things."

Anya bent her head dutifully over the page. Jill was still walking about. "It's too bare," she pondered. "It's lacking something…"

In fact the shop was anything but bare. Eggs, fruit and vegetables were arranged along the middle in a two-sided display unit knocked up by Jean and painted green by the children. There were leeks, cauliflowers, potatoes, onions, swedes, carrots, radishes and boxes of plump raspberries all sitting neatly in hay-lined compartments, while on top were assorted jars of Mags' tomato chutney, pickled onions, sauerkraut and blackberry jam. On a rug at the end near the door there were two chairs and a small settee, the wooden legs of which had been embellished by Dixie's hand, and upon these sat the cheerful dolls and bright cushions that Jill had always hoped for. In front was a coffee table piled with neatly-folded quilts and duvet covers, and in the corner an old wooden hat-stand that had belonged to Steven displayed the sequined shoulder bags. Under the window were several rag rugs in a colourful heap, and everything was labelled neatly in gold ink on black paper. The hat-stand was the only item marked "Not For Sale."

The opposite end of the building housed the door to the toilet, and on either side were selections of greetings cards, second-hand DVDs and CDs, and copies of Ellen's book. Behind the counter two white boards announced the week's bartering requests which had also been circulated by flyer: "OLD CLOTHES / SHOES / CARPET / FABRICS (INCL. DAMAGED AND STAINED) SCRAP METAL, FURNITURE (INCL. BROKEN), EGG BOXES, GLASS

JARS WITH LIDS, PLASTIC BAGS, DYNAMOS / ALTERNATORS, DUNG (HORSE, COW, CHICKEN), EMPTY DRUMS (METAL / PLASTIC), OLD SOFT TOYS AND DUVETS (FOR STUFFING)."

Dixie's carvings had a central position at the end of the vegetables with a huge eagle taking pride of place, and all the wooden masks he had managed to complete took up the remainder of the rear wall. Melyne's and Nadia's bracelets filled hooks on the front of the counter, along with some shell necklaces that Jill had made. The ceiling dangled with wire mobiles and wooden wind-chimes that rattled in the breeze from the open door. As yet there was still space along the outer wall – a few plans remained in the pipeline, the CD being the most exciting one.

"Bunting," said Nadia as she fiddled with the food display. She grinned: "Unique Ubuntu bunting."

"Brilliant!" cried Jill. She clapped her hands. "Go and ask Faye if they can knock some up quickly on the machines – with flowers and stripes and things."

Nadia left the room and headed towards the village gate. The clouds were shifting and parting as the day warmed up. Anya sat absorbed in colouring a big orange pumpkin. "I'm nervous," she said.

"Me too. I'll get us something to eat – that might help."

Jill strode across to the food van where Lizzy and Mags were chopping and chatting. The air was full of the sound of sizzling onions and the smell of garlic and herbs. "Any chance of a roll?"

"Jerry's not finished 'em yet," said Mags. The soup's ready if you want. You shouldn't eat so much bread anyway."

Jill rolled her eyes and waited while the soup was blended and served into mugs. Mags was absorbed in telling Lizzy one of her convoluted window-cleaning tales. Looking around, Jill tried to imagine how a visitor might feel coming through the farm gate. The little caravan was clean and neat and painted blue and white now, and bore the words "Ubuntu Café – Welcome" facing the road. There were four round tables, two with sun umbrellas. Nothing really matched but was loosely coordinated with blue seat cushions, and on each table there was a fresh geranium in a little vase. The sun blazed down, and Jean's playground was lit up like a modern work of art. Everything looked wonderful, thought Jill…. Or maybe it didn't. Maybe it didn't look that good at all. She hoped the visitors would like it. It had all been such hard work. She fought off Doubt that whispered: "What if *nobody* comes?" She sighed, feeling suddenly tired. Re-entering the shop with the soups she registered a faint plopping sound as a pigeon relieved itself on the roof. "That's definitely going to be a problem," she said looking up. "I said right from the start we shouldn't be under this tree."

At precisely ten o'clock Mr Rix appeared in the shop doorway smelling of aftershave and dressed in a smart pair of trousers, shirt and tie. "I'm going to open the gate – alright, Miss Ellen; Miss Jill? There's quite a little group formed out there."

"Really?" said Ellen, feeling as though she was about to sit her driving test. "Yes, of course Mr Rix. Go ahead." She looked at Jill, who was perched on the corner of the coffee table fanning herself with a flyer. "Well, this is it!"

"Should I sit down or stand up?" asked Anya from behind the counter.

"Stay sitting you ninny," said Nadia. "That's why you've got a chair."

Jill got up and peered outside to see around ten people wandering along the track towards the café. "God – there are loads of them!"

"You lot are hilarious," laughed Nadia. "It's only a shop. We aren't under attack or anything."

Ellen joined Jill in the doorway. With a buzz of excitement she saw a little queue beginning to take shape at the food van, and a couple of children running for the playground. A woman's voice could be heard asking questions: "What kind of biscuits are those?" and "Do you do takeaways?" Two elderly ladies had settled themselves under one of the sun umbrellas and were reading a menu. "Oh no," exclaimed Ellen, and her hand went to her mouth. "We've only gone and forgotten to decide whether it's counter service or not!"

"They'll be okay," said Nadia, still highly amused.

Anya frowned at her. "How can you be so insensitive? How can you expect us not to be nervous?"

"I'm not insensitive. It's you lot who are over-sensitive."

"Shh!" hissed Jill, seeing a young couple approaching followed closely by two more elderly ladies. They all stood to attention awkwardly as the people mounted the step and began looking round. The young woman smiled. She was a hippy-type with long dreadlocks, and was carrying a plastic bag. Ellen wondered if she was going to barter. She went immediately to inspect the bags. "These are beautiful," she said. "What would you ask for one of these?" She opened the carrier to show Ellen. "I've got two spare saucepans if you can use them, plus a bag of oranges. Oh – and some men's socks too. They're new but they're too tight round the ankle for Dave." She smiled again. "I couldn't resist it – it's such a novelty. I'm so glad you're doing this." Her partner joined her, carrying a cauliflower and a jar of pickled onions.

"You're so welcome to this lot," he told Ellen, handing over a bag of clothes. "They've been sitting in the cupboard since Christmas."

Ellen's mind was a spin. "Gosh," she said, totting up the approximate worth of what they were offering in her head. "Well the bags are six pounds, the pickles are one pound fifty, and the caulis are eighty pence, so that's... um – well, I think you're offering too much really." She gave them each a gratitude stone and asked a little anxiously: "Would you like to take a bit more veg?"

One of the elderly ladies was examining the dolls. She picked one up, turning it over: "These are very unusual."

"They're all unique," began Jill, spying an ornate gold crucifix at the woman's throat. She wondered briefly if the concept of the dolls might offend, but surely that was just silly? She cleared her throat. "You see, each one's a mixture of different races and religions. It's a kind of... anti-war statement."

"Oh, how wonderful!" exclaimed the woman. She called to her friend. "Brenda – Come and see these..." She turned to Jill. "I must get one for my new great grand daughter." Then her face dropped. "Horrible, isn't it – all the terrible fighting going on? I despair for this world sometimes, I really do."

Anya was standing next to Ellen, waiting eagerly to speak. "... I'm sure they'll be happy to do that for you," Ellen was saying. She turned happily to Anya. "These people want a takeaway lunch for every week day. Isn't that great?"

"That lady with the dreadlocks just bought one of your books!" cried Anya breathlessly, and flung her arms around Ellen's neck.

18

22nd November, 2019

Dear Janet

I'm so sorry that I haven't written for so long – we've been so busy. I know it's kind of my fault for not keeping in touch but I do feel concerned that I haven't heard from you for so long. I would phone, but I realise that might be awkward for you with the way Alan is. I know writing letters isn't everyone's cup of tea, but I do hope you're doing okay – I really mean that.

The village is finished now apart from odd bits here and there, and we are well and truly settling into our new lives. The shop and café opened in September and it's been quite a success. To begin with I was worried no one would come at all! October was frantic because people often come here for a cheap break over half-term. We have quite a few regulars at the café now who come for takeaways, which is nice. As more people hear about what we're doing they've started turning up with the strangest things, like old sinks and broken Hoovers – you name it – and they hardly ever take up our offer of something in return either. We've begun a dry food store in one of the old caravans which we ripped the seats out of: more wood and fabric (you see how everything gets re-used?) and we have all our chick peas drying out in there plus some cans and stuff. The shop and café will be pretty dead after Christmas so stores are essential. And then there's the getting off-grid thing to think about. It's all still an exciting challenge and we have a way to go yet.

My little house is great – I just love it. It's so homely and easy to heat. I thought I'd miss all my knick-knacks but that's not the case at all. In the end it was quite easy to pick out my favourites and I don't miss the others one bit, and have either given them to charity or put them in our shop. Same goes for books – I've kept just a few and the rest have gone to the village library so they're still around if I want them. I curl up in my chair every evening for a nice quiet read – talking of which I've sold about twenty copies of my book since the shop opened! It's strange to think of people reading about my ideas, especially when I've been thinking about them for so long. I feel pleased, but I hope I never have to struggle with "acclaim" – it's not about that – it's about actually doing it, and making it work. I got a really wonderful feeling last night when I was lying up on my roof. No one knew I was even there, and it was lovely to hear how happy people sounded all around, especially Jerry who's always laughing – it was such a lovely atmosphere.

We have got 3 new village members in the form of rescue cats to help keep mice down and scare the birds from our seedlings – not very nice but kind of natural and essential I guess. One of them lives with Jill and the other 2 live with Melyne and Nadia, although they pretty much roam all over the place really. Jill's one, called Mango, slept in Paul's house the other night without him realising until the morning when he found her curled up in a ball. My dogs go mad after them of course, but they'll get used to it.

There's not a lot to do in the allotments this time of year although we've just planted a ton of broad beans in the greenhouse. We have a root cellar which is an underground room with ventilation for storing fruit and veg for the maximum time. It's *working really well because (of course) Paul made sure he did it just right. His current project is a laundry room for when we go off-grid, and he's totally in his element planning it all. Several people are going to make do without electricity, including the children because they eat at their parents' and can always use a gas heater if desperate – but the winters don't often get that cold any more do they? It's really scary this climate change.*

I've started teaching the children yoga and meditation in the school twice a week and have also been giving our doctor some watercolour lessons. I reckon it must be in his genes somewhere because he's very good. At the start I volunteered to oversee our main store, and I have to keep that fully stocked for everyone which means a drive into town once a week – it's quite a bit of work. I've been helping in the craft-room too, and have to go beach-combing for stuff to use so I walk the dogs at the same time. I'm certainly kept busy!

Jill and Josh are an item by the way. I'm so happy, especially for Josh because I've known him a long time and he totally deserves it. I never would have put them together, but now when I see them it seems to fit just right. Personally I doubt I will ever have another relationship – I always seem to lose something of myself when I'm with someone. It's like you hand over your soul when you meet somebody. Or perhaps I just try too hard – I don't know. Anyway, I like being independent and the village is like my family and more than enough company for me.

We are having a get together in a couple of days because it's going to be Anya's 14th birthday. She is a stunning girl although she's very natural and modest about it, which makes her all the more beautiful to me. I'm so glad she's such a free spirit and has been spared the pressures of modern teenage life. She's always talking to me about having a boyfriend though. It's difficult because she's naturally a loner, so Mary's seeing about her volunteering in town to get her meeting more people, and she's joining Nadia's dance group after Christmas. Her dad's got her a CD player for her birthday and I've bought her a Sade album – I think she'll like that.

So anyway, we are all doing well and I feel the village is becoming a real place now and we're all evolving along with it. We chug along day by day and enjoy the natural work of surviving, as well as the thrill of creating our craft items. This place is about much more than just getting away from it all – especially as the mainstream way of living is unsustainable. My dream is that one day other people will feel driven to come together and build other villages like this one.

I hope to hear from you some time Janet but there's no pressure if things are difficult. I am with you in spirit. Much love – Ellen xx.

19

December, 2019

The town centre was swarming with Christmas shoppers and coloured lights glittered and flashed through the rain and on the wet roads and pavements. People jostled one another amid cumbersome bags and packages, shouting to be heard over the swells of music and laughter from open shop doorways and crowded bars. Maxwell kept his head well down and his coat collar pulled up round his ears, hugging walls and sliding into alleyways until he found himself in the quieter residential streets. Keeping a low profile had become as natural as breathing since being on the run.

Luckily the weather had not turned too cold yet, and he had gradually wended his way northwards sleeping in hostels, bus shelters, and the occasional warm railway waiting room when he could get away with it. Since using the ATM in Foxheath he had ditched his bank card, aware that it was an obvious way to track his movements. He had also disposed of his mobile, but was still reluctant to use a hotel or B&B, fearing his description may have been circulated. The police had caught up with him for vagrancy once when he had fallen asleep drunk in a shop doorway, but he had fled into a park and lost himself amongst the ruins of an old abbey – had crouched between the ancient stones, straining his ears for the slightest sound and cursing himself for having dropped his bottle. One day he had managed to steal an old lady's handbag as she sat on a bench feeding the ducks. Unfortunately it had contained only twenty pounds, but anything was a help in this clinging existence.

Hitch-hiking was risky and so he had followed Lancashire's flat rain-slashed roads listlessly, dropping out of sight into muddy fields whenever possible. Luckily he had found the address he was looking for in the phonebook, managing to prepare himself by strip-washing in a public toilet in the dead of night and changing into a half-decent outfit discovered dumped next to a clothes bank.

At long last he pressed the white doorbell button, giving it a good long loud ring. Then he dug his hands in his coat pockets to hide his fingernails. A figure appeared beyond the frosted glass, and the door was opened a crack. As one bespectacled eye stared over the silver security-chain, Maxwell immediately shoved his foot into the gap and grinned over his stubbly beard: "Hello Aunt Lill! Long time no see!"

The neat elderly lady didn't respond and stared blankly. Then she tried to shut the door, banging it violently and repeatedly against Maxwell's foot as she began to panic. He decided to made light of the situation, although the red flush of anger immediately flooded his face. "Aunt Lill – it's me: Maxwell!" He giggled childishly as if the whole thing was a birthday surprise.

"You can't stay here," the woman said firmly. "You'll have to go elsewhere. I can't help you." She abruptly vanished, and Maxwell pressed his bulbous forehead against the glass, searching for her. She was coming back…

He bellowed in pain as a huge old-fashioned hammer smashed down onto his toes. As he hopped and staggered and cursed she slammed the door and re-bolted it, drawing a thick curtain across with a determined flourish. The house fell into silence.

Maxwell leaned against the ivy-clad wall, overcome with the urge to punch something. He needed to get inside, so he mustn't make a scene: the house was overlooked from every angle. He shivered against the unhappy prospect of another night on the run. She hadn't recognised him – couldn't have done. He was sure she'd have let him in if she'd known it was him. He needed to calm down – obviously it wasn't her fault.

He took a couple of slugs of whisky and moved to the nearest window, where a well-lit room was visible behind pretty net curtains. Strings of cards hung on the creamy wall behind two cosy-looking damson armchairs, and on a polished table a china cup steamed next to two biscuits on a plate. A Christmas tree stood twinkling in the corner and silver tinsel was draped around a big oval mirror. With an empty feeling, the big man lent his head on the glass; but the woman immediately reappeared and dragged the curtains across. "I'll call the police!" she screeched.

He spoke into the glass, steaming it over. "But Aunt Lill, it's me – Maxwell. Don't you recognise your own nephew?" His smile felt real to him now, and it made his voice sound cheery. There was no way she'd turn him away once she realised who he was... Good old Aunt Lill...

There was a short pause. "I know who you are. Get lost!"

Maxwell was suddenly unstoppable in the face of insult. He felt himself swell and become broader; he pulled his shoulders back with a jerk and the old programming began playing through his head: "Always stand up straight, son –

people can't fail to show you the respect you deserve if you stand up straight." He strode around to the back of the house, smashed the window of the backdoor dripping blood onto the paving slabs, and then reached in to turn the key. In the dark kitchen he folded his huge hand over the woman's mouth before she could cry out.

20

December, 2019

Just as Anya was about to knock on Omasah's door he opened it. She laughed. "You always know I'm here!"

"Of course," he replied, indicating his chair. Then he said: "You prefer to walk I see."

"Yes please. I need to get out. We've been decorating the tree and Nadia talks too much."

Omasah closed his door and they took the cycle path towards the woods. There was a small gateway at the top end of the village that had been a last-minute thought on Ellen's part, mainly because of the enormous Sycamore that grew there. Its giant canopy soared above the surrounding trees and was so dense and hung so low that the underneath remained clean and dry for most of the year. Occasionally the villagers would congregate beneath for food and music, especially when rain threatened, and over time the tree had come to feel as much a part of the place as any house, shed or building.

They stopped together in the dim tranquil space. Anya knew that Omasah liked to touch the tree, and waited while he placed his hands against the trunk and closed his eyes. When he finally drew away she whispered: "What do you feel?"

"A calm and ancient soul."

Anya looked up at the bare branches just as the wind roused them, and felt she understood. "I know what you mean," she said. "I heard a new bird this morning, Omasah. I must find out what it's called."

He studied her face. "Why the need to label it? It is an individual life."

Anya pulled a face while she thought. "It makes them seem more friendly, maybe? More like we're close to them. I don't know, Omasah." She frowned at him playfully. "But you give us names and say it's important!"

Omasah placed his hands behind his back as they walked away from the giant tree, trying to understand. With a gentle look he answered her at last: "Naming is a most satisfactory art, yes. However, a label is not the same. Where I come from we each choose our own names for the people and creatures we love. And for each and every bird."

"Oh… that must be complicated, Omasah."

"We do not find it so. It is a traditional part of our creative process."

Anya placed her hands likewise behind her back, watching the man's feet as he walked; and she noticed how he was in touch with every step, and every single part of every step. Omasah smiled, reading her thoughts.

The girl tried to concentrate on her own feet. "So I should choose my own name for it then, so it's different from what everyone else uses?"

"Only if you wish it, and your expression is a fluid one."

Anya grinned widely at him. She liked the things he said and the way he saw things so differently. "So could I ask my dad to help choose a name," she asked. "Or wouldn't that be fluid enough?"

Omasah looked subtly amused. "That sounds most agreeable for everyone," he said. "Especially for the bird."

Anya giggled at the way his benevolence extended its gentleness around all living things. It made her hopeful and happy, but also eternally curious about his homeland and people. She alone was privileged in that she had learnt quite a lot about Sundara over time – a word meaning "world" as opposed to one particular country. There was no war, poverty or disease; the ecosystem was thriving and the birds and animals were tame. She kept these things mostly to herself; had dedicated several pages in her diary to it with drawings, and she had shown Omasah who had been very pleased. Then she had shown her father, and had noticed tears in his eyes as he read it.

They took a left turn and found themselves amongst the deciduous trees that formed the southern part of the wood, and where robins sang from the grey branches above the grassy path. The girl was still talkative and full of questions. "Don't you think that people are like birds, Omasah? Because some people always do and say the same things all their lives, just like a pigeon who only ever says 'coo.' But other people like my dad – well, he grows through his music and is much more interesting, like a thrush or a nightingale."

"I see your meaning," her friend replied, fondly. "But every bird… and every person… is interpreting the same life-force. All is an expression of the same thing."

Anya's mind ticked over. "So what is it they're saying, Omasah?"

The man took a breath at the racing clouds: "I am here. I am alive."

Anya gave another giggle. "Yes, I suppose they are. I like pigeons anyway. Maybe they're the wisest of all, because they don't need to overcomplicate things."

As they continued to stroll along Anya stopped to pick up a round patterned stone from the ground. She began to dig round it with her fingers, realising that it was a fossilized sea urchin – complete and almost undamaged. Omasah was immediately at her side. "Let me hold it," he said.

"Oh my God!" exclaimed the girl turning it over. "This is the best thing I've ever found… But we aren't by the sea." She looked up at him.

"This was a sea-bed. You see the little shells?" He took the fossil from her. "I have heard its voice before but my sight is greatly depleted in this place. Let us sit, and I will read it for you."

It didn't occur to Omasah that it wasn't the sort of weather for sitting in the grass. The sky threatened rain and a chilly wind whistled through the trees from the dark band of sea. Omasah put his hands carefully around the large weighty fossil; then he closed his eyes and got comfortable. He rested the stone in his lap and his eyes darted behind the lids as he breathed smoothly, unaware of time as it was passing for Anya. His features were calm, inexpressive of what he was processing as he searched for a distant time that was stable enough for total immersion.

The girl sat patiently watching his face, and at length Omasah murmured in a far-off tone: "This is a Golden Age. This memory is long by your count. There are many civilisations. Some people are remote and untouched while others gather in their thousands. Vast forests with river dwellings and boats of all kinds. Glorious cities in white stone. The seas and air are wholesome. There is great abundance, and the living is honest and free."

Omasah fell silent with his hands still encircling the stone, and his eyes moved again behind the lids. Eventually he spoke again: "There are visitors from many times and places whose knowledge and wisdom have helped shape this planet. However, this block of time has few links to your present. Most time-lines emanating from this block of time have formed histories that rarely touch your own, and have rarely seen fruition. It is a beautiful time I see in this stone." He opened his eyes and handed the fossil back to Anya. "Few souls have seen that era," he said.

The girl took the stone, which felt hot in her hands. "Is that era lost then?"

"Not lost, Navastri: rare."

That evening after the rain Anya biked round to Ellen's house with the stone in her pocket. Ellen was lying on her bed. "Come up sweetheart," she called.

Anya mounted the little ladder and sat on the bed. "I came to show you this," she said, placing the fossil on the quilt. "Isn't it lovely?"

"It's beautiful," said Ellen, putting on a pair of reading glasses and picking it up. "You lucky thing. Where did you find it?"

"In the woods with Omasah. He read it for me and said it's from a Golden Age, but I don't understand what he meant because he said…" Anya fell quiet, trying to remember. "He said that few souls have seen that era."

Ellen laughed. "You should know by now that Omasah talks in riddles, Anya. Don't worry about it."

"I'm not worried. Just curious."

"Well, ask him to explain. He won't mind. But I warn you – you probably still won't understand. I know because I've asked him things myself."

Anya took the fossil and held it in her lap. "I think he's wonderful and I believe everything he says. But I don't tell Nadia because she'd laugh. So would some other people."

Ellen took Anya's delicate hands in hers and looked into her wondering eyes. "Anya – I believe him too."

The girl's face lit up. "Really? You aren't just saying that?"

"No. I mean it."

They hugged.

21

December, 2019

My name is Ethan Timothy Wrenn and I am writing this because Ive been told to by the educational psycologist or there will be more trouble for me. She asked me to write how I see myself now and then how I reckon other people see me, and then how I imagine myself in the future living a normal life with out all these problems.

So right now I see myself as living a pretty dumb life really and it used to be much nicer when I was a kid. I don't really like much about life at home because its not like a real family and my mum drinks and my brothers fight all the time and nick my stuff or break it and my dad never speaks, so home is not a cool place to be right now. I like it better when I am out of the house, and I see myself as quite a normal guy really when I'm at school and I have a lot of cool mates, its nice to be popular. I am just your average guy to be honest who likes a laugh and to muck around really. I don't like school except for woodwork, I quite like football but I prefer the skateboard park where a lot of people hang out till its dark. I like to look good and get the latest gear when I can and thats one good thing about my dad because he gives me good pocket money. I like keeping my hair nice and flirting with girls but then who doesnt, I am pretty good-looking which is lucky because its pretty important these days to keep up your image spesially online, and I am pretty famous on there which is good.

I am glad I am not fat or ugly or really skinny because guys like that, well people act like they dont exist but I dont know, maybe they are even nicer or happier in the long run, but all the same I would still rather look good. I like movies and music and I have a big collection of both which I use to take my mind off things. I have some weights in my room and I work out most days to get the best body I can and I am pleased with how I look, spesially my abs, though thats not the inside is it. I like a drink or a bit of weed now and then because it makes me feel like nothing matters, sometimes I get a problem sleeping at night and sometimes I feel worried for no reason, so thats when its nice to have a drink or something but I don't ever go overboard like my mother because I thing its discusting, and I would never hit a girl like my dad even though I get angry, and so thats me pretty much at the moment.

I think other people think I am a lot cooler than I feel on the inside and they probably don't realize the work that goes into it and how much I worry about my body and that. I think other people see me pretty much how I want them to see me exept for my parents who think I'm a waste of space. Girls just see me as hot which is pretty cool I guess, but they are mostly totally up themselves anyway and just love themselves, but it rubs off on me and I get all stupid about it. Or they get really serious to quick which I don't want atall right now as I'm not up to it and it just makes me feel trapped. I think my teachers see me as a dead loss to be honest because I muck about a lot, but then they havent a clue whats going on in my head and if they did they might be a bit more simpathetic maybe. I think other people see me as fitting in ok which is what I want them to think although there are probably some people who will allways think I'm a dead loss, but I don't care about them because its my life and I'm doing the best I can even though it doesnt allways look that way.

In the future I see myself as having a nice wife and a couple of kids, and a good job that I enjoy like carpentry which earns well and which makes me feel good when I leave off. Perhaps I might even have my own business one day in carpentry and my own van. I would like to have a kind wife who is a good friend as well as a lovely wife and I wouldn't mind if she was not completely hot to be honest if she could make me happy. I want to be a good dad to my kids and a friend to them, spesially if they get troubles like I do because it must be cool to have a nice dad to talk to. I would like to have a nice semi on the outskirts of the city with a garden with some swings in for the kids and things. If I can stop feeling like the way I do now I think I might make a nice husband for a girl because I am very kind underneath it all and not at all like my dad who is a cruel bloke with a ton of problems although he doesnt admit it. I would like to have a nice Subaru in black with low profiles and stickers and I could help my wife with the shopping and things at weekends, and at weekends we could stay in bed late and cuddle up and things while the kids are playing. I would still keep my mates though but I would not be one of these husbands who is always at the pub or watching football because I dont see the point in having a family if you do that, and I would cook the dinner sometimes if I wasnt to tierd, you never know I even might be a house husband if I had little ones and my wife wanted a carreer, and then I could do carpentry just as a hobby in the garage or something. And sometimes I would like to go see a movie with my wife exept I dont think that will ever happen because my mum would never be up to looking after my kids anyway so I'd better find a wife with nice parents. And if I had some extra money ever I'd like to get my wife a nice silky nighty or some flowers sometimes and I'd really like a dog to so long as its not left on its own all day which is cruel because I really like dogs, and so thats kind of how I'd like to be one day in the future.

22

December, 2019

"Excuse me young man? Can you show me the way to the chief's hut?

Josh was busy scrubbing off the green algae that had begun flourishing on the mobile that housed the village store. Looking down from his ladder he saw a bizarre-looking woman with dark glasses and wild greying hair. How on earth had she managed to wander in? She was small and weather-beaten, with sunken cheeks and papery hands; and the most remarkable thing about her was her striped woollen tights – purple and blue – that wrinkled heavily around her tiny ankles. At her side she clutched a bulging violet and turquoise shopping trolley.

As Josh dismounted he noticed the woman's big hoop earrings, and recognised her face from Dixie's photograph – the one he had squinted at in the firelight back in the empty field a year ago. He smarted at the unmistakable smell of homelessness. Here was a challenge for Ubuntu. They couldn't turn her away: she was old and vulnerable and for some unfathomable reason she was supposed to be here. "Come with me," he said to her, taking hold of the trolley. "We'll go and have a look shall we?" The woman followed him with big bandy leaps, screeching urgently:

"Be careful with that! It's the colours of the Universe, you know!"

As Josh led the way up the driveway he caught sight of Jean digging over the large allotment. "Got a minute, Jean?" he called. He felt at a loss, but guessed that a medical opinion was a good place to start. Jean approached, puzzlement lining his forehead. The woman pointed a quivering finger at him:

"Light!" she cried, and then cackled happily. "I knew there was great light here!" Then her face sagged into seriousness. "But there is a bigger light than you and it is the chief who has it." She pawed a little at Jean's sleeve. "The light is warm," she whined.

Josh saw compassion soften Jean's face. "Grab a bike and go and get Steve, will you, Jean? Ask him to meet us in the centre."

Josh entered the yoga room at the rear of the centre building, where Ellen and Jill were absorbed in their practice and Anya sat reading. "Sorry to disturb," he said. "We have a visitor."

The woman's body odour quickly overwhelmed the room and Jill flung open a window. "Light… and a bright one at that!" cried the woman, indicating Anya with a knobbly finger. She turned to Jill, studying her closely through her dark glasses. "You aren't the chief. None of you is the chief."

Jill looked enquiringly at Josh who shrugged his shoulders. "Jean's getting Steve," he said. "Dunno what else to do really." Everyone fell silent, watching the peculiar figure as she walked slowly round the room examining the blank walls.

They had moved into the meeting room next-door where there were chairs. Steven left the woman sitting with Anya and spoke to the others with seriousness. "She says her name's Koomra and she's from the Pleiades star system. In other words she's schizophrenic. Could've been exacerbated by extended loneliness: the brain can play some funny tricks when it's starved of interaction..."

"Maybe she is from the Pleiades," grinned Ellen.

Steve clicked his bag shut, straight faced. "... But who cares what she's got? Truth is she needs TLC. She's very underweight, although she's got a pulse like a bull. We might be able to get her sectioned on the grounds that she isn't feeding herself."

"You can't," said Josh at once, and then checked himself. "Erm... I think she should stay here – at least for a few days." He took Jill's hand and pulled her aside. "She's *meant* to be here," he whispered. She raised her eyebrows. "I'll explain later," he said.

Ellen was watching the young girl with Koomra. Anya looked as though she was beginning to take to the old woman, who was gesticulating and drawing shapes in the air as she spoke. "And trees. Tall ones, but all blue. Very tall and skinny with trunks that are snaky. And the pyramids have glass walls and steep sides, and the sun is very low and murky compared with this one here."

Ellen drew up a chair and looked questioningly at Anya. "She's telling me about the Pleiades," explained the girl. "It sounds lovely." Anya leaned in close, whispering: "She might just be eccentric."

"I think it's a bit more than that," Ellen answered, glancing round at Jill who was hands on hips as usual.

"It's disgusting!" she was telling the whole room. "How can people call us a civilised country when our old and sick are left to wander about with nowhere to go until they just… pop off?"

Ellen felt the need for some clarity. "Would you mind fetching Omasah, Jill?"

At the moment his name was spoken he entered the room. Steven looked up and then down at his shoes. How did that man always manage to appear exactly when he was wanted? It made Steven uncomfortable, and he shoved the question aside.

"Chief!" screeched Koomra, jumping up like a flea. She trotted over to Omasah and got to her knees, shading her eyes. She grasped his clothes with one hand, pulling on them. "Dazzling!" She curled up in a ball at his feet, muttering. Then she spoke more clearly: "I am old and the dusk gathers, but the light is warm."

Ellen and Steven eased the woman back onto her chair and Omasah proceeded to lay his hands on her. After writhing and moaning as though in pain for a minute or two, she gradually became calm and almost slept.

"Her mind is scrambled, but she has second sight and sees my light-body," said Omasah. "Feed her and offer love. I will visit her again tomorrow." He went out, and Steven stared after him not knowing what to think.

"Well, I've got work to do," he grumbled, picking up his bag and making for the door.

They decided to settle Koomra in the school, because there were floor cushions there to sleep on and it was warm and peaceful. Since Omasah's visit she was relaxed, compliant and much more lucid, and, to everyone's surprise, had readily agreed to a shower and change of clothes. As Ellen sifted through spare garments in the store, the old woman followed her every move, repeating over and over that she must only wear blue or purple. An hour later she was almost unrecognisable: freshly-combed and perfumed, and insisting that Anya accompany her to the school. Once inside, the old lady made her way quietly round the classroom and kitchen, looking in cupboards and drawers and opening books. Her back had lost its hunch and her hands had ceased their restlessness. "She's completely different," Anya whispered to Ellen. "Omasah's healed her."

At around eight o'clock they left her absorbed in a big book about the universe. She had requested fruit and water for her supper, saying she refused to eat anything that had been interfered with by monkeys – a statement that left Anya giggling tearfully into a cushion for ten minutes.

Next morning Ellen was roused early by a loud knock at her door. Nadia's voice came up the stairs: "Ellen – The funny lady's gone. Anya and me went to take her breakfast but she's wasn't there."

Ellen sat up in bed and sighed deeply. She'd really thought that they had managed to make a difference – had been able to offer a lost soul some comfort and security. But no: it wasn't to be…

She showered and dressed and walked round to Omasah's house. As usual his door opened as she came near. "You are anxious for the woman, Kaphalya," he said to her at once. "There is no need."

Ellen sat down on the bed. "But she's gone. It's so sad. She would've been safe here with us."

Omasah appeared puzzled. "If she has indeed departed she will return shortly," he told her gently. "Not only does she belong here, but I sense a connection with you. May I hold the stone?"

234

"With me? But I've never seen her before." Ellen stood up and eased the green pebble from her jeans' pocket. Omasah took it and sat down at the table, holding it between his hands and scanning behind closed eyelids. "The connection is very faint," he said at last. "Her imprint is erratic and difficult to read, but her presence here is very strong." Ellen was about to speak but Omasah held up one hand. His face became faintly animated as he watched scenarios playing out. He smiled, but then suddenly smarted is if in pain, and dropped the stone on the rug. Ellen went down on hands and knees to retrieve it. The stone was almost too hot to hold.

"What is it? What did you see?"

The man was sitting with his great head resting in his hands. She touched his shoulder gently. "Omasah?"

"I cannot, Kaphalya." He took her hand. "I must bear these possibilities alone. Awareness on your part may force them into being. Remember – reality is fluid. Think only of things that please you, and never allow fear to pollute your heart."

It was noon before Jean discovered that the old lady had dragged a big floor cushion over to the roundhouse. There she sat, busily knitting in the semi-darkness, with wool from the classroom cupboards.

23

25th December, 2019
Anya's Diary

This has just been the best Christmas day ever because I have a new greyhound! She is pure black with a little spot of white at the top of one ear, like the yin and the yang Carlos says. She is quite small for a greyhound, and she has a fluffy bed from mum and a purple jumper that Koomra knitted. She is a little timid my dog, because she didn't have a very nice life in Ireland, where lots of the greyhounds come from, but I am sure she'll settle in quickly because she already knows that I love her. I asked Omasah to name her and he said Zoki which I think is beautiful, and it means "night" in his language.

I felt a bit funny about this Christmas because everyone has different beliefs. Jean and Melyne are Catholic, Paul says Christmas has become a hedonistic capitalist orgy and Jerry and Carlos agree with him, Tali's Jewish, and Koomra doesn't really seem to know what it means at all. Mum usually dreads it because of all the cooking (but this year Mags, Carlos and Lizzy did it all) and dad hates having to get up early. But anyway, it's all been so great! We had a fantastic lunch in the centre with crackers which Faye made, although they didn't go bang. Addy made up the jokes and some of them were really funny. Dad played guitar afterwards and sang his new Christmas song which went "Oranges and lemon slices; nuts in a cut glass bowl." I can't remember the rest but Mum says it's the best thing he's ever written.

All the dogs came and Zoki sat with her head on my knee. Mr Rix was there of course and Sage likes Zoki a lot, because usually greyhounds are used to being with other greyhounds in Ireland. Ellen bought me a beautiful embroidered collar for Zoki as my present in red green and gold. After the dinner Ellen gave a little speech about how the fact that we were all together at this celebration meant that Ubuntu is working, because however different people interpret things, Jesus's teachings are about universal truths like love and tolerance, and so is this village.

I got quite a few CDs for Christmas including a Joni Mitchell one from Dick and Lizzy because I like her a lot. Faye had made me a beautiful long pale blue dress which is all layered with no sleeves, and Jill gave me a shell pendant and Omasah gave me a stone with a crystal in it. I got a little carved CD cabinet from Dixie and Addy gave me 3 big pyramid candles because he got a kit for his birthday, and I got a book called The Power of Now from Paul. Steve gave me a picture he'd painted of Foxheath beach for my room and Nadia gave me a set of oracle cards. I got a whole box of John Steinbecks off Dad, plus 3 hair scrunchies from Melyne which she'd put beads on. Mr Rix gave me a clock with birds on it and from Jean I got a little wooden cross on a stand which he made me with a jewel in the middle, and he said it's for a blessing.

I made all my presents this year, and I did lots of my birds with bells and sequins because they are lovely and quite easy now I can use a machine. I gave Omasah my poem about Ubuntu Morning in a little frame and I also made some strings of holey stones, shells and driftwood which Jill says would be good for the *shop (Dick drilled the holes) and I gave Mum and Dad a drawing of a blackbird who sits on my roof a lot. The only present I bought was a French bible for Melyne from the RSPCA shop and which made her cry. Sandrine who runs it is ever so nice although she didn't like us at first, and I asked her to look out for a French bible ages ago, and it's pink with a matching box. But the best present of all was Ellen's because Jill's managed to get the Sounds of Ubuntu CD recorded with hardly any of us knowing! The cover is a night sky over trees and it looks wonderful.*

After the meal and presents we threw balloons about and played pin the tail on the donkey, and Dad drew a really funny cross-eyed donkey with huge teeth. I went for a walk with Omasah and Zoki afterwards and it was a lovely sunset. He said he'd enjoyed himself but that he always enjoys himself, which is how the Buddhists are because we've been doing them at school. I talked to him a bit about yesterday when I got a bag of newspapers given in the shop and there was so much sex and stuff in them. It just seems so childish to me, and I don't see why these things are always in the newspapers which are supposed to be about serious things. Ellen said it's just programming and I shouldn't pay any attention but I feel inadequate sometimes, and the pictures you see everywhere of these women — is that what a girl's really got to be like to attract boys? It's like they all want the same face, and what happens to all the people who can't afford it? I'd like a boy to like me for what's inside, and because of what you speak about and believe in, and then you can share all that forever. I think that sexiness comes from inside too, and it's beautiful like a flower, although more like a wild one than a gaudy man-made thing. Anyway, Omasah said that I'll know love when it comes, and that's all he really said.

After walking I went to the yoga room on my own and tried some of the things we have been learning. It was amazing because

I managed to meditate for the first time, meaning I felt a love feeling, like a floating bliss, and it was as though everything was completely perfect, and made total sense, and it made me cry. This has been the loveliest Christmas ever by a long chalk, and Zoki is asleep on my bed and I can hear the air whistling through her nostrils and it's really sweet. I heard a blackbird this morning too which is the earliest in the year I've ever heard one. I think he was a youngster because he wasn't a very good singer like some of them are, but that didn't matter because it's the feeling behind it that counts.

24

January, 2020

The new year brought heavy frosts, and birdsong was like a sparkling in the icy air. Villagers covered their crops with sheeting or cloches, while the greenhouse nurtured long lines of seedlings. Hungry pigeons were kept from the cabbages with nets and fed on the playing field where their dung was collected for fertilizer. Extra blankets and sleeping bags were transferred from the trailers to the store, and Nadia and Melyne moved into their parents' house temporarily. Anya insisted on staying put, sleeping in a hat and making use of an old gas heater that normally stood in Dixie's work shop. "The cold doesn't bother me," he told her truthfully. Years of off-grid living had taught Dixie to welcome the natural flow of the changing seasons.

Meanwhile Mary bit her lip and wrinkled her brows over Anya's outside toilet until Jill reminded her that people had used outside toilets for generations. "Anyway," said the girl; "It makes it *ever so* nice when you get back into the warm!" and her father's heart had rejoiced silently at her understanding.

As had been expected, trade slowed to a deathly crawl, and the time was used for forging ahead with the wind turbines and consolidating plans for the future. They met one cold but windless Sunday night around the new fire pit behind the centre and over mugs of mulled wine that Lizzy had made. "We had a load of really cheap plonk given us before Christmas," she told Anya. "I thought it'd be nice and warming. It's got cloves in."

Anya sipped the steaming brew gingerly. "It's very sweet," she said; "but nice."

Carlos stood up, Peruvian-looking in a patterned hat and blanket draped poncho-like round his shoulders. "I'm not going to talk about astrology," he announced with a smile to Steven; "But I'm convinced that a change is in the air. I feel it's time to expand our potential – for the village to begin to really evolve."

"How d'you mean?" Ellen asked quickly.

"Well… Most of us came here with a vague idea of escaping. But I knew that was never going to be possible, or even altogether a good idea. You see we're all part of the same thing…" He glanced at the hooded figure of Omasah, who gave a gentle nod. "We wanted to step back from the materialism and overuse of tech, which we feel compromise our natural connection to one another and the planet." He paused and sighed, and his long face looked forlorn in the firelight. "I watched a TV through a shop window the other day…" He gave a little chuckle, but his eyes remained far away. "I was shocked because I'm not used to it anymore. The adverts just kind of amused me to be honest, but the movie trailer… it was just… *violence*. Massive explosions one after the other; guys wielding machine guns… image after image almost too fast to keep up with… and every one *violent*."

Paul interrupted glumly. "Bet it was a twelve certificate too."

Carlos wrapped his blanket tighter. "Anyway – it was upsetting, and I felt isolated. But then I realised it's not me who's isolated: it's the people who are watching those… nightmares." He noticed Jean's arms move around his sister and pull her a little closer.

Carlos inhaled deeply, blowing a steamy cloud into the cold night air. "Anyway – that wasn't what I was even going to talk about." He gave one of his typical toothy grins, and continued more light-heartedly. "Ubuntu's about stopping the flow of this shit at the gate, right? But I'm starting to think we should have more of an osmosis kind of thing going on."

Addy piped up from Graham's side: "I know what that is! It's the movement of water from a high concentration to a low concentration through a membrane." Then his face creased up in puzzlement. "What's that got to do with Ubuntu?"

"Well, Addy – the term can also apply to ideas," Carlos explained. "What I'm saying is that I think we could give out more by letting in more."

Ellen was immediately interested. "In what way?"

He turned to her. "D'you remember when we spoke way back about a healing and massage room for visitors? Well, that kind of thing. We have expertise here that could benefit people. We could give classes in mindfulness and meditation – things like that."

"They'd pull us to pieces," said Paul.

Ellen flung him an angry look. "Why?"

"They'd call us charlatans."

"Don't be ridiculous," she said. "Hospitals already do mindfulness, but they're so strapped for resources. Carlos is right – we could help ease the load. And there's nothing quackish about massage."

Paul reconsidered. "Well, maybe," he ventured. "They'd probably have to sign something though, or we'd end up sued." Ellen rolled her eyes, but realised he was probably right.

"Yeah, okay, Paul."

Tali suddenly looked up at her husband, saying: "You could do your readings again as well!"

Carlos's face lit up in response. "I know!"

Nadia burst into excitement. "Oh my God – I know what we should do! We should do holidays for people. They could come and find out what it's like to do Ubuntu. They could stay in a roundhouse or something and have massages and do crafts and stuff, and it'd be really relaxing!"

Everyone stared at the girl's eager face. Paul became even more sceptical. "It'd be like an invasion."

"No! It's brilliant!" cried Ellen.

"How long would it take to build another roundhouse?" asked Jill. "Can we afford it?" It went without saying that Koomra could not be expected to move. She had considered the roundhouse her home from day one.

"We have the willow, wood, mud and dung," answered Jean. "We even have paint. All we need is thatch."

"It wouldn't be all year – just in the summer," urged Nadia.

"Retreats are very popular," said Mary calmly. "But we mustn't undercut other businesses. We'd have to charge roughly what they do."

Nadia's head was crowded with ideas. "Maybe we could do it all bartering," she told her mother. "And we could have a tree house for the children and people could peel potatoes and join in the music and use our funny washing-machines when Paul finishes them – it'd be fun!"

"Just bartering might be difficult, Nadia," said Jill. "You see, if a week in a roundhouse costs a hundred quid, well… that's a lot of stuff to bring."

"They could bring one great big thing, then," insisted the girl.

Paul stood up, taking the reigns. "Quiet everyone, please!" He began strolling up and down in the circle of light. "I get what Carlos is saying but we need to think it over carefully – yeah?" The ring of faces nodded. "We always knew the shop and café would be seasonal – even Dixie's carvings haven't really been selling since October…"

"They've sold some little ones and some masks," interjected Jill.

"… And ideally I'd like us to be able to support some charities one day, as well as prepping in case of crop failures and suchlike. So yes – I vote we take this further, as long as the whole place doesn't end up teeming with visitors… It's definitely a way of expanding our influence and upholding our concepts."

"But how will we advertise?" put in Dick. "We don't want to get roped into going online, surely?"

Anya sat beside her brother. "No – we can't do that. Someone would have to spend all day on a computer, and that doesn't fit with the village at all."

"I'll wear a sandwich board," offered Jerry. "I've always wanted to."

"We'll work it," said Carlos. "I agree we don't want hoards of visitors in any case. Every life we touch will make a difference – quality rather than quantity."

"Well done Nadia!" said Lizzy, clapping her gloved hands together.

"Humanity Towards Others!" shouted Tali over the cheers.

That night, Ellen lay in bed unable to sleep, and the excitement of Nadia's ideas had given way to brooding. She went downstairs and looked out of her east-facing window to see Carlos sitting by a small fire next-door. She quickly dressed in multiple layers and went to join him. "Baby alright?" she said by way of introduction. He nodded, she sat down, and they were silent for some time. She became reflective, looking up at the stars.

"Have you ever thought that Stone Henge might've begun with people putting rocks out to mark the stars because they realised they were moving, and then the rocks just got bigger and bigger?"

"Yeah, maybe," said Carlos, sleepily. "And eventually they calculated the movements of the heavenly bodies and shifted stones we can't lift now even with our technology. We aren't any 'peak,' Ellen. We should respect our ancestors more."

They were silent, looking up.

"I'm so glad I'm here, Carlos. It felt kind of insane in town at Christmas. But I don't know – other days it's nice to see all the people walking about…"

"Vibrational," said Carlos leaning against the house with his hands behind his head. "And astrological of course."

"You sound like Omasah," smiled Ellen.

"Everything's vibration, Ellen. That's science, not belief. The stars, those trees, you, me, our emotions… even our memories and hopes."

"And our fears," she murmured.

"And those, yeah. Light and dark. Black and white. Peaks and troughs. But you can't have one without the other. Ultimately they're still all part of the same thing. Like what

Einstein called the unified field. Everything's connected at an energetic level."

"I guess so, yeah."

He looked at her, knowing she wasn't feeling her usual self. "… Even if it feels like a huge balancing act to us."

"Between good and bad?"

"I don't think there really is any bad, Ellen: just fear and pain."

"Are you sure it's that simple, Carlos?"

He was silent for a second. "When you break it right down to its tiniest roots, yes. Or lack of love: it amounts to the same thing. Think of a stray dog. It's been chased away and hungry so many times it lives in fear. It bites, it's greedy, and it bears its teeth. But it'll still respond positively to a loving home. People are the same way."

Ellen was not feeling on Carlos's wavelength. "Not all dogs respond and some people are lost too," she said quickly, and steered the conversation towards issues that had surfaced in the meeting. "But where does all this blood-lust come from, Carlos? This acceptance of violence as normal… thrilling… sexy even? It's not bloody normal! It's *sick!* They just want to numb our children so they'll never think to question who starts the wars or who makes the weapons." She hung her head despairingly and her voice was devoid of hope. "The Elites must love this world the way it is. It suits them just fine."

Carlos draped an arm heavily across her shoulders. "Shh," he soothed. "It's from these tough times that change comes. It's got to be this way to force the transformation. Besides, horror is never the whole story. There's the kindness that can be given and received in bad times for a start. They prove the light never goes out."

Ellen still persisted: "But what about violence as entertainment? Some people can't get enough of it, and the film industry just keeps churning it out."

"Yeah, but only for as long as there's a demand," Carlos answered. He paused, mulling things over. "It's like people have become addicted. Like it's a buzz. But to me it seems like a mirror they can't look away from, reflecting their own fear. It's sad. We should send them love. They need it badly."

A warm inner spark kindled suddenly, and tugged at his heart. He breathed deeply, knowing that Omasah was awake and with them in spirit. "A Golden Age is coming, remember?" He placed his forefinger under Ellen's chin and tilted her head upwards. "Keep looking up at the stars, Honey."

25

February 24th, 2020

Hiya Ellen

Well here I am writing to you at long last. I hope you all had a nice Christmas in the village and thank you so much for the Ubuntu CD you sent me – it's so beautiful and I ripped it so I can listen to it when I go to bed. It's helped me a lot to relax and it makes me go all tingly. Sorry not to have written sooner to thank you, you've probably already guessed that things still aren't that good for me here.

Our Christmas was a bit hectic and very expensive because you know how kids are these days – they make all these demands on you and it's hell to pay if you say no, or at least that's the way it is in this house. Alan's been more sociable lately since he cleared the money problems, but it's still a very tense life for me and he's not really changed underneath it all, but he isn't quite so cruel to me since then because I guess he's not as stressed. He still hit me badly a few weeks back though, just for pulling the wrong face, and I can't challenge him about anything, so I just have to tow the line. I am not working any more because I can't handle it and I have been seeing a nice doctor who is very supportive, but I know I still drink too much between you and me. He lets me have sleeping pills but only a set amount so I often run out and then can't sleep atall, which makes life hard. Ethans getting to look like a real young man nowadays and so good-looking, I'm hoping that once he gets out of his teenage years we'll get close again because we always used to be before everything went wrong. He resents the bad marriage and most likely thinks I'm stupid for not getting out but it's not that easy when you are living in it, and especially when there are children. He is still seeing someone about his problems and still won't speak about it, but I get the feeling he's built up some trust in her which is good.

The good news is that Alan's decided to rent a big campervan this year at Easter because we didn't have a holiday last year atall, and we're going to go to the coast including Foxheath so I'll get to see the village at long last. He's got a bad back so we can't go too far from Norwich and there's no way I could ever drive a big thing like that. So anyway I'll let you know nearer the time about it.

I've started reading crime novels all the time which helps me feel a bit better. I'm glad I've found that because it's nicer than sitting on Facebook which I'd stopped posting on in any case. I don't do much else though and Ive gained no end of weight but then I guess it doesn't matter because no one really sees me anyway. I hope your book is still selling and that everything's going ok there and I really look forward to seeing you in April. Lots of love to you Ellen and thanks again for the CD and for all your lovely letters.

Love and hugs, Janet x

26

February, 2020

Milder weather had already returned with weeks of windless days and silent nights that kept the sea mists thick and murky. Unseen birds called from the damp tranquil branches, and the dripping land seemed to sleep in muted browns and soft grey-greens that lacked both the crispness of winter and the vibrancy of spring. The sun crawled indistinctly in the milky sky, and only the deeply sensitive such as Harry and Anya continued to see any beauty amid the endless gloom of what was beginning to feel like a no man's land.

There was no denying it any longer: Steven had flu, and the prospect of it depressed him. Every inch of his body ached, and he had lain awake half the night alternately sweating and freezing. In the midst of his discomfort his shower had felt small and inadequate, and for the first time since arriving in the village he missed the luxury of his old home. Wrapping a large scarf around his face in annoyance he headed out into the mist in search of milk, tea and bread for his breakfast, cursing himself for having run out of such obvious essentials. The store light was out and he rummaged irritably in the semi-darkness, knowing in the back of his mind that he really should find a bulb and fit it for the next person – but no: it just felt too much like hard work. On returning ten minutes later with his food in his arms he stopped dead beside the chicken run and fell abruptly to his knees. "Oh no," he said under his breath. "Bertha…"

There was a soft movement from the direction of the little gate as Omasah pushed it open. At once Steven felt angry – the strange man disturbed him, and he resented the way the villagers had built up such a respect for him. He knew it wasn't a good way to feel; he wasn't proud of it but he just couldn't help it, and he met the unearthly amber eyes with aloofness.

Appearing not to notice Steven's icy mood, Omasah crouched down to examine the sorry sight of Bertha's bedraggled little body lying lifeless on the ground. "Your bird is very sick," he said, lifting her gently. The strange eyes sought Steven's again: "As are you."

The doctor spun away and hauled himself to his feet. "My bird is dead," he croaked through his scarf, and marched towards the house slamming the door. He leant against the inside, immediately appalled at himself. "Christ – I sound like Ben." He thought shamefully of what Jerry or Lizzy would say if they had heard him and shut his eyes, longing for the lazy comfort of his bed. But at last, with the intention of apologising, he heaved a sigh and opened the door to find Omasah standing on his doormat with Bertha fully alive and struggling haphazardly in his arms.

"Please take your creature," said Omasah, wiping his feet and entering the room.

Steven felt drained and weak as his brain fought to process what he was seeing. He took the bird and felt her warmth through the white bony feathers, and then gave a spontaneous laugh as she pecked his hand and looked crossly at him. However dreamlike it might seem there was no disputing it: she had somehow been restored to health in ways that could not be explained – and even if Bertha had not been quite dead, she had certainly been very close: any fool could have seen that.

Steven dropped down on the sofa in a trance, still clutching Bertha awkwardly along with his groceries; but the next second decided to force himself into some kind of action. "I… er… I'd better put her back in the pen." His bread and milk tumbled to the floor as got up and went to the door, while Omasah stood silently in the centre of the room as though waiting for something. Steven slowed his pace and then turned round rather sheepishly. "Thank you," he said, suddenly close to tears.

Ellen pulled up just as Lizzy was closing up the café and wound down the window of the truck. "Take these to Koomra, would you?" she said, handing her a packet of almonds. "It's B vits and protein for her. I'm worried she'll disappear before long… Quiet day again?"

Lizzy peeled off her vinyl gloves and made a face. "Pretty much. We're getting those homeless blokes most days now. I can see us becoming a soup kitchen."

Ellen looked unperturbed. "Is that a problem?" she asked.

"Not at the moment it isn't. Jerry's doing extra rolls. It should be alright."

She watched the truck drive away, and through the thick mist recognized the figure of Mr Rix waving as it passed him by. He began heading in her direction, waddling a little over the rough ground, and so Lizzy went to meet him. "Hello Miss Lizzy," said the old man cheerily as she drew close. "I must tell you… You see, Miss Ellen looked in such a rush."

"What's up Mr Rix?"

"Oh, something nice I think. Something I think Miss Ellen will be very pleased about… at least I hope so." He looked momentarily doubtful, and then continued.

"Well, the lady Sandrine just rang me from the RSPCA shop, you know? And she's asking whether you'd like a couple of sheep to keep the grass tended. What do you reckon, Miss Lizzy? A good idea or not? Doopers they are, or some funny name. Special hairy ones what don't need shearing. Apparently they were in a dreadful state poor things, but now they're good as new!"

Lizzy smiled. "Well I should think that'd be very useful, don't you? Nice for the children and we could use the manure too." She put a hand on his shoulder. "Thank you, Mr Rix – I'll put it to Ellen as soon as I see her."

Lizzy turned towards the village with a bag for Koomra and a pan of food for home. Under the limp eucalyptuses the daffodils that Jill and the children had planted in November were pushing up long blue-green shoots, and below the misty tree-line in the corner of the playing field the old woman sat knitting outside her open door. The way she so often sat outside concerned the villagers, but she wouldn't listen to them and was adamant that it was good for her health. The bright eyes met Lizzy's as the needles clicked on and on at lightening speed. "For me my dear?" she said with affected surprise.

"All fresh and delicious and straight from Mother Earth," Lizzy replied. "Ellen's sent you some nuts. Please try and eat them, my love."

Lizzy entered the roundhouse where there was a small table covered in candle wax beside a mattress that lay on a blue patterned rug. She put down the bag and sniffed the air, wondering whether the bed needed changing. It would do for a couple more days she decided. Then she picked up a pile of knitting from the bed and went outside. "Your food's on the table my sweet. Thank you for these. See you tomorrow."

When Lizzy arrived home Anya was there playing Scrabble with Dick. Zoki the greyhound lay on the rug with her spindly legs in the air, and Dylan was stretched out at her side. "Anya's winning again," said Dick. "How did the butter beans go down?" He had a habit of tweaking Lizzy's recipes, and had suggested the beans as a replacement for potatoes in an stew she had been making.

Lizzy answered with a smile. "It's better. Everybody thinks so. And you were right about more turmeric too."

Anya's face was glowing. "You'll never guess what's happened, Lizzy. Omasah went to see Steve and cured his chicken and then cured his flu!" She giggled happily. "Now Steve's all confused because he doesn't believe in that sort of thing."

"Cured his chicken?"

"Bertha – the white one," explained Dick. "Steve swears it was a gonner. He left Omasah outside with it for a second and then it was okay again."

Anya frowned at him. "'She,' not 'it,' Dick." She went on cheerfully. "And his flu's almost completely gone, although he's still got the sniffles." She quickly became reabsorbed in her Scrabble tiles, and Lizzy mounted the steps to the kitchen to put the pan on the little wood stove to heat.

"I wonder if he saw the light," she whispered to the window.

She came to sit on the sofa beside Dick, nestling her head into his neck. "Who were those children with Addy and

Nadia today, Anya? They all seemed to be getting on very well."

Anya giggled again. "Oh, they're so funny," she said. "They call themselves the CAT Gang, for 'Children Against Technology.' They've got little badges and everything. They say their childhoods were ruined because their parents just sat on Facebook all day and stuck them in front of the telly. So now they don't want anything to do with technology. That's why they like it here so much."

"Doesn't sound funny to me," frowned Lizzy. "Sounds awful."

"Good that they realised that's no life for kids, though," put in Dick.

"I didn't mean it's funny the lives they've had. I meant they're just really funny characters," Anya explained. "You know – different… a bit like me, I suppose. I think they're great and so does Jill. She says they can visit whenever they want. Trouble is they want to join our school."

"Well, can they?" asked Lizzy.

"I don't know – maybe," said Anya. "I think it'd be nice…"

Omasah sat on Ellen's rug with his hands around the stone. He had paid her an unexpected visit at tea-time, and had been in a deep trance-like state for over half an hour. Ellen had grown bored with waiting and had curled up in her armchair with a book. At last Omasah stirred and turned to her, taking her hands in his usual way. She sensed a foreboding.

"You know Kaphalya that I am here as guide only. This density is hard for me, and it disconnects me. However be here I must. Operating from my own time is far too sporadic, and this loop of time needs to flow freely and establish its own vibration. Do you understand?"

"More or less," Ellen replied, excited at the mystery of it all. "But you're still very powerful, aren't you? I mean, compared with us."

"It is enough," he answered, and paused while he considered how to continue. Still holding her hands he said: "I have told you that reality is fluid. Thus by indicating to others the likelihood of what may unfold I risk its unfolding, and that is not my place. I am not here to manipulate the time-line, but to steer what already flows, like placing rocks in a stream."

"Is something bad going to happen?" said Ellen. "Please say."

His eyes gazed at her, and she felt the warmth of his love. "On this occasion I feel it is necessary to give you a warning. There is the high chance of a great storm in the month of April, and for this the village should prepare. I also sense the potential for… complications surrounding the event."

"Right," said Ellen. "Who should I tell?"

Omasah dropped his head in thought, and Ellen listened to his soft breathing. "Tell only Darad and Zalyam," he said at length – his names for Paul and Dixie. Again he fell into deep silence, still holding Ellen's hands lightly as he searched for something undefined. When he at last looked up into her expectant face he said quietly: "I hear a baby's cry."

27

March, 2020

The clock ticked on as the girl sat silently leafing through endless grim-faced mug-shots, while opposite her young PC Febland picked disconsolately at his fingernails under the desk. He looked again at the girl's young face: pretty girl no doubt, but nothing womanly about her. Whatever possessed these pervs to flash their privates at a little slip of a thing like that he had no idea. Whatever possessed them to flash their privates at *anybody*, come to that… The constable's mind was wandering. His eyes found the clock and he resisted the urge to sigh. "That's him," the girl announced in an expressionless voice.

The policeman leaned forward, craning his neck at the upside down image of a thick-set man with a bullet-shaped head. Nasty bastard he looked. "And before you ask, yes – I'm sure," she said, snapping the big folder shut. She crossed her arms and leaned back in the chair, sulky and dull-eyed.

PC Febland walked the girl along a corridor to her waiting parents and then hurried into his office, feeling a buzz of excitement now as he searched on the man's name. He waited while the computer whirred, always slow because of the heavy security software. Ah, here he was: no previous except for drink-driving. Ex-military – expelled for violent conduct… interesting. The constable scrolled down eagerly. Then he smacked the desk: Bingo! The guy was on the run, suspected of indecent exposure down south… illegal images found on his computer… Obvious next step: find out if he had any relatives living in the area.

With young PC Febland standing importantly at his side, Inspector Wilson rang the bell of the neat ivy-clad suburban house. The door of the neighbouring house immediately opened in response, and two owl-like eyes appeared over the hedge. "He's out," said the man. "Went out over two hours ago."

The officers were careful not to react. The woman was supposed to live alone. "And is Mrs Grader around?" queried the inspector.

"Haven't seen her for weeks. Reckon she must be ill. That chap what takes care of her won't speak to me though. Just marches off without speaking. Does her shopping though. Huge great bags he gets. Must eat most of it himself. Big beefy bloke he is. Don't see sight or sound of her any more. I mean, I hear the telly sometimes; but she don't potter about out here no more. Reckon she's bed-bound. Like to know what's going on with her, I would. Nice lady."

The two policemen thanked the man, who remained poised where he was, and went round to the back of the house. Febland immediately pointed out the boarded up glass in the door and dark spots of blood on the paving. They looked about, noticing that the garden had been carefully tended until relatively recently. There was a chair and wrought-iron table, several pots and ornaments, and the beds were well-stocked with weed-choked flowers and bushes.

"Loved her garden, she did," said the owl over the fence. "Shame he can't fix that up for her. Doesn't go to work. Heaven knows what he does all day. Looks after her, I suppose."

Inspector Wilson looked up at the second floor, seeing closed curtains behind grimy windows. He banged on the backdoor, calling the woman's name. Then he shouted louder, directing his voice at the upstairs. Not a sound, save the twittering of sparrows in the hedges and the distant drone of traffic.

"Should we get a warrant?" whispered the young constable. "She might be…" He stopped, feeling the owl-eyes upon him.

"Come on," said the inspector. "Let's get back." He turned to the neighbour. "Thanks for your help, Mr..?"

"Embick. Roger Marius Embick. Hope she's alright. Nice lady." The eyes dropped out of sight at last.

The two men made their way back to the car and drove away, unaware of the big man skulking behind a van parked opposite. Maxwell breathed fast, calculating. They'd be back – he knew that for sure. As soon as the car had disappeared from view he ran to the house and unlocked it, took the stairs two at a time, and grabbed an empty holdall. He proceeded to stuff it hastily with clothes from amongst a scattering on the floor and bed. Then he descended to the hall, where he snatched a packet of biscuits and bottle of whisky from the carriers he had brought back with him. As a last thought he opened the door to the cupboard under the stairs, and kissed his aunt wetly on the cheek. "Thanks for having me, Auntie!"

The front door slammed shut, and his heavy footsteps faded out of earshot. Lillian began to weep uncontrollably in the chair where she sat tethered and gagged – Maxwell's way of securing her whenever he left the house or got drunk. Tears streamed as she thought of her friends, all of whom had been somehow persuaded that she was too frail for visitors. She looked down at the cuts on her thin cold arms, and the recollection of Max's syrupy voice was nauseating. He had sounded so caring and compassionate as he had answered one curious phone call after another; so utterly self-assured and well-spoken. Even her best friend Helen had left the house convinced that Lillian was lucky to be in such safe hands, unaware that the smiling friendly man at the door clutched a knife behind his back.

The police hadn't heard her desperate attempts to cry out but it didn't matter now, because before long they would be back to set her free.

28

April, 2020

They were holidaying in Britain – something Alan found excruciatingly embarrassing – and to add insult to injury, Janet had somehow persuaded him to come to this dump. The excitement of the enormous flash camper had quickly waned, and every day had become a battle for decent food and entertainment.

In the evenings, Janet had noticed lines of cars parked on sweeping grass overlooking the sea, and realised that they were there to watch the sunset. She saw other children poring over rock-pools with nets and buckets as their mothers sat soaking up the sun, and she felt a terrible longing. Alan and the boys, meanwhile, were lost in the next bright distraction, but any actual enjoyment seemed fleeting and shallow. Janet didn't understand why, but thought sorrowfully how little her family relished its own company.

Alan had waited till the very last day before taking the family to the village so that Janet could visit Ellen. Even better, he had managed to hold off until tea-time, hoping the shop would be shut and the place deserted. He didn't want anything to do with a crazy bunch of hippies in any case, and he and the kids were in a hurry for chips and ice-cream…

Janet was brimming with anger and frustration, but underneath swam a cold fear. She'd had a sleepless night and had finally knocked herself out with wine and an extra pill at five in the morning. Her nerves were shredded and she was devastated at the thought of not seeing the village. "You waited till late on purpose!" she growled shakily at him, her eyes red and brimming with tears. "You bloody bastard!"

In the back of the camper the three boys sat absorbed in their screens, ignoring the shouting from the front seats. Feeling an emptiness take hold, Ethan glanced out at the spring bloom that peppered the trees and hedges. Everything looked bare and dull. His phone buzzed heavily in his hand – a small bright door onto an easy flow of smiles and love-hearts: a place where he mattered, like he'd mattered long ago. Numbly, the boy clicked off three pictures: the view from the window, his parents arguing, and his brothers next to him. Then he switched to selfie and laid one arm along the back of the seat. One more click. His fingers darted at lightning speed as he named the file *Ubuntu*, and uploaded.

Alan announced that they were going back to the campsite, and that he was driving straight past the farm. Without thinking, Janet grabbed the wheel, trying to steer into the entrance. Alan slammed on the brake and the van swerved dangerously up a grassy bank and down again, careering to a halt and causing the boys to sprawl on the floor. Out of control now, he lunged at his wife not knowing how best to hurt her. His hands found her forearm and he squeezed and twisted until she screamed. In the back Ethan wrestled with the locked side door as the youngest child began to cry hysterically. Then, feeling his fragile world crumble, he began shouting and kicking at the windows, first with his trainers and then with the fire extinguisher. Janet was trying to get out but Alan had her tightly by the hair, and her arms and body flailed and thrashed. He spoke into her ear in a low strangled voice. "You'll never regret anything like you'll regret this, you fat cow!"

Ethan didn't know how, but suddenly he was out of the camper and running between dark looming barns towards the farm gate, and calling for his mother to follow. The middle brother, Tyler, threw a sweet wrapper out of the window and plugged earphones into the DVD player. Then he curled up small, blotting out his brother's cries and the drama unfolding around him. Janet tore herself free with a yell and lost a shoe as she tumbled out of the van. She hobbled after her son, kicking off her second shoe and feeling the stony ground stinging her feet as she tried to run.

Ethan was arguing with an old man who was insisting that the shop had just shut. "No!" cried Janet, throatily as she caught up, her face running with mascara. "No, please! Please let us in. I need to see Ellen! She's my friend." Ethan started lurching about as he tried to force the man's hands from the gate. Mr Rix looked towards the camper to see Alan swaggering towards them, and immediately let the woman and boy through.

"No more, please!" he told Alan, waveringly. Janet and Ethan were running for the shop now, where Jill could be seen through the windows packing things up. Alan shoved Mr Rix aside and slid himself through the gap in the heavy metal gate. "Bad luck, old man. That's my family."

The crows were screeching over the woods and the child still cried in the back of the vehicle as Alan started for the shop himself – a dark hostile figure in the bright landscape.

Mr Rix's heart fluttered nervously as he heard Olive's voice in his head, reprimanding: "Oh, Stan. Why did you let him in? You could've stopped him… that poor girl, Stan!" He began following in desperation. Then to his relief he recognised Dixie framed in the shop doorway, and saw the lithe figure of Jean approaching from the direction of the village gate.

Janet pushed past Dixie, wild and out of place. Ethan held onto his mother roughly but protectively. "I need to see Ellen!" said Janet over and over, because it was the only thing she knew how to say. Alan mounted the steps, and Janet kept her eyes everywhere but on him as she edged behind the counter. Jill lowered the woman onto the seat and anxiously addressed the angry man.

"I think maybe you ought to leave your wife here for a while?" she offered, holding a hand in the air against him.

Alan's eyes blazed. "She's my *wife*! Why the *fuck* would I leave her with you people?"

Jill was alarmed to find herself between the warring parties. Alan's eyes were bulging and she could smell his breath. "I don't think she wants to see you right now. That is her right you know… You can come back later." Dixie moved forwards cautiously, pleased to see Jean who had appeared quietly in the doorway and was leaning with folded arms.

Alan suddenly raised his fists and bellowed like a mad bull. Dixie grabbed the man's arms and kneed him heavily in the stomach. Janet jumped to her feet sensing her escape as Alan groaned, momentarily winded, and then hit out wildly at Dixie but missed. Ethan forced his mother back down onto the chair and then ran full pelt at his father, aiming at his stomach with his head. Jean entered the fray as Alan got the boy round the throat, and there was a violent scuffle. Jill screeched in horror as one of the big carvings tottered and fell. Janet was up again and hurrying for the door. *"Ellen!"* she screamed, feeling oddly liberated. Jean and Dixie were still fighting to gain control of Alan as Ethan broke free. Staggering and coughing, he tripped down the steps and floundered on the dusty ground.

Janet was running again, just able to make out the village gate through the fog that seemed to envelop her. She could hear all kinds of shouting – her son crying in the distance – her husband swearing – Ethan calling. Her legs were leaden and it felt as though the ground was grinding upwards into her hips as dark trees bounced up and down and everything spun and roared in her ears. She reached the village gateway and heard sheep bleating as she carried on between the eucalyptus trees. She remembered those trees from Ellen's letters… they sounded nice in the wind, she'd said. Janet could hear them now, those trees, as she began to slow and stumble. Gradually she stopped, becoming aware that people were surrounding her. Sobbing and exhausted she sank down into a huddle on the path, certain at last of what she really wanted. "Please keep my husband away from me," she said into the gravel in a calm firm voice just as Ethan caught her up. The boy looked down at her and then back at the gate. The noise had stopped and his father was nowhere to be seen.

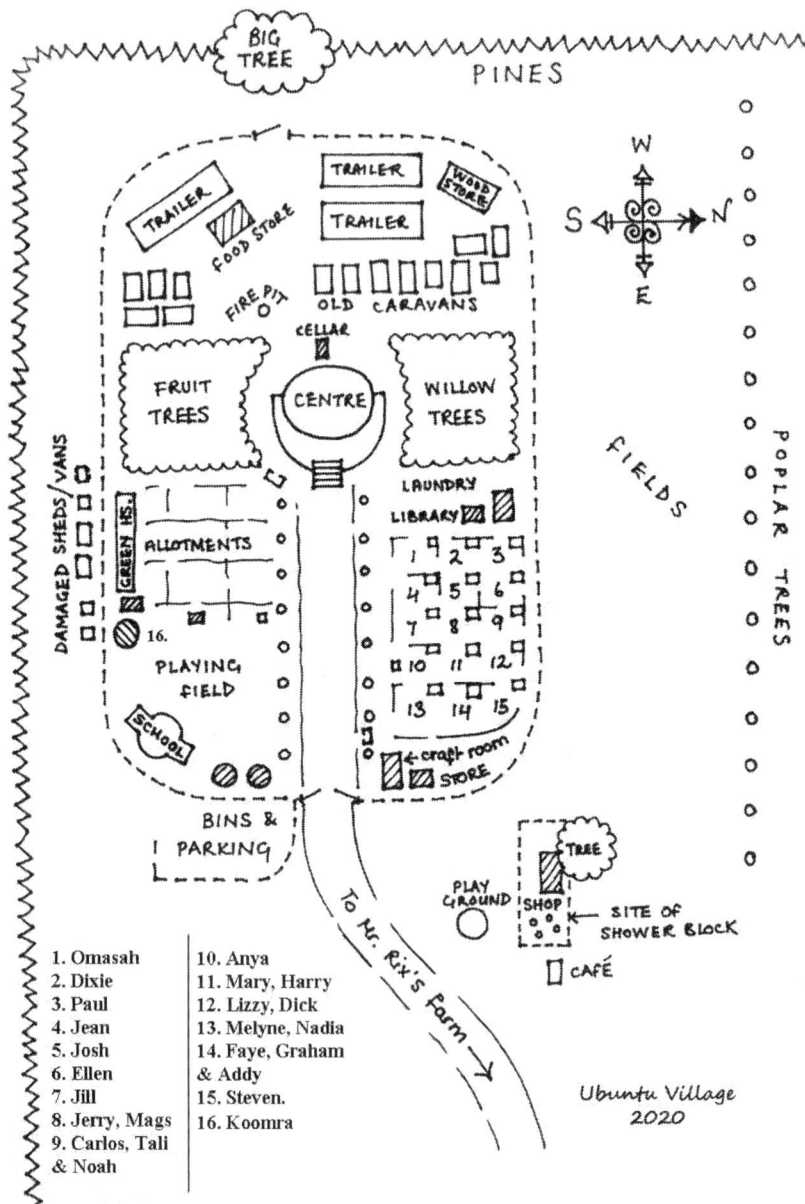

BIG TREE

PINES

TRAILER

TRAILER

WORD STORE

TRAILER

FOOD STORE

FIRE PIT

OLD CARAVANS

W
S — N
E

CELLAR

FRUIT TREES

CENTRE

WILLOW TREES

FIELDS

DAMAGED SHEDS/VANS

GREEN HS.

ALLOTMENTS

LAUNDRY

LIBRARY

1 2 3
4 5 6
7 8 9
10 11 12
13 14 15

16.

PLAYING FIELD

SCHOOL

← craft room
STORE

POPLAR TREES

BINS & PARKING

To Mr. Rix's Farm →

PLAY GROUND

TREE

SHOP

SITE OF SHOWER BLOCK

CAFÉ

Ubuntu Village
2020

1. Omasah
2. Dixie
3. Paul
4. Jean
5. Josh
6. Ellen
7. Jill
8. Jerry, Mags
9. Carlos, Tali
& Noah

10. Anya
11. Mary, Harry
12. Lizzy, Dick
13. Melyne, Nadia
14. Faye, Graham
& Addy
15. Steven.
16. Koomra

Part 3

1

April, 2020

The breeze made the white curtains billow and the air smelt of spring. Gina liked it when the curtains did that because it gave her a nice feeling inside. It was lovely weather for the time of year – good for dog-walking she thought, stroking her Bull Terrier's big warm sleepy head. She needed to get up; should have got up ages ago in stead of just taking her pills and getting back into bed to watch the telly. She sighed and turned the set off. "Better get going I s'pose, Ghostie," she told the dog, and sat up fighting against the pain in her back and upper arms.

She picked up a book lying on the bedside table and leafed through the pages to where her marker lay. No, she mustn't start reading again now. Ghost needed her walk, and the fresh air would do them both good. The woman walked stiffly to the music system and pressed PLAY; then she crossed the hall to the bathroom. As she put the plug in the bath and turned the tap, a soothing murmur of wind through trees filled the air, punctuated by the twittering of birds. She fetched her phone from the lounge and sat on the laundry basket, scrolling down to "MUM."

"Hello love," said a voice very like her own.

"Hiya. Only me. Thanks for the book and CD and the stone. I was reading that book till quite late last night. It's quite interesting. And that CD's so nice and relaxing – I've got it on now."

"Oh, that's good, Gina. You should go up there, you know. The shop's full of the kind of stuff you like. Really nice bags and masks and things, but I didn't want to choose for you. You'd love it, honest."

"What, African masks?"

"Yeah, and candles and wind-chimes and stuff. All homemade. Perhaps you could ask to help out up there. It wouldn't affect your money."

"Oh, I don't know, Mum. I wouldn't have the guts… Couldn't you ask them?"

The reply was firm but kind: "No."

"Anyway, they aren't going to want someone like me with all the problems I've got. What if I have to take loads of days off?"

"They're nice people, Gina. Just go up and get a feel for it. You'd only be volunteering – helping out. So what would it matter if you took time off?"

"But I hate letting people down, Mum. You know that."

There was a pause at the other end of the line. "You're assuming the worst again, Gina. They're animal-lovers; they've got the same interests as you. If you read the book you'll see what I mean. Just go and look at the shop. You look round shops in town, so what's the difference?"

"Yeah, but I'm used to them. I'd get all anxious, Mum – you know me."

There was another pause. "Well, how about we go up the café one day next week and take Ghost? We'll have a baked spud or something and you can go and look round the shop, and then I'll be there in case. How about that?"

Gina held the phone against her shoulder as she unscrewed a bottle of bubble bath. She watched the long rose-pink string as it flowed into the water and started to froth. "Oh I dunno, Mum. I'll have to think about it. Anyway, I'm going to have my bath now. I'll probably pop round later." She pulled the band from her hair and scratched her head. "Thanks Mum. Love you. See you soon."

The sweet sugary smell of the bath foam blended with incense from the lounge. A slim black and white cat curled in and out of the woman's legs as she went to select clean clothes, and as the curtains billowed again she thought how pretty the bedroom looked. Today was a good day... to think that only a week ago she had hardly been able to get out of bed. And then her doctor's voice had sounded cold and uncaring on the phone, which had made her feel even worse. Still... what could he do for her anyway apart from give her more pills, and she was adamant she didn't want to go any further down that road? She sighed as she laboured indecisively over what to wear. It might be a better day but still nothing looked right. But as she hung her pink dressing gown on the back of the bedroom door she remembered something, and picked up a smooth flat white pebble from the bedside table. She held it in her hands and closed her eyes. "Thank you for my Mum and my animals and my nice hot bath," she said, and slipped the stone into the pocket of the jeans she had picked out to wear.

2

April, 2020

Maxwell stopped behind the corner of a big post office building and leaned against the wall. His chest heaved, and he felt exhausted, crushed, and close to giving himself up. But no – he couldn't hear anything… must have lost them at long last. Good job too, because he was nearing his destination… had unfinished business down in Norfolk. It was a better place for him in the long run, he realised that now: there were fewer homeless and barely any cops. These days he felt sure no one would recognise him either: his hair and beard were getting long, and the few times he had braved a mirror recently had startled him.

He opened the blue leather handbag and fished about inside: powder compact; keys; lipstick; tissues… he pulled out a purse eagerly. Bingo! A stack of notes! At last he could buy some booze again. He counted them, panting heavily: forty pounds and some coins. He stuffed the lot into his coat pocket and searched about for somewhere to dispose of the bag. With a glance left and right, he crossed the quiet street and peered over the wall into the river. Another quick look about, and then he tossed the bag over, watching it spin slowly and start to fill with water as it floated away.

He washed his face roughly with an old cracked bar of soap in a chilly Victorian toilet block and ran his fingers through his hair. The streets weren't too busy with it being a week day, and Maxwell soon found a corner shop where a stony-faced Indian man sold him a cheap bottle of whisky and a large meat pie. After a few grateful sips he headed towards some trees, eventually finding himself in an enormous graveyard where tall pale statues stood sentinel-like between the smaller stones. Once inside, he made for the remotest corner which was overhung by a twisted tree, and where he found traces of previous rough sleepers: burnt wood, dog ends, empty cider cans and a thin damp mattress covered in pine needles. Pleased, he sat down and pulled out his bottle.

At around midnight Maxwell sat up, stirred from a thick dreamless sleep by voices. He searched about for his bottle and took a couple of generous slugs to wake himself up and ease his aching head. As he replaced the cap he listened intently. Voices on the breeze... young girls' voices.

The unspeakable desire dropped upon him like an unseen hunter as he got to his feet and urinated luxuriously against the low cobbled wall. Then he slunk hulk-like towards the sounds, wiping spittle from his beard. There was no plan in it – just an aching burning need. Such an irresistible, titillating, exhilarating act, and well worth losing his sleeping-place for. He stopped behind a large obelisk, smelling marijuana smoke... could see them now: two girls sitting on a low tomb, giggling together. Maxwell was consumed with a powerful urge to laugh as he began fumbling with his clothing.

3

April, 2020

The warm evening had become still and soundless. Janet and Ethan sat in the shade of apple saplings on the long wooden bench that hugged the curved wall of the centre building. Janet was red-faced and mascara-streaked in her gaudy dress, and Ethan slouched alongside her with his hood up. For the third time his hand dipped into his pocket in search of his phone, and found nothing. He found himself studying his mother's legs and finding them repulsive.

The boy looked away to his left to see Ellen approaching with a black dog and a slim young girl in a long pale blue dress. With a kind of electric shock Ethan recognised her as his old crush from the chip-shop, and hid his face. She was older now: taller and even more beautiful than he remembered, and suddenly everything felt surreal, like a strange movie playing at half-speed.

"Janet!" cried Ellen, running up and hugging her. The girl had slowed her steps, and was hanging back uncertainly.

Janet immediately became a cacophony of wailing and coughing, and although Ethan felt embarrassed for her he realised that some of her tears were for him. His neck burned and ached and he felt hot and stupid in his thick hoodie, but he couldn't face anyone's reaction to his injuries – wanted so much to be left alone, and yet…

Ellen was talking kindly to his mother, offering a bed for the night; a bath; a meal and a glass of wine… "Don't give her wine!" blurted Ethan before he could stop himself. Janet looked crazily at him. "Sorry, mum," he said to her, meaning it. "But please try not to have any wine…" Feeling his voice begin to break, he sank back inside his hood, seeing the girl's pretty bare feet on the decking.

"You must stay Janet," said Ellen. "We'll look after you. You don't have to do anything. You can just rest. You won't have any worries. There are people here who can help – we've got a doctor… and a masseuse."

Janet blew her nose noisily. "I'm such a mess, Ellen. And I haven't brought my phone… or my pills." She began fanning herself with her hand.

Ellen looked into her friend's face. "The silver lining is that you're here. Trust me – this is meant to be." She hugged her again, stroking the hunched shoulders. "Anya – take Ethan to see Paul and them, will you?" Then Ellen addressed the boy for the first time. "You can have something to eat if you like. Don't be afraid to ask, will you?" And suddenly he was alone with the girl in the pallid light.

The girl was watching him with an expression he couldn't read as he wondered where to put his hands and feet, and all around her face fine sun-kissed hairs had drifted gently free. "Where did you go?" he said at last. Anya didn't answer, but stood fondling the dog's head.

Ethan stared miserably at the trees, feeling her eyes upon him. "Where did you go?" he repeated, looking into her eyes for a second. She still said nothing and he hung his head. Perhaps she didn't understand what he meant. Or maybe she despised him. He didn't know how to impress her – didn't know how to speak to her. Hot and flustered he pulled his hoodie up and off over his head, making sure he exposed his flat muscled stomach as he did so. Then he looked towards her again.

Seeing his bruises she came forwards, her face full of tenderness. Without thinking she raised a hand to his neck, saying breathlessly, "What happened?" The hand dropped away limply.

Ethan kept his eyes on her face. "My dad did it."

Her lips parted slightly as her eyes searched his face. "I can't imagine… My dad… would never hurt me." And then she was gone, and disconnected from him again.

"Where did you go?" he said, missing her closeness. Her mouth immediately became sulky, and it made him want to smile. "Please tell me," he said, standing up and taking her arm. She shook him off.

"I'd better take you to see Paul."

"But what if I don't want to?"

"Well, you have to."

"Who says?"

Anya looked pained and Ethan felt it acutely. They stared at each other in emotion. "Please," he said finally. "Please let me stay with you for a while."

She didn't move, but he registered the fleeting twitch of a smile. She was becoming readable. Ethan sat down again and looked up at her beseechingly. Bit by bit and little by little she moved towards him, joining him at last on the bench and resting her head against the wall. A soft breeze stirred through the saplings and the boy began to speak as though roused by them. "I spent a fortune in that place. I went in there every Friday for months hoping to see you again. My mates thought I was nuts." He sighed very slowly and very deeply, hanging his head again. "I know what it must be. I know why you stopped coming in. I bet you saw me acting like a jerk…" He turned to her quickly. "Is that it? Is that what happened? Because that wasn't me. That wasn't the real me, you know. You must believe me, Anya."

The smile tugged at her lips again at the sound of her name, and her hands slipped into his as though they had always been there. She was searching his face deeply again. "How can you not be the real you?"

Ethan looked into the blue-green eyes and saw such kindness and such beauty and such innocence that it rent his chest and stole his breath. "I am now," he said.

4

April, 2020

Steven stared out at the subtle lavender sky and then down at his painting. His mind began juggling the mix of colours in the evening clouds along with the dubious composition of his latest picture. He needed to switch off.

He laid his paper down and went outside to feed the chickens. He had spent the afternoon listening to a play on the radio as he worked, and tucked away in the corner of the village he was unaware that anything out of the ordinary had taken place – any occasional shouts had been absent-mindedly processed as children's games. His nose sniffed the air as he checked his watch. The coup needed cleaning but it was too late to do it today. As he walked down his path he caught sight of Ellen weaving her way between the little houses, followed by a woman in a bright dress. Seeing her wave he leaned against the shed, waiting.

Ellen spoke in a low voice as she passed him: "I need your bedside manner." Steven followed the two women into the house in uncertainty. Janet was already seated on his sofa, looking woeful. As he sat down opposite, he had never felt less like a doctor. Ellen explained quickly: "This is Janet, Steve. She's here for a rest. She's just out of a violent relationship. You obviously haven't heard… there was a big showdown in the shop earlier. She might need to discuss her pills with you because she's left them in the camper."

Steven registered Janet's startled reaction to the words "just out of a violent relationship." He crossed his legs and tried to feel professional. "So what's been going on, Janet?" he said, in the most relaxed manner he could muster.

"Ask me another of your funny questions," said Ethan from the beanbag.

"Don't take the pee."

"I'm not. I could answer them all night."

Anya made a little flirtatious act of considering as she swung herself from side to side on the big black chair, pushing with her bare toes. "What's your favourite tree?"

The boy smouldered at her; amused, but loving the vision of her. "I dunno. What's yours?"

"Well," she said; "the silver birch is prettiest, but I like the huge big ancient ones too – they're like old souls that have seen so much." She leaned forward, and her happiness was infectious and flooded through him. "Would you like to see our big tree where we have barbecues?" She got up out of the chair and offered him her hand. He hauled himself up and lingered at the table by the window, gently stroking her closed diary with his palm. "That's private," she said as she joined him and laid her head against his upper arm. She smelt like she had always been there. "I can show you this though…" She lifted the book and let it fall open at several loose pieces of paper. She took one out and held it up. He took it, wonderingly.

"It's me…"

"I often drew you… before I went off you." She laughed, snapping the book shut and taking his hand again. "Come on."

279

"If you go back now things will carry on just the same, Janet. There are refuges for women like you. You must let us contact social services. Things changed today when your husband attacked your son. From what Ellen says it was quite brutal." Steven sat with his elbows on his knees feeling fraught, and his hair was untidy from running his fingers through it.

Janet's eyes were stinging behind their closed lids. She couldn't visualise anything but her old bedroom and the safety of the drawn curtains. The vision still felt like home – it had been her sanctity for so long – and Alan still held the leash firmly, as though seated beside her, breathing down her neck.

"You used to be free," said Ellen. "You used to be your own person, remember? Yes, we were young and directionless; but back then you were often more together than I was. You deserve joy in your life, Janet; just as much as anyone does. Is that so foreign to you? He's stolen you from yourself. He's convinced you there's no life outside, when the opposite is true."

"Ethan attacked Alan first," said Janet, not knowing what else to say and feeling the statement fall flat and useless in the quiet room. She smoothed her dress over her thighs and looked tragically at the doctor. "I need to sleep so much, and I know I just won't be able to without my wine and pills."

Steven leaned back in his seat, looking at Ellen. "Could Omasah help, d'you think?"

"I'm sure he'll call by. But first I'd better help Janet and Ethan get settled."

Steven knew that a sudden withdrawal from alcohol and sleeping tablets could be nasty, and guessed that like most alcoholics Janet had probably been drinking far more than she would admit to. He got to his feet and moved Ellen aside. "Maybe a few sips of brandy or something here and there," he whispered quickly. "Or she could get palpitations and sweats and heaven knows what by morning. She's stressed enough as it is." He dug his hands into his pockets with a grim look. "The way some of these GPs dish out pills is criminal."

Ellen nodded and addressed Janet with a smile. "Let me take you somewhere to rest. We'll talk more tomorrow."

"What about my other boys?" Janet snivelled tearfully. "Zack was screaming and I just… ran away."

Ellen was starting to feel exhausted with the pressure of saying the right thing. "I'll call your house and check on them if you like." She didn't want to, but was prepared to do it if it helped. Alan didn't frighten her.

Janet looked uncertain as she rubbed her face with a soggy tissue. "I'll think about it," she said.

Ethan, Anya and the dog nestled together on the cool earth beneath the great tree as a lone blackbird's song rang out between poignant silences. The sun was setting behind them, and the windows of the village and farmhouse burned orange under the dark eastern sky. Ethan's head rested on the girl's shoulder as she spoke to him freely and unaffectedly about her life, her family, her village – her likes and dislikes. As he absorbed her words he felt them fill the empty spaces inside him, and with the soft tone of her voice reason crept into the world. The girl fell quiet, and he kissed her very gently on her forehead, breathing her in. "Tell me about your life," she said to him.

"No," he answered.

The blackbird called again, finishing with an audacious

upward whistle that split the night air and made Anya giggle. "They're so funny sometimes." She looked at him, suddenly flustered and wide-eyed. "Oh, my God."

"What?" He stroked her cheek with one finger. "What is it?"

"I don't want you to go!"

They stared at each other for an interminable moment, turning the ugly scenario over in their minds. Ethan looked at the soft curve of her neck and the shadows of her eyelashes and the swell of her lips. He ached for the whole untouched part of her, and yet she felt sacred. What he'd had with other girls had been all sweat, noise and conquest; but this was different. This was excruciatingly tender and it made confused tears burn and quickened his breath.

"I'm not going," he said and kissed her again, softly like a feather.

"I'm afraid there's no electricity," said Ellen, pushing open the door to the one of the new roundhouses. The sweet clean smell of fresh new thatch filled the air inside. Ellen put a small glass of brandy on the wooden table where three of Addy's big candles sat on a plate. She lit them one by one and the cosy room filled with rosy light. There were two single beds, two chairs and a small cupboard with a few books on top. The beaten earth floor had a rug in its centre, and on the newly-painted wall hung a couple of Steven's watercolours. At the side of the door-frame dangled a string of red sequined birds. "It's so lovely," said Janet sitting down on one of the beds. "Thank you!"

Ellen took a chair, crossing her legs. "How're you feeling?"

"Like nothing's real." Janet's eyes looked far off, and then she smiled fondly. "We did used to have fun, didn't we?

Whatever went wrong… for me, I mean?"

"It wasn't all roses. But yes, we did have fun." Ellen sighed and looked up at the cavernous roof, and the smell of the straw was comforting. She let her past life play out in her head for a minute. "It's so hard being human. We all make such awful mistakes – or at least most of us do." She winced. "D'you know, Janet? I still remember the incredible feeling of love when Maxwell took me in his arms for the first time. It was like… honey."

A pigeon began calling loudly from the woods. The two women sat listening. "Alan used to shoot pigeons," remarked Janet in a croaky voice. "I just don't know how he could ever do that."

Ellen hung her head for a moment. "You rest while I find Ethan. Just a sip of that brandy if you need to take the edge off, Janet…" Ellen kicked herself for sounding tense and bossy. Softening her tone she said, "The loo's outside I'm afraid, on the other side of the playing field. There's one in the school too, but mind the sheep. I'd better bring you a torch." She paused. "Would you like me to ring him?"

"I'm still not sure."

"Alright. See you later." Ellen went out and pushed the door shut, and Janet stared after her.

Several figures were crouched near the small fire glowing warmly outside Dixie's workshop, and the sound of Paul's guitar carried gently. Ellen approached the group and stopped. "Where's Ethan?"

"Haven't seen him," said Dixie around an unlit cigarette.

Ellen's blood ran cold, but before she could think how to react she caught sight of Anya's long pale skirt moving towards them in the half-light from the direction of the centre. The two youngsters emerged into the firelight, and Ellen saw that Anya was wearing Ethan's hoodie. Her heart sank – wherever had they been? She couldn't help glaring at Ethan, instantly full of suspicion. She loved Anya as her own. The boy met her gaze calmly, and she noticed a strange confidence about him that was hard to place.

A sturdy breeze pushed at the nearby tree-tops and the men heard it and looked up as one. "Welcome Ethan," said Jean. "How you feeling?"

The boy's reply came thinly: "Okay, thanks."

Ellen strode forwards, taking his arm. "Come on. Your mum's waiting."

Anya's face was strained and pleading. Ethan turned to her and smiled tenderly. "I'll see you tomorrow." The girl stood watching with Zoki at her side as they disappeared into the night. Then she turned to the men, wondering whether or not to sit down. Paul began tuning his guitar with his head cocked low towards the strings. The air stirred, and the fire sparked and swelled for a second.

"You know, Anya," laughed Jean, wanting to cheer her; "Paul keeps a pair of socks inside his guitar to make good the sound. It's the truth!"

The wind gusted powerfully again in the trees, and the group looked skyward except for Paul. He didn't move, but the ex-sailor in him registered it over his strings. "Don't like the sound of that," he said.

As soon as they were out of ear-shot Ellen turned to the boy so aggressively that he raised both hands in defence. "Nothing happened, Ellen. I swear to God. She's… too precious… for that."

Ellen stood stock still, trying to catch sight of his eyes. She believed him, but still felt like her world was falling apart. She couldn't think of what to say. Her anger rose again and she pointed a finger at him. "You don't touch her Ethan! You don't bloody touch her!" She marched away. "Come on…"

At the roundhouse door Ethan pulled at her T shirt, struggling to see her face under the big black overhang of thatch. "I won't Ellen. It's not like that. I… don't even want to. I don't see her like that. She's too young anyway."

"Yeah, like that bothers you. Like that bothers anyone your age. Your mum's told me how you've been recently, Ethan. You think she doesn't know what you've been watching? *And* doing?"

His voice was gruff with emotion. "What I've been doing with girls has nothing to do with how I feel about Anya. But that's just the way it is. That's life these days. I'd be a bloody freak if I'd never…" He tailed off and Ellen sensed tears as he said very quietly: "I'd give anything now… to have waited for someone like her. I don't give a toss if you believe me or not."

Ellen sighed and shut her eyes, wanting to trust him. She touched his shoulder lightly and opened the door to see Omasah seated on Janet's bed. The woman lay peacefully under the blankets, and Ellen saw that the brandy glass was untouched. Omasah stood up to take Ellen's hands. "Your friend will sleep now," he told her softly. Then he glanced at Ethan, who had thrown himself on the second bed and lay facing the wall. "His heart is pure."

The wind was rising outside and stirred the flames of the candles as it whistled through the half-open door. Ellen followed Omasah out into the night, registering a sudden drop in temperature. She watched the eucalyptus trees reeling with each gust and hugged herself. "So here comes the storm."

5

April, 2020

The children's bedroom was neat and tidy, and the floor was freshly vacuumed. Dark blue star-speckled curtains were closed against the violence of the wind and rain, and atop a large bookcase burned a large pyramid-shaped candle in shades of green. A stocky curly-haired boy entered carrying a box of white candles, a bag of food and some blankets. "I found some," he said. "Why have you lit it already, Pinky?"

His sister sat on the bed, leaning against a big poster of the solar-system. "Because it makes a nice atmosphere, like in Anya's shed. Anyway, I didn't light it – Shiny did. You know I can't do matches."

A toilet flushed out in the hall and a short-haired girl in dungarees strode through the door. "I've got blankets and more candles," the boy told her. "Why did you light Addy's? We need a store in case the lights go out."

The girl clambered onto the bed next to Pinky. "Because it's important to feel peaceful at a time like this. Anyway, we've got loads now so we'll be okay."

The wind howled outside and buffeted the window, and the mumbling of a television could be heard through the floor. Pinky fiddled nervously with her friendship bracelets. "What should we do?" she asked. "Are you going to read, Shiny; or should we play something, or just talk?"

"Well, let's have a conversation now before I read."

"Let's wrap ourselves up in our blankets," said the boy eagerly.

"You're being over the top, Fudge," Shiny told him. "We've still got heating. They're just in case."

"Yes, well we've got electricity. I wish we could have a proper fire. Then if it all went off we'd be warm while everyone else was cold."

Pinky giggled. "I don't think mum and dad would be very pleased if we lit a fire."

"They probably wouldn't even notice for a week," grumbled her little brother. His face looked briefly sulky and then lit up. "After school on our first day Addy's going to teach me to make those candles, and if mine are good enough they're going to sell them in the shop next to his ones."

"I think we should help in the craft-room after school in any case," said Shiny. "Jill said we can, and it's like a contribution for letting us join." Her eyes dulled for a second. "It's better than going home," she added.

Pinky became reflective. "I never thought I'd want to go to school, but it's so different with Jill, especially because of the freeness of it, and the sorts of thing we talk about."

"In my first free-time I'm going to draw a big robot where you can see all what's inside its body," said Fudge. His mind ticked over. "On a really huge piece of paper."

Shiny beamed at her two friends. "I'm so glad I'm here with you two tonight. It's kind of exciting, don't you think?"

They fell silent as the mumbling from downstairs was interrupted by applause and whooping. The wind grew suddenly frenzied, and whistled shrilly through the vents at the top of the window. "I'm going to make these," said Pinky, showing off her bracelets. "What are you going to make, Shiny?"

"Everything, but I'm particularly interested in the dolls. I like those best because of the concept."

"What's a concept?" asked Fudge.

"Well, it's like an idea. You can't see it or touch it. Like our gang is a concept."

"You can see me and I'm in our gang."

"Yes, but the ideas behind it are a concept. Like Ubuntu is a concept."

The rain beat aggressively at the window. "I hope the village will be alright," said Pinky quietly. "It'd be terrible if it all got ruined."

A faraway look passed over Shiny's face. She sighed and got off the bed, fetching a huge tatty copy of *The Lord of the Rings* from the bookcase. She stood leafing through the pages for a few seconds, and then turned to face the others. "Ubuntu will always be alright. Wind can't destroy a concept. Nothing can."

6

April, 2020

"Hello?" said a young voice. Ellen felt relieved – perhaps she wouldn't need to speak to Alan after all.

"Is that Tyler?"

"Yeah – d'you want dad?"

"Er… Can you take a message?" Ellen immediately became doubtful. What if the boy forgot? She was being irresponsible. "No, actually… can you get him, please? It's Ellen." She waited, hearing muffled voices. The phone was grabbed noisily.

"Yes?"

"Hi, Alan. I just wanted you to know that Janet and Ethan are okay and they're spending a few days with us in the village."

"Yes."

"In case you were worried, that's all."

"Right." There was a tense silence and he hung up. With a sigh Ellen turned to Mr Rix in his armchair.

"He hung up," she said. "But at least he knows."

"Anything I can do, my dear?"

"No, thank you Mr Rix."

"Big storm coming they say. People have been panic-buying."

"We'll be alright. I'd better get back. Good night, Mr Rix." She stroked the greyhound's head. "Good night, Sage."

As Ellen took to the dark farm track, the intensity of the rising wind made the lights of the little village seem all the more welcoming. Stopping outside the gateway, she looked up at the big fence with its long fronds waving and Steven's wind turbine whirring away to her right. And then her eyes gleamed as she saw the fruits of her dreams as though for the first time. "We did it! We built it!" she called out to the speeding clouds, and pushed open the big wattle gate and latched it behind her.

Passing by Koomra's house she felt she must call in, and found her raving with Omasah at her side. The noise of the wind wasn't helping, and the old woman continually shifted and wound herself up in her bedclothes, and her hair was a grizzled mess. She was complaining of a headache and was much more confused than usual. "There's a huge shift coming across from the west!" she moaned, wild-eyed from her pillow.

"I think you mean the storm," smiled Ellen.

"I will sit with her," said Omasah. "She senses much."

She looked into his face in curiosity. "You feel a very deep bond with her, don't you?"

He tried to take the old woman's hand but she wrestled it free. "She is a diverse and ancient soul, Kaphalya. She will continue in many ways, through many lives and many times."

Outside the wind was swelling and crying as Koomra held her head and wailed. "The vibrations are getting stronger! To let the people know we must save Gaia! Everything is dying! Everything is plundered!" Her voice became thin and heartbroken. "The rape of the mother. The rape of the land…"

She closed her eyes at last, allowing Omasah to touch her brow, and Ellen slipped back out into the turbulence of the night.

Next morning Mr Rix came trotting in at the village gate in his wellies and made for the craft-room. "Oh, Miss Faye," he exclaimed hoarsely from the doormat, wiping his boots vigorously and shaking his big umbrella. "Please – you must tell Paul. This storm is getting terrible. It's all over the news…"

The sound of wind and pouring water deadened Faye's soft voice. "We know, Mr Rix. Everyone's busy making safe right now." From somewhere the noise of hammering reached them before being swallowed again by the rain.

Mr Rix was quite frantic. "But Miss Faye – it's category three!"

The rain had begun falling in the early hours – no steady pattering but a monstrous roar. They had worked in waterproofs to alleviate the mess, digging channels and throwing down sacks and boards. The sheep had been shut inside a stripped-out caravan that stood lodged against the north-side of one of the heavy trailers, but the children worried for them terribly. At first light Josh had taken the tractor and towed the café van to the north-west end of the fence, hearing crockery tumbling and smashing as he went, and kicking himself for not having thought to pack it away first.

Since Omasah's timely warning, Paul and Dixie had been preparing the homes one by one, adding metal loops to the roofs and concrete bases. Luckily, Paul still had a good deal of rope from his sailing days, and they had passed a request among local fishermen for more. The two new roundhouses had been built with raised doorways and all the new turbines could be lowered to the ground in high winds. Finally, Paul had built up a store of sandbags, taking the truck down to the beach in the evenings and filling a few plastic bags at a time.

Opinion quickly became split as to whether they should sit the coming hours out in the village or take refuge in the farmhouse. Paul, Dixie and Josh insisted on remaining, claiming they would be safe in the root cellar. Jean wanted to stay with them but eventually agreed to take his sister to the house. Jill was ambivalent, finally choosing Josh and the cellar, and Koomra wouldn't budge an inch. As one villager after another appealed to her over the roaring of the wind she became even more confused and frightened. "We must let her be! We can't make her come!" shouted Steven frantically, and with reluctance they left her weeping and rocking over her knitting in the dark. As the last stragglers took to the open ground beyond the fence Ellen looked back, and was relieved to see the windswept figure of Omasah entering the roundhouse.

She struggled after the others, almost losing them in the dark sheet of rain as she held her two trembling dogs close to her body. The wind suddenly upped itself and ahead of her she saw someone fall and flounder. "God," she thought, as water streamed down her face and into her hood. "How are we ever going to get through this?"

Inside the big cosy farmhouse Mr Rix was doing his best to feed and entertain everybody like Olive would have done, while Lizzy and Mags fought for control of the kitchen. "Sit down and relax, Mr Rix," said Mags over the clattering of cups and spoons. "We do this every day. We're used to it."

Jerry leaned against a cupboard gloomily with his hands

in his pockets. "Should've brought the bread-maker... it'd gimme something to do."

"I got some extra bread yesterday," announced Mr Rix, proudly. "The shelves were nearly empty, you know. People panic when there's anything like this."

Next-door the crowded lounge smelt overpoweringly of rain and mud from the piles of wet boots heaped on newspapers, and the many dripping coats that hung on hooks and chairs. Mr Rix wandered in with a packet of biscuits and sat down at last, lamenting the damage from the nails that held boards over his windows. Ethan and Anya sat quietly together, safe in the comfort of each other, while Ellen and Steven chatted quietly with Janet. Harry had commandeered Mr Rix's ancient banjo and was experimenting with it, lost in concentration, while at his side Mary sat fretting and pale. In the corner the muted television played out a repeating satellite image of the huge weather system as it crawled across the country, while the death-toll ran again and again across the bottom of the screen.

As the storm approached its zenith they ate sandwiches dejectedly for lunch and waited. The din became torturous. Addy cuddled up to Faye and sucked at his thumb with his eyes shut as she blocked his ears against the shuddering thunder. Through the cracks in the boards the sky could be seen streaming overhead as branches and debris hit the house with bangs and crashes that made the children scream and sent baby Noah into a fit of crying. Then with an almighty hammering the lights went out, and they huddled in the dim room devoid of a single candle.

Seated beside Anya, Ethan shut his eyes and gazed into the soothing dark. He gradually became aware of his breathing, and it felt slow and comfortable. "I feel funny," he told her.

"Funny how?"

"Just completely different. Being with you, especially. I don't know, Anya. It's like I already know you. Like I feel completely with you, and like you understand all about me."

"Maybe we met in a past life."

"Do you believe in that?"

"Not believe exactly. But I like to think it's possible."

Ethan's brow furrowed as he picked through his emotions. "You're so kind and nice and real... and happy. It's like... fresh air."

He breathed her in and held it, not wanting to let go.

She waited, listening. "Breathe out!" she giggled. They touched foreheads in the dark as he exhaled gently. "I'm here, Ethan. You don't have to hold onto anything. Just imagine we're in a boat together, floating downstream."

The remainder of the day passed numbly and slowly, with it being too dark to read and too noisy to speak much or play music. When, towards nightfall, the wind at last began to abate, spirits rose little by little. Conversation felt like a long-lost luxury, the children began chatting together, and there was the welcome sound of Nadia's giggles from the corner. Tali slept with Noah in her arms, Mr Rix dozed in his chair and Mags put a large pan of water on the gas for hot drinks. Ellen went cautiously to one of the windows and peered out between the cracks. A dark battlefield met her eyes, strewn with broken branches and soaked with puddles. Through the gloom, she caught sight of the lone tree waving blackly in the wind behind the shop. She laid her head against the glass feeling grateful that it had survived as the conversation around her gained in momentum.

"Let's draw straws to see who goes to get some candles," said Nadia.

"Oh, I'm such a fool for not having any," groaned Mr Rix.

Addy's voice was indignant: "There are hundreds in the shop. And in my house."

"Who's got the biscuits?" asked Dick.

"I think you've had quite enough of those, my sweet."

Ellen picked her way across to where she had been sitting as Mags entered the room with a tray of cups in her hands and a torch between her teeth. Jean sat cross-legged on the floor wearing a peaceful expression, his fingers working at a rosary in his lap. Ellen touched his arm fondly as her other hand turned the stone over and over in her pocket. "The worst of it's over. I guess we'd better think about trying to get back soon, don't you?"

At the kitchen table Ethan sat holding Anya's hand in the dark. "What do you think your friends will say when you tell them you're staying?" she whispered, stroking the softness of his palm with her thumb. Ethan felt a chasm yawn momentarily between them.

"I don't know. Maybe I won't tell them," he said, avoiding the question. The idea of sharing Anya with anyone felt nauseating. He automatically pictured his online world, once so dazzling and vibrant and now so far away. Sharing, liking, commenting. None of it was real. No breath or tender perfume like this new and most private space he now shared with her. Everything had dropped away when he had looked into her eyes, and the world had become reassuringly simple.

Being, not doing. Seeing, not watching. Feeling, not fleeing. Loving, not lusting. Savouring, not enduring.

Ethan felt the seconds nudging by, and said: "You know I thought you guys were totally nuts before I came here. I didn't want to come at all; I wanted to go to the arcades. I can't believe how I feel now."

Her voice was eager. "How *do* you feel?" Her hair touched his face and he spoke into the fragrant wisps.

"I feel like I understand why you've done it. I love it here. It makes my heart soar."

Anya laughed. "What?" he said, keen to know.

"That you can be so happy sitting in the dark in a hurricane." She laid her head on his shoulder. "It's good. It's all life. None of us knows why we're here. Carlos says we're part of the big bang that's still expanding, and Jerry says we're just here for the experience, but I guess it's up to you. But it's all life, and it's nice to share it."

"I feel ready for anything," he told her determinedly. "We'll fix that village up in no time." Ethan wished he could see her eyes: the way they always held him for an inviting second or two before letting go.

"Of course we will," she said, contentedly. She gave a small sigh then, seeing Ellen hovering in the dimly-lit doorway. Her voice altered its tone. "Hi, Ellen. You okay?"

"Mind if I sit?"

"'Course not," said Anya. Ethan dropped her hand and she re-took it. They heard the chair squeak as Ellen sat down and leaned back in the dark room. Ethan sensed her coldness and without a thought turned and spoke fearlessly, barely conscious of words that seemed to come from another place.

"Please don't be like this, Ellen. Please listen to me. I'm

not a threat to Anya. I'm not a threat to anyone. I've had a horrible life. I mean, it was okay when I was a kid, I guess. You know – all toys and games and everything's wonderful. But then I grew up. I'm not blaming mum, honest. Like Anya says – we all do our best, and she couldn't help it, and I think my dad's been a lot worse to her than she's let on. She must've been through hell, and with trying to cope with us… and me. But the good thing is it's brought me here. I want to be here more than anything. I love the people and… and I…" He tailed off, hanging his head in his customary way.

Ellen sat still and silent as though waiting for more, and the boy eventually continued, lost inside himself. "Please don't laugh. Please believe that I know that… it can't be any other way. I know I've only just met Anya, but sometimes you just know something is true. I feel like I'm… like I'm… melting." He choked. "Please let me stay, at least to help fix up the village. I'm sixteen soon, and if you send me away I'll just come back on my birthday, because then it'll be my right." He stopped speaking, not remembering any of it.

Ellen meanwhile had heard every word, and a softening passed unseen over her face. She folded her arms on the table and leaned towards the boy in the darkness. "You're alright, Ethan. You can stay."

At that moment a hearty cheer went up from the next room as Paul and the others came through the front door, and everyone waited tensely to hear their news. Paul spoke first, perched on the arm of Mr Rix's chair: "Well, it could've been a lot worse," he began in a peculiar voice that juggled optimism and worry. "The pines to the south drove the wind over us, which helped. We've lost some solar panels but we've still got tons in storage. The boards held the windows, but your turbine's down I'm afraid, Steve, and a few of the sheds are in a mess. Dixie's lost his workshop roof and both loos are gone… but all the homes are still standing." A second lesser cheer went up.

"A few trees have been ripped up but we should be able to replant," added Josh. "Three vans have gone over like dominoes." He turned to the children. "But the sheep are fine. Oh, yes… and erm… Jill and I are going to have a baby."

There was a fleeting silence and the room fell into uproar. Everyone rushed forward to talk at once and offer congratulations. Delight took Ellen's heart. Funny how things always seemed to work out so neatly: if Ethan was staying then presumably he'd need his own place, and now that this had happened Josh was sure to move in with Jill. As if reading her thoughts Josh jostled his way over to her and spoke in her ear. "The boy, Ellen – he's supposed to join us. Omasah knew about him before I even bought the land."

She smiled and hugged him. "I'm so happy for you, Josh. And yes – I guess it's meant to be.

7

April, 2020

After a second difficult night's sleep the salvage operation began in earnest the following day. The villagers gathered early, summoned by Paul banging lengthily on a metal dustbin lid. Normally the schedule for the day was loose and pliable, but this situation required them to organize. The only absentees were Koomra, whose mind still wandered; Omasah, who sat with her, and Harry, who was in bed. Mary was a flutter of worry and embarrassment until Paul reassured her that her husband's presence would in fact be more of a hindrance than a help.

By eleven o'clock Mags and Lizzy had already returned the café to its rightful spot and were fixing it up from boxes of spare crockery transferred from the trailers. As soon as it was shipshape they began work on a big pan of soup, while Jerry was reunited with his bread-maker. Janet helped the children with the work of clearing debris into bags – Ethan, meanwhile, hovered round the men and the damaged buildings until he was made use of. "Keen as mustard," were Josh's words as he took a well-earned coffee-break with Jill.

Most of the young chickpeas that filled a quarter of the outer field were flattened and broken, but it wasn't too late in the year to plant more. Fortunately, the rest of the ground was still waiting for sowing or lying fallow, meaning nothing more was lost. The allotments were in a sorry state, but Mr Rix said that some of the crops might survive the water-logging on the back of several dry weeks. Everyone celebrated this piece of news during what had become a precarious seesaw ride between good and bad. Ellen found herself feeling buoyant and grateful amid the stress and shock. Not only had Omasah's warning saved most of the village, but Paul's never-ending dedication and quietly-nurtured common sense had given them the root cellar and dry store – complete life-savers at a time like this.

At midday the CAT Gang arrived, heavily laden with garden brooms, bin-bags and a box of tools. "We're here for as long as you need us," announced Fudge proudly, and Jill ushered them off to help with the re-planting and general tidying. As she stood looking after them she felt a sudden flood of contentment. Presumably these children heralded the "osmosis" that Carlos had spoken of back in January. She touched her lower abdomen tenderly, wondering briefly how the school would manage once she had the baby.

At lunchtime the villagers crowded exhaustedly into the centre streaking the floor with mud, and Harry did his bit on the guitar. Ellen sat with Mary, attempting to reassure her about Ethan over Mags's and Jill's clattering and endless chitchat. "You know – my cousin met his wife when they were both fourteen, and they're still together."

Mary stared into her mug of tea. "Well, yes of course I know it could work, and he seems like a nice boy. I mean he's giving up everything he knows to stay here."

Ellen considered, rubbing her eyes and already looking forward to her bed. "What does Harry think about it all?"

Mary gave a doleful kind of smile as she fiddled with the hairpins in the little bun at the back of her head. "Oh, he hasn't said anything, but I can see something in his eyes. He kind of goes with the flow, does Harry. Doesn't really like to interfere. It's strange how he is – I can't really explain it."

Work ceased at six in the evening, but Steven still pottered about trying to fix his turbine and avoid everyone else's company. He'd lost two chickens in the storm – their tiny necks snapped like twigs – and was finding it heartbreaking. From the peak of her roof Ellen surveyed the day's work with satisfaction before wandering down to find Ethan and Anya in Dixie's newly-repaired workshop. "Looks pretty good," she said, inspecting the corrugated iron roof which had ended upside-down in her own allotment.

"It's just a bit dented," said Anya, taking Ethan's hand.

Dixie had changed back into his shorts and was busy chipping away at a fresh lump of wood. "Working again already?" smiled Ellen.

Dixie laughed gently. "You know this isn't work to me. And anyway, I said I'd give Ethan a lesson."

The boy dropped his head self-consciously. "Woodwork was the only subject I ever liked," he said quietly.

Ellen leaned against the wall wondering what to say.

"Is my mum alright… with me?" asked Anya a little sorrowfully.

"Yes, my dear. Of course she is."

Ethan fondled Zoki's head, and his brow furrowed. "I'm causing a lot of trouble, aren't I?"

"It's not trouble, Ethan; it's an opportunity – yours and ours." Ellen stalled, seeing Dixie's emotional glance: it was obvious he'd already bonded with the boy, and she took his look to mean that she should lighten up. "School starts next week," she went on, brightly. "Your mum's going to speak to your headmaster on Tuesday, Ethan. We've got three other children joining as well."

"I've told him," said Anya. "We've gone from four to eight in one jump."

The boy stared down at his trainers, still stroking the dog. Ellen somehow knew then that there was nothing more to say, and no need for her worrisome hovering... because an aching need for love and home was all she would ever find here. She turned to him and he noticed a difference in her. "Thank you so much for all your hard work today," she told him, and was gone before he could reply.

8

April, 2020

The store light was out and Ellen figured the grid must still be down. She yawned as she quickly noted what was running short: it had been a long, long day. Descending the steps she noticed that the farmhouse was in darkness, and went to peer through the wind-shredded gate. A single candle burned in the lounge window, and Ellen wondered suddenly how the town was coping… the supermarkets probably wouldn't even be open. She tried to shove the subject from her mind as she started for home – there was certainly nothing she could do this late in the day, and the power was sure to be restored soon. But then she stopped and waited, thinking she heard a shout.

Yes – there it was again: a woman's voice. Ellen returned to the gate and unlatched it. "Hello?" she said, spying a figure advancing towards her in the dusk.

The newcomer was middle-aged, thin, and was weighed down with two enormous carrier bags. She wore a large fur-trimmed camouflage coat, and multicoloured leggings inside big lace-up boots. Her eyes were plaintive, and they drew Ellen in. "I'm sorry to be a pain," began the woman; "'Specially after this storm and everything, but my mum bought me the book and I was just wondering if you had any baby formula?

I don't want to be cheeky but the shops are shut till the power comes back, and my downstairs neighbour's got Bipolar and she's nearly run out and she hasn't even got any normal milk, and I don't drink it so I can't help. I can give you all this stuff here…"

She dropped the bags at Ellen's feet and the eyes became sadder. "It's my fault really. I should've checked. She don't know what she's doing half the time, bless her. But take the bags anyway… I'm sick of the bloody things cramming up my wardrobes." Gina stopped speaking, overcome with uncertainty.

Ellen felt faintly amused; she didn't know why. She also sensed a lumbering kind of sincerity in the woman, and a genuine desire to do the right thing – a heavy, humble compulsion as opposed to any smug obligation. Ellen immediately liked her. "Come on in," she said. "We have got some but it's right at the other end of the village." She picked up the heavy bags. "Gosh – this'll keep our craft-room in fabrics for a whole year."

"Well that's me," said Gina with a defeated look. "Always buying the wrong fuck… wrong stuff." She hesitated. "Are you sure you don't mind?"

Ellen looked into the blue eyes, searching for a connection. "I'm positive. Come on." She led the way through the tall gate and re-latched it. She didn't feel tired any more. "So did you like my book?"

"Oh, was it you what wrote it?" Gina exclaimed. "Well, I haven't finished it yet but it's very interesting. I don't blame you for wanting to build this place and get away from all the crap. This world's gone fucking nuts." She stopped. "Sorry – I shouldn't swear." Emotion took hold of her. "It's just awful.

I can't watch the news no more. It just makes me feel so awful."

Ellen turned to her in the gathering darkness. "Most of us don't follow it either," she said. "We're just trying to do some good and not cause any more damage. It's mostly fear-mongering anyway. I mean it'd be better if they balanced it out with a bit of good news, but they never do..."

Gina began warming to her subject. "Exactly, but everyone says you should know all what's going on, but you can't do nothing... apart from send money I s'pose, but then how d'you know the poor buggers are even getting it? 'Cause I can't sleep if I think about stuff too much. I lie awake all night thinking about all the poor little kids and climate change and cruelty to animals, and then I'm good for bloody nothing. I've got my neighbour and pets to look after."

"And that's good work," said Ellen. "What animals you got?"

Gina's voice turned warm and syrupy. "Well, I've got a blue Staff called Ghost, because I believe in them – ghosts and stuff – and two cats called Sugar and Spice. One of my cats has got three legs but it don't bother him. They're all rescue. I always get rescue ones. I think it's stupid the way they keep breeding dogs when there's so many what need homes."

"Me too. I've got two Jack Russells... called Jack and Russell!" They both laughed and began moving up the drive. Then Ellen put down the bags and pointed. "Look: we've got sheep over there. Come and see." Ellen took the newcomer's hands and they were soft and warm, and she suddenly realised she didn't even know the woman's name. "They're called Dorpers... they're quite rare. The RSPCA gave them to us. They're called Bumble and Phyllis."

Gina brightened even more. "Oh, how lovely."

A box of baby formula stood in the centre of Ellen's coffee table following an hour-long tour of the village by torchlight. Gina had made a big fuss of the sheep and any cats or dogs they had happened to meet. She had sat in the old Rover, admired the school and library, and tried out the washing machines – and the more she had seen the more talkative she had become. But as Ellen made drinks she dropped quickly back into self-doubt. "Are you sure I'm not being a pain?"

Ellen came down her kitchen steps. "The only thing that's a pain is you keep worrying about being a pain." She put down two mugs of ginger tea.

Gina smiled, trusting again. "You know I've really enjoyed looking round. I wanted to come up here and see, but I never had the guts before. But then tonight I couldn't think of no one else to ask… I guess it was meant to be." She picked up her mug. "Well, in any case I s'pose I'd better get back soon."

"I'll drive you if you like."

"You're alright. I'm used to walking."

They were quiet, sipping at their hot drinks.

"I was wondering…" ventured Gina with her most forlorn face. "I don't s'pose you want any help round here, do you? I could maybe look after them sheep and walk the dogs and stuff. I'd quite enjoy that… 'cause I prefer animals to people to be honest, 'cause they're so trusting and loving. I just love them." Her voice dwindled.

"That'd be great," said Ellen at once. "When could you start?"

Gina drained her cup. "Dunno. I'll let you know. Tomorrow maybe. I, er…" she glanced quickly at Ellen and then reached for the cushion next to her. She took it and hugged it to her chest. "I get depression. Really badly sometimes. I thought you should know."

"That's okay, Gina. Just come when you can."

Ellen unlatched the ragged gate and took Gina gently by the arm, saying: "I know exactly what you mean about animals, you know. There've been times when I've been so low that I couldn't bear to be awake, and so I'd just sleep and sleep." She paused, and her face relaxed. "A lot of times it was my dogs that pulled me through. Their warmth and their touch. The beautiful souls in their eyes, loving me… without condition."

"You don't seem like you could be depressed," said Gina in surprise.

"I've kind of learned to live round it. And to see things differently. But it was a long road."

Gina hesitated. "Would you talk to me some time, d'you think… about how you did it?"

They began walking through the gateway together. "Of course, although I think different things work for different people. And at the end of the day you still write your own story, Gina. The secret's in how you tell it…" She was turning the stone in her pocket, warm and smooth.

"I don't feel like I'm writing anything. I feel like it's writing me."

Ellen laughed. "Yes – it can feel like that. Or Paul says it's like a huge jigsaw and we're just one tiny piece. Trouble is it's not our picture – but that doesn't mean we don't matter."

Gina's face was frowning and serious. "I know what you mean, but life just seems so hard to me. And so pointless."

They were ambling along the dark farm-track now, unaware that they were moving. "Maybe it is pointless," sighed Ellen, realising that she was accepting ideas that had once disturbed her. "But is that so bad? Couldn't that be seen as… liberating?"

Gina suddenly stopped. "I do like you!" she exclaimed. "You're very interesting." Reserve crept back into her voice. "Sorry – is that a bit forward?"

Ellen hugged her. She smelt of perfume – sweet and fruity. "I like you too, Gina. And it's because you don't try to be anyone other than who you really are. You're a hell of a lot stronger than you think."

9

April, 2020

Inspector Maude clutched his takeaway coffee to his chest as he looked up at the big sprouting willow fence. He had heard about the project of course – mainly through his wife, who sometimes gave the village unwanted items and had bought a number of gifts from the shop. Passing through the gate he almost fell over a wheelbarrow as he became distracted by two sheep. The animals chewed slowly and stared as the policeman collected himself and looked about. They'd not fared too badly in the storm he thought, noticing a man at work on a nearby roof. He called to him through the silence: "Excuse me, sir – can you tell me where I might find Ellen Turner?"

The man descended his ladder and offered his hand. "I'm Paul Turner," he said. "Can I help at all?"

"Inspector Maude from Foxheath Police. It's nothing to be too concerned about, sir – but if I might just have a word with your wife?"

Ellen sat in her armchair trying her best to relax. Talking about Maxwell always disturbed her. "The last time I saw him was… er, the year before last I think," she said. "He was hanging around here quite a bit but then he stopped."

"Yes – he's been causing problems up north," the inspector replied between slurps of hot coffee. "Quite nasty. But now he's running again and we may've had a sighting. All I ask is that you let us know if you see him, alright? And pay attention – his appearance might have changed."

"I'd know him anywhere, believe me," said Ellen glumly.

The inspector got up to go, speaking with gravity. "Please take care, madam. And don't let your young girls out unaccompanied – he's been exposing himself. If you see him don't challenge him, will you?"

Ellen felt slightly sick. "No, I won't inspector – don't worry."

The policeman stopped on the doorstep to look up at the house as a ginger cat began snaking round his ankles. "Nice little homes these, aren't they? Nice little set-up you have here. My wife's very fond of your shop. She gets all her birthday presents there."

Ellen met Omasah in his allotment and he led her inside. "Do not fear, Kaphalya," he said. "The man is not close."

She smiled at the accuracy of the man's second sight, thankful as always for his quiet presence in the village. "You know I doubt we would've survived here without you, Omasah," she said, sitting down. "I think we would've argued too much. And the storm would've ruined us."

"This is my work – to see that all goes well for you."

"And Jill's baby's coming – you heard it crying, remember? There's lots to look forward to." Omasah's face changed almost imperceptibly for a second. "What's wrong?" Ellen asked him.

"Nothing is wrong, Kaphalya. But the child I sensed is not the one of whom you speak."

Hearing voices outside, Ellen didn't have time to react. Steven entered with Janet, who was looking radiant in a fresh pink dress and pale green cardigan. She flung herself on Ellen. "Oh, how can I ever thank you and Steve enough for everything you've done for me?"

"I'm just running Janet to the station," said Steven, peeking at his watch. "The refuge is expecting her."

"Bury's a lovely place," smiled Ellen. "It'll be a brand new start for you. You deserve it so much." She hugged her friend emotionally. "How was Ethan?"

"Fine," answered Janet tearfully. "I'm so happy for him. This is just what he needs… but I will miss him." Her voice dropped to an urgent whisper: "I'll stay off the booze, Ellen – honest. I can't go back to that now." Then she turned to Omasah. "Thank you for looking after me."

He took her hands lightly. "All is as it should be, Sweet Lady."

As Ellen stood looking after them, Janet stopped under one of the eucalyptus trees and called out, putting her hand on the trunk: "I'm going to plant one of these in my new garden when I get it." Ellen laughed with happiness at how things had turned out. It was uplifting to know that they had managed to help Janet find the strength to regain control of her life. When she re-entered the small room, Ellen found Omasah waiting at his table.

"May I hold the stone?"

She handed it to him, and then headed out in the direction of Josh's caravan to see if he had a spare glass of wine. She needed to get Maxwell out of her head. When she returned ten minutes later Omasah had not moved and so she sat on the bed, sipping at a glass of cheap Pinot. At last he broke off his mind-link, repeating the same words with the same composure:

"The child I sense is not the one of whom you speak."

10

21st May, 2020
Anya's Diary

Yesterday was just about the best day ever! Ethan moved into Josh's old caravan, and now all the stuff he collected from his mum last weekend is here, although there's not very much of it. Steve gave him a picture for his wall which already has some hooks in it for pictures, and then we went to the shop and trailers to look for other things for him, like pillows and stuff. Lizzy told him to take one of her small rugs too so it looks quite nice already although he says it needs a woman's touch, which is true. The best thing was that Ethan finished his first proper carving which is of a flying bird and it's for me, and I've hung it over my table near the window. We still see my shed as our main place together but we'll get used to things, and I think Dixie's pleased to have his workshop without a camp-bed in it.

Another good thing is that we have got some new people here after only just meeting them. After school yesterday I saw Ellen talking to a young couple at the café, and it was the girl with the dreadlocks who was our first ever customer and bought Ellen's book. Her name's Amanda and her boyfriend is Dave, and they had their yellow VW camper parked near the café. So anyway, after Ethan and I finished moving his stuff we saw the van behind the centre and wondered why, but no one was around and I had to go dancing. When I got back at 9 there was quite a party going on around the yellow van, with a fire and food and everything. Ellen told me that Amanda and Dave have just got back from travelling round India and have nowhere really to go. They didn't plan on staying here – it just happened. Ethan told me that Ellen had been dancing on top of the VW and that she'd told him that it was the first time she'd danced in public since that bloke beat her up. Then things got even nicer because Dave plays an Indian pipe and Amanda taught Carlos and Tali a new Hindu Mantra, and we're all going to learn it. Dad and Paul played guitar and Jean drummed on a wooden box – it was just so great. I asked Ellen if they are staying and she said she hopes so, and she told me they still have the gratitude stones she gave them on the first day of the shop. She was quite high which doesn't bother me because she's nice on it, and she kept hugging me and saying how Ubuntu's evolving into something wonderful. Paul looked a bit off and Josh said it's because he thinks Ellen's being reckless just letting Amanda and Dave into the village even though she was the first person to read her book.

Another new person is Gina who came after the storm to get baby milk. She has mental health problems and fibromyalgia which makes all your muscles hurt. She has got a beautiful blue-grey Staffie dog called Ghost because she is very interested in ghosts, and she comes every day to look after the sheep and walk some of the dogs although actually she does a lot more than that, and she and Ellen are thinking about starting a hedgehog hospital. She is really lovely and she has been talking a lot with Ellen about her problems, and is pleased people understand which Ellen does a lot because she's had them herself. Ellen told me that you can't understand that sort of thing unless you've had it yourself, and that depression is like living a half-life.

The only bad thing that's happened is that quite a big carving of a crow went missing from the shop yesterday. We can't understand how anyone could have got out with it, but it's definitely gone and it was worth quite a bit. Dixie tried to be "Ubuntu" about it, saying "I hope they enjoy it," but then he said "Bloody bastards," and laughed. Anyway, it's not the end of the world as mum always says.

Talking of the book, nearly all the first hundred have sold now and so Ellen needs to print more. Hopefully the holidays that we are starting in June will pay for it. We will be offering stays of four to seven days in the two new roundhouses, and the people will get free food and yoga, free massages, and a free astrological reading. They can also do crafts, cookery, meditation, agriculture and anything else they might want, but if they don't want to do anything at all then that's okay too. There are also some young people who want to come at weekends and put their tents outside and have fires. The council say it's okay if we do extra water butts. I hope it won't cause trouble and that they'll be quiet. I don't know why they even want to come – Ellen says it's because most campsites won't let you light a fire, but Ethan thinks that maybe they like our ideas.

After the party in my shed Ethan touched me a little bit you know where but not much and then he cried but wouldn't say why. In one way I quite like it that he's experienced but in another way I don't, and it makes him quite exciting to me so long as I don't think about it too much. I know I'm unusual these days with never having had a boyfriend of any sort, but he says it's a gift for him and he wants to wait till my sixteenth birthday. I think those are just human rules about the age limit, and they are just like an idea and so can't really be held as fact, but he says he really wants to do it this way to prove something to himself, so I guess that's okay if it's so important to him.

This afternoon after school we sat in the garden with Dad, and we listened to the blackbirds which he said are like jazz musicians. Ethan doesn't feel embarrassed with Dad anymore, but he's very much in awe of his talent and can't understand why he doesn't want to get famous. He asked him to play guitar and liked it when he did blues with a slide especially, and then he sang us his new song called Clapweed Junction which starts: "Mr McAnn grows big blue cabbages that rock in the morning wind." Mum likes it even better than the Christmas one and says he's reached his peak, but Dad says he doesn't care if he stops getting better so long as he enjoys it. Ethan knows that Dad misses me sometimes and he always goes to see Dixie so we can talk about books and things. I'm reading East of Eden at the moment and it's so great that I desperately need to speak about it with somebody. I don't think Dad is sad. I hope not, because although things are changing they aren't changing badly.

11

May, 2020

Overloaded with a pile of books, Jill fought with the school door, dropping a large atlas on her foot and swearing under her breath. Picking it up she edged in backwards and headed for the kitchen – she hadn't even had a cup of tea yet. Tossing a teabag into a mug she stopped, hearing shouts and recognising Shiny's voice. Leaving the kettle boiling she hurried outside into the promise of a fine warm spring day.

There was a dark knot of children at the big farm gate, and Lizzy could be seen leaning out of the café van. "What's going on?" asked Jill as she dashed past.

"Some kind of argument," said Lizzy. "Be careful, Jill."

As Jill neared the gate Pinky ran into her arms, sobbing. "Oh, please do something. They've been following us all week, taking videos and throwing stones."

The uniformed school children had formed a band beyond the gate and began punching the air and shouting in unison: "Fuck-ing-freaks! Fuck-ing-freaks!" A big stone landed near Jill's foot and rolled to a halt along a dry wheel-rut.

The hands went to the hips at once. "Now just cut that out! Leave now or I'll be straight onto the school," she shouted, determined to call their headmaster in any case. Mr Rix appeared behind the group wearing a startled expression and Jill waved him away, shaking her head. He lingered for a moment and then disappeared back into the yard.

Shiny stood defiantly, taking advantage of the lull. "Us freaks? *You're* the freaks, stuffing sweets all day and staring at your phones. You think you're all so cool, don't you? Well, you're *not* – you're just *victims*, desperate for attention and desperate to escape reality. Desperate for your parents to buy you the next stupid thing you don't even need. You're just *victims*, all wearing the same shoes and the same jackets. Don't you realise how *boring* that is? So stop bullying us because we're smart enough to be *different!*" She turned and strutted away with Fudge trotting behind her, clinging to her coat. Then she spun round again, no longer caring whether she made any sense. "You're irrelevant to me!" she screamed. "You're invisible to me! I'm fresh and I'm new and exciting, and you can't hurt me!"

Jill followed the three children towards the village without looking back. As they neared the café Shiny slowed her pace and collapsed onto one of the seats in a flood of tears. Jill held the shaking girl close, stroking her back as she spoke between choking sobs. "I'm sorry. I'm so sorry. It's not their fault. It's not their fault…"

Lizzy came and sat down, taking Shiny's hand and looking at Jill with a gleam in her eye: "Well, that told them!" She turned towards the gate and saw that the children had gone, and Mr Rix was ambling towards them.

"My dear child," he said in his kindly manner. "Don't cry so hard or you'll start me off."

Shiny managed a trembling smile. "I'm sorry," she repeated. "I shouldn't have got angry."

"Don't be silly, my love," Lizzy told her, stroking her hand. "You were just speaking up under attack. We all lose our tempers sometimes – we're only human."

"But Ubuntu's supposed to be a peaceful place," snivelled the girl, looking shamefully towards the gate where several concerned villagers had gathered.

"It is," said Lizzy. "Listen."

Jill handed Shiny a tissue. "That's right. Let it go, sweetheart. Bring yourself into the now-moment like you've been learning with Ellen. Hear the skylark? He didn't mind you shouting – he was singing the entire time!"

"Really?"

"Yes, really."

During morning break the children sat in the old Rover with the doors flung open and the two sheep came close, nibbling at the grass. Fudge took the wheel proudly, leaning back so he could reach the pedals. He leant on the horn, making the sheep jump. "Don't, Fudge!" growled Shiny through her teeth. "I'll cut the wire if you keep on."

"Why have you all got such funny names?" Addy asked from the back seat.

"Your name's funny too," said Pinky.

"Mine's because my name's Adam, but yours are just silly."

Shiny was drained from her temper-fit; hungry and defensive. "They aren't silly," she scowled. "They've all got very good reasons actually. Pinky's is because she likes pink, Fudge's is because that's his favourite food, and mine's because I'm Polish."

"I didn't know you were Polish, Shiny," said Nadia from the bonnet where she lay sunning herself.

"My parents came here when I was two."

"Do you ever go back?"

"No."

"Would you like to?"

"One day maybe, but not with them."

Addy was frowning in his typical way. "So why are you called Shiny, then?" Nadia sat up with a grin.

"Shiny... polish... as in Mr Sheen, Addy."

"Oh – that's clever," said Addy. "So what are your real names?"

Pinky sat with her head down, turning her bracelets round and round. "We never say. We don't use them any more."

"You really feel that badly about your families?" Nadia enquired, turning onto her front and looking through the windscreen.

"I consider myself neglected," Shiny answered, getting out of the car huffily. "My parents hardly ever spoke to me and they still don't. They're Tech Heads first and parents second. And reality...?" She took in the sky and grass and trees with a sweep of one arm. "All this? Well, it's just a side-show to them, and a very dull one at that. Are we allowed a sandwich?"

Nadia slipped off the car and followed her towards the school. "It could be worse, you know. My adopted sister saw her entire family slaughtered in front of her with a machete."

Shiny whirled round. "This isn't a competition about who's worst off. I'm just saying that I've been neglected – that's all." She made her way to the kitchen and opened the little fridge. Then she froze. "I'm sorry..." she said. "About Melyne, I mean." She leaned against the cupboard with her head in her hands: "I don't know what's wrong with me. Those children reminded me of things I just don't want to think about. How school was… but more than that…" Tears began to roll again, silently this time. "I had toys that spoke you know, and when the batteries ran out I used to panic…"

"You're here with us now," said Nadia reaching for her. "Why don't you ask Jill if you can go to the craft-room? It always helps to be creative. It was right what you said to those kids, anyway. Just try and forget all about it." Nadia hugged the girl close. "Shh. You're here with us now."

The oppression of the morning's events died away with the freshness of the breeze and the blueness of the sky, and the larks sang endlessly over the fields. Having heard all the details from Lizzy, Ellen went in search of Shiny towards the end of the school day. "She's doing crafts," whispered Jill, who was marking books at her desk. Ethan was bent over his page and Ellen exchanged a private look with Anya. The girl was proud of him, and he was enjoying making her so until the time arrived for him to go into apprenticeship with Dixie.

Ellen found Shiny chatting with Faye amongst wool, felt, scissors and beads. She looked up happily. "I've been putting the faces on the dolls," she said. "And I've pinned all Koomra's squares into blankets. She's started knitting baby clothes now – did you know? Really tiny, they are! Oh, and I keep forgetting: Pinky and Fudge's parents want to give you their old beach-hut, which got wrecked in the storm. You can either mend it or use it for wood."

Ellen looked with contentment around the cluttered craft-room. "That's great, Shiny. Thank you." With the ongoing repair-efforts and first Ethan's and then Amanda, Dave and Gina's arrivals, a shift in dynamics was in the air.

Suddenly there were increased comings and goings from the town alongside the prospect of summer visitors. Since the storm, they had accumulated a number of damaged sheds and vans plus an old car, all of which had been placed between the south fence and the pines. Paul had traded a cooker for some window glass and had ended up by helping a couple of people get fixed up in town, and a group of youngsters had requested tent pitches on the fallow field at weekends. As she felt the leash of Ubuntu slip just a little from her, a thrill was beginning like a new breath.

"Would you like to come and visit someone with me, Shiny – while you wait for the others?"

"Okay," agreed the girl. She slid off the stool and tidied her workplace hurriedly. "Can I see the washing machines on the way, please?"

"You can do a load if you like, but you might need help to get it going!"

They descended the steps and took the cycle-path round to the laundry room. Shiny looked up in fascination at the ramshackle building with its huge water-tank, mishmash of solar panels, and racing turbine that hummed over the corrugated roof. She ran to one of the machines eagerly, opening the drum and peering inside. "I guess it keeps you quite fit," she said, getting on and lying back in the seat. She easily got the empty drums spinning. After a couple of minutes she got off and went to the shower curtains, pulling one aside. She tapped one of the metal baths with her fingernail and it made a tinging sound. Then she leant against it forlornly, remembering. "I'm not in trouble am I?"

"'Course you're not, darling. I just want you to meet a very nice man, that's all." She took the girl's hand and they walked round the laundry room, turning right towards Omasah's house. He was waiting for them in his garden, but as soon as she saw him Shiny stopped dead in her tracks. "Oh dear! It's the space alien."

"He's not a space alien, Shiny. Who told you that? Was it Nadia?"

"Well, yes… but she was very nice to me this morning."

As they approached, Omasah moved inside to wait. He offered both hands to Shiny as she entered the room. "Hello, Harina."

The girl accepted his hands at once and looked into his face. As she scanned the strange features she seemed to realise something that completely overpowered her. Her mouth dropped open, she gave a kind of moan, and both knees buckled as Ellen rushed to support her. The girl's body sank some more; her eyes swam a little and then she murmured, "How did you know my name?"

Omasah lifted her quickly onto the bed, where she lay as though watching something blissful. She whined and two small tears formed. "What's happening?" whispered Ellen.

"She is feeling the Oneness. She is watching the light."

Shiny half-woke for a second, disorientated; then she immediately fell asleep. The man gave a subtle smile and covered the child with a blanket. "Oneness is the natural human state," he said. "Children especially are never far removed from it." He began unrolling a thin straw mat along the floor. "You need healing, Kaphalya."

As Ellen lay down she noticed that the sleeves of Omasah's silken top were patterned with pink paisley, faint against the cream background, and that the same fabric covered its three buttons. The man knelt beside Ellen and took hold of her right leg, saying: "You have tension in your legs and buttocks. It is affecting your knees. Relax completely..." He bent her leg and pushed it gently across the other one, answering her previous thought with a look into her face. "I have begun experimenting with clothes as a form of expression... as do my people, though I myself have never before felt the need. This is also my journey, Kaphalya."

Ellen let out a quiet cry as pain sliced around her hip-joint – pain that was mixed with pleasure. How could she be carrying this much tension without knowing? Omasah softened the force of his hand. "Stop resisting. Allow the muscles to stretch."

When he had finished with her leg he slipped his hand under her buttock and massaged deeply and quickly. Before Ellen had a chance to feel embarrassed, he had removed his hand and was shaking her whole leg like a lump of jelly. She laughed as it became warm and limp with relaxation. A tingle ran up her spine and, to her confusion, she became suddenly sexually aroused. Awkward tears burned, for she knew the man would know what she felt; then more tears mixed with smiles as she realised that she need never fear Omasah's judgement of her. She took his hand, gripping it tightly, and her face was a knot of emotions. "Is everyone like you where you come from?"

Somehow his gentle affirmative reached her, although he hadn't spoken out loud. "The other side will be more difficult," he told her with a gleam in his eyes.

When Ellen finally sat up she found herself half-watching the birds through the window, knowing in her heart that she had once had an experience very like Shiny's. "Why did she say that... about her name?" she asked.

"She connected with its eternal meaning. The child senses much."

"And what does it mean?"

Omasah answered in a playful, almost childlike voice – soft tones that carried on a wave of overwhelming distance. "Its meanings are many: Belonging. Snow-berry. Night bird. The colour of the moon…"

Ellen turned from the window and saw that a sparrow had entered through the open door and was perched on the man's hand, and he was talking as much to the bird as he was to her.

12

May, 2020

From his beloved armchair Mr Rix had a clear view of the village. Seated there in the evenings, he would often watch the lights twinkling through the fence, and trace everything back to its small beginnings – to a field and a few caravans – to an idea discussed around a fire. Although he no longer owned the land he was just as much a part of Ubuntu as any of them. They depended on him for his phone, his computer, and his fatherly presence; while he depended on them for company and entertainment. It had all worked out so perfectly that sometimes Mr Rix wondered at it, believing secretly that the benevolent spirit of Olive must have given them a helping hand somewhere along the line.

To Mr Rix's surprise, the older he was getting the more he wanted to live. Dutifully however, he had recently been giving his will some consideration – and with it, his son. He had not seen Charlie since selling the land, and had barely spoken to him. The lad had taken offence at what he saw as a cold slash to his inheritance. So what of the future? Perhaps he should speak to Dick and Jerry about doing a couple of barn-conversions. The buildings weren't being used and it would mean a steady income for Charlie… a good investment too. He really wanted to leave the house to the village – otherwise his son was sure to either rent it out or sell it. The thought of "just anyone" living there felt unsavoury, whereas he knew he could trust his friends to respect Olive's memory, and use the house for something good.

Mr Rix was startled out of his reverie by a brief but determined rapping at the backdoor. Funny – the villagers normally came to the front, so whoever could it be? Sage trotted eagerly into the kitchen as the old man struggled out of his armchair and hobbled across the room. On opening the door he was dazzled by a full moon sailing in a clear sky, but there was no one to be seen. Then, hearing noises, he spied a dark figure getting into the passenger seat of a car parked out in the road. The car drove off at high speed and Mr Rix looked after it, feeling vaguely puzzled. Perhaps it was a mistake. Perhaps it was a prank. An owl hooted loudly from the big hollow barn nearby, and Mr Rix went back inside with a sigh.

Returning to his armchair he crossed his hands comfortably over his stomach, wriggled a little, and closed his eyes in contentment. Enough of thinking about all that sort of thing. He may be old and stiff but he wasn't going anywhere just yet, that was for sure. But just as he began to drift off into a pleasant doze there was another knock – this time at the front-door. It was a much softer sound, and plainly not from the same hand as before.

Before Mr Rix could get up Omasah entered the lounge, carrying a cardboard box. "Oh, hello Mr Om-sah," exclaimed the old man in surprise. "Well, I've never seen you here before. It's nice to have you visit, I must say. Can I offer you a cup of tea?"

Without answering Omasah placed the box on the table saying in little more than a whisper: "See what has been given?"

Speech failed Mr Rix as he looked but seemed not to see. It was a pair of shoes under a cloth. No, it was a blanket bundled into a box. No, it was a doll belonging to one of the children. No, it was a tiny sleeping baby, and there was a note with it. He picked it up, and his hands trembled as he read the words scrawled aggressively across the page: *"GIVE THIS TO ETHAN ITS HIS."*

Mr Rix became suddenly breathless and Omasah helped him back into his seat. "Oh, Mr Om-sah!" he cried in distress. "If you hadn't come… why, the poor little thing might have… might have… Oh dear, now what'll we do? Whatever will we do?" Then he realised the even greater seriousness of it, and began despairing more with each quickening breath: "Oh, my poor dear Anya. Oh, the poor dear girl. Oh, whatever will we do?" He descended into tears as Omasah took a chair and moved to his side.

As the large hand folded gently over his brow, Mr Rix felt a lazy warmth seep through his body. His eyes closed, and he saw fields of wildflowers showered in light from a dome of sky. He heard birds singing and felt a summer wind carry the music into his heart, and he smiled. But drifting into a tranquil half-sleep he still murmured, reluctant to let go: "Whatever will we do..?"

13

May, 2020

The girl was curled up pale and exhausted on the sofa, gripping two wet handkerchiefs. At long last it felt as though everything there was to say had been said, and Anya's bitter tears had finally run dry. Mary sat opposite, elegantly sorrowful; and at her side, Gina, who had stayed late in the craft-room. From upstairs Harry could be heard tinkling on his guitar, pausing now and then to scribble in his notebook. The dogs slept on the floor, peaceful and unaware.

Gina brandished her cushion as though to ward off further disaster. "P'raps it won't be so bad, love. If he wants to keep it then at least you've got lots of support in a place like this." She sighed tragically, wondering what to say for the best. "And I'll always help you out – you know that. I like babies."

Anya placed a ball of handkerchief firmly over each eye and breathed shakily in and out. "I feel like my whole life has gone."

"No, my darling," Mary said. "It's all life, and you've got it all to come. Lots of happy times. You've said you still love him. You forgive him, and you think he should keep the baby. The big decisions are over with, and you're already moving forward."

"It's not his fault anyway – it's society," interjected Gina.

"I do love him... so much... and it's not his fault, I know. I don't know if anything's anybody's fault really. People just can't handle things and then make mistakes." Her face contorted. "But it still hurts... And then I think of him thinking he's lost me, which is even worse." She leapt up in desperation: "I must go and see him!"

"Not yet, dear," said Mary. "Try and give it until Ellen comes."

Too weak to protest Anya sank back down, her face struggling with the idea of Ethan's pain. Gina moved tearfully across the room with her cushion. "Just stay with me and your mum for a little bit longer, love."

"But I must see him soon. He needs me..." A knock at the door interrupted them. It was Steven. Anya jumped up again in alarm. "Where is she? Where's the baby?"

"Tali's feeding her, sweetheart. She'll be keeping her tonight. We're lucky – breast is definitely best, you know." He closed the door and leaned against the wall with his arms folded. Anya's mouth twisted with emotion as she pictured a sad angry girl out there somewhere, her breasts swollen tight with precious milky fluid. She looked up as Harry's soft footsteps sounded overhead, and a robin sang on the night wind that hummed steadily against the window.

Ethan and Ellen sat at opposite ends of Anya's shed. He had cried; he had cursed; he had thrashed at the cushions and hurled them round the room. Finally he had broken the little wooden bird into pieces. Omasah had retired after bringing the news and had so-far stayed away, leaving events to play out on their own. Ellen felt the burden of the situation acutely. She had watched Ethan's outbursts uneasily without responding, and now the boy had finally dropped into a numb stupor. At last he met her eyes with a shattered expression. "What's going to become of me?"

"This isn't just about you, Ethan."

Anger distorted his handsome features as he digested this ugly truth. He put his head in his hands, growling like a mad dog. "I'll kill myself. I'll just go from here and kill myself."

"You have a child."

He stood up, shouting again. "I'm a bloody kid myself! I can't look after a bloody baby! Anyway, my life's *nothing* without Anya, and she must hate my guts now." Pain surged and became intolerable. "I need a knife!" he croaked, heading for the little drawer where Anya kept a few pieces of cutlery.

Ellen jumped up in terror, willing Omasah's arrival just as the shed door swung on its hinges and a tall figure appeared in the moonlit opening. Oblivious and beyond caring, Ethan extracted a knife from the drawer with shaking fingers, but then immediately flung it from himself with a cry. He clutched at his hand while the knife spun uselessly on the rug; looked up as Zoki slinked into the room and Anya's tear-stained face peered from behind the man at the door. Her voice was remote and only half-remembered to him. "Please, Ethan. I still love you," she said. "Why shouldn't I?"

Before Ethan could lose control again, Omasah pushed him quickly down onto the bed. He laid his hands on the struggling body and, with a great exertion of will, subdued the boy until he was barely conscious. The man rested his forehead on the covers. "I am not accustomed to such anguish," he whispered. "Some water, please Kaphalya."

Ellen hurried to the outside tap and Anya moved to the bedside. She touched Ethan's face tenderly, and then laid her head on his chest, listening. "His heart is slow," she told Omasah. "How can I make him realise I still love him?"

Omasah drank thirstily before answering: "When he sees what he has been given he will see all."

Ellen felt a strange undefined emotion flood through her. "How is… the baby, Anya?"

"She's fine. Very small, but Steve says she's fine. The cord wasn't clamped. She can't have been born in hospital." She paused to stroke the boy's head and he moaned gently. "I love you, Ethan," she said. "Can you hear me?"

His eyes searched for her and focused with difficulty. "What's happening?" he muttered, taking her hand. Anya held it fast and buried her face in the blankets.

At just after midnight Dixie pushed the door open with a gentle hand. Ethan still slept with Anya at his side, Omasah sat on the beanbag and Ellen had finally taken herself off home. Dixie touched Anya's shoulder. "How is he? Should I see him to bed?"

The girl looked up at him in anguish. "I don't think he can leave. I think he might hurt himself."

Omasah opened his eyes. "I will stay. Take Navastri somewhere to sleep."

"No," said Anya.

"Then lie here. I do not require sleep." Omasah got up fluidly and coaxed the girl towards the beanbag just as a quiet tap sounded at the door. It was Mary carrying blankets.

"Just what we need," said Dixie, taking two and covering Anya as she curled up.

He left them and started for his house, pondering at the clear bright moon. Then he stopped as the faintest cry meandered on the pristine air: small and feeble, with barely enough strength to make itself heard. He saw Carlos's light switch on. Of course – Tali must be nursing the baby. A shiver passed through him as he closed his door against the cold night.

Anya was woken by quiet voices – or rather by the sleepy backseat awareness of a very long conversation. She struggled to place herself for a few seconds; then she heard the bed creak as Ethan shifted his position. His voice was exhausted and hoarse: "I can't! It's horrible!"

Anya started to get up but Omasah subdued her with a thought. She stayed huddled where she was, listening as she watched the candlelight flicker over the coverings, and the soft tick of the clock seemed to select the same moment over and over again.

"It is the abyss," said Omasah in the gentlest voice.

Ethan panted out the same words several times: "I can't! It's horrible!"

"You must look in, Komala. We cannot leave this place until you do." The bed creaked again as the boy turned over with a pitiful moan. Then Anya heard a sudden indrawn breath…

At first his body fought against the fear of falling, until all sensation dissolved into patterns and light. There was no falling because there was no space. There was no fear because there was only love, and he wept without knowing. "There's a light. It's very deep. It's a green light," he whimpered.

"It is the colour of love," said Omasah.

"No… it's white. It's dazzling…" whined Ethan.

"Stay in the knowing of it, Komala." Omasah bowed his head and fell silent for a moment, and when he spoke again his voice allowed for new understanding on the part of the boy. "Do you see?"

The reply was barely audible: "Yes."

"Resist any urge to name it or to understand it. Know that you are worthy of it."

Ethan sobbed and Anya felt tears on her face. Omasah continued quietly: "See all in its Oneness. See how it is already made good and ended and begun again in an instant, like the breath of the ocean. Be at peace, Komala."

Anya continued to lie still, hearing Omasah rise. The candle went out and the door was closed.

Morning brought a heavy silence that hung with the grey clouds. Ellen jumped awake late, sensing something terribly wrong and then remembering. She sat up feeling nothing was real; she splashed her face with some water and went to put the kettle on. Standing in her doorway and watching her dogs she felt like flopping back into bed; took a few deep breaths and looked at the sky.

A door clicked open to her left and Tali stepped over the low willow fencing into Ellen's allotment, carrying the baby. She came close, her expression tender and maternal. "It make me want another. You seen her already?"

Ellen shook her head feeling blank, and watched as Tali pushed aside the swaddling to reveal two long crescent eyelids lightly closed above a small globular nose and pink dot of a mouth. "Wow – she's tiny. Is that one of Koomra's hats?"

"Yes. She been knitting baby things all the week. Strange, no?"

Ellen's eyes filled up under a weight of mixed emotions. Instinctively, she reached for the comfort of the stone in her pocket, relieved to see Dixie heading up the path as Tali took her leave. "I come bearing good tidings," he grinned.

Ellen forced a weak smile. "What?"

He took her arm. "I know it must be hard for you," he said, suddenly serious. "Jill's pregnancy and now this."

"No – really, Dixie," Ellen insisted. "I don't think about it in that way. I never thought of it like a… like an actual baby. I could never really see past the violence. Perhaps I'm blotting it out, but… I could never have loved it." She fell onto his chest, weeping. "I just couldn't have…"

Dixie rocked her. "It's all going to be okay, Ellen," he said warmly. "Ethan's much better this morning. Says he got to face up to the responsibility. Anya's says she'll learn to love the baby because it's a part of him; says it happened before they met when he had a different life. God – I've never seen so many tears and now you're at it as well! But anyway, you know what I keep remembering?" He held her away from him, and looked happily into her face.

Ellen's hands shook as she unfolded a tissue and wiped her nose. "What?"

"Well, I keep remembering when you and I sat near the fire over the other side of the field, and Paul was asleep on the grass, and Josh was in bed – remember? And I said how Ubuntu was going to help heal the world like you healed your life. Well, you've got to hand it to Ethan and Anya because they've managed the whole shebang."

"What shebang? I remember the evening but not what was said."

"Acceptance – gratitude – forgiveness – love," said Dixie, pushing a bent roll-up into his mouth and entering Ellen's house in search of the coffee jar.

14

May, 2020

At least the floor was dry and quite clean in this place, and for the second night in a row the other homeless hadn't argued with Maxwell's arrival. They were grouped around a bottle not far away and so he quickly curled up in a dark corner, afraid of bringing attention to himself. Street people remained largely alien to him: part of an odd fluid culture that he struggled to get to grips with. Hostile; over-familiar; silent and brooding; drunk… you never knew what you were going to get, and yet he was drawn to the places where they gathered. Circumstances had forced Maxwell into their world and they were the authority. They made the rules, such as they were; and ultimately they were more likely to meet his needs than society. All society wanted was to lock him up: a fear that haunted his every step.

During the long chilling nights when he slept little and thought much, he would often picture his previous life. The images that filled his aching mind were vivid and lively, whereas reality had become a cold grey watercolour world. Red carpets; glittering chandeliers; shining cars; sun through a bay window. He no longer bothered telling the others though, and had quickly realised that his story was of no interest to them. They either didn't believe him or simply didn't care. For someone who thrived on sharing jokes and anecdotes, it was hard and desolate. Increasingly, Maxwell was suffering from panic attacks, as the truth of who he was, and what he he'd become, began to strangle. He needed an outlet where none was to be found. He needed to re-create himself but no one wanted to watch.

There was a rough cough and a rustle as a bedraggled moonlit figure appeared. The voice was guttural and rasping. "Mind if I kip?"

Maxwell's voice sounded loud inside his head. "That you Squiffy?" He felt pleased. Of all the homeless Squiffy was just about as good as it got. He didn't talk too much or too little, he shared his booze if he had any, and he didn't get angry. Somehow, it felt as though those baggy bloodshot eyes might just harbour some fragment of promise, and Maxwell craved it.

"Oh, it's you…" grunted the man as he took the opposite corner. He began untying a putrid sleeping bag. "Got any butts?"

"Got quite a few, Squiffy. Got them 'specially for you." He searched his pockets, pulling out a handful of stinking cigarette ends. He leaned towards the other man in the dark, offering them to him. Squiffy took them with another grunt, saying:

"Should've put 'em in suffin.' Bag or suffin.' Not much good all loose and bent, like."

Maxwell felt his anger begin to seethe. One thing he couldn't stand was ingratitude, but neither of them had anything to gain by fighting or insults, and they certainly didn't want to lose a nice dry place through making a scene. Huffily, he began making ready his own bag and cushion. Hell – what a desperate shambles his life had become! It had been quite good for a while up north, what with his aunt's pension to spend and a nice house with plenty of booze. He lay down, getting as comfortable as possible and wondering whether to speak. The other man was just visible, a shaft of moonlight illuminating his blackened bag. Then Maxwell caught the glint of glass and smelt spirits. His mouth burned with yearning as he lay perfectly still.

"Wanna drop?"

Maxwell fought with his sleeping bag in a hurried attempt to sit up, but as he stretched out his hand something heavy hit it, smashing his thumb. He screamed, fell onto his front and writhed in pain. Rolling over to face the door he saw a crazy sight picked out in pale blue light: a small scrawny goblin-like creature, wild-haired and ravaged with age. One arm was raised, wasted and angular in its flimsy sleeve, and a huge bird perched dead-still on a bony hand. Maxwell hid his face against the dirty floor, screeching for help. Then he fell quiet, petrified and waiting.

"Hello Maxwell," said a voice from long ago, as the weapon crashed into his skull and everything collapsed into black timelessness.

Outside, Omasah took Koomra's little arms gently from behind and closed his eyes while she seemed to look at nothing. At the same time a group of people appeared round the corner of the big fence, making for the disturbance in panic and causing the homeless to flee into the pines. Paul got there first. "What the hell's going on?" he gasped.

"I am late," said Omasah. "The man is hurt."

"I'll get an ambulance," said Jean, running off at top speed. Everyone began speaking at once.

"Who is it?"

"A tramp."

"Did anyone know they were here?"

"I didn't. Must have come through the woods."

"Is he alive?"

"Should we get Steve?"

"Whatever possessed her?"

"Why, Koomra?" demanded Ellen.

The old woman turned to her calm-faced, and her voice was that of a younger woman recalling the ease of better times. "For his own good, my dear. You see, he always was a bad egg I'm afraid, and terribly unhappy deep down. Luckily I escaped to the stars, where I lived in a cave of indigo rocks. Happy times, they were… It was there that I first learned to knit, you know. But now that we have little tiny babies and other sweet creatures roundabout, I thought I'd better put his troubles to rest. A mother always knows what's best for her son." Omasah let her loose, and she patted Ellen's hand fondly before hobbling off in the direction of the gate.

"She is no danger to the village," said Omasah.

Ellen heard muffled movements and a groan from inside the old beach hut, and felt rising panic. Her thoughts were whirling – grasping at something elusive that kept slipping away. As Maxwell's blood-streaked head and unmistakable profile with its scraggy beard crept into view, she went dizzy and lost control of her bladder. She hurled herself at Paul, taking his arm. "I've got to go," she said in a strange gruff voice. "It's Max. Get the police."

As she hurried away into the darkness, several nasty coughs came from inside the hut and someone spoke: "Anyone got a light?"

Dixie edged forward, placing a reluctant hand on Maxwell's shoulder. "Ambulance is coming," he said, feeling numb as he held out his lighter towards the other man. The flame picked out something jagged on the floor. It was his carving of a crow that had gone missing. He picked it up. "I'd better ring the cops," he told Paul under his breath, and followed after Ellen.

Paul was busy calculating scenarios. Maxwell would go to jail – no doubt there. But the thought of Koomra in prison or an institution was unthinkable. How could they get round this? He made a snap decision just as giddy blue lights began dancing over the field from the farm-gate. A second later he was close by the second man, stifled by the smell of grease and whisky as he spoke rapidly into his ear. "We don't want any trouble for the old lady. This guy's a wanted man. Raped my ex twenty years back. Real sick piece of work. Just make yourself scarce and keep shtum and we'll see you good. Stay away for a week. We'll tell the cops it was a fight between homeless and then you come back. But none of you saw anything, right? We'll give you soup and leave you be. You can light a fire as long as you use a hub. How about it?"

Squiffy didn't need long to consider. "Alright. Real nice, that soup. 'Ad me suspicions, I did. Saw rage in 'is eyes, I did." The man crawled out of the door like an animal and vanished into the trees just as the ambulance bumped to a halt and turned off its engine.

Paul let out a sigh and leaned his head against the wall. Maxwell had collapsed again into an unsightly heap, and Paul could hear his shallow breaths coming and going. A kind-faced ginger-haired paramedic appeared in the doorway, weighed down with equipment. She gave Omasah an odd sideways glance and then squatted down beside the injured man.

Ellen went straight home and fetched some fresh clothes and two candles. With her dogs at her heels she headed for the fire pit, where she used a big pair of tongs to fill a metal bucket with hot stones. The yellow camper stood nearby in darkness. Ellen couldn't remember the last time she had felt such a need to be alone.

Weighed down with her hazardous load, she made her way to the laundry room and let the bucket drop onto the concrete floor with a loud clunk. Then she pulled one of the curtains aside, laid a pipe in the bath and turned the valve. As the water began to run slowly and soundlessly, she took a bike round to the store and grabbed a few sprigs of dried lavender. Returning to the laundry room, she lit her candles and stuck them on the wide metal rim – she wasn't in the mood for electric light.

The stones hissed noisily as she placed them in the water one by one to boost the heat. When they had done their work she removed them hurriedly, threw in the lavender, and lowered herself at last into the hot steaming water. Then she laid back, closed her eyes, and let the silence of Ubuntu embrace her weary mind.

15

May, 2020

As soon as Omasah sensed that Ellen was ready, he paid her a visit. "It is over, Kaphalya. What is often called the wheel of Karma begins again."

"You mean things will calm down and get back to normal?"

"I mean all is renewed. Do you feel it?"

She smiled rather wearily. "Yes."

"I am sorry I did not warn you of the man's presence. I was exhausted, and his vibration had altered. He is not the same man as before. But all is well."

Ellen looked doubtful. "He'll remember her," she said. "He'll tell the police and they'll come looking for her."

Omasah took her hands. "He will remember nothing, Kaphalya. Think no more of it." And with that he left her, and she snuggled up in her chair and closed her eyes. Her dogs jumped onto her lap and they all dozed together until mid-morning.

She found Tali holding the baby in the doorway of the yellow camper while Noah rolled on the grass with his chubby little legs in the air. Amanda hugged Ellen warmly and gave her a compassionate look. "Omasah's named the little one."

"Anya ask him," said Tali. "Her name Aruna."

Ellen sat down next to her. "That's lovely."

"Are you alright?" Amanda asked gently.

"Pretty much."

"I can't understand how the woman knew he was there."

"Her house is right behind where he was sleeping. I guess she heard his voice."

"So do you realise that your kindness to the old lady ended up protecting you from...?"

"Yes, I know. Where's Dave?" said Ellen, eager to change the subject.

Amanda sat down cross-legged on the grass to roll a joint. "He's having a big debate with Paul. Don't worry. He's totally fine with us. It's just that Paul says you've reached maximum capacity here, and..."

"You're not going?"

Amanda lit up and laughed. "No, we're not going, Ellen. They're just having a philosophical talk. Dave's partial to a bit of philosophy too, you know. But Paul's right: get too big and you risk losing something... or gaining something you don't want."

Ellen considered as the sun came out from behind a big white cloud. "True. I guess we have to draw the line somewhere. But please stay, at least for now."

"We're staying for as long as it feels right," smiled Amanda. "Three days – three decades..." She shrugged. "Is there a limit to this experiment?"

Ellen sighed. "We need to re-apply after ten years but it shouldn't be a problem. I just wish we could do it properly, but you need to go to Africa or somewhere to do that. Somewhere without all this blasted legislation."

Amanda eyed her with a spirited expression. "So who knows? Maybe that's what we'll do."

"You're smoking too much pot, Ellen," said Paul later as they sat on her porch. "It's making you cough. You know too much of something's never any good."

"Oh, bugger off. You don't own me any more."

"Don't talk rubbish," he argued. "I never owned you."

She shot him a hostile look and they sat in an awkward chilly bubble for an instant. Then it softened.

"Look," said Ellen; "normally I'm sensible but it's been such a funny time. It gives me some peace and helps me sleep…" She coughed. "Oh, sod it! And makes me cough!" She stubbed the joint out and flung it on the grass. Paul was right as usual. She was starting to rely on cannabis for the first time in twenty years, and from somewhere came the strength to admit it: "I don't want to come down, Paul. I never thought I'd feel like that again. It's beginning to make me feel trapped."

Paul was wondering what to say. "Amanda and Dave aren't helping matters," he ventured. "It's different for them you know, only being in their twenties."

She didn't get angry. She just sounded sad. "You don't like them."

"You're wrong, Ellen," he told her truthfully. "I love them to bits."

She put her head in her hands. "I wish I could be more like Carlos… you know – take it or leave it."

"You can… and you will again. I know it's been tough. And everyone's got a poison. Mine's coffee. And beer. And food… that's three."

"I should practise what I preach," groaned Ellen. "I'm

always talking about how people over-indulge. But life's hard you know. Even here it's still hard."

"You can't escape," said Paul. "We always knew that. Life will always catch you up and nudge you to move on." He got up a little stiffly. "Well – I need a coffee."

16

June 13th, 2020
Anya's Diary

This weekend is the last before the visitors start coming and everything is very busy. It feels a bit like a new beginning after all that's gone on. I think Ellen feels better knowing that bloke's locked up for a start and I don't think she realised how much it bothered her. I asked her if she ever told the police and she said it happened abroad and afterwards he told her he'd done it to other women and acted all ashamed. Then she told me that she got pregnant from it and had an abortion, and I was very shocked about that. I thought that seeing Aruna must be upsetting because afterwards Ellen had the menopause really early and never had another chance. She says it is hard sometimes because it reminds her, but mainly it makes her happy because she can share our baby now. Ethan says Ellen must definitely be God mother if we get Aruna christened but I'm not sure because it feels hypocritical if you don't go to church. But then again it would be lovely if Jean could do it but he's Catholic and I don't know if that matters or not. Tali is going to start a little nursery to help with the babies because she and Carlos want another one so there will be four eventually. This means that Ethan can still train with Dixie when Aruna gets a little bigger and until I leave school. So this means extending the school, which we'll look at after the summer.

Aruna has started smiling and she gets completely transfixed by your face. Ethan is just over the moon with her, especially as he's been spending time with Omasah who's very good at telling people the best way to look at life. Although she is Ethan's baby it kind of feels like she's everyone's, and Ubuntu's such a lovely environment for a child. She likes hearing the birds and you can really see she's listening and sometimes she makes her mouth into a tiny little "O" and opens her eyes all wide – it's really funny the faces she pulls.

Janet is coming next weekend to see the baby and she is doing really well apparently. Amanda has started working in the craftroom sewing all Koomra's squares into blankets for the homeless and charities because she knits so fast that we have far too much! Now she's on the baby clothes we can sell some of those too – she's been making tons of little hats and cardigans and tiny booties. Ellen said how it was her big knitting bag that let her hide the crow carving, and that she was sent here to protect us. Ellen sees a lot of patterns in life.

Dixie has made a sign saying "Homeless Row" and he's nailed it on the old beach hut and Jean and Dick have done a few repairs and put some old bits of carpet down. There are two caravans, an old car, two old sheds plus the beach hut, and they've got wheel hubs for fires plus a dustbin of water and a bucket. Mr Rix is a bit dubious but Carlos says you have to trust people because more often than not they respond best to that. Paul spoke to the man called Squiffy at morning soup yesterday and he said there are only a few people who know about the place and that they'll keep it quiet. You would never know they were there unless you go round the edge of the fence which no one does except for us.

Mum has joined Foxheath Operatic who do musicals on the pier so she is rehearsing a lot, and Jean and Melyne have joined the Gospel Choir. Melyne wants to get them here to sing, and they have asked Faye to make their new robes. The materials they have chosen are yellow for the sand and blue for the sky. So everything is suddenly getting very musical, especially with the mantra most evenings. It really cheers you up singing and the weekend campers like it too. The Sounds of Ubuntu CD is selling well and Amanda says we should do a music one with Dad on it, and Mum said that would be nice so long as he doesn't do Squeeze my Lemon.

The holidays begin on Monday and we have six bookings just from flyers, word of mouth and an advert in the paper. Of course Mr Rix is our sort of secretary and he has a diary for the bookings. It's a funny set-up and makes you wonder how we'd ever manage without him. Carlos has asked me to do a poster for his astrology readings and I am really looking forward to it because I can draw all the star signs round the edge. Everything seems to be taking off suddenly and I think it's going to be a wonderful summer this year. We're getting a lot of nice weather for a change and it's lovely to take the pram and Zoki on the beach in the evenings and watch the sun set. Ethan and I have been collecting round stones – only the really perfect ones – and every time we find at least one. We have eleven lined up on my window sill and Ellen says they symbolize unity.

I've got sunflowers in my allotment this time, and this year we're going to sell the seeds as well as the flowers, and in October we might do pumpkin seeds too. School is much nicer since the CAT Gang came and I really like Shiny and I can talk about books with her even though she's only twelve. We're going to enter our poems in a competition soon and if you win you get a book token for fifty pounds and some art stuff. Shiny's best poem is about her life but everyone thinks it's too sad so she's going to choose another one, which will probably be a bird one like most of hers.

Talking of birds Ethan has been making bird-boxes for the shop which is a great idea, and he gave me a new bird last night and it's really beautiful and much better than the last one although I still wish I had that one sometimes. Now he's working on an owl for his mum and a pendant for Jean at the same time. I'm so pleased he's found his gift. He gave me a card too that he got Ellen to sketch of our tree, and inside it just said "Thank you x."

17

June, 2020

Hi Mum

I hope you are feeling well and will soon hear about a house. I also hope that my brothers are OK. We are all fine and little Aruna is so sweet and I just can't help feeling that my Anya is her mum which I really wish was true. Well, I guess she is her mum really because she will always be there for her like the other one won't. Thank you for not going ape about whats happened, everyone has been very kind and understanding even though its all my fault, I know I was stupid and out of control but I see her as a gift anyway now that I am used to it and have started to love her. I have been talking a lot to Omasah because he helps me gets stuff straight in my head, and he says that happiness is mostly about how you look at things which I guess is true. I think my baby is lucky to be here because this village is a nice place for babies and Tali who is Israeli and has been looking after Aruna while I'm at school has gone all broody. I think this is a nice place for me too and I couldn't stand to leave it ever, its funny how time goes slower here which seems like I see Anya more, although I know it's just a feeling. She told me last night that her brother and his wife have got HIV which was a big shock, it upsets me to think about that but I'm glad that I can be here for her, I don't want her to ever be sad. I stop school on the 26th which will be nice in a way but in another way I'll miss it, because it's not like a normal school and Jill is good fun and we do cool stuff. Yesterday we did old civilisations and how all the world has pyramids and stuff so they must have known about one another, and how it's impossible how they built them because you can't do that even now with our technology, and we saw pictures of bore holes and tons of other things which you can't do with a copper chisel. Addy is such a funny kid too, he makes me laugh the way he always eats the same stuff like cheese and onion sandwiches which really stink and then he makes a ton of stripy candles after school every single day, I'm glad I'll still see him and the others around the place. Anyway I don't suppose youve heard from dad, I haven't, I'm so glad you are out of that shit relationship mum, you deserve better and having nobody is better than being with a bigheaded bully like him and its better for my brothers too for sure. We have got holiday makers now in the village which is OK I guess just for the summer, and it's nice to see a few different faces walking around plus we have homeless blokes who have soup and a roll before the café opens and at tea, I spoke to one of them called Squiffy and he wasnt a bad sort of bloke even though he smelt bad, it must be a strange sort of life. Me and Anya have been on the beach every evening and its really nice down there, I wish I had the money to get her an engagement ring because I know I will never want to be without her ever. Silver would suit her best and something a bit unusual and Dixie says I can keep the money from my bird-boxes towards it, they are selling really well and I like doing the details and making them all different. I am reading a book in bed at night, dont fall off your chair, which Ellen got me from the village library called day of the jackal, and I tell you what its so bloody exciting I was reading it till 1.45 last night which was stupid because I need lots of sleep with everything Ive got to do these days. Anyway I'd better get on with stuff as I have a load of nappies to wash which will be fun. I said to Anya I wish I had a little radio to listen to in the laundry room and so we looked in one of the trailers at the back and found quite a few in a box, so I got one for free. I am working on a present for you which I hope I will do by the time you visit next week, I miss you, love from Ethan x

18

June, 2020

The wind swept the long grasses along the cliff-top as though by brush-stroke and the large poppies shrugged their big red heads at the wild bright arc of the sky. Steven began setting up his equipment with a practised hand: easel, paints, plate, brushes, cloth and bottle of water. Paper, tape, tin cup, bulldog clips. Sun-hat, lunch box and, lastly, an old shirt he had often worn for surgery. Then his worst nightmare: a walker approaching with a swinging gait from the direction of the beach. He pretended not to notice, and began squeezing blobs of colour around the rim of his plate. Surely no one would want to stop and chat about a blank piece of paper?

"Hello there!" cried the man in greeting. He was wearing a wax jacket, a corduroy cap and walking boots. Steven smelt money.

"Hi," he answered moodily.

"You the artist from the Ubuntu set-up? Someone told me you'd been working up here."

"Yes, that's me." Steven offered a rather limp hand. "Steven Wallace."

"Marcus Frank. Pleased to meet you, Steven. I've been wanting to speak to you. The lady wife and I are opening a gallery in town next month – good central position near the church. A friend bought one of your works. You're very talented, I must say. Not many people bring a landscape alive like you do. Would you be interested in exhibiting at all?"

Steven felt far more interested in the turbulent panorama of grass, cloud and sky than the man's words, but he laid down his brush and turned to him as politely as he could. "I paint for the village," he said flatly. "We aren't interested in making big profits."

Marcus wasn't a bit perturbed by this reply. "I'm aware of the concept. My daughter's read the book. But surely the more money you have the more you can put your ideas into practice… print more books or help some good causes… or even put it towards starting another village?"

The words hung in the air despite the wind. Steven hesitated. "Well, I don't think we can spare the cash right now for a gallery slot, but thanks anyway. I'll certainly bear it in mind…"

"You get to place two works for free, but as it's you make that four. We take twenty percent."

Steven took his hat off and ruffled his hair. "Well, in that case… alright, Marcus. You have a deal. Thank you!"

The other man shook his hand warmly. "It's a pleasure, really. I'm so glad you've agreed. Your work's absolutely top-notch." He waved over his shoulder and took to the little sandy path that led along the sunny cliff-top with an energetic step. "I'll be in touch," he called.

Steven flopped his hat back onto his head and dipped his brush, and a broad smile lit up his face as he watched the colours begin to run together on the plate.

19

July, 2020

The dog bolted as the heavy black swell collided with the walls of the promenade with a reverberating boom. Gina bent down, talking kindly: "It's alright, love. It's alright."

They walked swiftly away from the brightly-lit pier towards the emptiness of the west beach, dodging the white salty spray that rose as much as thirty feet before slopping in frothy swathes upon the wide walkway. Beyond the chaos of the lamp-lit concrete, the huge waves fell rhythmically onto tumbling stones. Gina sat down with her head in her hands and wept.

It had all been going so well, what with the village and everything. But gradually the inevitable rot had set in. They didn't really like her. How could they? Why should they? They were just entertaining her because she'd turned up more-or-less demanding it. They could easily do without her. They probably hadn't even noticed her absence. Trust had fled, and in its place a seeping fearful loneliness. She'd said all the wrong things. She'd upset people without meaning to, and now it was too late to mend it. She was back in this place again, struggling to avoid thoughts of an unthinkable future. Stupid to ever dream that she would never return here… to this blacker than black hole. Her sobs were swallowed by the sound of the sea.

Ghost finished her nonchalant sniffings and scratchings and came at last to sit close, leaning her heavy body against the woman. Gina draped her arms around the dog and laid her face on the smooth short fur. "Oh, what would I ever do without you?"

Getting up to go, she looked out at the crashing waves and dark cloudy sky and dug her cold hands into her pockets. Her fingers found the stone her mother had given her, and she pulled it out contemptuously. So much for that... So much for gratitude, and faith, and love and positivity. As it lay in her hand, useless and hopeless, she saw Ellen's face and heard her voice: "The Universe never stops giving, Gina. We should remember to be grateful whenever we can." The stone was warm and weighty in her palm. She wanted to fling it away like a small nothing but couldn't quite bring herself to. She re-pocketed it, recalling the feel of Anya's arms around her neck as the tears began again.

Walking home, the town felt overly busy, and everywhere black hulking figures seemed to lunge at her. She could hear the roaring of the sea in her ears and the sweeping beam of the lighthouse dazzled her into confusion. Gratefully she mounted the stairs to her flat, but then her heart missed a beat at the sight of a pale blue envelope protruding from her letterbox. She pulled it out and turned it over, immediately recognising Ellen's handwriting. Her blood ran cold. No doubt she'd called round to see why the hell she'd failed to turn up for two whole days without even bothering to phone Mr Rix. But how could Gina have ever explained her weakness, her exhaustion and her pain to someone like Mr Rix who had worked so hard his whole life? Dear Mr Rix, to whom joy flowed so effortlessly on the back of a life well-lived. How could she ever admit to these crushing emotions when it was obvious that she should just get her act together and get on with things?

Phoning up would have made the whole disaster even more real, but pushing it away was the beginning of forgetting it. Yes… the phone had been unplugged first thing yesterday, and then an extra tranquilizer had brought on an uncomfortable sleep fraught with nightmares. Her hands shook as she unfolded the short one-page letter and read:

Dear Gina

We love the honesty of your face and the goodness of your heart. We love the way you make us feel safe and nice when things are going badly. We love the way you swear and then clamp your hand over your mouth. We love the way your voice goes all gooey when you speak about animals and babies. We love the way you get so excited when you open a present. We love the way you just can't do enough for other people. We love the way you always call Steve "tasty." We love the way you puzzle over the meaning of life, and frown while you're doing it. We love it when you laugh till you cry and then sit with mascara all down your face. We love the way you moan about your hair, your clothes and the pigeons. We love the way your eyes go all big when you get your dinner. We love the way you worry about silly little things because then we can reassure you. We love the fact that you came to us, and are proud to know someone who has such a large dose of Ubuntu spirit. Please let us know if you need our help.

Miss you - Ellen xxx

Gina slept soundly, tired out with weeping, and awoke at six o'clock with her hand still curled around the gratitude stone.

By seven o'clock she had taken a bath, dressed in an outfit that pleased her, and let Ghost out for her morning toilet. She picked up the phone, knowing that Mr Rix still kept a farmer's hours.

"Only me, Mr Rix… I was wondering if you'd mind picking me up. I thought maybe we could watch 'This Morning' together. You know I wouldn't ask for a lift normally, but…"

Mr Rix's voice was gruff with joy: "Oh, Miss Gina. Oh, I have been worried, my dear. Thank goodness! You just wait there and I'll be round as soon as I can hobble my way round to the truck…" He laughed heartily. "I'm so pleased you've rung. We have been concerned."

For once Gina resisted the urge to apologise for making him "hobble" because he sounded so happy. "Thanks, Mr Rix," she said.

She went to fetch her coat and the dog's lead. She left the *Sounds of Ubuntu* CD playing for the cats and slammed and locked the door.

20

July, 2020

It was almost seven o'clock and Ellen sat yawning in Mr Rix's second armchair. She adjusted her position and stroked Sage's head which was draped over her thigh. The old man had fallen asleep as usual, and Ellen was regretting not bringing her book. Then she heard a car on the gravel outside, and stood up to go and meet it.

A middle-aged well-dressed bespectacled gentleman lowered the window of the smart black Mercedes and smiled. Gosh, these people looked well-off, thought Ellen. He offered his hand through the window, and she took it, feeling conscious of her own roughened skin. "Hello, Mr Gasgoine; Mrs Gasgoine: I'm Ellen. Welcome to Ubuntu."

She pointed to the village entrance and swallowed as she noticed Squiffy lurking about under the trees collecting sticks. She cleared her throat. "You can park behind that bit of fence to the left of the main gate. The roundhouse is just through the entrance on your left. I'll meet you there shortly."

She watched as the car crawled towards the village on the newly-repaired track-way, willing Squiffy to disappear. Then she dragged the heavy farm gate shut, grinning to herself. Oh, well – presumably they had come in search of a unique experience. She made a mental note to take some wood round to the Row and went inside to say goodbye to Mr Rix.

"It's so wonderfully peaceful," declared Mrs Gasgoine. "I haven't heard so many birds singing for a long time." She took the leaflet from the table and started reading.

"What time would you like breakfast?" Ellen asked. "The café opens at nine but we're happy to bring you something earlier."

"Nine is perfect as far as I'm concerned," said Mr Gasgoine, looking at his wife. She nodded cheerfully.

"I'll leave you to it, then. Sleep well, won't you?" Ellen left the door open onto the sunlit playing field where the sheep stood sleepily side by side. She gave Koomra a wave as she turned towards the craft-room and popped her head in at the door. "You're working late," she told Faye and Nadia.

"We're stocking up," said Faye. "We've sold a lot this week."

Nadia was fastening lavender bags with purple ribbon and the sweet soporific scent pervaded the room. "Aruna's been looking at stuff. She can really focus now. Mum cut her nails because Anya was too scared, and Shiny wants you to read her poem but she's gone home. Gina said she'll bring that cat shampoo tomorrow but she won't be in till two because she's got the dentist, and Paul's got a surprise but I mustn't say."

Ellen was tired and not altogether in the mood for surprises, it being one of those days when the inescapable camaraderie of the village was starting to grate a little. She headed for the centre where Amanda and Dave lay on the sunny grass. "Mary's rehearsing tomorrow so are you two okay to do the shop while I sort out the holidays?" asked Ellen.

Amanda sat up and stretched herself. "Sure thing."

Dave said: "Paul's got a surprise for you."

"Yes, I heard," said Ellen. "I'm just going to get some wood and then I'll drop by…"

At that moment Carlos came out of the yoga room. "I've got a client!" he announced with a huge smile. "I honestly didn't realise how much I missed it till now."

"Maybe you shut it out while the village grew," suggested Amanda.

Ellen hugged him. "That's brilliant, Carlos." Spying Dave opening his tobacco tin she hurriedly took her leave and threaded her way through the old vans to the wood store. She selected as many logs as she could carry and exited the village by the top gate. Anya and Ethan were sitting under the big tree with the pram, and she quickened her pace. "Can't stop," she called to them. "I've got to see Paul about a surprise."

She found Paul on his little veranda stroking his beard thoughtfully. "So what's up?"

A strange unreadable smile began on his face and his blue eyes glinted. "The BBC wants to interview me."

"Really? What, about the village?"

"Yup!" He got up and hugged her.

"But I can't believe that many people know about us."

"Holiday-makers and campers. Why do you think we're suddenly so booked up? Someone flew a drone over here when you were in town the other day… I guess no one dared tell you." He laughed gently. "The village has entered the cyber-world. I wonder what they're saying."

Ellen frowned. "I don't."

Paul was watching her, sensing her emotion. Ellen couldn't help viewing Ubuntu as her own creation, as well as a refuge. "Should I do it or would Carlos be better?" he asked, his face uncertain. She could see his mind ticking over. "Or should I say no?"

Ellen considered. "I think Carlos might be too... verbose." She grinned and then became serious again. "I hope they don't make us out to be freaks."

"I thought you weren't bothered. See – you're starting to worry now. You mustn't Ellen. I can be very good in an argument, you know."

"Yes, I know you can. I'm just saying... But yeah – of course it doesn't matter what people think."

They sat down and watched the evening sky as it blushed and then deepened. Paul sighed and picked up his guitar, polishing the wood with his T shirt. "Don't know how I'll begin to explain it," he said.

Against the dark trees a pale blue ribbon of smoke rose from the Row and from somewhere nearby the baby let out a thin cry. The crows cried and tumbled over the black pines; a dog barked; somebody coughed and began whistling tunefully; a soft breeze pushed at the willow stems and then abated.

"Heaven," sighed Ellen.

21

August, 2020

Dear Rene

I do hope you are well my dear – I just had to write and let you know how our trip went. The Ubuntu Long Weekend was a most unusual holiday and quite amazing in its own way. Derek says it makes you realise how disconnected we've all got with one another and our surroundings, and by the end of the four days I was so relaxed I could hardly stay awake! The roundhouse was a lovely building – really the homeliest little space despite not having any windows. The walls were painted with a couple of landscapes hanging, and there were beautiful patchwork quilts on the beds made in the village workshop. It felt quite roomy with the big high roof, which smelt of straw with it being a brand new house. The evening we got there we just went straight to bed and slept like logs, and it was so nice to wake up to so much birdsong in the morning. Now Derek's adamant that we're moving to somewhere away from a road as soon as possible, and I really think he's serious!

In the mornings we got our breakfast from the food van: freshly-baked rolls and fried eggs from the village hens. The man brought the rolls just as we got there on our first day, and I must say they were all such a cheerful bunch that in some ways it reminded me of the old days. It's such a long time since I heard a man whistling!

So we just sat with our newspapers and the door open a lot while we were there Rene, and the children would play cricket on the field and I felt such peace – that definitely reminded me of the old days too, and they were such lovely happy children. In the afternoons the adults sometimes came for a game and they always invited us which I thought was kind, but Derek kept saying we weren't up to it. It does annoy me when he says that because I'm sure he's just being starchy. I felt sure I could have had a go because it was only for fun.

The classes and treatments on offer over the four days were very good. I had a massage on the first day to loosen up all my shoulders and then I had a superb soup for lunch with carrots, potatoes, kale and beans in. The cook said the secret is fresh thyme. They had several cooks there and everyone seemed to do a few jobs each, but it was all very relaxed. No one ever seemed to be rushing about because they just did what needed to be done in their own time. So after lunch on the first day Derek and I drove to the coast and had a wonderful walk along the beach. Then I had a yoga class at 4 o'clock – just one-to-one because I've never done it before. It mainly focused on relaxing and breathing with a few simple stretches. Well, Rene – I felt such a fool because I fell asleep twice and woke myself up snoring!

On the second evening the villagers invited us to their barbecue and we had some very strong homemade gooseberry wine that someone had given the shop – they allow you to pay with whatever you like there, you see. We had a lovely spicy vegetable burger each and even Derek liked it. This time the cook told me that the secret was a desert-spoon of peanut butter to keep it moist. The guitarist who played after the food was simply amazing, and I chatted a little to his daughter who has recently adopted a baby. She only looked about fifteen but I didn't feel I should ask the reason.

So anyway my dear I shan't bore you with every single meal, only to say that my favourite dish was the roasted aubergine with humus made from the village's own chick peas – delicious! The other classes I did were meditation and crafts, and then I had my horoscope done and two more massages because they were free for as many as we wanted. There was some hardship of course but that was the point, and we easily got used to candles and an outside loo. We used rainwater for bathing, heated with solar panels, and the washing machines were pedal-powered with special soap they use on the land afterwards – I was really impressed with the amount of stuff they manage to reuse. But oh, I did laugh sometimes Rene and wish you could have seen it, especially when Derek got all starchy.

On our last night they had singing and toasted us and said how lovely it had been to have us there, and it really did feel as though they meant it. I don't know if I would like to live quite like that with no TV at all and having such a tiny house as they live in, but I do agree with Derek that we must move somewhere quieter. I bought one of their Sounds of Ubuntu CDs before I left to remind me, plus a rug for the conservatory, and I got a bird-box for Heather's garden and a patchwork doll for little Amber.

Look forward to seeing you soon for morning coffee –

Much love

Stella Gasgoine x

22

September, 2020

They had watched a starling murmuration in town; had stood hand-in-hand with a gasp as the birds flowed together for a second to form a perfect heart. Then they had trekked along the beach almost as far as the next small town. Ethan started hammering the windbreak into the sand as Anya parked the pram and looked for stones for a fire. As the boy piled sticks, Anya extracted the beloved bundle from its sleeping place and held it close as she moved towards the sea. It was her favourite kind of sea: large quiet undulations that toppled and broke at last onto the pebbles, sucking them back with a foaming soaking hiss before sighing hugely and beginning again. The sun was sinking bright red into the western waters but Anya had already spotted the low bank of cloud that would subdue any real drama at the last moment. Sure enough, she watched as the rolling ocean lost its fire to heaving shadows and glinting peaks. The eastern sky drew darkness to itself as the shimmering red disc became a thin lone arc of flame. Nearby a cormorant was poised on a post, drying its great wings.

They sat on the soft sand with the sleeping baby, enjoying the small bright fire. "I'm so happy," said Ethan into her hair. "Thank you for being here, my beautiful secret magical creature." He smiled self-indulgently, savouring the moment. "I've got something for you."

She beamed at him: "What?"

The boy dug into the pocket of his shorts and handed her a small wooden box with a heart etched neatly into the lid. "Oh, Ethan…" she said, opening it slowly. He moved closer.

On a bed of red velvet sat a pretty silver ring adorned with curls and moonstones. Without hesitation she slipped it onto her finger where it caught the light. "Oh, Ethan; I shall never want anything else." They kissed, long and gently. "You don't miss anything do you… about your other life? I don't want to have taken anything away from you."

He laughed a little. "Well, I suppose I miss being lazy sometimes – being able to lie in bed a bit more."

"You can lie in bed."

"No, it's not fair on the others. Anyway, it's okay once you're up."

"My dad lies in bed all day."

"Yeah, but he's an amazing musician. They're allowed."

"Dixie won't mind if you go in later so long as you finish later."

"It's fine, Anya."

The baby whimpered and her father picked her up with a practised hand. Anya took a blanket from the bag and made it into a pillow. She lay down with her hands behind her head, hearing the sea come and go. "I wish all the world could feel like us," she said. "Omasah says that one day it will and that this is just one stage along the journey and we're all playing our parts… only it's such a little bit isn't it, when you think about the size of the world and the amount of sadness?"

Ethan was watching his daughter's tiny face. "Hey – I

keep forgetting to tell you about Amanda's idea... A big meditation every Sunday with anyone who wants to. We could do it on the field and the weekenders can come and people from the town. A meditation for world peace, and you can do the poster."

"That's a good idea." Anya's eyes were full of firelight. "I can do a big dove or something. That kind of thing can bring down crime rates and stuff, because they've done experiments: Paul told me."

"Yeah, Amanda said that too. She reckons it's human consciousness causing all the shit in the first place, so it's kind of got like a vicious circle."

Anya lay back down and sighed. "She's probably right. Too much fear and not enough love."

They fell into comfortable silence, getting up eventually as one to begin their walk home; and the small fire was a tiny speck of orange on the long dark shore, and the dark shore lay still and waiting for the long slow rising of the sea.

23

September 23rd, 2020
London

Paul hurried through the tall glass doors of the BBC centre, ducking his head under his jacket against the grey London rain. Lights flashed through the blur of traffic, and the few straggling people were dark-suited with big black umbrellas. Women's heels echoed like gunshots between the tall buildings and everyone was too rushed to look at anyone else. He wasn't used to this. He felt alone – alien – and he was smarting and exhausted from Frank Piper's duelling.

The rain suddenly increased, and Paul took shelter under a Romanesque frontage: all smooth marble and soaring pillars… "Like the trunks of trees," thought Paul, looking up. Other people stood about singly, each absorbed in a screen save one girl who stared out at the rain without seeing or hearing.

Rain was the sound of Ubuntu. Throughout so many recent evenings the village had listened to the rain, struggling to accept it in the face of what it was doing to their crops. And then they had found joy and laughter one dull muggy afternoon – had had a mud fight, and Carlos and Josh had taken off all their clothes.

Paul felt alone; alien.

He looked around again. He saw the pillars like trees and marvelled at the logistical and artistic achievement they represented in human terms – and both impressions were beautiful and One. He saw the people and regretted their disconnectedness, but sensed also their spirit: perfect; powerful… One. Paul noticed that he no longer seemed to hear the rain or roar of traffic, and his ears felt cavernous and his head hollow as he hung between worlds. He closed his eyes. Silence was the sound of Ubuntu.

Back again in a breath, and a dissolving into the rain-chimed wind-sweeping moment where everything was sound and sensation. It rained on.

Love reined.

Suddenly unable to wait, Paul ducked his head again and surrendered to the streaming water. Five minutes later he climbed dripping into the truck. He started the engine gratefully, enjoying its ugly roar. He felt good: he was going home.

A cork exploded from a bottle of Champagne and there was a hiss of bubbles and the chink of bright glass. Everybody clustered close, cheering and speaking at once. "You were brilliant!" Ellen said into his ear.

"I can't remember much," he answered. "Never again…"

Carlos grinned toothily. "You were perfect. A total triumph!"

Paul caught sight of Janet holding the baby on the other side of the room. He jostled his way over, biting hungrily into the fat slice of fruit cake that Mags handed him. "Oodles of sherry," she whispered. "Just keep it away from me and 'im."

He sat down next to Janet. "Can I hold her?" he asked, surprised at himself. He took the unfamiliar bundle carefully, nestling it into the crook of his arm. The baby opened her eyes and gazed.

"You know it's funny," said Ethan taking Anya's hand. "Things are different when you look back. 'Cause now it feels like it's the baby that's made everything alright."

Acknowledgements

With thanks to: Michael Tellinger, Timothy Halloran, Abraham Hicks and Jim Lingwood.

rosinagray-thevillage.com